Kathleen McGurl lives near the sea in Bournemouth, UK, with her husband. She has two sons who are now grown-up and have left home. She began her writing career creating short stories, and sold dozens to women's magazines in the UK and Australia. Then she got side-tracked onto family history research – which led eventually to writing novels with genealogy themes. She has always been fascinated by the past, and the ways in which the past can influence the present, and enjoys exploring these links in her novels.

After a thirty-one-year career in the IT industry she is now a full-time author, and very much enjoying the change of lifestyle.

When not writing she likes to go out running. She also adores mountains and is never happier than when striding across the Lake District fells, following a route from a Wainwright guide-book.

You can find out more at her website: http://kathleenmcgurl. com/, or follow her on Twitter: @KathMcGurl.

Also by K

The Emerald Comb
The Pearl Locket
The Daughters of Red Hill Hall
The Girl from Ballymor
The Drowned Village
The Forgotten Secret
The Stationmaster's Daughter

The Secret of the Château

KATHLEEN McGURL

ONE PLACE. MANY STORIES

This novel is entirely a work of fiction. The names, characters and incidents portrayed in it are the work of the author's imagination. Any resemblance to actual persons, living or dead, events or localities is entirely coincidental.

HQ
An imprint of HarperCollins*Publishers* Ltd
1 London Bridge Street
London SE1 9GF

1
First published in Great Britain by
HQ, an imprint of HarperCollins*Publishers* Ltd 2020

ISBN: 9780008380489

MIX
Paper from
responsible sources
FSC˚ C007454

This book is produced from independently certified FSC™ paper
to ensure responsible forest management.

For more information visit: www.harpercollins.co.uk/green

Printed and bound in Great Britain by
CPI Group (UK) Ltd, Melksham, SN12 6TR

For Jo, Pete, Simon, Fiona and Bruce, who were all present on the night that inspired this novel

Prologue

Pierre, 1794

Pierre Aubert, the Comte de Verais, could see the mob coming in the distance, up the track towards the château, brandishing flaming torches, shouting and chanting. There were perhaps fifty or more men, in their rough brown trousers and loose shirts. Most of them were carrying weapons – farming implements, sticks, pikes. He clutched his young son close to his chest, hushing the child and trying to ignore the pains that shot through him as he hurried along the path that led away from the château, towards the village. The girl was ahead of him, holding the baby. They had to get the children to safety first; only then could Pierre concentrate on saving himself and his wife.

Catherine. His heart lurched as he recalled her white, frightened face as he'd hurriedly told her his plans. If she did what he'd told her, she'd be safe from the mob, and soon the family would be reunited and they could get away. Into exile, into Switzerland.

France had changed over the last five years or so. The old ways, the *ancien régime*, had gone. There seemed to be no place in this new France for the likes of Pierre and Catherine. In the past it had been their class who ruled, but not anymore. If this mob caught them, they'd be imprisoned, summarily tried, and very likely executed – by guillotine.

But the mob would need to catch them first. Pierre had received a warning and was a good way ahead of them. The men hadn't reached the château yet, and they wouldn't find Catherine there. She was safe for now, and he'd return to her later. It would all work out.

It had to. It was their only chance.

Chapter 1

Lu, present day

It all began one drunken evening at Manda and Steve's. We were all staying with them for the weekend, as we often did. Three of us – that's me (I'm Lu Marlow), my husband Phil and our mate Graham – had arrived on Friday afternoon, and Steve had cooked a stupendous meal for us all that evening. We'd all brought a few bottles of wine, and I admit by the time this particular conversation began over the remnants of dessert we may have all had a tad too much to drink.

'What are you going to do, now you're retired?' Phil asked Steve. Steve had been forced to retire early – given a choice between that or relocating to Derby. ('Nothing against Derby,' he'd said, 'but we've no desire to live there.') He was aged just fifty-nine. We were all fifty-eight or nine. We'd met forty years ago, during Freshers' week at Sussex University and had been firm friends through rough and smooth ever since.

Steve shrugged. 'Don't know. I didn't want to stop work. Not quite ready to devote myself to the garden yet.'

'He needs a project,' Manda said. 'Something to get stuck into.

He's lost without a purpose in life. House renovation or something.'

'But your house is beautiful,' I said. 'It needs nothing doing to it.' We were sitting in their dining room, which overlooked the garden. They'd bought the house over twenty years earlier when their daughter Zoe was a baby. Zoe had recently sent Manda into a tailspin by moving to Australia on a two-year work contract. They'd done up their house over the years, turning it from a tired old mess into a beautiful family home.

'Yes, and I don't see the point of moving house just to give me something to do,' Steve said. 'More wine?' He topped up everyone's glasses.

'Can you get any consultancy work?' Phil asked. 'I've had a bit, since I got my redundancy package.' He'd done a few two-week contracts, and a part-time contract that lasted three months.

'Probably. But it's not what I want.'

'What *do* you want, mate?' Graham, who we'd always called Gray, asked.

Steve looked out at the rain that streamed down the patio doors. 'Better weather. Mountains. A ski resort within an hour's drive. Somewhere I can go fell-running straight from the house. A better lifestyle.'

'Relocating, then. Where to?'

'I fancy France,' Manda said.

'Yeah, I do, too.' Phil looked at me, as if to gauge my reaction. First I'd heard of him being interested in living abroad – we'd never talked about anything like that. We went to France or Italy a couple of times every year on holiday – always a winter ski trip (Phil's favourite) and usually a couple of weeks in the summer exploring the Loire valley, the Ardeches, Tuscany or wherever else took our fancy. Very often these holidays were with the other three people sitting round the table now.

'France?' is all I managed to say. An exciting idea, but my life was here in England. Even though there was less to keep me here,

4

since Mum died. I imagined visiting Steve and Manda in France for holidays. That'd be fun.

'I like Italy,' said Manda.

'But we don't speak Italian,' Steve pointed out.

'We could learn …'

'Where in France?' Gray interrupted, leaning forward, elbows on the table. I knew that gesture. It meant he was Having An Idea. Gray's ideas were sometimes inspired, sometimes ridiculous, always crazy.

Steve shrugged. 'Alpes-Maritimes?'

'It's lovely round there,' I said. Phil and I had had a holiday there a couple of years ago, staying in a gîte in a small village nestled among the Alpine foothills. We'd gone walking in the mountains, taken day trips to the Côte d'Azur, dined on local cheese and wine and all in all, fallen in love with the area.

'It is lovely,' Manda agreed. 'But I'd hate to move somewhere like that and be so far from everyone. Bad enough having Zoe on the other side of the world but if I was a plane ride away from all our friends too – you lot, I mean – I'd hate that.' She sniffed. 'You know I hate flying.'

'We'd all come and stay often,' I said with a grin, 'if you got a house somewhere gorgeous like that.'

'We'd move in,' said Gray. I looked at him quizzically and he winked back.

Steve laughed. 'Ha! I'd charge you rent!'

'Maybe we should all just chip in and buy a place big enough for all of us,' Gray said. 'Sell up here, buy ourselves a whopping great property over there that's big enough for all our kids to visit us, and retire in style.'

There was laughter around the table, but Gray looked at each of us in turn. 'No, really, why don't we? Makes perfect sense. It'd be more economical overall – shared bills and all that. Property is cheaper there than here – at least cheaper than it is in the south of England. And imagine the lifestyle – we'd be out cycling and walking, skiing in the winter, growing our own veg. We should do it now, while we're still fit enough. None of us have jobs to keep us here anymore.'

'We could employ a cleaner,' Manda said, ever the practical one.

'And a gardener. And a chef.' Phil grinned.

'We could keep chickens and have fresh eggs every day.' Steve's eyes lit up. He's such a foodie.

'I'd get a dog.' I'd always wanted one.

'Can I have a horse? Let's get a place with stables,' Manda said, to a bit of eye-rolling from Steve.

'It'd need somewhere to store all our bikes,' Gray, our resident cyclist, chipped in.

'There needs to be plenty of spare rooms for guests. Our kids would want to come to stay.' Me, again.

'Imagine at Christmas! All of us together – we'd have a ball!' Steve said – actually, if he wasn't a bloke, I'd have said he squealed this.

We were all speaking at once. The idea had taken shape, invaded all of our minds, and yes, the quantity of wine consumed had helped but as the conversation went on, I could see it taking root. At some point Gray and Steve both pulled out their phones and began searching for properties to buy.

'You can get an eight-bedroom château for about a million euro,' Gray said, peering at a list of search results. 'That's about the right size for us five plus visiting kids.'

'We could afford that, if we all sold our houses here. That's two hundred thousand per person. Your place is worth, what, six hundred thou?' Steve looked at me and Phil.

'About that, yes. And the mortgage is paid off.'

'So you two put in four hundred, that's euro not pounds, and you'd still have a huge wodge of cash over. Manda and I do the same, Gray puts in two hundred.'

'Look at this place! It's got a medieval defensive wall!'

'This one's got a tower, like something from a fairy tale.'

'Rapunzel, Rapunzel, let down your hair!'

'Who's Rapunzel? Steve's bald as a coot, can't be him!' Manda teased.

'You, dearest! Always wanted you to grow your hair long!'

We were passing phones around, looking at the various large properties currently on sale across France. There certainly seemed to be a lot of intriguing-looking châteaux that were within the ball-park price range Steve had suggested. It was a fun evening, and as we indulged ourselves in this little fantasy of selling up and moving to France together we laughed and joked and I felt so happy and comfortable with my friends around me.

It'd never happen, of course. It was just a bit of a giggle, a way to spend the evening with lots of laughter. That was all. We were all far too settled in our current homes and towns. And I, for one, was not good enough at French to be able to manage living abroad.

We'd met during Freshers' week, the five of us. We'd all gone to the Clubs and Societies Fair, and had signed up for the Mountaineering Club. The county of Sussex does not actually contain any mountains of course, but the club arranged weekends away travelling by minibus to north Wales, the Lake District, Brecon or the Peak District for camping, walking and climbing trips. The first meeting of the term was at the end of Freshers' week, where first-years were welcomed and the programme for the term was laid out. I signed up immediately for a trip a fortnight later to Langdale in the Lake District. So did Manda, and we agreed to share a tent. By the end of the meeting we were chatting with the other first-years – Phil, Gray and Steve – and the five of us decided to go on to one of the student bars for a beer. And that was it. We bonded. We were practically inseparable from that moment on, sharing digs during the second and third years, although it wasn't till after university that Phil and I finally paired up, closely followed by Steve and Manda.

'No one left for me,' Gray had said, with a mock-tremble of his lower lip. He was best man at both weddings. And there was never any shortage of girlfriends for him throughout the years. Melissa was the one who lasted longest. They never married but had two daughters together before splitting up when the kids were little. Gray shared custody of the girls with Melissa, having them for half of every week throughout their childhood. He was a great dad. Then there was Leanne who lasted a while, but Gray's commitment phobia sadly finished that relationship in the end.

Phil and I had two kids as well – our sons Tom and Alfie. And Manda and Steve had their daughter Zoe. All were now grown-up, finished with university, earning a living, flying high and happy in their chosen lifestyles. They didn't really need us much anymore, other than for the occasional loan from the Bank of Mum and Dad.

So the five of us were all pretty free, free to do what we wanted with life. We were still young enough to be fit and active, although Phil was a bit overweight and not as fit as he ought to be. We were old enough to be financially secure. We were all recently redundant or retired. Our kids were grown-up and independent. We had no elderly parents left that need caring for – my mum was the last to go of that generation.

So I suppose if we had been at all serious about upping sticks and moving to France, it was the right time to do it. But of course we weren't serious, and in the morning we'd all be dismissing it as a joke, a good giggle but nothing more. At least I hoped so, as I lay searching for sleep in Steve and Manda's spare room that night. I didn't want to move to France.

I was the last one up next morning. That's not unusual – I've never been a morning person. The others were sitting in the kitchen, drinking coffee while Steve organised breakfast. All the men in our little group are great cooks. And Manda can bake amazing cakes, cookies and breads. It's just me who's a klutz in the kitchen.

'Morning, Lu,' Steve said. 'The full works for you this morning? Phil said you were still out for the count.'

'I was. And yes please.' I scanned their faces. Was everyone wondering, as I was, whether the conversation last night had been serious or not? Or had they all forgotten it after a night's sleep? The latter, I hoped.

Phil put out a hand and pulled me to a seat beside him. 'All right? There's fresh tea in the pot. Want some?' He didn't wait for an answer but picked up an empty mug and poured me a cup, adding just the right amount of milk. The advantage of thirty years' marriage is that we know exactly what the other person likes and needs. I smiled a thank-you at him and sat down.

'How're everyone's heads?' I asked.

'Surprisingly all right,' Gray replied. 'Think we drank about eight bottles between us so we've no right to feel good this morning. Not at our age.'

'Speak for yourself, Gray.' Manda gave him a playful punch on the arm. 'You may be knocking on a bit but I'm still only fifty-eight.' She'd always been the baby of the bunch – youngest by all of two months.

The banter was all very well, but I was dying to know. Were they about to start house-hunting in the Alpes-Maritimes? Or anywhere in France for that matter. I hoped not. Steve was busy flipping fried eggs, and Manda was taking trays of sausages and bacon out of the oven and putting them on the table. There was a bowl of cooked mini tomatoes, racks of toast and a pan of sautéed potatoes. I couldn't help but grin. A good old fry-up the night after a skin-full of wine was my favourite thing.

Could you even get bacon and sausage in France?

It was as we finished eating, as Manda was making more coffee and I began stacking plates to load the dishwasher, that Steve spoke up. 'So. This house in France. Are we going to do it, then?'

'Were we serious?' Phil asked.

'I was,' Gray chipped in, as he munched on the last of the toast.

'You're never serious,' Manda told him.

'Well' – he waved the crust of his toast at everyone – 'I was last night. Honestly, it'd be awesome. We could breakfast like this every day!'

'We'd be fat as fools in no time,' I said. My stomach gave a lurch. If they all wanted to do this, I couldn't be the one to spoil the party. Not now. It'd all fizzle out soon enough anyway.

'I'm up for it,' Phil said, looking at me with a raised eyebrow, and I swallowed and nodded. 'Er, yeah. Sure.'

'Manda and I discussed it this morning, while we waited for you lazy lot to show your faces,' Steve said. 'We think we could make it work. Manda needs something to take her mind off Zoe being away. Phil needs a healthier lifestyle. Sorry, mate, but you do. And you, Lu' – he nodded at me – 'need to do something for yourself, after all your years caring for your mum. As for me, I need a project. So I'm happy to do the legwork.'

No one was better than Steve at organising things. He'd been a project manager in a finance company for years and was good at it. And he spoke better French than the rest of us.

'What about me?' asked Gray. 'What do I need?'

'A new hunting ground,' Phil said, with a wink. 'Maybe you'd meet the perfect woman in France.'

'Mmm, I like the sound of that!' Gray laughed.

'Well then,' Phil said. 'Let's go for it!'

There was much cheering and clinking together of coffee mugs, and by the time I had that dishwasher loaded Steve had opened his laptop and begun a search, and a shortlist of potential properties was being drawn up. I watched them crowded around

10

behind Steve and smiled. It would probably all come to nothing, but in the meantime I had to admit it was fun dreaming and planning. In the end the whole thing would no doubt just fizzle out, thankfully, but I wasn't going to be the one who said no to it. Not while they were all so excited.

Phil and I discussed the idea on our drive home later that day.

'Moving to France, eh? At our age! Great idea, isn't it?'

I bit my lip for a moment, not sure how to respond. It was one thing going along with the excitement when we were with all the others, but surely I should be honest about my misgivings with my own husband? 'Yeah. Lovely idea, but I can't see it actually happening, can you?'

Phil glanced across at me and frowned. 'Don't see why not. You know what Steve's like when he gets his teeth into a project. There's no one better than him at getting things organised and done.'

'Do you really think we should do it? Sell our house and everything?'

'Well, what's the alternative? Neither of us are working anymore. I'm not ready to just vegetate in front of daytime TV for the next thirty years. So, yes, I think we should put our house on the market as soon as possible. We've been saying we should thin down our possessions ready for downsizing anyway. This'll force us to actually get on and do it. And living with Steve, Manda and Gray will be awesome. It'll be like being twenty again – regaining our youth!'

'Ha. Except we are nearly sixty. But I agree, we do want to downsize and release some equity. So we might as well get on with sorting our stuff out. I reckon the boys will take some of the spare furniture. And it's probably time I threw out all their old schoolbooks and nursery artwork.'

'God, Lu, have you still got all that?'

I grimaced and nodded. 'In the attic. About five boxes of it.'

Downsizing. Not moving to France. That's all I'd agreed to, wasn't it?

So the following week I began clearing the attic, while Phil started on the garage and arranged for valuations from estate agents. We cleaned and tidied ready for the agent's photographer, and then put the house on the market. It felt good to make a start on this – we'd been talking about selling up for at least a year.

A week later we heard that Gray already had an offer on his place, and that Steve was away in France looking at potential properties.

'Already!' I said to Manda, when she phoned to tell us. I couldn't believe they were really this serious about it all, but it looked like Steve was, at least. My heart lurched. I'd accepted the idea of selling our family home, but moving abroad was a much bigger step, one I didn't entirely want to take.

'He spent days online scrolling through endless possibilities, then two days ago said to me it'd be easier to be "on the ground", and next thing I knew he'd booked a flight to Nice.'

'Didn't he want company?' I asked. I'd have thought he'd have taken Manda or Gray with him.

'I think his plan is to whittle his short list down to a proper shortlist – there are over a hundred on it at the moment – and then let us have a look at the details. Then if any really stand out and we're still all keen, we can go en masse to view them.'

'Sounds good.' The rest of us hadn't the first idea how to buy property abroad, but Steve would have looked it all up already, spoken to suitable people for advice, and would know exactly what he was doing. He was a born project manager.

'Lu, I'm so excited about this, aren't you?' Manda said. I detected a tiny bit of worry in her voice, as if she was frightened Phil and I might have had second thoughts. She was right – I'd been having second thoughts all the way through. But I refused to be the one to spoil things.

'Definitely! Just can't wait to get on with it now!' I forced myself to sound enthusiastic. Whatever happened, I was not going to put a dampener on it. There was still a strong chance the plan would fall apart.

'Phew! I told Zoe, too. She thinks it's a great idea. I was worried, you know, that she'd somehow think we were abandoning her ...'

'But she lives in Australia – actually you'll have moved a little closer to her!'

'I mean more that when, or God help me *if*, she comes home to England, we won't be there.'

'No, but you'll be a short flight away. And she can come "home" to France. Home is where her heart is.'

Manda answered with a little wobble in her voice. 'You're right. It's the only thing that worries me, though. That our kids won't like it.' She took a deep breath. She'd struggled with empty nest syndrome ever since Zoe first left home to go to university. 'What do Tom and Alfie think?'

This was my chance. I could offload to Manda here, now, tell her my misgivings about the whole project, using the boys as an excuse, perhaps. She'd talk to Steve, and maybe it'd all be quietly put to bed, for surely if we weren't all happy with the idea, we shouldn't do it? After all, moving to another country is a big step, at any time of life. But no. I wasn't going to be the party pooper. They'd never think quite the same of me again if I did that now. And I was still convinced the plan would die a natural death if I just let events run their course.

I smiled, to make my voice sound happy. 'They're delighted. Tom sees it as a base for cheap holidays. Alfie's dictated we need to have a swimming pool, and a butler serving iced cocktails at all hours.'

'Fair enough. I'll let Steve know the new requirements.' We had a giggle about this, before going on to talk about Gray's house sale.

'Steve and I have said he can move in here if need be, if his sale goes through really quickly. Actually that'd give us some capital for a deposit, if we need it. It's all working out, Lu. We've got the skiing holiday coming up, then it's possible we might be ready to move in the summer!'

Well, I hoped Phil and I would be ready to move by the summer. But with luck, not to France.

Chapter 2

Catherine, 1785

Catherine Aubert, the new Comtesse de Verais, smiled and curtsied to her husband Pierre as he entered their bed chamber. They had recently married and moved into an apartment in the great Palace of Versailles. Catherine could not believe she was living here, in the greatest palace of all Europe, being in the company of Her Majesty Queen Marie Antoinette daily. But with her husband being one of King Louis XVI's advisers, living at the palace was part of the job, and she knew she needed to get used to it. As a girl she'd dreamed of living in a great palace, wearing magnificent clothes and eating the finest foods, and now, look, here she was!

'My love, you do not need to curtsy to me. I am your husband!' Pierre crossed the room and took both her hands in his, raising them to his lips to kiss. 'You know, I still feel so blessed that you accepted me. I'm old, and you're so young and beautiful, and yet you agreed to marry me. Thank you once again, my dear.'

'It is I who should thank you,' she replied. 'It is through you that we are able to live here in such luxury and style.' Catherine looked around her at their opulent chamber, the cornices and woodwork picked out in gilt, the sumptuous wall hangings and bed coverings, the elegant furniture with its shapely legs and silk upholstery. She leaned into him and raised her face so that he could kiss her. He was much older than her, and she was his second wife, but there had been no children from his first marriage, and her family had thought it a good match, impressing upon her the need to be a good wife to Pierre and to provide him with heirs. There had been no sign of children so far, but she was young and there was plenty of time, and surely it would happen eventually. Pierre was a handsome man even if he was already in his fifties, and Catherine liked him. Indeed, she felt she was growing to love him. He cared for her, he would do anything for her, and she felt safe and secure in his arms. She trusted him.

'We are fortunate indeed,' Pierre said. 'And you shall make a good impression on our Queen. I am sure you will become a firm favourite of hers in no time at all.'

'That would be marvellous,' Catherine whispered. Imagine being the favourite of Marie Antoinette! Pierre already had a position of some significance and Catherine would love to feel equally as important, within the Queen's court. She resolved to do everything she could: first of all to not embarrass herself in any way for that would reflect badly upon Pierre, and secondly to try to get the Queen to notice her and like her. 'But how do I manage this?' she asked. Rules of etiquette at Court were notoriously complex, and she was terrified of making a faux pas.

'Just be yourself, my dear. No one can fail to love you, just as you are.' He pulled her close into his embrace and began kissing her face and neck. 'Shall we retire? Shall I call your maid to help you undress? Oh, my sweet. I am surely the luckiest man alive.'

The Queen, Catherine noted the next morning, had dressed her hair in a new style. It had a little less height than usual, with a few tendrils left loose, hanging down in corkscrew curls just behind her ears. There were tiny pink silk bows pinned into her hair, to match the silk bows on her sleeves and skirts. She was wearing one of her new, shepherdess-style dresses, the skirts flounced and pinned up into drapes, decorated with more bows, the bodice trimmed with another flounce, a pink sash around her waist.

Catherine committed every last detail of the dress and hairstyle to memory. One way to impress the Queen was to emulate her style. She resolved to ask Pierre to pay for a new gown in this wonderful, country style. It was essential to keep up with the latest fashions if she was to play an important part in the Court. Besides, Catherine loved wearing the latest fashions, and this one she thought would particularly suit her. Yes, she must persuade Pierre to let her have a new gown.

As Catherine followed the Queen and the other ladies of the court through the great halls of Versailles she took careful glances out of the corner of her eye, checking what the other ladies were wearing. One or two of them had already dressed their hair in a similar way, and three were wearing colourful sashes with matching bows in their hair. Pierre *must* agree to pay for a new dress. Catherine must not get left behind. She may be one of the youngest, newest members of Marie Antoinette's court, but she was also one of the prettiest and determined to make a success of it.

'Madame, may I ask where we are going?' Catherine asked the lady walking alongside her. It was Madame de Polignac, the Queen's favourite, and a lady who'd been kind to Catherine when she'd first arrived at Versailles, after her marriage to Pierre. She twisted the large garnet and diamond wedding ring that she always wore, so that the stones were on the top of her hand, clearly visible to all.

'I believe Her Majesty wishes to visit the Petit Trianon, this afternoon, and then walk down to her hamlet. She has received a report that lambs have been born and wishes to make the acquaintance of the dear little creatures.' Madame de Polignac smiled indulgently at Catherine.

The Petit Trianon! Catherine loved going to the Queen's personal palace, and her hamlet. To think, the Queen had built an entire, perfect little village and farm, within the grounds of Versailles! It had dear little cottages, tiny fields containing snow-white lambs gambolling and frolicking merrily in the sunshine, and a pretty doe-eyed Jersey cow that wore a blue ribbon bow on its head. Catherine smiled happily at the prospect of their visit to the farm. It was a sunny spring day, bright but not too hot – perfect weather for a little trip to the hamlet. She trotted alongside Madame de Polignac, until the older woman sped up a little to be alongside the Queen herself. Catherine kept her place behind the great ladies. It was enough that Madame de Polignac had walked alongside her and spoken to her. She didn't expect to be noticed by the Queen, although there had been that glorious day the previous week when the Queen's head had turned her way, and nodded slightly in acknowledgement. Catherine had blushed and curtsied. She was still learning the etiquette of the court, the subtle cues and hidden meanings behind every word, every look, every gesture. Her *maman* had tried to instruct her before her wedding, Pierre too, and on a couple of occasions Madame de Polignac had taken her aside and explained a social nicety to her, but it was so difficult to keep up with it all. Catherine's greatest fear was of making some sort of faux pas and accidentally offending the Queen, and in so doing, harming Pierre's reputation at Court.

There were carriages awaiting them for the short drive through the grounds of Versailles, to the Petit Trianon. There it sat, the most adorable little palace, in Catherine's opinion. While Versailles was of course magnificent it was too big to feel truly comfortable in. Catherine would love a palace for herself, like the Petit Trianon.

Pierre owned a château somewhere, far away in the mountains. One day, he said, he would take her there. Perhaps when they had a family, it would be the place to bring up their children. She knew Pierre longed for an heir. His first wife had been unable to bear him any children. Catherine looked forward so much to the day when she would be able to fulfil his dreams. But for now, their place was at Court, not hundreds of miles away in rural France. Catherine hoped Pierre's château was about the size and grandeur of the Petit Trianon. If or when they moved there, she intended setting up her own court, like the Queen's but of course on a smaller scale.

The ladies alighted from the carriage and accepted the bows and curtsies of the people who'd gathered to see them arrive. Among them were several children. The Queen liked to surround herself with children and hand out bonbons to them that she kept in the pockets of her gown. She'd even adopted one poor little boy and doted on him, until she'd had children of her own.

Catherine smiled to see how the Queen interacted with the children, stroking their hair and giving them sweets. She was so lovely, so kind, such a perfect monarch. France was lucky indeed, that this Austrian princess had married their prince, and become the most beautiful, loved and worshipped Queen of all time. Long may she reign!

The Queen began strolling towards her little hamlet, a short distance from the Petit Trianon palace. Catherine followed, excited to see the dear little lambs on their unsteady legs. When or if she and Pierre moved to his château in the south, she would build a similar hamlet for herself, so that she too could play with pretty lambs in the springtime.

The hamlet looked so lovely in the spring sunshine. Every building was perfectly maintained, the grass was cut short and free of weeds, there were flowers blooming everywhere. And in a little pen behind the sweet little farmhouse, a peasant stood proudly with his flock of sheep – just three ewes, each with a lamb at her side. Each mother sheep had a blue bow tied around its neck. The Queen called forward one of her ladies, who passed her a set of new ribbons, these ones pink, matching the Queen's own bows and sash. There was one for each sheep and narrower ribbons for each lamb. The peasant tied them on, making a hash of the bows until one of the ladies stepped forward to help.

There. At last they were all done. 'Aren't they just so very lovely?' Catherine remarked to the lady standing beside her.

'Delightful, I'm sure,' came the response. Catherine glanced sideways at her. The other woman looked faintly bored by the proceedings, although when the Queen's gaze swept around over her she plastered a smile on her face and clapped her hands as though in utter joy at the occasion.

Well, whatever the others thought, Catherine adored the lambs. She'd like to pick one up, she thought, but no one else had done so, and unless the Queen set the example, they could not do it or even suggest it.

Late that evening, as they returned to the small apartment in the Palace of Versailles that Catherine shared with her husband Pierre, the Comte de Verais, she recounted her day to her husband.

'Truly, was there ever such a queen?' she asked. 'So elegant, so refined, so kind to her people. And they love her, do they not? She will reign alongside her beloved Louis for a thousand years!'

Pierre smiled and stroked a finger down Catherine's face. She turned into his hand and kissed his palm.

'Oh, my dear wife. You are so young and have much to learn. The Queen is indeed elegant and refined. But I fear not all the people love her or the King as you do. Come sit with me.' He gestured to a richly upholstered sofa set by the fireplace in their apartment. Catherine motioned to her maid that she should leave them for now, and joined her husband, relaxing gratefully into the cushions and his arms, pleased to be off her feet at last.

'How can they not love our monarchs? Are they not chosen by God to lead us?'

Pierre laughed indulgently. 'Yes, my dear. That is what Louis believes.'

'Then it is so,' said Catherine firmly. 'The King is always right. And we love our monarchs truly, don't we?'

'Of course, my love. Perhaps they spend a little too much …' He broke off and bit his lip.

'What do you mean, they spend too much?'

'Oh, nothing. I did not mean to say anything.'

'But you did.' She frowned. 'Please tell me what you meant. Your words worry me.'

Pierre smoothed her frown with his thumb and smiled. 'My love, you need not worry. Louis has good advisers who will steer him in the right direction, I am sure. It is not your concern. Now tell me more about your day. How was Her Majesty?'

Catherine snuggled up to him. 'The Queen today was wearing the most adorable shepherdess gown. I should so like to have one that's similar, though of course I should not look nearly as beautiful as her. Pierre, won't you pay for my new gown, so I can keep up with the current fashions?'

Pierre twisted so that he could kiss her cheek. 'Of course, my darling. You shall have a new gown. You may visit your dressmaker at your earliest convenience and charge it to my account.'

Catherine clapped her hands with joy. 'Thank you! You really are the dearest of husbands. I am very lucky. Now, what colour bows and sash shall I have? The Queen had pink, but perhaps I should not copy her exactly. I like pale blue, but the Queen no longer seems to wear pale blue ribbons.'

'Yellow, maybe? The colour of sunshine?'

She pondered this. 'I have not seen any other ladies with yellow. It would look lovely, but I would fear being the only one in yellow. It wouldn't do to be unfashionable.'

'No, my dearest, it wouldn't do at all. Come now. Let's retire

21

to bed. Call your maid and I will see you in your chamber in a short while.'

Catherine did as he had asked, and the maid Claudette came to help her undress, prepare herself for bed and for the attentions of her husband. Maybe tonight would be the start of a baby. She hoped so.

Chapter 3

Lu

There was a 'gang gathering' as Steve called it, about a month after the crazy idea had first taken shape. We met at Steve and Manda's again, on a rainy Wednesday afternoon in January. Manda had baked an enormous carrot cake, and Steve had printed off details of a short list of six properties in Provence – mostly in the Alpes-Maritimes *département* which is the southwestern end of the Alps where they meet the sea, not far from the French–Italian border. A couple of properties were on the edge of the Mercantour national park, two more were further west near the Verdon Gorge, and the other two were in between, one off the Var Valley and the other near Entrevaux which I remembered well as a beautiful walled medieval town with a magnificent citadel up on a hill.

We passed around the details, exclaiming over each, comparing numbers of bedrooms, acreage, proximity to towns, villages and mountains. Steve opened up his laptop on Google Street View and showed us the access to each property. They weren't all châteaux – two or three looked more like modern, large houses. I peered at each of them with some trepidation, resolving to join in properly and make sure I had my say. I was still sure the whole idea would eventually fade away but in the meantime I at least wanted to be sure we picked a property I could really love. I had in mind a proper château, with turrets and towers and perhaps even a moat. One or two of those Steve had picked out were pretty disappointing in that respect.

'So what I suggest,' Steve said, after we'd all seen all the options, 'is that we all pick our favourite and see whether there's any consensus.' There was a glint in his eye that made me look sideways at him, but he looked away and began organising us with pens and slips of voting paper.

I picked the one near Entrevaux. A bit further from the high Alps than I'd like, but it was the most castle-like of the options. It had mullioned windows and was ivy-clad. I tried not to look over Phil's shoulder to see if he was picking the same one, but it looked to me like he'd gone for the one nearest the Alpine ski resorts. I might have guessed that.

Steve gathered up the responses. 'Well, we had six properties and there are five of us, so at the minimum we'll have ruled one out.' He opened up the slips of paper and piled them up, then guffawed. 'Well done everyone. We've all picked a different one, and Gray here has chosen two. So none are ruled out.'

We all laughed. I felt a surge of relief – if we couldn't agree on a property then surely that would be the beginning of the end of this crazy idea.

But Steve had something up his sleeve. He gathered up all the property details and stacked them to one side. 'Alternatively,' he said, with that twinkle in his eye again, 'we could consider *this* place. Ladies and gentlemen, I present to you the Château d'Aubert.' With a flourish he passed us each a copy of another property's details. As I read it, I found myself grinning more and more broadly at every paragraph, despite my misgivings. This one was perfect. It had, not just everything I would want, but everything I was sure the rest of the gang wanted too. It was about an hour and a half's drive inland from Nice, in the Alpine foothills, and was situated a short distance outside a village. It had a couple of acres of land, including some outbuildings. It dated back to the 1600s. It had a tower. There was a small ski resort a little further up the valley, or some of the major resorts could be reached in an hour or two's driving. The opportunities for cycling (Gray), fell-running (Steve), riding (Manda) and hill-walking (me) were endless. It had been in use as a small hotel until a year or two ago but was a little run-down and in need of renovation. There were eight bedrooms plus another small room in the tower, so it was just the right size for us and all our kids. And it was pretty as a picture, built of creamy stone with terra-cotta roof tiles. If we were serious about moving, this one would be perfect. But were we serious? Was I going to have to admit I didn't want to do this after all?

I hardly dared look at everyone else to see their reaction. They'd all gone very quiet. Steve had Google Street View open for the new property, so I leaned over to take a look. There was a small gatehouse off the main road – and I say 'main' but it looked like a quiet lane leading along the valley floor from the village. A track led past the gatehouse up to the château. Street View, of course, did not go up the track but you could see tantalising glimpses of the tower from the road. There was woodland either side of the track and a steep hillside rose behind. A small river ran through the valley along the edge of the château's land.

'Bloody hell, Steve,' said Gray quietly. 'It's … amazing …'

'I love it,' Manda whispered. I glanced up at her, and saw her eyes shining. I realised it was the first time she'd seen this possibility too. Sneaky Steve, staging a dramatic moment when we all saw the details for the first time.

'How much?' Phil asked, bringing us back to earth with a bump. I frowned. Surely Steve wouldn't have offered up this one if it was out of our budget? But then, if it was too much, maybe that'd put paid to the idea and we'd all just stay in England after all.

'It's bang on the million euro that we've already worked out we can afford,' Steve answered, and there was a collective sigh of relief from everyone else, though I felt a rising surge of panic. This was all happening too fast. 'So shall we all go over and view it? We're off on our ski holiday next week but maybe we could go after that? We could use the week away to really think hard about this to be sure it's definitely what we all want to do. At the end of the week we can have a proper, frank, chat about it all, and decide whether to go ahead.'

'Course we're going ahead!' Gray said. 'You're talking as though someone's not happy with the idea. I thought we were all on board? I'm about to exchange contracts on my house sale!'

'Yeah, we're all happy as far as I know,' Steve said. 'But no harm in having a final discussion, make sure all our ideas and dreams are on the same page, just before we commit to actually buying something. So hold off exchanging contracts till after the ski trip, Gray. Just in case.'

I kept quiet. Maybe I shouldn't have. Maybe that was the moment I should have spoken up and said, *actually, guys, I'm not happy with this plan*. But I didn't. There would be another chance – at the end of the ski trip, when we would all speak openly and honestly about what we wanted for the years ahead. I'd use that opportunity. I'd talk to Phil beforehand. If we pulled out, the other three could still move to a smaller place if they wanted, and we'd simply visit them once or twice a year. They'd understand. We all had to be happy and comfortable with this plan.

'Right, well, where's the bubbly? If we've found the perfect château, we need to toast it!' Gray said, and Manda got up to find the glasses. Prosecco was poured out; we toasted each other and our collective future. But I noticed Phil turn a little pale, and then he quietly got up and left the room, his hand clutched against his chest. No one else seemed to have noticed – perhaps they all thought he'd gone to the loo – but I followed and found him sitting in Steve's study, breathing heavily.

'Phil? Are you all right?' I knelt beside him.

He nodded. 'Just a little twinge. A stitch, I think. Been laughing too much and too hard, I guess.' He grinned at me as if to prove his point, then went back to join the others who were still sitting around the dining table, surrounded by property details. There was nothing I could do other than follow him and keep a worried eye on him for the rest of the evening.

Our annual ski trip was the following week. We'd been skiing together almost every year for about twenty years – ever since the kids were old enough to be put into ski school. The kids, now they were grown-up (and now that their parents would no longer pay for them), no longer came, but the five of us still kept up the tradition. It was Phil's favourite sport. Unfortunately, he wasn't actually at all fit. His cholesterol levels were sky-high owing partly to his habit of eating stacks of cheese after every meal, and drinking too much red wine. And skiing was generally his only exercise. When we got together with the gang, others would go for walks or bike rides, but Phil so often found an excuse – the rugby was on, he had a hangover, he wanted to read the Sunday paper – and stayed home. He'd do a fortnight of squats and wall sits to 'get fit for skiing' and that was it.

It was midway through the ski holiday, high in the French Alps, when it happened. The day had started out with glorious sunshine and eye-wateringly blue skies, but by mid-afternoon clouds had begun to gather and the light was becoming flat. Manda, Steve and I decided to call it a day and head back to the hotel for a *vin chaud* and a shower. Phil talked Gray into going up one more time. 'One last run down from the top,' he said, and Gray, after a longing look at the rest of us heading off for our drinks, nodded and followed him onto the chairlift.

Phil started feeling unwell on the way up. Gray later recalled him tugging at the collar of his ski jacket, pushing his goggles up and wiping sweat from his face, grunting a little. 'You all right, mate?' Gray asked him, but Phil brushed him off, saying he was fine.

They had planned to take the most direct route from the top of the lift back to the hotel – a steepish red run that linked onto the blue return route near the bottom. But once off the chairlift, Phil said he'd rather take the meandering, easier blue run all the way from the top. 'I'm feeling a little iffy,' he said, and Gray agreed. If you're not feeling great when skiing, it's always best to pick a more gentle descent.

They set off, but after just a couple of turns Phil fell behind. Gray stopped and waited for him. 'Take it slowly, Gray,' Phil said, when he reached him. 'I'm really not feeling right.' They ended up snow-ploughing and side-slipping down the next section with multiple stops; at one point Phil even sat down on the edge of the slope, gasping and clutching his chest.

'Mate, we need to get you to the medical centre,' Gray said. 'See the top of that chairlift over there? Let's cut across to it and go down by chair.' He led Phil to it, but just short of the chairlift Phil collapsed and was unable to get up. Gray waved his arms and shouted, and the chairlift operator ran over to them. 'He needs help,' Gray shouted. '*Au secours, il sont mal.*' Dreadful French, he said later, but all he could dredge up at the time. The lift operator got on to his radio and shortly after, a ski-stretcher – or 'meat-wagon' as they are affectionately termed – arrived. Phil was loaded on and taken down, with Gray following. 'Amazing how fast those chaps can go when they're towing,' Gray reported later.

I was sitting in the hotel bar sipping a *vin chaud* with Manda and Steve, still in our ski gear but having left our skis and boots in the boot room, when Gray phoned. 'Phil's not feeling so good. He's going to the medical centre to get checked out,' he said. 'Can you meet us there?'

I could tell he was trying to downplay the seriousness of the situation, and I remembered Phil's breathlessness and the way he'd complained of 'a stitch' at Steve and Manda's a week before. And with mounting horror I guessed what had happened.

I told Manda and Steve, and we all abandoned our *vin chauds* and headed over to the resort's medical centre which thankfully wasn't too far from our hotel. We arrived at about the same time as the meat-wagon with Gray not far behind.

Phil's face was grey and clammy, and I clapped a hand over my mouth with shock. Manda put her arm around me. 'He'll be all right. Stay strong for him.' But her voice was shaky. Steve collected Phil's and Gray's skis and boots while Gray followed us into the medical centre and filled us in on what had happened.

The next hours were all a bit of a blur to me. The medical centre suspected a heart attack and arranged for Phil to be taken by helicopter to the nearest hospital. I followed in an excruciatingly expensive taxi. Manda came with me as interpreter as her French is so much better than mine. The taxi journey was horrendous – it took well over an hour to negotiate the hairpin bends leading down from the resort to the valley then along the main road in rush-hour traffic to the hospital. And all the while I kept up silent prayers that Phil would survive. We'd been married thirty years and the thought of life without him was unbearable.

It was indeed a heart attack, and Phil was operated on quickly, to insert a couple of stents.

I was distraught throughout. 'I can't lose him, I can't,' is all I kept saying. Thank God Manda was there to comfort me, to talk to the doctors when I couldn't, to make sure I ate and drank, to chat to me about random topics while we waited in a futile attempt to take my mind off it all. She kept Gray and Steve updated by text.

It was nearly midnight before we were finally allowed in to see Phil. There were tubes everywhere, and bleeping machines flashing numbers that detailed his life forces surrounded his bedside. He was barely awake, but managed a half-smile at me, and to squeeze my hand as I leaned over to kiss his cheek. I was trying not to show how distressed I was but failing miserably, as tears streamed down my face.

'You've got one job,' Manda told him, putting on a strict, parental tone, 'and that's to get yourself better. Now get on with it, Phil, or you'll have me to answer to.'

He smiled wanly and managed a nod, and then we were ushered out by the nurse. There was a cheap hotel nearby that we checked in to for the night, and then the following day was taken up with arrangements to get Phil home. There were many discussions with doctors between brief visits to see Phil who thankfully looked less grey and was more responsive each time. Manda headed back to the ski resort but Gray came by bus to the hospital with Phil's and my luggage, and then finally we took a flight home a couple of days later with Phil in a wheelchair. He was admitted straight to hospital back home, where they declared the French operation to have been a success, and a day later he was discharged, armed with several leaflets on how to lower his cholesterol and get his heart fit again.

Tom and Alfie visited soon after we got home, shocked by what had happened, but determined not to let their father see how worried they were. 'Come on, Dad, stop lazing around in bed all day,' Alfie joked. 'Get up, lose some weight and get fit. By next Christmas or there'll be no visit from Santa for you. That's loads of time. Surely even you can manage to sort yourself out by then.'

Of course, with all this going on, I gave no thought whatsoever to our potential move to France. I couldn't talk to Phil about it as I'd planned. I assumed, I suppose, that Phil's heart attack would be the end of that idea, and we'd be buying a sensible suburban bungalow instead.

A week after Phil came home from hospital the gang came to visit us, with Steve insisting on doing the cooking and Manda giving the house a thorough cleaning. Even Gray, not known for his domestic skills despite having been a single parent for years, chipped in and did a load of chores, including the food shopping. I was not allowed to lift a finger. Phil, by this time, was able to get up and dressed, doing his gentle exercises as prescribed by the physiotherapist.

The discussion I'd been expecting came up over dinner – a hugely tasty fish and vegetable concoction that even Phil enjoyed, despite it being low fat and low calorie. 'Kind of thing I suppose I need to get used to,' he'd said, glumly.

'So,' Steve began, 'the plan had been to head over to France again to look at Château d'Aubert, and if we're all happy, to go ahead and make an offer on it. But – I guess it's all off now.' He nodded in Phil's direction.

There was a moment's silence. I did not want to be the first to speak. Manda looked at Gray, who was biting his lip as though trying to decide how to respond. Steve looked as though he was fighting to keep his expression neutral, and not show his disappointment.

'Pity,' Gray said at last. 'It could have been fab.'

Manda nodded. 'Yeah. But Phil's health is the most important consideration. We could have lost him.' She reached over to squeeze his hand, a tear in her eye.

We all sipped our drinks in silence for a moment. Phil's glass contained sparkling water – he was off all alcohol until he'd made a full recovery. I'd never known the gang seem so lost for words.

In the end it was Phil who spoke up. 'Listen, guys, this is only a minor setback. I'm still keen. In fact, I'm even more keen than before. I'm supposed to be getting myself fitter, and what better way to do that than to live somewhere amazing. The doctor suggested I adopt a "Mediterranean diet" so the nearer I am to the Med the easier that will be. We had a great idea, we found – well, Steve found – that château. Can't let a little thing like a near-death experience stop us. Lu, what do you think?' He turned to me and took my hand.

This was my moment. If I said no, I didn't think we should do it, we should stay in England where it'd be easier for Phil to get medical treatment and live a quiet life – then that would be it. The others would accept it, Gray would buy himself a flat near Steve and Manda, and we'd continue as we had been, moving gracefully into the 'third age' of our lives. I shook my head and opened my mouth to speak, but then I caught Phil's eye.

He was gazing at me with an expression chock full of hope and pleading. I suddenly realised that moving to France, a big, radical move to a completely new area, was just what he needed to change his lifestyle and protect his health. If we stayed in England he'd slip back into his old ways, eating the wrong things and not exercising enough. But living in a château in the French mountains just might force him to change. It'd be a new lease of life for him. So of course we should still go ahead with it. If I hadn't wanted to be the one who stopped it before, I definitely wasn't going to now. I took a deep breath before answering.

'I want what's best for you, Phil. If moving is what you want, and you'll promise to look after your health, and everyone else still wants to do it, then yes. We should go ahead.' I smiled at everyone.

'But … are you sure?' Manda still looked worried.

'Mate, you'll be away from your doctors, the NHS …' Gray said.

'They have doctors in France. And hospitals. Good ones – I should know,' Phil replied. 'Question is, are you lot happy to move in with me, given that I'm going to need a bit of help and support over the next few months, until I get myself sorted?'

'We'd do anything for you, old man.' Steve clapped him gently on the shoulder. 'So … do we go ahead with the plan?'

'Yes,' said Phil emphatically, lifting his glass ready for a toast.

'Yes,' I said, realising the others would need me to be as certain as Phil was, for their own peace of mind.

'Too right!' Gray grinned.

'To France!' Manda said, and we all clinked glasses, then began a detailed discussion of how to get the plan back on track.

In the end, Manda and Gray went to France with Steve to look at Château d'Aubert again and begin the process of buying it. Phil was still in recovery and not yet well enough to travel, so he and I stayed home and were the only ones who didn't see it ahead of our moving date. We'd had an offer on our house and were busy packing up and sorting things out, with Alfie and Tom helping us. The boys were also collecting some of our spare furniture.

Before they returned from France, and with our blessing, Steve made an offer on the château which was accepted, signed the *compromis de vente* and paid a ten per cent deposit, mostly using Gray's money from the sale of his house. Ten days later the contract was legally binding. No going back now – not if we wanted to keep Gray's friendship!

The others came back gushing about the château and its environs, and I found myself getting excited about the move, and genuinely looking forward to it for the first time, especially as Phil's health was improving in leaps and bounds. He was coming out with me for daily walks – just around the block at first but gradually progressing to longer distances. He was losing weight, too, and the doctors were delighted with him. 'I need to be as fit as I can be before we move,' he said. 'It's all hilly around the château, isn't it?'

It certainly was. I felt a pang of worry that it might all be too much for him, and he'd end up housebound. But it's what he wanted to do, and I'd support him in every way I could.

Chapter 4

Catherine, 1785

It had been a difficult few weeks at Court. The Queen seemed fractious, stressed and distracted by the ongoing trial, although she continued to maintain her innocence, declaring frequently to the ladies of the court that she'd had no knowledge of the transaction to buy the diamond necklace, she'd never received the necklace, it was not her signature on the instruction to buy it. She'd been duped, she said. Catherine's heart went out to her. The poor Queen, with so much resting on her shoulders, having to deal with this terrible, sordid affair. None of it was her fault, none at all!

Catherine had pieced together what had happened, with the help of Pierre's explanations. A diamond necklace, costing millions of *livres*, had been originally commissioned by the old king Louis XV for his mistress, Madame du Barry. But Louis had died before the necklace was finished. The jewellers, hoping to recoup costs, had tried to sell it to the current king, Louis XVI, for him to give to Marie Antoinette. But the dear Queen had refused, saying it was too much, and the money would be better spent on ships than necklaces. Privately to her ladies, and in Catherine's hearing, she'd said she found the idea of wearing a necklace designed for another woman distasteful. 'If it was not ordered with me in mind, then it is not for me,' she'd said, and Catherine had agreed. The Queen could not ever be considered second best, the second choice to own the diamonds.

And then a woman named Jeanne de la Motte, along with accomplices, had concocted a plan to defraud the Queen. Jeanne had become the lover of Cardinal de Rohan, who was anxious to regain favour at Court after having insulted the Queen's mother, the Empress of Austria. Jeanne de la Motte had told the Cardinal that if he were to help buy the necklace on behalf of the Queen by negotiating with the jeweller, the Queen would be prepared to be reconciled with him.

'Her plan was audacious, and the Cardinal so stupid, that it worked,' Pierre had said. Audacious indeed, Catherine thought. After passing forged notes purportedly from the Queen to the Cardinal, Jeanne de la Motte had arranged a meeting after dark in the grounds of Versailles, between the Cardinal and a prostitute who bore a resemblance to the Queen. The Cardinal had believed he was meeting the great Marie Antoinette herself, and had pledged his own credit with the jewellers to secure the necklace for the Queen. Jeanne had sent a man pretending to be the Queen's valet to collect the necklace from the Cardinal, and that was the last time it was seen. 'I expect it was sent abroad, and broken up,' Pierre had said. 'There were a lot of diamonds in it.'

The deceit had come to light when the Cardinal failed to pay the first instalment to the jeweller, who had then applied directly to the Queen. She had denied all knowledge of arranging the transaction, had denounced the correspondence as forgeries, and stated she had never set eyes on the necklace itself.

'But people do not believe her,' Pierre had said, shaking his head sadly. 'She spent so much money in the early years of her reign, not least on that hamlet of hers that you love so much, that the people believe she has the necklace and is only trying to wriggle out of paying for it.'

'It is shocking,' Catherine had said, 'that they believe her capable of such a thing, when she has shown her people nothing but kindness and compassion.' She'd sighed. 'Our poor queen is much misunderstood.'

The Cardinal had been arrested and imprisoned, but acquitted. Jeanne de la Motte and some of her accomplices were not so lucky. She had been found guilty and sentenced to flogging, branding and life imprisonment. The ongoing scandal had been the subject of court gossip for weeks, and the worry had taken its toll on the Queen. She looked tired, Catherine thought. There were lines on her face where there had been none before. There were rumours too, that under the powder her hair was beginning to turn white.

But Catherine would continue to support her. She still believed in the overarching goodness of the Queen. She was innocent in this affair of the diamond necklace. She had done nothing wrong, and had been duped by a charlatan. That Jeanne de la Motte! If Catherine ever saw her again, she'd tell her exactly what she thought of her. But now that the trickster was in prison that was never likely to happen.

As she mused on what had happened to the poor queen, Catherine twisted the ring that never left her finger – her own most precious piece of jewellery. A garnet and gold ring, with a ring of diamonds around the central stone. Inside, known only to her and Pierre, their initials were engraved to mark their wedding.

'It is so unfair on the Queen,' Catherine lamented to Pierre, as they lay in bed one night, propped up on several pillows in satin pillowcases. 'She is innocent. She had nothing to do with the theft of that necklace. Why do the people blame her?'

He sighed and pulled a sumptuous woven coverlet a little further up over them. 'They believe it is in keeping with her character. They see her as extravagant and uncaring about the poor.'

'But the dear Queen is so kind to the poor! Look at the people who live in her little hamlet. They want for nothing. She bought them all new smocks only last week.'

Pierre kissed her. 'My love, you are so sweet and so young. The people of the hamlet are indeed well looked after. Do not worry. I am sure this affair will soon blow over.'

Catherine smiled happily and snuggled up against him. 'I think you are right. This is just a blip, then, and all will soon be well. At least that terrible woman who defrauded the Queen is now in prison and paying for her crime. The people will realise who the true villain is in this affair.'

'I hope so,' Pierre agreed.

'And tomorrow, I believe we are to pay another visit to the Petit Trianon and the hamlet. I shall wear my new shepherdess gown. I am so glad that I determined on pink ribbons, in the end. They look just right. I believe the Queen will notice them and may even pay me a compliment. I should be so happy, were that to happen!'

'I'm sure she will,' Pierre said, leaning over to kiss her long and deep. 'Your happiness is all I want, my love. I shall do all in my power to secure it.'

She kissed him back. He may have been much older than her but he was a good, kind husband. One day, after she'd borne him an heir, perhaps she would take a lover, as so many at Court did, but not yet. For now she was content with Pierre. It had been a good match.

'Catherine, my sweet, I would like your portrait painted,' Pierre said. 'An artist will come here tomorrow to consult with us. Perhaps you can give some thought as to which gown you will wear, and how you would like your hair to be styled?'

Catherine was delighted. 'Thank you. I have always wanted to be painted. Tell me, is the artist the very best there is?'

He laughed. 'Of course. Only the best for you.'

'Then I shall wear the shepherdess gown. With my hair piled high, with matching ribbons … no, perhaps a few locks left loose, curling down. Oh! I shall never sleep now. I am too excited, and my mind too full of how I shall look for my portrait!'

A few weeks later, Catherine's excitement over the painting of her portrait had worn off. While she had loved the initial consultations, deciding what to wear and how to dress her hair, and where to sit within their apartment to allow the most opulent backdrop to the painting, she had found the actual sittings to be tedious and boring.

'Madame, please turn slightly to your left, no, the other way, and incline your head just a fraction. Ah! That is perfect. Now, please stay still while I capture your exquisite beauty.' The artist fussed over her position every time she sat, and showed irritation when for one sitting she arrived wearing a different gown. 'Madame, I have started the portrait with you in the other gown. I cannot paint you in this one. Ah, maybe I will concentrate on your face today, and next time you will wear the other gown, yes?'

She did not like being told what to wear and how to sit, but Pierre had asked her to do what the artist wanted. He had assured her the end result would be worth it, and so she resolved to suffer the discomfort of the many sittings for his sake, as was fitting for a good wife. Within the Palace of Versailles were other portraits painted by the same artist, and she had to admit they were good likenesses. Her own, she hoped, would show her to be one of the most beautiful women at Court, second only to Her Majesty Queen Marie Antoinette, of course.

Finally, after far too long, the portrait was complete, and Pierre declared himself delighted with the result. It was hung in their apartment, though Catherine would have liked it to be hung in a more public part of the palace. Nevertheless, she enjoyed gazing at it every morning and evening. She looked almost regal in it, she thought. And the portrait would live on, preserving her beauty for all time, even after she aged and died. That was a comforting idea.

Chapter 5

Lu

The next weeks were a whirlwind of activity, and I had no time to think any more about my own feelings about the move, between nursing Phil and organising our own affairs. I kept checking – several times a day – that he was all right, still happy to be going ahead with it all, but he remained excited and confident we were doing the right thing.

We spent a weekend with the others working out what we needed to keep to furnish the château – between us we had ten sofas, five of them Steve and Manda's, which seemed a bit excessive. We all had items we knew we couldn't part with, but there was a lot of thinning down needed before we moved. Gray moved first – driving his own furniture in a hired van, all the way through France. He also signed the final *acte de vente* and arranged to transfer the balance of payment to the *notaire*. This time it was mostly our money, as Steve and Manda were still waiting on completion of their property sale. We'd drawn up legal documents stating who owned what proportion of the property, and who would pay what and when. We trusted each other of course, but Steve insisted we make everything watertight.

'In case we all drop dead suddenly,' Steve had said, 'and our kids are left dealing with it all.' He'd looked at Phil and blushed. 'Sorry, mate, that was tactless of me.'

'It's OK. I'd expect nothing less from you,' Phil had replied, laughing. It's good to have friends so close that we can joke about our mortality.

We went a day after Gray, driving down through France ahead of our removal company, spending a night in a small hotel on the edge of Dijon on the way. Steve and Manda were doing much the same, though were booked on a different ferry to us. I did almost all the driving, as although Phil had been signed off from the doctor he still found it tiring. As we headed into the mountains the scenery became more and more spectacular and despite chattering non-stop earlier in the journey, Phil and I found ourselves falling silent, each absorbed in imagining our new life in France with our best mates. When we reached the village of Saint-Michel-sur-Verais I gave a little gasp – partly of excitement and partly of trepidation – and Phil turned to grin at me.

'This is it, then! Hope we like the place!'

'I'm sure we will,' I replied, but not without a pang of worry. What if the château didn't live up to its promise? What if we didn't actually like it, after all? But the village at least was appealing. It looked familiar from so many passes through it on Google Street View. There was the *boulangerie* where we would buy our bread. The little Carrefour Connect supermarket. A central square, named Place de la Révolution, containing a *pétanque terrain* shaded by plane trees, and a war memorial. A *tabac* that also served coffees in the morning and beers in the afternoon, and a friendly-looking bistro overlooked the square. A squat church at one end of the square, with a little *mairie* behind, the French tricolour proudly flying alongside the EU flag. A *patisserie*, with a delicious-looking display of cakes and pastries in the window, and the ubiquitous pharmacy with a flashing green cross. I made a mental note to check where the nearest hospital with an emergency department was, and to register with a doctor as soon as possible.

We parked in the square, then crossed to the bistro, where Steve had suggested we all meet so we could arrive at the château together. The other three were already there, sitting at a table near the window. Manda waved excitedly as we entered, and they all leapt up to hug, kiss, shake hands as we took our places at the table.

'So this is it! We're here!' I said. My stomach gave a flip as I said the words. There was no going back, now.

'We'll have a late lunch, then let's go up to the château. Gray's got the keys and has checked it's still standing,' Steve said.

'Did you sleep there last night?' Phil wanted to know.

Gray nodded. 'Yes. In my sleeping bag on the floor. It was dark by the time I arrived and there was no one to help empty the van.'

'Oh, you poor thing. On your own in a château all night? Weren't you scared?' Manda teased.

Gray was about to answer when the bistro *propriétaire* arrived to take our order. He was a portly man with an impressive moustache, and must have overheard part of our conversation. Despite our attempts to order in French, he answered us in good English.

'You are the English who 'ave bought the château, yes?' he asked.

'Yes, we are moving in today,' Steve answered. He introduced each of us, and we all shook hands.

The man nodded. 'My name is Paul Christophe. I am pleased to meet you. I 'ope you will be vairy 'appy living 'ere.'

I adored his accent. There's something about a Frenchman speaking English – I could listen to him all day. 'Thank you. We're very excited to be here, and I expect we'll be regular visitors in your bistro.'

He laughed. 'But you 'ave not yet eaten my food. You will be 'ere *every* day when you 'ave tried it.' He went off to pass our order to the kitchen, but was back a moment later with the tallest liqueur bottle I have ever seen – it must have been about three feet high, tapering from a six-inch base. 'Pastis, on the 'ouse, to celebrate your arrival,' he said, pouring us each a shot.

What a welcome! We laughed, clinked glasses, downed the shots (or in the case of Steve and Phil – who both still needed to drive a short way – sipped it) and toasted our new life in France. Monsieur Christophe joined us.

'I am glad the château is occupied again,' he said. 'It should not be empty. I think the ghost does not like to be alone.' He winked as he said this, but I felt a shiver down my spine.

'Is it haunted? Did you meet the ghost last night?' I asked Gray.

'Well, I heard a few odd noises,' he said with a laugh. 'Bound to be some, in an old property.'

Noises, or ghosts? Ghosts wouldn't be good for Phil's heart condition. I wasn't sure what Monsieur Christophe meant and was about to ask, when he spoke again.

'You must go to say 'ello to Madame la Maire. Do not wait for 'er to come to you. She likes to meet all the people of the village.'

'Madame la Maire?' Manda said. 'Where does she live?'

'Do not go to 'er 'ouse. The *mairie* is in the village, behind the church. You must go this week.'

'We spotted the *mairie* when we drove through,' Phil said. 'OK, we'll go soon.'

Monsieur Christophe nodded, and left us to our meals. It was a joyous occasion with lots of laughter, but we didn't linger as we were all desperate to arrive at Château d'Aubert and get started with our new life.

It was a short drive from the village to the château. Gray had walked down, so he took a lift with Phil and me. We drove out of the village, along a quiet lane running beside the river along the bottom of the valley, past rich pastures. There were lofty peaks on both sides of the valley, their slopes mostly covered with coniferous forest, giving way to deciduous trees on the lower levels. Numerous streams cascaded down the mountain sides feeding the main river – I imagined that in early spring when the winter snows were melting they'd be torrents rather than trickles.

We rounded a corner and then there were the tiny gatehouse and gravel track I'd seen on Google Street View, leading off to the left. A hand-painted wooden sign pointed the way to Château d'Aubert. Our château. My heart beat faster as Phil turned off the lane. The sun had come out as though to welcome us to our new home, and I craned my neck for every glimpse of it through the trees as Phil navigated the winding track. And then suddenly, there it was in front of us, yellow stone looking warm and welcoming, ivy climbing up one wall, glass in the tower windows glinting in the sunshine. Shutters painted in a faded, peeling blue paint at every window. It took my breath away. I couldn't believe this was to be our home.

'I parked just round the side, in front of the old stables,' Gray said, pointing to the left. Phil drove round and parked our car next to Gray's hired van. There were a few outbuildings there, and also some ruins – something the others had mentioned seeing when they viewed the château but which I'd not seen on the property details. It looked as though the château had once been much larger, and only a part of it was still standing. I wondered what had happened to it.

There was a side door into the château but Gray led us back around to the front, and the main door. 'You should enter in style,' he said, as Steve and Manda's car appeared around the corner and parked next to ours. Gray pulled out a huge old-fashioned iron key and unlocked the studded oak door. It looked to be original – probably several hundred years old. How many different people had passed through it, through the centuries? Who were they, and what were their lives like? I may have stopped teaching history some years earlier but I was still a historian at heart, always wanting to know what and who had come before.

'This is it!' said Manda, hooking her arm through mine as Gray pushed open the door. It gave a gentle creak but swung easily, and we crossed the threshold into a cool stone-flagged hallway with wood-panelled walls, lit by a full-length leaded window at the far end, which looked out onto a courtyard garden.

'Oh my goodness,' I said, but my words seemed totally inadequate to convey my feelings on setting foot in this amazing new home. I glanced at Phil, who was standing with his mouth open, looking around in wonder. I'd been mad to worry it might not live up to expectations. It was simply gorgeous.

'Like it?' said Manda with a grin.

'Impressive!' I opened the nearest door – it led to a large kitchen with dated but usable fixtures. One end of the kitchen had a curved wall – the base of the tower that rose up in one corner of the château. There was a change in level, with the tower part being a few steps above the main part of the kitchen. Below, in the base of the tower was a cellar, that would be perfect as a wine store. The next door off the hallway opened into a huge room with a massive fireplace. At the far end, patio doors opened onto the garden.

'Living room. Probably also dining room,' Manda said. She'd followed me in, while the fellas had gone straight into the kitchen to put on the kettle.

A third door from the hallway led to a short corridor with more doors off. 'Various small rooms – utility room, boot room, pantry, whatever,' said Manda. 'But come upstairs now.'

The stairs led up from the hallway. They were carpeted in a worn red-patterned carpet, and had dark wood banisters. On the first floor were four bedrooms, each with an en-suite bathroom. 'The advantages of it having once been a hotel,' Manda said. The bathrooms were in need of updating but usable. One bedroom also incorporated the tower, so had a curved end wall and again, a difference in floor level. On the second floor were four more bedrooms, and at the end of a passage a narrow spiral staircase led to a small circular room that was wholly within the tower, above the curved corners of the kitchen and bedrooms. I went in, picking my way through rubbish left here by the previous owners, and peered out of its small grubby window which looked out of the front of the château. You could clearly see the entrance track and the gatehouse from here, and the lane to the village. It was a good lookout post – if you were waiting for someone to arrive, you'd catch glimpses of them from here long before they reached the château.

But it was the view over the mountains on the other side of the valley that really excited me. It was April, and there was still a bit of snow on the distant peaks, contrasting against the deep blue sky and the vibrant green of foliage on the woodlands of the lower slopes.

'I know, right?' said Manda, who'd come to stand beside me. 'I can't wait to be on a horse, hacking up those hills.'

'I'll be on foot,' I laughed. The possibilities for hill-walking were, to my mind, one of the best things about this move.

'Steve's already planned a fell-running route, and Gray said he'll be out cycling tomorrow. We just need Phil to take up some kind of exercise beyond skiing.'

I nodded. 'Something gentle for him.' He needed to build up a bit of fitness, for the sake of his health, and to reduce the chances of another heart attack. But he'd need to be careful. I was glad the château was at the bottom of a valley, and that the walk to the village was more-or-less flat.

'Lu? Come and choose a bedroom!' Phil was yelling up the spiral stairs. I turned away from that incredible view and went down to help pick which of the eight main bedrooms would be ours.

It was surreal, that first evening in the château. We unloaded the few things we'd brought with us in the car – clothes, sleeping bags, towels and toiletries – and put them in the room Phil and I had chosen, that had a view over the valley revealed after we flung open the shutters. Gray had bought some food and rustled us up a cold supper, and of course we'd all brought bottles of bubbly to celebrate moving in. Gray had to rummage through his still-unpacked hired van to find the box with glasses in. Phil wasn't supposed to drink, but he poured himself a small glass. I kept a careful eye on him. We sat on the floor on our pillows, in what was to be our sitting room, and toasted each other.

'Well, here we are!' said Steve, raising his champagne glass high.

'To our future! To us!' I said, and everyone joined in. 'To us!'

It was at that precise moment, as we cheered and clinked glasses, that it happened. A knock, a creak and a momentary flicker of the electric lights.

'What was that?' Manda said.

Gray looked thoughtful. 'Same sort of thing occurred last night, when I was here on my own. Just an old building settling itself down for the night, I suppose. And elderly electrics.'

'Or that ghost,' Phil said, unhelpfully, 'the one that Monsieur Christophe spoke about.'

'Don't be daft,' I said, glaring at him to shut up. Manda, I knew, was nervous about the idea of anything supernatural. The last thing she wanted was to think that she'd just moved into a haunted house.

She took a long sip of her fizz. 'Let's just hope if it's a ghost, it's a friendly one.'

'How could it not be?' said Steve, as he adjusted his position to put an arm around her. 'This is the most beautiful place in the world. Any ghost living here would be a happy one.'

'I wonder if anyone did die here,' Gray said.

'Almost certainly,' I replied. 'This place is what, three or four hundred years old? People are bound to have died here. Doesn't mean there are any ghosts though. There's no such thing.' Even as I said it, I wondered if I believed it. Since Mum died I'd often felt her presence somehow, as though she was just behind me, watching what I was doing, smiling and lending a hand. If there was life beyond the grave, I liked to think Mum was happy, fit and able-bodied again, enjoying herself.

Manda shuddered. 'Well, if they died here, I just hope they didn't decide to hang around. Hey, you ghosts – this place is ours now, all right?'

'Ooh er, don't antagonise them,' Gray said, widening his eyes at her. 'Or they'll come and haunt your bedroom tonight. Wooo!'

He got hit with Manda's pillow for that, and before long we were all in a pillow fight, laughing and giggling as though we were twelve years old rather than almost sixty. Only one glass of champagne got spilt, which wasn't too bad considering. And there were no more spooky noises. As Gray had said, it was probably just old-house noises and some dodgy wiring.

That first night, we slept in sleeping bags we'd brought in the car, on the floor of our new bedroom, closing the shutters to block out the light. The château creaked a few more times as we got settled. I supposed we'd just have to get used to it.

'Happy?' I asked Phil, as we snuggled down together.

'Very,' he replied. 'You?'

'Mm-hmm,' I said. Was I happy, now that we were here, and the château and its environs were all I'd hoped they'd be? I was excited, certainly, but those misgivings were still there. Would we fit in to the local community? Would this work as a long-term move?

'Good. That's good.' Phil shifted position so that I could put my head on his shoulder, the way he knew I liked to sleep. It was a little uncomfortable lying on a hard floor, but I slept amazingly well, waking only when Manda tapped at the door and came in with a couple of cups of tea for us.

'Morning. It's a beautiful day!'

'Thanks, Manda.' I rolled over in my sleeping bag, sat up and took the tea from her. Phil was still snoring gently beside me. Manda smiled and crept out of the room, as I wriggled out of the sleeping bag, threw on some clothes and took my tea downstairs. The rest of the gang were outside, on a patio. They'd flung open the patio doors from the living room. There was an old wooden bench and table out there – tatty but serviceable – and the sun was already warming the patio flagstones. I sat down and gazed around at the garden.

'Amazing, isn't it?' said Manda. 'Gray's inside cooking bacon and eggs.'

'That's even more amazing,' quipped Steve and we laughed.

The patio looked out onto a sweep of lawn that fell away down to the right towards a copse of trees. The grass was a little overgrown now that the new growing season had begun. There were shrubs along the edges, and an old stone wall on the left side, with a peeling painted gate set into it.

'What's through there?' I pointed.

'It goes through to the courtyard,' Steve said. 'And the ruins.'

'Ruins?' I recalled I'd seen something of them the day before.

'Apparently the château was once much bigger. There was a fire, a couple of hundred years ago, that consumed a lot of it, leaving only this wing.'

'Ooh. Wonder what caused the fire?'

Steve shrugged. 'The estate agent said it was something to do with the French Revolution but knew nothing more. Also he said there's some mystery about a woman – a member of the aristocracy – who lived here and vanished. You're the historian, Lu. Maybe you could research, and find out for us?'

I smiled and shrugged. Ruins, a fire, a ghost, a woman who'd disappeared. What other mysteries were associated with this château?

'Breakfast is served, ladies and gents,' announced Gray. He was carrying a tray, which he put down on the table. 'We'll have to eat it out here as it's the only table, until we unload my van and the other furniture arrives.'

'Frankly I'd like to eat out here every morning,' I said. It was all simply perfect.

Phil turned up, still in his pyjamas and with his hair flattened on one side, sticking up on the other. 'Did someone say breakfast?'

'Yep,' said Gray. 'Your turn to cook tomorrow, mate.'

We'd need to agree some rules, I realised, to make sure everyone did their fair share of jobs. And we needed some financial arrangements for buying food or shared items for the château. We were here, we owned the building, but we were a long way yet from getting our new life properly organised. But there was plenty of time. For now, I wanted to simply sit here, enjoy the sunshine, bacon and eggs, and the company of my favourite people. It had felt like a long time since I'd been able to fully relax and take time for *me*. The move had of course taken a lot of time and energy, and before that had been Phil's heart attack, and before that I'd spent most of my time looking after Mum up until her death.

Mum had always been so fit and active and independent that when she was diagnosed with multiple sclerosis – the primary progressive form of the disease – and told she should no longer drive, it was a shock. Dad had died of cancer a few years earlier so Mum was on her own, although she lived just an hour's journey from Phil and me.

Soon after her diagnosis she became unable to climb the stairs in her home. I'd been doing her shopping for her at weekends, and then I helped move a bed downstairs for her. Before too long she began needing help with basic things such as getting undressed and into bed, and it was then that I had a serious chat with Phil.

'I don't want carers for her, Phil. She's my mum. I want to be her carer.' It felt right. She'd done so much for me throughout my life – here was my chance to give something back. And I knew she'd much rather have me tend to her needs than a stranger.

'But Lu, she lives too far away for you to go to her every day. You have a full-time job.' Phil looked worried.

I paused, weighing up my words. I'd thought about this hard during several sleepless nights before I'd come to my decision. 'I think I should give up work, Phil. To free up time to care for her. I also would like her to move here. We can put a bed for her in the dining room – we never use it.' We had a downstairs loo and shower room that would be suitable for her to use – it'd be perfect.

'You stop work? Move her here?' Phil repeated, with a frown. I nodded but said nothing more, just gave him time to process what I was suggesting. It was a big change – my salary from teaching was nothing compared to his so financially we'd be all right, but moving his disabled mother-in-law in was a big step.

At last he smiled and put out a hand to me. 'If it's what you think is best, and you are sure you can cope with it all, then I'll support you.'

'Thanks, darling,' I replied. I'd expected him to say this – after so many years together I was pretty certain he'd be supportive. But it was good to get confirmation that he was as lovely a son-in-law and husband as he could possibly be.

Within a week, I had handed in my notice and was due to leave at the end of term. We'd rearranged the house to make space for Mum, squashing the dining-room table into one end of the sitting room and putting bedroom furniture into the dining room. She was overwhelmed but delighted when I'd suggested the move to her.

'Oh, darling, are you sure? I don't want to be a burden ...' There'd been a smile on her face but tears in her eyes as she spoke.

'I'm sure, Mum. Least I can do.' I had hugged her, but been careful not to say too much as I knew it would make me cry, and then she'd worry I was only doing this out of a sense of duty and didn't really want it.

'And Phil's all right with it, is he?' Mum loved Phil. They had the same sense of humour, and I'd often come across the two of them giggling together over the silliest thing.

'He's looking forward to seeing more of you,' I replied.

And so she moved in. The first few weeks while I was still working were tough. I'd get her up and dressed in the morning, then leave her settled on the sofa with a walking frame near to hand before going to work. When I returned home, she'd be desperate for me to sit and chat to her after a long lonely day, but I'd need to be cooking the tea, putting some washing on, unloading the dishwasher – all those jobs that working people have to squeeze into evenings and weekends. Phil did his share – more than half of the cooking and housework – but even so, it was tough getting everything done. And then it'd be the bed and bath routine for Mum. It reminded me of when Tom and Alfie were small and I was working – there was very little free time for me.

It was much better when I'd given up work. I was able to enjoy spending time with Mum. We'd go out – to garden centres, cafés, shops. I bought a wheelchair that easily folded into the boot of my car, and then we could go anywhere as long as it was flat. For a couple of years we had fun, and I loved having her with us. We sold her house; she insisted Phil and I should take half of the proceeds – 'towards the cost of looking after me,' she said. But eventually the inevitable decline came, and it became more difficult for her to transfer from armchair to wheelchair to car. Our trips out became less frequent. And she was tired most of the time – wanting to nap in front of the television while I mooched around the house looking for jobs to do.

If I'm honest, there were times during this period that I began to feel resentful. I'd given up my job and put my life on hold for Mum, and while I didn't regret my decisions it was hard at times not to feel that life was slipping away from me. I'd occasionally meet old colleagues for a coffee and they'd chat and laugh and regale me with stories of the latest shenanigans at school, and I felt left out. I'd see Steve and Manda going off on holidays while Phil and I stayed home, or Phil would go skiing with Gray while I stayed home with Mum. I did have a couple of holidays, managing to book Mum into a nursing home for respite care, but she was never happy there and I wasn't happy either knowing she was being looked after by strangers.

When she caught pneumonia and had to go into hospital the first time, I felt a mix of emotions. Worry, of course, for her. But tinged with a guilty feeling of relief that while she was in hospital she was no longer my responsibility. I visited her every day of course, but in between there were hours for myself. I went shopping for new clothes. I spring-cleaned Mum's room. I visited a couple of National Trust properties. I went for long walks in the country. In short, I had a life, without Mum being there.

But when she was discharged from hospital and I brought her home, my overwhelming feeling was one of relief. She'd survived. I had my mum back where she belonged. Who cared about having time to myself – it was more important to spend time with her. Her brush with death had made me realise she would not be with me for ever. And indeed, it was only another six months before she had another bout of pneumonia, another hospital stay, and this time was the last.

I sat at her bedside for five days at the end, holding her hand, doing little things for her like holding a drink for her to sip, straightening her pillows, brushing her hair. She slipped into a coma on the last day, and a nurse checking on her put a hand on my shoulder and gazed at me with compassion. 'It won't be long now,' she said quietly. 'But your mother is aware you are here, and that will be a comfort to her.'

The nurse was right – it wasn't long afterwards that Mum's breathing slowed, then stopped, her lips turned briefly blue and then she was still, sleeping forever. I think I let out an anguished wail – I was vaguely aware of a nurse poking her head through the gap in the curtains to see what was happening, and then leaving me to hug my mother for one last time. 'Love you, Mum,' I whispered, as I kissed her cheek.

It was odd going home that day. Home to Phil, but no Mum, and no need for further trips to the hospital. Just a funeral to arrange and her possessions to deal with, probate to apply for, her room to convert back into a dining room and then nothing. She was gone, her life had been dismantled, and there was I with little to do.

I could have gone back to work I suppose, but I had been out of teaching for several years and felt out of touch. The syllabus had changed. My old school had no vacancies and the thought of trying to settle in at a new school, possibly far from home, did not appeal.

Besides, it was not long after Mum's death that Phil got made redundant with a healthy payout, the whole move-to-France project began, and then Phil had his heart attack, giving me a new set of carer's responsibilities.

And now, as Phil was beginning to recover, I would have more time for myself at last. Time to pick up an old hobby, or start a new project, after we had settled in, of course. Maybe I could rekindle my love of history, and try to research what happened to that aristocrat who went missing from the château?

Chapter 6

Pierre, 1789

All was in uproar at Versailles, as Pierre Aubert was summoned to the King's chambers along with the ministers for urgent discussions, one day in June 1789.

'They have locked themselves into an indoor tennis court, of all places,' the King was saying, as Pierre entered the room and bowed to his monarch. 'They say they will not leave until they have agreed upon a constitution. My authority is no longer good enough. The Third Estate – the commoners – are now calling themselves the National Assembly, and as I understand it, some of the nobles and clergy from the First and Second Estates have joined with them. My power is being eroded!'

Privately, Pierre thought this was no bad thing. It wasn't right for all power to be vested in one man. Sometimes that worked – when the country was prosperous and when the man was strong and wise. But Louis XVI was not strong and wise. He'd been a weak prince – hadn't he taken years to consummate his marriage? As King he'd been indecisive, yet stubbornly clinging to the ways of the *ancien régime*, insisting that he was answerable only to God. He'd overspent hugely, partly in supporting the American War of Independence, despite the poverty of his own people. His Queen had spent yet more money, on her clothes and jewels and indulging herself with her ridiculous little toy farm that Pierre's wife loved so much. And Louis had raised taxation in an attempt to pay off his debts or at least the interest on them, but the burden had fallen largely on the poor, and the King had been resistant to any reforms that would redress the balance.

And then there'd been the failure of the harvest the previous year. Horrendous hailstorms across northern France had destroyed the crops in the fields. Any grain reserves they might have kept had been exported, in an attempt at raising funds. The price of bread had risen enormously. People could barely afford to eat, let alone buy other goods, leading to unemployment. To top it all, the winter had been vicious.

At Versailles they'd been comfortable of course, living in luxury that Pierre was beginning to feel embarrassed by, as he saw what was happening to the poorest members of French society. At least convening the *Estates-General* had been a step forward, but without reform, without the Third Estate of the common people being given equal voting rights, there would be no progress. And now the Third Estate had formed themselves into the National Assembly and were seizing control themselves.

How Louis managed this crisis was all-important, and could mean the difference between a smooth transition to a more equal, modern form of government and … Pierre didn't like to consider what the alternative might be. The monarchy had existed for hundreds of years. The current king could trace his ancestry back for generation upon generation, some better and some worse, but all having absolute power. But times were changing, and Louis must allow things to change, for his own safety and that of his family. And his ministers and courtiers.

'Sire, the National Assembly will not stop until they have the reforms they seek,' the Finance minister, Jacques Necker, told the

King. 'I fear you may need to agree to their demands, and at the very least, recognise their authority. We must work together with them, not against them, and gradually move towards a new ...'

Pierre thought he was about to use the word 'regime', but Necker appeared to have stopped himself before he went too far. Everyone knew that of all the ministers, Necker was most sympathetic to the National Assembly and their demands. He was popular with the people too, Pierre knew. So far the King had tolerated Necker in his government, but as he scowled now at the finance minister, Pierre wondered how much longer that would last.

Personally, Pierre thought Necker was right. If only the King would listen to him and take his advice – there could be a way for the reforms to be made while keeping the monarchy intact, albeit with less power. At least he hoped so.

It was mid-July. Pierre had been sent into Paris, to report back to the King on the mood there. Three days earlier, on 11th July, the King had sacked Jacques Necker, and reorganised his government completely. Pierre had privately thought this was a bad move – sacking the well-liked Necker had only served to inflame the situation. Despite Necker's best efforts, the King had not taken his advice in terms of acknowledging the authority of the Assembly. Worse, the King had deployed loyal, mostly foreign, troops on the streets of Paris, ostensibly to keep the peace and quell any riots, but the Parisians believed the troops were there to break up the National Assembly. The situation was tense.

Pierre's job was to ride around the city, checking on areas where mobs were building, and return to Versailles to provide a first-hand and trustworthy account to the King. 'I will deploy the Royal Guard wherever the worst mobs have formed,' the King had said. 'I will not allow lawlessness in my capital city! It will not do!'

As Pierre rode his grey mare into Paris, he wondered whether that would be the best course of action. Surely if the Royal Guard were there in too large a number, and used force to disperse the mobs, that would only inflame the people more? All summer the tensions had been rising and now it seemed they were at breaking point. The King's dismissal of Necker had certainly not helped at all.

Even on the outskirts of the city Pierre found gangs of men brandishing sticks, hoes, pikes – anything they could get their hands on – and heading into the city centre. He passed by them cautiously. He had a half-dozen of the Royal Guard with him as protection. One mob jeered and yelled as they passed, and at one point Pierre was afraid they would grab for the horses, and perhaps pull the men off.

'Look, the Swiss and German soldiers – they have come to shut down our National Assembly!' one man called out, to roars of anger from the others.

'No, there are only seven of them. They can do nothing,' another voice cried out. 'Let them pass. We will do better to join with other groups before we try to take any of them on.'

Pierre was sweating, but thankfully the man was right. There were about a dozen in this mob, on foot against himself and the six guards who were all on horseback. The mob would have had no chance. Pierre and his men passed by unhurt, although the mob jeered and brandished their improvised weapons as they passed. One threw a clod of horse manure, which hit Pierre on the shoulder. He wanted to turn back, find who had thrown it and punish him, but instinct told him that he'd come off worse if he did, even with the guards protecting him. This mob, these *sans-culottes* as they were beginning to be known because of their attire, had nothing to lose and as such would fight harder and dirtier than himself and the guards. His mission was to observe and report, not fight.

Around a corner, on a quiet street, Pierre pulled up his horse and spoke to the captain of his guards. 'This won't do. I will be able to provide better reports if I am on foot, blending in a little with the common people.' He dismounted, and handed the reins to the captain. 'Go back, with my horse. Wait just outside the city on the Versailles road. I will spend a couple of hours finding out what is happening and will return to you there.'

The captain nodded, looking relieved, Pierre thought, to be given such an easy, safe task. Any danger would be to Pierre himself. He looked down at his clothing. He'd not put on his finery for this mission, but even so his jacket marked him out as a member of court. He slipped it off and handed it to the captain. He'd continue on in his shirt sleeves.

The roads were filthy, filled with mud and stinking of sewage, and Pierre had to tread carefully. If ever he had to do this again he'd need poor clothes and commoner's boots, not the fine breeches and white hose that he was wearing. He should make himself look like one of the mob himself, maybe even carry a stick, and not his sword. But right now, the sword lent him courage. He was a good swordsman. If anyone attacked him, he'd make short work of them. He continued into the city, hand on the hilt of his sword, keeping a look out on both sides and with frequent glances behind. He was aware of people peering out of windows, women hurriedly closing shutters, ushering children inside. There was tension in the air – a feeling that something momentous was about to happen.

Pierre hid in a doorway as a mob ran past, whooping and yelling. Behind them came a wagon filled with sacks of grain. A warehouse had been plundered the night before, Pierre had heard, and its contents seized by the hordes. The Royal Guard had done very little to stop them.

Pierre went first to the *Hotel des Invalides*. Until recently it had been used to store thousands of muskets and hundreds of barrels of gunpowder. The commandant there had advised that the gunpowder at least be moved somewhere safer, and so a few days ago it had been moved to the Bastille – that huge, ancient fortress in the middle of the city. It would be safe there. At the *Invalides*, there was uproar. The Paris militia, under the command of the National Assembly, had stormed the palace, no doubt in search of the muskets and gunpowder. They'd taken it over, apparently meeting little resistance. Pierre moved on, travelling by the back streets, crossing the river under the shadow of the great cathedral of Notre Dame, hiding from mobs in shadows, until he reached the Bastille, where he found a vantage point in the doorway of a boarded-up building. There were hundreds of people gathered, chanting, brandishing weapons of various types. They were calling for the removal of the cannon and gunpowder from the fortress. Pierre listened to conversations around him and gathered that representatives of the people had gone inside earlier that morning, to negotiate the surrender of the prison, which only held about half a dozen inmates, mostly forgers. But nothing had happened yet, and the crowd were impatient.

It was early afternoon when all hell broke loose. Some of the crowd had climbed onto a roof and broken the drawbridge chains. More had run inside. There was gunfire from all directions. Pierre cowered back into the doorway where he'd been standing, his hand on the hilt of his sword, just in case. All was pandemonium. The crowd had become a chaotic mob with no one seemingly leading it. A gunshot whistled by Pierre leaving a musketball lodged in the door over his left shoulder. It was not safe here. Head down, he ran for better cover, hoping he would still be able to observe what was happening.

Dodging musket fire he ran around a corner, straight into a handful of men. They were wielding sticks rather than muskets, he was thankful to see.

'Who's this?' the leader of them said. 'One of the Royal Guard? Are you Swiss or French?'

'French,' Pierre replied, his fingers curled around the hilt of his sword. 'On your side, my friends.'

'You're no common man,' the leader said. 'That fine shirt, those boots. You're a King's man. Spying, perhaps? At him, lads!'

There were four of them. As the first couple stepped forward and thrust at him with their sticks, Pierre drew his sword and easily parried them – disarming one and flesh-wounding the second. The other two men were behind him. Pierre spun around, his sword held in both hands, and snarled at them. 'Four of you but you'll come off worse. I suggest you let me go.'

Two of them ran – the wounded man and one other, but the leader of the little gang stood firm. 'Listen to him talk, lads. He's an aristocrat, all right. Taking the food from the mouths of your children, to pay for that Austrian bitch's excesses. Make him pay!' The man swung at Pierre, aiming at his head, but Pierre blocked his thrust, swinging his sword around and up, catching the man under the arm. He could kill him, so easily, with another swing and a thrust. But he chose not to. The man was wounded enough that he could no longer attack.

'I warned you. Now run,' Pierre said, holding his sword ready in case the other man decided to have a go. But the other man was already halfway down the street behind him. Only the wounded leader was left, clutching his wounded right arm with his left.

'You'll pay,' the man growled. 'In the end, you and all your like will pay. The future belongs to the common people, not just the over-privileged few.' He spat at Pierre's feet, and stumbled away after his comrade.

Pierre clutched at his chest – a sudden, sharp pain, a tightening like a band around his chest. He'd felt it before after exerting himself but had paid it no attention. This was more intense. Catching his breath, he looked about him, and sheathed his sword. The mob in front of the Bastille was uglier than ever. Some men were holding a pike aloft, and on the end of it was a severed head – he knew not whose it was. He realised if he stayed in the area, there'd be more confrontations like the one he'd just had. He'd end up either being hit by musket shot or killing someone. Or even his own head might end up on a pike. No, he would not

61

risk staying longer. He had to think of Catherine and keep himself safe. She was too young and innocent to become a widow. He'd done his duty and would be able to provide a good eyewitness account. Moving as quickly as he could despite his pain, he retreated away from the Bastille, heading west, once more sticking to the quietest streets he could find. He found two of his guard, thankfully with his horse, on the edge of the city as instructed. The captain admitted with some embarrassment that when a group of *sans-culottes* had approached, some of the guard had decided to join their numbers and had deserted.

'They'll be punished when or if they return to barracks,' Pierre said. He was too exhausted now to think about it. He mounted his horse and spurred her into a fast trot, back along the Versailles road. He'd need to wash and change before reporting what he'd seen to the King. All he really wanted to do was collapse on a sofa in his apartment with Catherine, and let her stroke away the demands of the day.

Back at Versailles, Pierre handed his horse to a groom and hurried inside. Enquiring as to the whereabouts of the King, in case he was expected to report immediately, he was told that the King was in his private rooms and did not wish to be disturbed. That suited Pierre. He climbed the stairs and negotiated the long corridors to his own apartment, and sent a footman to summon Catherine to him. He kicked off his muddied boots, and tore off his shirt, stained with the blood of that rebel leader, before she arrived.

Even so, she was visibly shocked at his appearance.

'What has happened, dear love?' she said, her face etched with worry as she stepped towards him.

How much should he tell her? He always wanted to keep the perilous state of affairs from her, keep her as innocent and naive as she'd been when he married her. But this time was different – this was so much more, and sooner or later Catherine would hear of what had happened anyway. Better that she heard it from him. He took a deep breath before answering. 'There is an uprising taking place in Paris. I got … caught up in it, a little. It's all right, I am not hurt. Just weary.' He sat down heavily on the sofa, and she perched on the edge beside him, taking his hand in her smooth, white ones.

She stroked the back of his hand. 'My poor, brave husband,' she said, and a tear rolled gently down her cheek. She had never looked more lovely. If only they could capture this moment and stay in it for ever. But what he'd seen that day made him fear for their future. The people were rising up, against the natural order, against the rich and powerful. The aristocracy may have the power now, but the ordinary people were by far the more numerous, and if they worked together, they would change the natural order. The *ancien régime* would not last much longer.

As he regarded his wife's sweet, innocent face, he wondered how much of his fears he should share with her. She needed to be aware – if he was right then their days living in luxury at Versailles would be numbered. They should start making plans to go to his château in the mountains. His father had died the previous year, and although the estate was well managed Pierre knew he should visit it again soon. Perhaps he should also tell Catherine of his chest pains. Or maybe not until he'd had chance to consult with a physician. He opened his mouth to speak, but she got there first.

'Dearest Pierre. There is something we must speak about. Our lives are about to change forever.' She had an endearing coy smile on her face.

'You're right, I believe they are,' he replied. If she'd understood what was happening in Paris too, that would make it easier to suggest they leave Versailles soon.

She snuggled up to him, snaking her arm around his chest. 'My darling, you are to become a father.'

He jumped up, startled by her words. He'd been so deep in

thought about the people's uprising he hadn't for a moment thought that she might have meant something else by her statement that their lives were about to change. 'Oh, Catherine …' was all he managed to say. In the corner, the maid Claudette was sitting with some needlework. As he caught her eye she smiled shyly before looking away. Catherine had clearly already confided in her.

'What is it? Are you not happy? We have been married for some years already, and I was beginning to lose hope … surely this is marvellous news? Of course, we will need to reconsider our place at court, but it is not impossible for us to stay …'

'It is … marvellous news, as you say …' Pierre knew he should react with happiness, take her in his arms, kiss her and share her joy at the news, but he couldn't. Not just yet. He needed to think … Would they be better off leaving court now, travelling south as soon as possible? Or should they hold on, and see what happened? It would undoubtedly be safer for Catherine to give birth here at Versailles, with the best physicians in attendance. Safer for the birth, that is. But could he guarantee their safety from the mob? Surely … surely the people wouldn't come out to Versailles. Surely all here would be safe? He looked around at their opulent apartment, their fine furniture, clothes, decor. What he'd seen today in Paris, outside the Bastille, didn't seem real any more. This was real – this life, here in comfort, with Catherine. There'd be reforms to placate the people – surely even the King would understand that now. Maybe he'd reinstate Necker. Pierre made his decision and turned back to Catherine with a smile.

'My dear, I am so happy for us. I am sorry – I was distracted. We will of course stay here at court, where we are comfortable and where you can have the best medical attention possible. I am delighted you are with child. Truly delighted.' He crossed the room and sat down beside her once more, ignoring the pain that once more tightened around his heart, taking her in his arms, inhaling her fragrance as he kissed her soft neck. An image of that hideous head on a pike came unbidden into his mind but he pushed it away. He would not tell her of that. Nor about his fears for his own health. Nothing must worry her, not now that at long last she was carrying his child.

Chapter 7

Lu

It was mid-afternoon on the day after we arrived at the château when the removal vans arrived – both ours and Steve and Manda's within an hour of each other. By then we'd unloaded Gray's hired van, Gray and Steve taking the heavy items in while Manda and I carried boxes in. It was hard work, but fun as we went back and forth to the van. We'd sent Phil into the kitchen, unpacking boxes rather than lifting heavy items.

But when our own stuff arrived it was a different story. Phil insisted on helping with the shifting of furniture. He didn't go so far as to carry it in from the van and up the stairs, but once the removal men had deposited a piece of furniture in a room Phil was there shifting it into position, sometimes by himself, sometimes with Gray's help.

'Phil, darling, I don't think you should be doing that heavy lifting,' I said, as he and Gray man-handled a large sofa into a space along one wall.

'I'm all right,' he said, or rather, he grunted, with the effort of moving the sofa. And he glared at me, a look that I knew meant, *shut up, we'll talk about this later in private.*

I tried to get to each piece that needed moving before Phil did, to either move it myself or ask the men from the van to do it, but it was all a bit of a rush. The removal men seemed to want to dump all the furniture in approximately the right rooms as fast as possible and then get on their way. I knew they'd had a long journey and had to drive back – a couple of days each way – but we were paying them well and it wasn't too much to expect them to place furniture and boxes where we actually wanted them.

'What are you doing?' I yelled, as I spotted Phil carrying a heavy box upstairs, puffing and panting. He'd had a heart attack just a few months before – he shouldn't have been doing this sort of thing.

'It's books, but it's the ones I want in our bedroom,' he said, as he struggled on.

'Here, let me take it,' I said, coming up beside him to take the box from him. It was as heavy as it looked, and it was all I could manage to carry it up the rest of the stairs to our room. I put it in a corner by the bookcase and turned to Phil who'd followed me up anyway. 'You go and sit down on that sofa you and Gray were heaving about. I'll come down and make you a cup of tea. Leave the rest of the unloading to the men.'

'Lu, it's all right. I'm fine. And I want to be involved.'

'But you shouldn't. In your condition—'

'I'm fed up of *my condition*, as you put it.' He made air quotes around the words with his fingers. 'The heart attack was months ago. I've been perfectly all right for the last seven, eight weeks. Look at me, I'm as capable of moving furniture as Steve or Gray.'

It's true he was already looking slimmer and healthier than he had for years, but still – he'd had that heart attack. He'd had stents put in. He was on medication. Immediately after the operation he'd been told not to do anything that would put a strain on his heart – and surely carrying a heavy box of books up a set of stairs counted as straining your heart?

'Love, I am only trying to take care of you,' I said. I hated it when we had cross words. It didn't happen often. We had a strong, happy marriage and had very rarely rowed. But since his heart attack, Phil seemed to get irritated with me on occasion. Like now, when he just threw up his hands, shook his head, and walked away from me.

I followed him downstairs to make that cup of tea I'd promised, but he didn't go to sit on the sofa as I'd suggested. He went out to the removal van, hefted one of the remaining boxes into his arms, and carried it inside.

'It only contains cushions,' he said as he passed me, before I could object. 'Light as a feather.'

There wasn't much I could say to that. Well, if he stuck to the lighter boxes, he'd be all right. I kept an eye on him during the rest of the unloading period, earning myself a few winks and smiles from him as he passed me, carrying bags of duvets, a box labelled 'coats and hats', a small rolled-up rug. As soon as the van was empty, the men had drunk a cup of tea and been tipped, they were off, with a couple of hours' drive to the hotel where they were booked in for the night.

I went inside and was relieved to see Phil sitting on a sofa, his feet up on an unpacked box.

'Good job, well done,' said Steve, passing him and me a cup of tea each. 'Just a lot of unpacking and sorting out to do.'

'I'll get started on our stuff in a minute,' Phil said. 'Need to get some of these boxes unpacked to make space to live in!' He kicked the one his feet were resting on, which was labelled Books and DVDs.

'No, Phil, you take a rest,' I said. 'You've done enough today. I can unpack the boxes in here.'

He gave me a look. A look that told me once again to shut up and stop fussing. Steve caught the look, glanced from me to Phil and back again, and then discreetly left the room, muttering something about sorting out something in the kitchen.

'Lu, just stop fussing, will you? I'm not an invalid. I'm not your mother.' Phil stood up and walked out with his tea, to the patio where Gray and Manda were arranging the outdoor furniture we'd brought.

I shrugged to myself. I was only trying to help. It was a spouse's job, wasn't it, to care for your partner and make sure they didn't do anything to harm themselves? That was all I was trying to do. We should have had fun today, as our stuff arrived. But instead I'd irritated him once again. I hoped this wasn't going to set the tone for our new life. I blinked back a tear and went to help Steve in the kitchen, where he was ripping open boxes of kitchen equipment and trying to find homes for everything.

By evening we had furniture scattered throughout the château and what looked like a thousand half-emptied cardboard boxes. Three households merging into one. Soon we found out that we had three kettles but no toaster, ten fish slices and no can opener. The château was a hive of activity as we all began organising the kitchen first – as Steve pointed out, the sooner that was up and running the sooner we'd be able to cook full meals.

Phil and I had made up, thankfully. We'd both been in our room, silently unpacking boxes on opposite sides of the room, when he'd stopped, come over to me and put his arms around me without saying anything. I leaned into him, tucking my face into the crook of his neck, and knew he was both apologising and letting me know he understood and that I was forgiven. Words aren't always necessary after thirty years of marriage.

It felt odd, looking around the rooms at our own furniture arranged in the château. Once again it made it all seem real – this was not a holiday home; we had actually moved in, and were here for good, for better or worse.

We had a late dinner (cooked by Steve today) by which time we had the kitchen and our own bedrooms more-or-less organised. There were still piles of boxes in the sitting room, and a stack of mismatched bookcases that needed to be constructed and filled. I was dreading the rest of them finding out that at least fifteen of the boxes were filled with my books that I'd been unable to part with. I had a bit of a reputation among them for hoarding books. Mum had been the same. I remembered her sitting room, which had one long wall completely covered with bookcases jam-packed with paperbacks. I used to spend ages in there, browsing her shelves, picking out books to read a few pages and then discovering with shock I'd read a hundred pages and had been in there for hours.

Ah, Mum. I missed her so much, still. While her last few years had been difficult as I took on more and more of her care, I still missed that sunny smile she'd always had for me, even when she was totally bed-bound. I missed her unconditional love, her gratitude for every little thing I did for her, her boundless optimism that however we might feel at any given moment, *no doubt the universe is unfolding as it should.*

Getting over her death had been a wrench for me. I knew that many people, my best friends and husband included, privately considered that her death was actually a relief, that she was never going to improve and her continued existence was making my life hard. But I never truly resented a moment that I spent with Mum. She'd done so much for me throughout her life – caring for her at the end was my way of repaying her, just a little. She'd never complained, not once. She'd smile and reach out her hand to me, and apologise that she couldn't do more for herself. She'd try so hard – she'd take the hairbrush from me and try to brush her own hair; she'd undo the buttons of her nightie ready for me to change and wash her; she'd carefully stack her used cup on top of her breakfast plate on her bedside table to make it easier for me to clear up. If I had any small sewing job that needed doing, she'd offer to do it for me. 'I can still see well enough, and my hands are steady enough to sew,' she'd say, and I'd go round the house looking for small things to mend, buttons to sew on, little tears to repair. She'd do a good job, despite her illness and disabilities, and her smile of pride at her work, at being useful, was beautiful.

I missed her so much. I missed the work, caring for her. I missed her company, her smiles, her presence. It was true I had more time for myself since she'd gone, and fewer demands on me, and life was less stressful – at least up until Phil's heart attack. But I'd take any amount of demands and stress to have her back with me again. The others didn't seem to understand this. I was the only one who'd become a carer of an elderly parent, the only one of us who'd given up time and money to do this.

And the only one who'd then had to care for a spouse through a serious illness. I just hoped we were through the worst now and could relax as we got used to our new lifestyle in France. If indeed I would ever get used to it. Every now and again I felt a wave of panic that I'd never feel at home here, never truly fit in with the local community.

We were back in the bistro a week after moving in, celebrating the end of our first week in the château. Monsieur Christophe greeted us like old friends, kissed each of us on both cheeks ('that's *ten* kisses!' Phil whispered in my ear) and opened a bottle of red wine on the house for us, before we'd even sat down.

It was a lively meal, as we were all in high spirits, talking about the things we'd done already, the things we were going to do, what the summer would be like, what the following winter would be like, our plans for the coming weeks.

'I want to visit some of those cute little hilltop villages,' Manda said. 'There are loads in this area. I was reading up on them. Carros, Gourdon, Tourrettes-sur-Loup …'

'The Loup river? Oh, there's a fantastic gorge on the Loup, and a bike ride up through it. I've got that on my list too,' Gray said. 'Lu, there's some fab walking around there as well. Especially from Gourdon which is quite high up. I went there on a holiday about ten years ago. Stayed in Tourrettes. They grow lots of violets in that area.'

'Violets?' Phil frowned.

'For perfume, and for flavouring sweets.'

Phil's eyes lit up. He was partial to sweets of any kind, and violet flavour was not something he'd ever tasted, as far as I knew. 'Well, we'll have to take a trip to that valley sometime soon, eh?'

'Definitely. I'll drink to that.' Steve raised his glass and we all clinked ours against it.

'You are 'aving a good time?' Monsieur Christophe asked, as he brought our desserts (crème brûlée for Gray and Steve, chocolate mousse for Manda and me, and sadly nothing for dieting Phil).

'We certainly are!' We all grinned.

'You 'ave met Madame la Maire?'

'Er, not yet,' I admitted. I remembered he'd suggested we go to see the mayor as soon as possible, but it had slipped my mind. And probably everyone else's too.

Monsieur Christophe tutted. 'You must. You must all go to see 'er. She ees quite, 'ow you say, *formidable*. She was 'ere last night. She ask me, 'ad I met the Eenglish from *le château* yet, and I say I 'ave, and she make a face, like thees.' He turned down the corners of his mouth. It was comical but we dared not laugh, realising we were being told off.

'Let's go tomorrow?' I said, looking at everyone.

'Hmm, can't, got the chap coming about the electrics,' Steve said. We'd had a few problems – lights flickering, fuses blowing, and wanted someone to check all the wiring, tell us what we should get done and what we *must* get done, and quote us. We weren't prepared to accept the explanation that it was a resident ghost. Not quite yet.

'OK, well, soon then.' I smiled at Monsieur Christophe, and

72

then the conversation moved on to whether or not we should start baking our own bread.

We forgot, of course we did, in all the excitement, to visit Madame la Maire as Monsieur Christophe had suggested, twice. We'd talked about it after the trip to the bistro but that was all.

'Gray, you go,' Steve suggested. 'You're best at turning on the charm, and your French is pretty good.'

Gray widened his eyes. 'Why me? I don't want to go and see the old battle-axe.'

'She might be young and blonde and gorgeous,' Steve said, with a wink.

'Huh. Doubt it. She'll be eighty, with a steel-grey perm. She'll have one of those terrifying stares that make you die inside, like a junior school headmistress. I think we should send one of the girls. Lu, you go.'

'Me? Not on my own,' I said. 'My French isn't up to it. What if she doesn't speak English?'

'Why do we have to go anyway?' Phil asked.

'Because Monsieur Christophe said we should. The mayor likes to meet everyone in the village. There are probably forms we've got to fill in. You know what they say about French bureaucracy. Besides, we want to make a good impression here, don't we?' Steve had poured out more wine, and somehow the entire conversation was forgotten about. Over the following days we were busy settling in, emptying boxes and walking around the village to get our bearings yet somehow not managing to remember about calling on the mayor whenever we were near the *mairie*.

Before we knew it, we'd been there a fortnight and we still hadn't visited to introduce ourselves, and then one morning the huge iron ring set into the front door was rapped smartly against the wood three times. I was in the sitting room at the time, organising books onto the bookcases. Manda was out on the patio with some paperwork, Steve was baking something that smelled amazing in the kitchen. Phil and Gray were somewhere in the garden.

Steve went to open the door, and a moment later ushered a smart fifty-something woman with a blonde bob, who wore glasses with pink sides that should have looked tacky but somehow looked fabulous on her, into the sitting room.

'And this is Lu Marlow,' he said. 'Lu, this is Aimée Leblanc, the *maire*. I'll ... um ... make some tea.'

'Coffee, please, for me,' said Madame la Maire, and Steve nodded, ducking quickly out of the room, leaving me to ... what? Make the apologies for not having visited her first, I suppose.

'Please, do sit down, Madame,' I said, then realised there were books on every surface as I'd been trying to organise them before shelving them. I gathered up a pile to make a space and ended up dropping some. The *maire* took a skip backwards to avoid having them land on her foot. 'Oh, I'm sorry, *je suis désolée*,' I said, cursing myself inwardly. What would she think of us?

'It is all right,' she said, moving another pile of books without a hiccup and perching herself on a sofa. She was wearing a pair of perfectly pressed loose linen trousers, a silk blouse and a scarf draped artfully around her neck. It was the kind of look I have never, ever been able to pull off. On me the trousers would be horrendously creased (life's too short to iron linen, has always been my motto), the scarf would be slipping off and the blouse would have a coffee stain on it somewhere. But our *maire* looked elegant and poised and, to me, absolutely terrifying. I've always felt slightly intimidated by elegant women.

'Let me just call the others in to meet you,' I said. I couldn't face sitting alone with her, and who knew how long Steve would be with the coffee. I could see Gray and Phil poking at a flower bed at the end of the garden. I crossed over to the patio doors, opened them and yelled for them to come, startling Manda.

'Bloody hell, Lu, I thought the château was burning down or

something,' she said, then spotted the *maire* and clapped a hand over her mouth. 'Ah, *excusez-moi*, I didn't realise ...'

'Manda, this is the mayor,' I said. I'd forgotten her name already. Manda stepped forward, a huge smile on her face, and air-kissed the *maire* on each side, the French way. I cursed inwardly yet again for having forgotten this social nicety. Not a good start.

'Pleased to meet you,' said the *maire*, in perfect but accented English. 'I like to meet the people of the village when they move in. To say hello, to offer my help with anything you might need. As you are English perhaps you do not know ... how to say ... how everything works here. I can help. The *mairie* is there to help all the people.' She smiled graciously. I felt as though I was in the presence of royalty. 'You are settling in? It is a beautiful château, is it not?'

'Thank you, yes, we are very happy to be here,' Manda said. 'It is such a beautiful area, and the village is gorgeous. We can't wait to get out and about and explore a bit. Cycling, walking, skiing – it's all right here! And riding. I love horses.' She was rambling a bit, as though she too couldn't wait for the others to join us and take over. Thankfully at that moment Steve came in with a jug of filter coffee and a plate of cookies he'd just taken out of the oven, and Phil and Gray came in through the patio doors.

The atmosphere improved immediately, as the fellas began chatting with the *maire* about the château, places to go, things to see. I had the impression the *maire* was one of those women who get on better with men than with women. Or perhaps Manda and I in our faded jeans and baggy overwashed T-shirts were just not her type of women. Whatever, I was happy to sit on the edge of the group and listen to the conversation, nodding now and again as I sipped my coffee, rather than take an active part in it. Manda did likewise. Once or twice she caught my eye, smiled and raised an eyebrow. I smiled back but wasn't sure what message she was trying to convey. There'd be time later to dissect it all.

I did notice, however, that Gray seemed to be making an especially big effort to charm our visitor.

The thing about Gray is, he's commitment-phobic. He had a seven-year relationship with Melissa, whom he'd met shortly after we left university.

Since then, other than one relationship that we all thought was going somewhere, he's never stayed with anyone more than a few months.

I think, from having had many an in-depth conversation over late-night wine with Gray over the years, that his problem stems from his own parents' failed marriage. They divorced when Gray was little, and he grew up spending weekdays with his mum and weekends with his dad, plus whichever 'stepmum' his dad was shacked up with at the time. There were at least fifteen different women, Gray says, from the time his parents divorced to the date he went to university. All of whom his dad wanted him to call 'Mum'.

When Gray and Melissa split up, he resolved never to put his daughters through that same level of pain and confusion. There would be no 'stepmum' living in his house when his daughters stayed. There'd be only him, and the girls would have his undivided attention.

He's a great dad and has the best relationship with his offspring of all of us. Open and honest, and truly loving. But it's come at the expense of his personal life, his love life.

There was one woman after Melissa, that we all thought was The One. Her name was Leanne, but we refer to her as The One That Got Away. Gray and Leanne were together for over five years, but he never let her move in. She wanted more – she wanted to marry and have children with him, but he wouldn't let her stay with him if the girls were there. She'd go out with them on day trips but would then have to return home. Even when Clemmie reached her teens and told him, 'Dad, it's OK, we don't mind if you sleep with Leanne when we're there', he would send Leanne back to her own flat after dinner and before the girls went to bed.

Eventually it all became too much for poor Leanne. She gave Gray an ultimatum. Let her move in, or she was leaving. He agonised for weeks, stringing her along, and then eventually made what he thought was the right decision – the girls must come first. He would not live with another woman until both had left home and were settled elsewhere. Leanne tried to talk him round. She pleaded with him. She phoned each of us and asked us to intervene on her behalf, and we tried, but he'd made his decision. In the end, for the sake of her dignity Leanne accepted his decision, found herself a new job in Vancouver, and moved. Now she's still there, married to a Canadian, with three children of her own and a lifestyle that involves sailing all summer and skiing all winter. She and Gray are still friends on social media, and frankly, I think he regrets losing her. But, as I've counselled him, he made what he thought was the right decision at the time. Now he needs to look forward not back, as you can only move forward starting from where you are.

There'll be someone for him, somewhere. Now that the girls are grown-up and he's on his own, he can be more relaxed. Of course, now he's acquired new housemates – but we won't mind in the slightest if he invites someone to stay over! Not saying he won't get a bit of stick for it, when the lady in question is out of earshot, but we'll be delighted for him, if it ever happens.

'You have met *le fantôme*?' asked Madame la Maire, as I tuned back in to the conversation. 'The last owners of the château said it was friendly but sad. So you have nothing to worry about.' She smiled at us all.

'*Fantôme* – ghost? Not sure I believe in them,' said Steve, with a nervous laugh. Nervous because of the idea of a ghost, or because he feared insulting the mayor? I wasn't sure.

'No, they probably do not exist, but we do not know for sure,' she said, with a gracious nod in Steve's direction. The conversation then moved on to other things.

I felt the mayor been holding something back, not telling us everything. Did I even believe in ghosts? I'd always been a bit in two minds about it. I'd 'felt' the presence of my mum more times than I could recall, since her death. But I'd always dismissed this as my own wishful thinking, missing her, wanting to believe she was still near me, watching over me. And there'd been a time, once, when I was a teenager, I was cycling along a country lane on holiday and saw a small boy wearing a red jumper, followed by a little white dog, run across the road and vanish into the hedge. When I reached the spot there was no sign of boy or dog, and strangely, no gap at all in the hedge on either side. Nowhere they could have come from or gone to. I still remember feeling spooked by the experience, so much so that I didn't sleep for the next few nights for thinking about it. I told Dad at the time, but he just laughed and said there must have been a gap in the hedge I hadn't spotted. Mum had looked thoughtful, but made no comment.

But were we now living in a haunted house? That mysterious missing aristocrat still hanging around, perhaps? I wasn't entirely sure how I felt about that idea.

Chapter 8

Catherine, 1789

As the summer progressed, and Catherine's pregnancy blossomed, the outbreaks of violence in Paris continued on and off. Despite Catherine's protestations Pierre was sent to report on them a few more times, but he had learned his lesson and went on foot or by cart, dressed in rough, dirty clothes. She hated seeing him dressed like this – like a peasant, like a city-dwelling artisan. He was nobility, he should be dressed accordingly!

Each evening Pierre returned to their apartment exhausted and worried, after making his reports to the King. He looked ill, she thought, but whenever she'd questioned him about his health he had smiled, kissed her and told her not to worry. He had, though, told her something of what was happening in Paris, and she'd gleaned more from some of the ladies of the Court when Pierre had refused to tell her details. She knew he was afraid of upsetting her, in her delicate condition. He was becoming concerned, he said, with events in Paris. The people were complaining that bread was too scarce and too expensive. There were rumours that the nobility were plotting to destroy the wheat crop in an attempt to starve the people.

'I asked a man why he thought the nobility would do that,' Pierre told her. 'It was at a market, where scuffles had broken out over the shortage of bread. The man told me he believed the nobility wanted to keep them subdued, and that if they were hungry they'd remain submissive. But he said they wouldn't – they were taking control.' Pierre sighed. 'I believe he is right. Even the King will have to accept the reforms in the end.'

Catherine snuggled up to him. 'Which reforms? Tell me again, dearest.' She still couldn't believe, even after the events of July and Pierre's continued reporting of rioting in Paris, that any of it could affect her, or the rest of the court here at Versailles. They were close to Paris, it was true, but removed enough to be safe, as Pierre had continually assured her. And they had plenty of bread here. Catherine was, as always, taking her cue from Marie Antoinette. The Queen was going about her life exactly as she always had, although perhaps there were fewer visits to the little farm at the Petit Trianon, than before. But this year's lambs had grown so the farm was less pleasurable to visit now. 'I have heard something from the other ladies, about potential removal of privileges from the clergy and nobility? Please tell me the details, so I can join in with the conversations at Court.'

'Ah, my sweet, I would prefer not to bother you with all this,' Pierre replied. 'It is nothing you need be concerned about.'

'But if the nobility are to have privileges removed then surely that affects me directly, and I do need to be concerned about it.' Catherine stroked her hand over his chest. 'Please, my love. Tell me a little of it.'

Pierre wrapped an arm around her as he answered with a sigh. 'I told you, I think, about the August decrees issued last month by the National Assembly? The aim is to ensure a more equal distribution of wealth in our country. And then there's the Declaration of the Rights of Man and the Citizen. The National Assembly want Louis to recognise the legitimacy of both of these, but he's resisting them, so far, despite being advised to the contrary.'

'What will all this mean for us? For you and me, and our baby?' She patted the little bump that was almost visible now, beneath her gowns.

Pierre sighed. 'If Louis accepts the reforms, then there may be little change here at Versailles, though Louis will have less power and influence, and he and the Queen will need to curb their spending. If he doesn't, then who knows what will happen. We may need to leave.'

She pouted. 'I thought you said we could stay here.'

'We can, for as long as it's safe to do so.' He kissed her. 'But I can't promise it will remain safe.'

It was early October, the leaves on the trees were just beginning to turn to their autumn colours and there was a distinct chill in the air, when things came to a head. Pierre had been reporting that the riots in Paris were becoming worse, and that there were calls for an organised march to Versailles.

'What do the people want now?' Catherine asked him. All she wanted was for life to go on as it had, while she awaited the birth of their child. She wanted to be focused inwardly on the new little life growing inside her, and not to need to worry about external events.

'Bread. The assurance that bread will be more easily available and priced more cheaply. And that the King should dismiss his Swiss bodyguard in favour of the National Guard.'

'How dare they tell him who he may have to guard him!' Catherine was outraged.

'The National Guard are patriotic, and generally more sympathetic to the Revolution,' Pierre replied. 'Although their commander, the Marquis de Lafayette, remains loyal to Louis. There's talk too, that the King should move to Paris, to be among his people, rather than removed from them here at Versailles.'

'And where would he live? Tell me, Pierre, where in Paris is there a palace fit for a king such as Louis, and a queen such as Marie Antoinette? No.' She shook her head vehemently. 'The royal family must stay here. Versailles is the greatest palace in Europe, in the world, even! There is nowhere else suitable.'

'They may end up with no choice,' Pierre said quietly. Catherine stared at him, but his expression was closed, as though he wanted no further discussion on the subject. She thought back through what he had said. He'd used a new word to describe the situation – *revolution*. Was that really what this was? Was there no way back?

It was the following day when a messenger arrived, sent by Lafayette galloping hard from Paris, with the news that the march was underway, and that the people would arrive at Versailles that same afternoon. Catherine, along with the Queen and the other ladies of the court, were ushered into the palace for safety.

'There are several thousand marching, as I understand it,' the Princesse de Lamballe said to Catherine. 'Led by women, from the markets, would you believe it! And all because they want for a loaf of bread.'

'Why do the National Guard not stop them?' Catherine asked, as the ladies took their places gathered around the Queen in a drawing room.

'The National Guard march with the people,' came the response. 'I only hope if there is violence, the guards will remember their place and defend us rather than turn against us. Oh! I am sorry, I have worried you.' Princesse de Lamballe put a hand on Catherine's arm. 'You're so young, and with child, I believe? You will be safe. Please do not fear. The royal bodyguard will protect us all.'

Catherine peeked out of the window as the march arrived. There were many thousands of people, some holding pikes aloft. For one terrible moment she thought there were heads on the ends of the pikes – she'd heard gossip that that had happened to defenders of the Bastille on that terrible day in July. But no, it seemed the mob had speared loaves of bread with their pikes. She didn't understand. If this march was all about wanting more bread, why did they waste so much in that way? And if there wasn't enough bread, why didn't they eat something else? Brioche, perhaps? Surely no one was so poor they couldn't afford to buy anything to eat at all?

The marchers were accompanied by drummers, and the constant rhythmic beat permeated the palace, even though the people were kept at some distance. Catherine felt as though it was forcing her heart to beat in time too. 'Oh, how I wish they would stop!' she said to one of the women. 'I can't bear it!'

'Listen, they are shouting now,' the other woman said, and Catherine followed her to a window. What she heard made her blood run cold.

'Death to the Queen! Death to the Austrian bitch!'

Catherine glanced over her shoulder at Marie Antoinette, who looked worried but otherwise calm, as she sat with her closest ladies-in-waiting, playing a game of cards. It was not clear whether she could hear the chants, but as Madame de Polignac leaned over and whispered in her ear, the Queen visibly paled, and she put down her hand of cards, stood and left the room.

'She should stay near Louis,' Catherine's companion said. 'The people still love him and will not hurt her while she is with him.'

It was a long afternoon and evening, but eventually the members of court were informed that all was quiet and calm, negotiations had been reasonably successful and the immediate danger had passed. They could retire to their chambers in peace, protected as usual by the Swiss guard. Catherine was grateful to be reunited with Pierre, who'd spent the day with the King, advising him. He looked tired and grey.

'Louis agreed to accept the August decree reforms, and most importantly, the Declaration of the Rights of Man,' Pierre told her. 'That is what they wanted. And he'll do what he can about the bread situation, ensuring we build up as much reserves of wheat as we can. It's hardly his fault though, that the last harvest was ruined by those violent hailstorms! But I think we are safe for now. Sleep well, my darling.'

Catherine was woken early next morning, while it was still dark, by a commotion in the corridors outside her chamber. And was that … yes, it was gunfire! She scrambled out of bed, along with Pierre who urged her to go immediately to the Queen. He needed to find out what was going on. Catherine tugged a shawl around her shoulders and ran barefoot along the corridor, to the Queen's chambers. Other ladies-in-waiting were there too, and all were in disarray.

'What is happening?'

'Some of the crowd gained access to the palace,' one woman said. 'The royal bodyguard are holding them back, but we must get the Queen to safety.'

Catherine recalled with fear the chants of 'Kill the Queen' she'd heard the previous day, and shuddered. At that moment Marie Antoinette herself, attended by a couple of ladies, emerged from her chamber, barefoot just like Catherine.

'Come,' called Princesse de Lamballe to the rest of them. 'We must find safety!'

'To the King's chamber,' the Queen cried, and the group began running through the corridors of the palace, trailing their shawls, dropping nightcaps. Behind them they could hear the intruders getting closer, more musket fire, screams and cheers, and once more, shouts of 'Get the Queen! Kill the bitch!' It was terrifying. Catherine wished she'd stayed with Pierre – they could have locked themselves in their chamber, perhaps. She feared for the Queen's life, for her own … As she ran, she held a protective hand over her swollen belly. If she was killed, this child would never even take its first breath. But surely she could not be in danger of death here in Versailles, where she had always felt so safe!

They reached the King's chamber but it was locked. Marie Antoinette at once began pummelling on the door, screaming to be allowed in, but the din around them had intensified and no one inside could hear. Catherine pressed herself against the wall, looking back along the corridor they'd run down, and saw the first of the mob rounding a corner at the far end – they'd be upon the ladies within seconds … She crouched down, hands covering her face, awaiting the feel of a musket shot or the thrust of a pike between her ribs.

'Get up, come on!' Hands hauled her to her feet and pushed her through the King's door, opened at last and with only seconds to spare. The women piled inside, collapsing onto chairs, sofas or the floor, as a footman slammed the door closed behind them and locked it. More hammering on the door, this time accompanied by male shouts, 'Give us the Queen! The King is safe!'

The Queen had run into her husband's arms, and was standing with him, shaking, yet still somehow dignified, Catherine thought, as she watched. She too was shaking, and to her horror realised she was going to be sick – here, in the King's private apartments, in front of the Queen … But there was no stopping it. She heaved, and when her stomach was empty, she wiped her mouth with the corner of her shawl.

As daylight broke, word came that the intruders had been overwhelmed and the palace was once more secure, although the crowd of many thousands were still gathered outside. The Marquis de Lafayette came to consult with the King, and the ladies were allowed to return to their own chambers, to freshen up and dress. There were many more Swiss guards inside the palace now, on every corridor and at every door. Catherine felt a little reassured, but still apprehensive as to what would happen next. As she glanced out of a window, she could see the crowd was bigger still than it had been the previous day. The night's events had shown the royal family and all members of court were vulnerable, even inside the greatest palace in Europe.

Pierre was not in their chambers to Catherine's dismay. How she wanted to be held and comforted by him! But she had to make do with the attentions of Claudette, who helped her remove her soiled nightwear, wash, and dress for the day.

'Madame, it must have been very frightening,' Claudette said, in her thick Provençal accent. She had been lady's maid to Pierre's first wife, travelling with them from Pierre's château in the mountains when he'd first come to Paris.

'Yes. The poor Queen.' Catherine was still shaking.

'I mean for you. You should not have had to be caught up in it all, Madame.' Claudette gently brushed Catherine's hair, soothing her and making her presentable for whatever lay ahead. Who knew what the day would bring? Catherine had a sense that nothing would ever be the same again. An era was ending.

Later, the Court gathered in the Hall of Mirrors as the King consulted with his advisers. Catherine stood with the Queen and the other ladies, and was relieved to see Pierre across the room, safe, but looking tired and fearful. She managed a brief, whispered conversation with him.

'The King is going to appear on the balcony,' he said. 'He must face the people. They have the power.'

Catherine was horrified. 'What if they attack? They might fire a musket upon him!'

Pierre's expression was grim. 'He must take that risk. It is the people who are now in control, and he must show himself to be compliant. I think also, he must agree to their demands that he go to Paris. The Tuileries Palace is habitable. And my sweet' – here Pierre lowered his voice still further, so that Catherine had to strain to hear his next words – 'if that happens then you and I will take our chance and leave the court. Claudette will come too.

I have spoken to her. It will be safer for us, in the long term. We have our little one to think about.'

'Go to your château in the south?'

'Yes. Let us see what the day brings first, though.'

Catherine couldn't believe it. Leave Versailles, leave the Court, leave her beloved Queen? A few months ago she'd have absolutely refused. But now, with this new life growing inside her, she realised the most important thing was their child's safety. Pierre had always said they should move to his family château when they had a family. Perhaps now was the time.

A little later, as Pierre had said, the King went out to the balcony to appear in front of the crowd. There was a tense moment as everyone waited to hear the crowd's reaction, and then relief as a cheer went up, '*Vive le Roi!*' It was soon taken up by the whole crowd.

'They love him still,' said Marie Antoinette, her eyes glistening with unshed tears as she clutched her children, Madame Royale and the Dauphin, to her.

'But do they also love you?' asked Princesse de Lamballe.

A new chant was heard: 'Bring us the Queen!'

The Marquis de Lafayette approached. 'Will you step onto the balcony, your Majesty? With your children?'

Catherine watched as the Queen straightened her back and nodded, then followed him out to the balcony, still clutching her children to her sides.

Her reception was different to that of the King's. There were jeers and insults, muskets pointing at her and calls for the children to be taken back inside. *They want to take a shot at her*, thought Catherine, in horror. *They want the children removed to keep them safe, to allow them to take a clean shot at her.*

But the Queen stood firm, her arms crossed over her chest and her head slightly bowed, as though she was her own effigy, and she kept the children at her sides. Gradually Catherine, peeping from another window, sensed a change in the atmosphere. The crowd were beginning to appreciate the Queen's courage, her steadfastness in standing there, despite the fact many in the crowd were pointing muskets directly at her. Gradually the guns were lowered, and then, to everyone's astonishment, a new cry went up, tentative at first but soon gaining in volume: '*Vive la Reine!*'

'They love her still,' Catherine whispered, echoing the Queen's words about her husband. The crisis was over for now – the royal family were safe. Perhaps they could stay at Versailles after all? Perhaps things could go on as they were?

Across the room, she caught Pierre's eye. He looked faintly relieved, but still grim-faced. He gave a tiny shake of his head, as if to tell her, *it's not over yet.*

Chapter 9

Lu

Life began slipping into a comfortable routine, as April progressed into May. Steve had started a wonderful habit of getting up early, donning his running clothes and going out for a morning run with an empty rucksack on his back. He'd loop round so that he returned through the village and on the way stopped at the *boulangerie* to buy fresh bread, croissants and occasionally also something from the *patisserie*, for our breakfast. We usually had a stock of local cheese and fresh fruit in the pantry. The perfect French breakfast! Only Phil, who'd been advised to give up eating cheese, couldn't partake of it all, but he'd proclaimed himself happy with a fruit and yoghurt breakfast. He'd never have touched such a thing in England.

We'd spend the morning doing jobs around the château – cleaning, painting, gardening. Phil had always quite liked gardening and now was planning to dig up the lawn in the sunniest corner of the garden to make a vegetable patch. 'We'll be self-sufficient in no time,' he announced, after sowing a line of lettuce. The exercise was doing him good, though I fretted sometimes that he would overdo it, and had quietly asked Gray to help him with any heavy digging.

In the afternoons we'd go out – either all together to a local tourist spot or nearby hilltop village, or separately. Gray and Steve for bike rides, Manda and I for walks. Phil would most likely stay home and continue gardening, and we'd come home later to find him asleep on a sofa. I had to admit it was good living here in the summer. Like an extended holiday. But I still fretted about how well we'd fit into the community in the long term, and how we'd cope with the winter months.

Manda and I went on several walks in those early weeks along the well-marked trails in the hills above the village. One of them, we were pleased to see, ran right past the top end of our land. 'We must get a couple of rooms ready as guest rooms,' she said. 'Wonder who'll be our first visitors?'

'Tom's talking about coming soon,' I said. Our eldest son was working for an engineering company in Liverpool, and ready for an early summer holiday in Provence. He was a keen walker and cyclist, and as Gray had brought three bikes with him Tom was hoping to borrow one and cycle up and down a few Alpine passes in the area.

'Great – so he'll be our guinea pig! Which room shall we put him in?'

I laughed. 'He's already said he wants to sleep in the tower.'

'That dirty little circular room? We've no bed in there and I'm not sure how we'd get one up that spiral staircase.'

'He says he'll sleep on a blow-up mattress, or on the floor. He's determined.' Tom had always adored castles, ever since he was four years old and we'd first taken him to Carisbrooke Castle on the Isle of Wight. I smiled remembering how he'd run up every spiral staircase, peered into every room, brandishing the little wooden sword we'd bought him in the gift shop at his imagined enemies.

'Ha! Well, we'd better give it a clean, then,' Manda said. The tower room had obviously been used only for storage when the château functioned as a hotel. The previous owners had left some rubbish up there – boxes of chipped crockery, bundles of decades-old magazines tied up with string. Nothing of any interest, but so far we hadn't found time to take it down and dump it. We'd have to, before Tom slept there, as the room also needed a good scrubbing.

'Tomorrow's job,' I said, as we paused at a turn in the path. There was a convenient bench set just off the track, positioned so that it faced across the valley. We didn't need to say anything – we both knew that the bench was there just for us, to take a seat for a moment, rest and enjoy the view.

'Look, you can see the château from here,' Manda said, pointing. She was right. Tucked among the trees the roof was visible, the tower with its little pointed turret, the main building, part of the lawn. And the outbuildings, plus the charred ruins from the fire hundreds of years ago. I wondered who had lived there when that happened, and whether anyone had perished in the fire.

It was only a fortnight later that Tom arrived. Manda and I had cleared out the tower room – dumping all those boxes and bundles which had indeed turned out to be nothing but rubbish accumulated over the last thirty years or so. I'd been vaguely hoping there might be some gem among it all – some remnant of the château's older history, some papers hinting at a mystery to be solved – but there was nothing. It all dated from the château's time as a small hotel. The only thing of interest was a poorly executed watercolour painting of the château, silhouetted against what appeared to be a fire. The painting was dated 1963 and a sticker on the back read: *L'incendie du Château.*

'Shall we hang it up downstairs?' I asked.

Manda shook her head. 'No. Even Steve can paint better than that, and he hasn't an artistic bone in his body.'

Once the room was cleared, we lugged buckets and brooms and mops up the spiral staircase and set about cleaning it. There were no electric sockets up there so we couldn't use a vacuum cleaner but with a little effort we soon had the room dust free, the cobwebs gone, the window sparkling to reveal a stunning view. The walls were partly covered with cracking plaster, and partly clad in wooden panelling. The whole lot had been painted a dull grey, and the paint was badly peeling in some places. I picked at a bit of the painted panelling with my fingernail and exposed a warm-looking wood beneath. It'd be nice to strip the paint off and restore it to its original state. Big job, though. That would have to wait a while.

We laid a rug on the floor, brought up a blow-up bed and made it up, added a chair and a bedside table and it looked quite homely. The floor creaked loudly as we moved around, but we paid it no attention, being well-used to the various sounds the château made by now. There were no curtains or shutters for the window but we'd found a piece of board which could be slotted into the window recess to block out most of the light. It would have to do for Tom's visit. And an old paraffin lamp Phil had bought in the Saturday market would do to light the room.

Phil drove to Nice airport to pick up Tom, while the rest of us sat impatiently awaiting our first visitor. We had plenty more lined up – all the kids (except Zoe, who was still in Australia) were booked in, and several friends wanted to come too. The summer was going to be busy.

At last the sound of a car outside alerted us to their arrival, and we all went to the door to welcome Tom. I gave him a huge mum-hug at the door. 'So good to see you! Our first visitor!'

'Great to be here, Mum,' he said, leaning back so that he lifted me off my feet.

'Arrgh! Put me down!' I laughed, and once my feet were back on the floor I led him through to the sitting room where, it being late afternoon and the 'sun over the yard-arm' as Steve liked to say, we had a bottle of bubbly chilling and ready to celebrate his arrival. Steve, who was fast becoming our resident baker as well as the bread-buyer and chef for most meals, had made a cake. Chocolate, decorated with French flag icing.

But Tom wanted a tour before he'd agree to sit down and eat cake. 'Show me round, Mum,' he said. 'From the outside this place looks awesome!'

'It is,' I agreed, and took him off for the tour.

Of course, it was the tower he liked best. He said the little circular room was perfect, as he dumped his rucksack down beside the chair we'd hauled up there. He peered out of the little window, exclaiming at the view just as I had on the day we'd moved in, and turned to me with a grin. 'This place is fabulous, Mum. I hope you are going to be really happy here, all of you.'

'So far so good,' I said, 'and no reason it shouldn't get even better, once your dad gets the veg plot going.'

'Mmm. Dad as a gardener, who'd have thought it,' Tom said. 'Well I'm already considering which of my friends I want to move in with when I'm old, so I think you've set a precedent.'

'Oy, less of the "old",' I said, throwing him a mock punch. 'None of us are sixty yet.'

'Dad's birthday next month?'

'Well, yeah.' Phil was the oldest of us. Then Gray. The rest of us were, as we still liked to say even after all these years, a 'school year' below them. Both Phil and Gray had taken a gap year before going to university, travelling for a few months each, and working. Phil had done bar work in Australia and Gray had done voluntary work setting up a school in Malawi. The rest of us had gone straight to university after sixth form.

'Anyway, be careful with that paraffin lamp,' I said. Being a mum, I couldn't help but advise caution to my kids at every possible opportunity.

Tom rolled his eyes. 'I'm a grown-up, Mum. I know how to use a paraffin lamp. Of course I'll be careful.'

'I know, but the château's already burned down once,' I muttered. I turned to go back down the spiral stairs. As Tom followed me the floorboards gave an enormous creak.

'I'd be more worried about the state of this floor than me

setting fire to the room,' he said, taking exaggerated tiptoe steps the rest of the way across to the door.

The day after Tom arrived I took him for a walk. We'd planned to go down by the river path, explore the village, and then come back along the higher path. And maybe on and up the mountain, if the weather was good enough. It usually was.

It was only about three kilometres to the village, and I'd promised Tom coffee and a cake from the *patisserie* when we got there. They did a mean *mille-feuille* I knew he'd love. We headed off not long after breakfast, down the château's driveway, across the main road and down a small path that led to the river and then followed it down to the village, chatting companionably of his latest adventures, his plans, and how life was shaping up for us oldies in the château.

The path meandered alongside the river, sometimes bounded by lush meadow and sometimes through a band of deciduous woodland that flanked the banks. It was a delightful route, and I felt vaguely ashamed I hadn't already walked it. It was part of Steve's regular morning run to the village to buy bread. When we were approaching the village, we came across a small stone building that overhung the river a little. There was an information board mounted beside it – written all in French but with a bit of effort I could translate enough to get the gist of it.

'It's some sort of wash house,' I told Tom. 'The women of the village would bring their laundry here to wash it in the river.' We entered the little building, which had a wooden floor, and some sort of rusty mechanism mounted on one wall.

'Looks like the floor is movable,' said Tom, touching an iron handle which turned a cog wheel. 'Presumably it was raised and lowered depending on the water level. An ingenious design – aren't the wash houses usually just large stone basins fed by a stream? I've never seen one over a river like this.'

I went outside and tried to translate more of the information board. He was right. The wash house was an unusual design for the area, apparently, and had been built by Victor Aubert, Comte de Verais, in 1760 for the use of the villagers.

'Aubert? As in Château d'Aubert? Did he live in your château then?' Tom asked.

'I suppose he must have.' Funny to think our home was previously owned by a French aristocrat. All aristocratic titles were abolished during the French Revolution, of course. I wondered if this Victor Aubert had survived that period, or met the fate of so many of France's nobility. 'Perhaps there are Aubert tombs in the village graveyard.'

'We could go and look for them sometime, if you like?' Tom raised his eyebrows at me and I smiled. Of course I would like to, and he knew it. I'd always had a bit of a thing about old graveyards. I love reading the inscriptions and wondering about the lives of the people buried there. Especially when they'd probably lived in the château we now owned.

We didn't manage to get to the graveyard that day, but enjoyed a cake in the *patisserie* (Tom adored the *mille-feuille* as I'd known he would) and then headed up a path that led to a mountain ridge above the village.

'Fantastic view,' Tom said, gazing southwards. 'Is that actually the Mediterranean?' He was pointing at a distant strip of shining blue.

'It is indeed,' I replied.

'You do live in an amazing place. I'm so glad I was the first visitor – beat Alfie to it! Are Gray's girls and Zoe booked in to visit?'

'Clemmie and Hope are coming later in the summer. Zoe can't – she's in Australia.'

'Oh yes. Forgot she was there. I bet Manda's missing her, isn't she?'

I nodded. 'She certainly is, poor woman. She's terrified Zoe will end up staying there permanently when her contract's up.'

'Will she, do you think?' Tom frowned. 'That'll be hard for Manda and Steve. Zoe's all they have.'

I think Manda and Steve would have loved to have had more children. Manda was always the perfect hands-on mum: taking days off to attend sports day and nativity plays, spending weekends baking with Zoe and evenings helping out with Brownies then Guides, always putting Zoe ahead of her job. She was better than the rest of us at juggling the demands of career and parenthood, so it always seemed a shame she only had the one daughter. She'd had another three pregnancies, one before Zoe and two after, all ending in early miscarriage. In the end she and Steve decided they couldn't face any more heartbreak and it was better for Zoe to grow up a loved, only child with relaxed parents rather than keep trying and failing to provide her with a sibling.

And yet Manda managed not to be too over-protective. Zoe was encouraged to be independent from an early age. She went on every Guide camp possible, and on Outward Bound courses run by her school. Aged seventeen, she asked if she could spend the summer holidays travelling in Italy with a mixed group of friends, and Manda agreed, on the condition she paid for it herself from her Saturday job and babysitting earnings.

It was no surprise really that after completing her degree Zoe looked further afield than the UK for a job. She applied for jobs in Germany and France, but ending up working for a UK-based company to Manda's relief. However, the company had offices in Australia, and it wasn't too long before Zoe was offered a two-year placement in Sydney.

'I've got to take it, Mum,' she said, her eyes shining. 'I'll be able to travel the country in my holidays, maybe also get to New Zealand. It's such an opportunity.'

We all agreed, it was an amazing opportunity. Steve thought so too, and Manda said she did, but I could see misgivings behind her expression when they told the rest of us Zoe's news, about a year before we decided to move to France. Later that evening, I'd taken Manda to one side and asked her if she was really happy about it.

To my horror she'd instantly welled up. 'I'm terrified, to be honest. Terrified the two-year placement will turn into something permanent. Terrified Zoe will meet some tanned Australian surfer-hunk and decide to marry him and settle out there. I'll never see her again, Lu! I don't think I can bear that!'

I hugged her and patted her back. 'Don't be silly. You'll see her. She'll come back for visits, and you can go out there, see Australia for yourself.'

But she shook her head. 'You know I hate flying, Lu. I couldn't go there.'

'You fly all the time! You flew to Venice with Steve a few weeks ago …'

She wiped her tears on a tissue. 'I can manage short haul, just about. But the idea of a twenty-four-hour trip to the other side of the world …' She shivered. 'I couldn't do it, Lu. And then I'd never see her.'

'There's Skype. And her visits home. And anyway – it's a two-year contract. She'll most likely stay only two years. Don't worry about what might not happen.'

Manda had smiled through her tears. 'You're probably right. It's just … so hard. Letting go.'

She'd surprised me, with those last words. Of all of us, she'd seemed to be the best at letting go, giving her child wings and the freedom to use them. Funny how you can know someone for forty years and they are still able to surprise you.

'Zoe will come home after her contract is up, I bet,' I said to Tom, hoping I was right for Manda's sake. We turned away from that stunning view and headed down the hillside, back to the château and a much-needed cup of tea.

*

Later that day, Manda returned home looking tired but jubilant after having been out all day.

'What have you been up to?' I asked, taking in her grubby cotton trousers and sweat-soaked T-shirt.

'I've found a riding stables!' she announced with a grin. 'It's down the valley, past the village and then up a little lane. I've been there half the day, and they've agreed that in exchange for a couple of hours' work twice a week, I can take a pony out riding whenever I like!'

'Fantastic! I thought you were thinking of buying your own pony to keep here, though?'

She shrugged. 'I was, but it's a huge responsibility. I think this is probably better. They've a lovely grey mare named Argent that suits me well. This way I can ride her, and work with the others, and all without having to spend a fortune getting the stables here up and running. Steve was looking at the roof – all needs replacing before we can house any animal in there through the winter.'

'That's great news,' Steve said, giving her a hug. 'Good to have something to keep you busy.'

He needed something himself, I thought. Steve's not a man who can keep still for long.

Manda nodded. 'Who'd have thought it – I've got myself a job. No pay, but for me the chance to go riding means so much more.'

'Good job you've all got good pensions,' Tom said. He sighed. 'Oh, you are lucky. You can do what you want, when you want. I can't wait to be retired myself!'

Manda laughed. 'Don't wish your life away, Tom. But yes, we're lucky, and I am going to enjoy this job.'

It'd also help take her mind off Zoe, I thought, but decided not to say out loud. I was glad for her.

It was the third day of Tom's visit when we discovered something odd about the château. Actually it was Tom who spotted it. Tom, the visitor – not we unobservant five who'd lived here for a month. He was at the front of the château, doing a bit of weeding of our gravel driveway. I had brought him out a glass of iced Orangina.

'Here. Getting hot, isn't it?' I said, as I handed the drink to him.

'Thanks. Yes, it is.' He was gazing up at the tower. 'Odd, isn't it?'

'What?' I looked up at the tower too, but it seemed the same as ever to me.

'The windows. In the tower.'

I looked again. There were the large windows of the kitchen and bedrooms, then above that the small window of Tom's tower room, and then above that but further round the tower, another one … 'Oh! That top window – where did that come from?'

Tom laughed. 'Well, I suppose it's always been there. How do you get to it, though? It must be a room above mine.'

'There's no room above yours. Well, there's no staircase or anything. Are you sure that's not your window?'

'Sure. Mine looks out this way, that one is further round to the south side, looking down the driveway. I'll prove it.' He thrust the Orangina back at me and sprinted off into the château. A minute later as I stood there watching, his face appeared at the lower of the small windows, waving at me. I waved back, then gasped as I briefly glimpsed something else, at the higher window …

Don't be stupid, I told myself. It was just the light. The sun, glinting off the glass, giving the impression that someone was up there. But that window – what was behind it? How did you reach it? We'd explored every inch of our new home, and there was no way to climb any further up the tower. And yet, there was a window up there.

Chapter 10

Claudette, 1789

Versailles was in uproar, on the afternoon after the women's march. Claudette was trying to keep abreast of the fast-moving events, listening to servants' gossip as well as gleaning what she could from overhearing Monsieur and Madame Aubert's conversations. She had perfected the art, she thought, of blending into the background of their chambers, quietly getting on with work yet remaining near enough to listen in to what they said.

When she heard them discussing the way the King and Queen had bravely stood on the balcony and how the crowd had chanted *Vive le Roi* and *Vive la Reine* she had felt a mix of emotions. Relief that perhaps the moment of danger had passed, and that life could go on comfortably as it had been. And disappointment underlying it all – did this mean nothing would change after all? Despite her job, working in the grandest palace in all of Europe, despite her comfortable room, good food and manageable workload, she wanted to see France change for the better. It was time for a more modern way of life, where people were treated equally. A fairer split of the country's wealth, so that no one went hungry. Ever since that day in July when her master had returned to Versailles looking tired and ashen-faced, reporting that the great fortress of the Bastille had been stormed by a mob, Claudette had secretly hoped that it would all lead eventually to the end of the *ancien régime*, and France would become a more equal society. She'd taken great care never to discuss her beliefs with anyone, not even her best friends among the hundreds of staff that kept the enormous palace running smoothly.

And now, it seemed that the King had agreed that he and his family should go to Paris and live at the old Tuileries Palace. Most of the Court was to go with them, and nobles and their servants were scurrying about trying to pack for the move. Carriages were being made ready and everyone was talking at once, wondering what their future held. Claudette made her way quickly to Madame Aubert's chambers, to do her duties. Monsieur Aubert had spoken to her briefly and in private that morning.

'Do not tell your mistress yet, but if the King is taken to Paris, we will not be going with him. We will be leaving here.'

She'd stared at him, wide-eyed, but had nodded silently as he handed her a pile of peasants' clothing, telling her to hide them in Madame Aubert's chamber, in readiness.

As she hurried into Madame's chamber, she realised now was the moment. Both Auberts were there – Monsieur was holding Madame's hands and she was gazing fearfully at him.

'Must we leave? Can no one stay here?'

'Of course no one can stay here. We are leaving. Ah, here is Claudette. She will help you dress – Claudette, where are those clothes I gave you earlier?'

Claudette hurried across the room to the chest where she'd secreted the items and pulled them out. Madame looked at them with distaste.

'I cannot wear those! They are the clothes of a peasant woman!'

'You will wear them,' her husband said, his voice sounding sterner than Claudette had ever heard it. 'Prepare yourself quickly.'

101

Claudette began unfastening the bows and buttons on Madame's gown. There were so many, and her fingers felt slippery with sweat. Ordinarily she'd have taken care not to stain the gown but she suspected Madame would never need it again, so she chose speed over care.

Soon she was fastening the coarse woven brown gown around Madame.

'The fabric is so scratchy! It is not at all like silk. Oh, I don't know if I can wear this!'

'You must, Madame. Monsieur said so, and he is right. You will not be safe if you look like a member of the nobility. This is the only way.' Claudette fought hard to keep impatience out of her voice. It was not Madame's fault. She was young – a good ten years younger than Claudette, barely out of her teens. And she was carrying her first child. Of course she was scared – the situation was tense and who knew what the immediate future would hold? Claudette was not sure how much Madame understood about what was happening in France. How there was no going back. The old ways were gone for good, whether Madame liked it or not. But all she could do was focus on what needed to be done now – preparation for the journey, hoping that Monsieur Aubert had made good enough plans to get them away from Versailles, praying that no mob would accost them as they left the palace, steeling themselves for the long journey ahead.

They were going to Monsieur's château, in the south. The Château d'Aubert, near the village of Saint-Michel-sur-Verais. The village where Claudette had been born, and where her mother still lived. It had been eight years since she had been there – since she'd travelled north with Monsieur Aubert and his first wife to Paris, for Monsieur Aubert to take up his position in Louis XVI's court. Claudette was excited at the thought of seeing her mother again, being back among the people of the south, speaking Provençal, but apprehensive about the journey.

'Madame, your boots,' she said, holding out the pair of rough leather boots Monsieur Aubert had provided.

'I cannot wear those!' Madame Aubert turned her back on them and reached for her dainty silk slippers.

'You must, to blend in,' Claudette told her. 'Madame, many of the peasants go barefoot, in all weathers. That is your choice.'

It did the trick. Grumbling, Madame Aubert sat on an ottoman and allowed Claudette to slip her feet into the boots and buckle them. They were not bad boots. Many of the Parisian women who'd been on the march would have been grateful for them. Claudette bit her lip to stop herself saying anything more, reminding herself once again that it was not Madame's fault she'd been born into the aristocracy. She was not a bad person, just young and naive, with much to learn about the world beyond the luxury of Versailles. Claudette suspected Madame would learn much over the coming weeks and months.

At last it was time to leave. Monsieur Aubert returned to the chamber, dressed now in workmen's clothes, looking like one of the *sans-culottes*. He nodded his approval at Madame's attire. Claudette tied a simple cape around Madame, another around herself, and stood beside her, ready to leave.

'Just one moment,' Monsieur Aubert said, crossing to the cabinet where Madame kept her jewellery. He picked up the box, and emptied its contents into a leather bag which he tucked into a pocket inside his coat. 'I have money, but we may need more. Hide your ring, Catherine. Put it in a pocket. Come, we have no time to lose.'

He checked there was no one about in the corridors, and led the way out of the palace via a side door, and from there across a courtyard and into the crowds where they quickly blended in. Madame Aubert was clinging tightly to Claudette's hand, and the two of them stayed as close as possible to Monsieur. There were thousands of people about – more even than the day before.

Monsieur began taking up some of the chants – 'To Paris! Liberty for all! Equality for all!' and following his lead, Claudette did the same and nudged Madame to join in.

She caught glimpses of carriages leaving the grounds, no doubt carrying other members of court into Paris. Thank goodness her employers were not among that number – who knew what their future would hold? Claudette wondered if she'd have stayed with the Auberts if they had gone with the royal family, or if she'd have quietly disappeared into the crowd and left them to their fate, whatever that might be. But the chance to return to her home village, and her mother, had persuaded her to stay with them, throwing in her lot with them for a while longer. Besides, she liked Monsieur, and Madame was nothing but a product of her spoiled upbringing and privileged position in life, not a bad person.

The crowds finally began to thin out as they wove their way through, moving in a different direction to most. Around a corner of the lane they came upon a farm, where a man stood holding the reins of a pony that was harnessed to a farm cart. Monsieur Aubert approached him, handed over a small coin purse, and ushered the women up onto the cart. A couple of coarse blankets were folded at their feet.

'You are sisters, and we are travelling south to attend your mother, who is sick,' Monsieur Aubert told them. 'If we are questioned by anyone, say nothing, leave me to do the talking.'

Madame looked terrified but nodded her agreement, as did Claudette. Monsieur climbed up, flicked the reins, and the pony set off at a slow walk.

'When we are far enough from Paris we will find an inn for the night. Catherine, it will not provide the level of comfort you are used to, but we will be sheltered and fed, and will have a place to sleep.'

'How long will it take to reach your château? I assume that is where we are going?' Madame asked, her voice sounding small and scared.

'Yes, it is. It will take a week, perhaps a little more. We will pick up a stage coach at Orléans which will be faster. But for today and tomorrow, make yourselves as comfortable as you can.' He nodded at the blankets by their feet, and Claudette reached down to tuck them around herself and Madame.

It was a long and uncomfortable journey. The inns they stayed at were basic – even Claudette found the straw-filled pallets they slept on uncomfortable and the stews of stringy meat unpalatable. But it was more than many people had, she reminded herself, and she should count herself lucky. Thankfully no one had questioned them, or guessed that they had come from the court at Versailles. There was talk everywhere of the removal of the royal family to Paris where, it was said, they were effectively under house arrest. There was much speculation in the inns about what would ultimately become of the King and Queen. Along with the Auberts, Claudette listened carefully to everything but commented on nothing.

As soon as they had eaten at each inn they retired to their rooms. Sometimes all three were in one room, in others the two women shared a chamber while Monsieur Aubert slept elsewhere, Claudette suspected sometimes he'd slept in the stables.

'I'm afraid,' Madame said to Claudette one evening, 'that all this jolting in the coaches is harming my baby.' She put a protective hand on her midriff.

'No, Madame. Babies are hardy little things. It won't mind the travelling at all. Don't worry, I am sure it will be fine. And it will be a lucky child – growing up in the fresh air of the mountains around Saint-Michel-sur-Verais. It is where its father grew up.' She smiled reassuringly at her employer.

'I hope you are right. Oh, these horrible clothes!' Madame scratched at her neck and shoulders. 'How I long for a hot bath, and a silk gown to put on afterwards!'

'It will not be long before we reach the château. And then you shall have your bath. There will be some clothes left by the previous Madame Aubert, and I am sure your husband will soon buy you more. Stay strong, Madame.'

Madame caught hold of Claudette's hand and held it to her cheek. 'Thank goodness I have you, Claudette. I don't think I could have stood this without you. You will stay with us, won't you, when we reach the château?'

'Yes, Madame, I will.' Claudette looked away. She hadn't quite decided. It depended what the mood of the people was like, in the south. She didn't wish her employers any harm, but she wanted what was best for the country. And she wanted to be safe.

At long last they reached the mountains, and transferred from stage coach to a rough farmer's cart once again, for the final part of the journey up the winding road that led to the high valley along which the river Verais flowed. Claudette felt a thrill to be nearing home, to be passing through scenery she'd grown up with. They passed farms that looked familiar, twists in the road she thought she recognised. And then through the village of Saint-Michel-sur-Verais itself – looking exactly as she remembered it. There was the church, the village square, the row of cottages leading up the hillside towards the cemetery. At the end of that row was her mother's house. She wanted to stop the cart, climb down, run up that hill. But Madame Aubert would need help when they arrived at the château. There was time enough for her to visit her mother. Monsieur Aubert had written to the château's housekeeper, he said, to inform her that they would be arriving. Word might have reached Claudette's mother, and she might possibly have guessed that Claudette would travel with them. As the cart passed through the village Claudette tried to calm her growing excitement. Surely she would be able to visit her mother the next day? A horrible thought occurred to her – was her mother even still alive? Claudette and her mother could not read or write, so had sent each other no letters over the eight years since Claudette had left the south. She sent up a little prayer that she would find her mother alive and well.

A little way out of the village Monsieur Aubert turned the cart up a familiar driveway, around a corner, and there it was, Château d'Aubert, looking much as it had when Claudette had last seen it. A little less well cared for, perhaps. She knew that Monsieur Aubert's father and mother had both died a few years earlier, and apart from a housekeeper and a retainer, no one had lived at the château since then. There was ivy growing up one wall, weeds in the gardens that encircled the building, and peeling paintwork on the window frames.

'Oh! Is this it?' cried Madame Aubert. 'It is … perhaps a little smaller than I had thought …' Claudette glanced at her. Madame was looking at the original, older wing of the château, with its little tower.

'There is a second wing, behind,' Monsieur Aubert said, sounding a little defensive. 'More modern. My grandfather added it. It is where all the principal rooms are.'

Madame turned to smile at him, looking relieved. 'That is good to hear. I shall need a full tour, as soon as I have had a hot bath and changed into some other clothes.'

A bath and change of clothes – that was exactly what Claudette wanted too, but she knew she would not get the chance for anything more than a quick wash. At least she knew what her first duties would be, and she smiled reassuringly at Madame.

They alighted from the cart, groaning and stretching after the long journey. No one came out to meet them, and Monsieur Aubert tugged impatiently on the bell pull that hung beside the front door. A woman, dressed in a drab brown gown, her untidy hair pinned at the back, answered the door.

'Tradesman's entrance is round the back,' she said in the Provençal dialect, as she attempted to push the heavy oak door closed.

'Madame, it is I, Pierre Aubert, Comte de Verais, and this is my wife Catherine,' Monsieur replied in French. 'We require a meal, baths and clean clothes, at once.'

The woman squinted at them, suspicion clouding her eyes, then she turned and called out. 'Henri! Fellow here says he's Aubert. Come and deal with him, will you?'

A stooped old man, dressed in worn but good quality clothing, shuffled into the hallway. 'Henri! At last. We are exhausted,' Pierre said, stepping past the housekeeper into the line of sight of the old man. Claudette smiled too, recognising the man who'd served as butler when she had last worked here.

'Monsieur Aubert! It is good to see you, sir. Welcome, Madame. And Claudette! We were not expecting you. Nevertheless, we can quickly make everything ready for you. Might take a day or so to get up to speed. It's been empty so long, you see. Madame Bernard, this is the master.'

The housekeeper dropped into a curtsy, but her face was still stony and disapproving. Madame Aubert looked furious, but her husband tried to smooth things over, ushering his wife into the hallway. Claudette followed, kissing Henri on both cheeks as she passed and smiling and curtsying at Madame Bernard. The woman would be her superior, so it was as well to get on the right side of her if possible.

It was two days after they arrived that Claudette was finally able to ask Madame Bernard for an afternoon off, so that she could visit her mother. The time was grudgingly given, but only after the housekeeper had consulted with Monsieur Aubert. 'If my wife can spare her, then of course she may go,' he'd said. 'Claudette has been a good and loyal servant to us for many years.'

Claudette had managed to procure a cheese and some ham from the kitchen, to take as a gift for her mother. She'd found clean clothes in one of the old maid's rooms and had had a good wash. With a basket over her arm she set off for the walk to the village, choosing to take a high level path that contoured along the hillside, from the back of the grounds. It was the way she'd always taken when she lived here before. It was overgrown, but still usable. Monsieur Aubert had asked Madame Bernard and Henri to employ more staff, to get the château running as it should. When that happened, perhaps someone would be sent to clear the path.

It was a fine autumn day, and although it was chilly Claudette enjoyed the walk, remembering some of the twists and turns of the path, picking her way over the stream that it crossed, and eventually dropping down into the village via a steep lane. She reached her mother's cottage and knocked on the door, feeling apprehensive at what she might find.

But she needn't have worried – the door was opened by her mother, who looked fit and well and excited to see her.

'Claudette, *ma petite*! I had heard you might be coming, along with the Auberts. You are here!' She kissed Claudette on both cheeks and then pulled her in for a hug, in which all the longing and loss of the previous eight years seemed to be released.

'*Maman*. It is so good to see you,' Claudette replied, relishing the chance to speak her native Provençal dialect once more.

'So come on in, drink wine with me, and tell me all about your life in Paris. There is a new Madame Aubert now, I think? Not the one you were first employed by? What is she like?'

Claudette allowed herself to be led inside and seated at the rough table by the kitchen hearth, the same table that had always been there, the same hearth. She handed over her gifts and began to tell her mother all that had happened over the previous eight years. Although Monsieur Aubert had told her not to tell people that the Auberts had been at Court and living in Versailles, for their own safety, Claudette judged that her mother was trustworthy. She described court life, told her all the details of that last horrific couple of days, and detailed their escape and their journey south.

'But, *Maman*, if anyone asks say the Auberts lived near Paris.

Do not say we were at Versailles. Monsieur Aubert is fearful of what might happen, if this revolution progresses, and maybe it would not be safe for us if the people turned fully against the royal family and anyone associated with them.'

'We know little of the Revolution here,' her mother replied. 'We are so far from Paris. But I will keep your secrets, if you think it is best.'

Chapter 11

Lu

That mysterious extra window ... Tom and I were intrigued by it. He'd clearly inherited my overactive imagination.

'Probably just a loft space,' Steve said, shrugging. He and Manda had come across us outside, with a ladder propped up against the tower. Tom was up it, right at the top, but still far short of being able to see into that topmost window.

'But how do you access it?' I asked, watching Tom carefully. He was too high up the ladder for my comfort.

'Don't know.' Steve wandered off, looking for something to do. A few minutes later he was off on a run, his second of the day.

The thing about Steve is he likes to be busy. I mean, really busy – the kind of busy that makes normal mortals feel stressed and overwhelmed. He loves to have several projects on the go at once, flitting from one to the other and somehow keeping them all moving forward – plate-spinning, he calls it. He'd been a superb project manager at his work, and was always able to have something else on the go at the same time – DIY projects at home, restoration of old cars, clearing out his parents' old house and eBaying furniture.

When Steve had first heard about his redundancy – a result of his company deciding to outsource some departments including his – he'd thought he would get another job. He approached job-seeking with all his usual project management skills and sent out dozens of CVs, but no one was hiring. At least not at the kind of salary he was used to.

'I mean,' he'd said, 'I could get a job for half the money I was on before. But I don't want to work as many hours for half the salary.'

'And he doesn't *need* to work,' Manda had told us. 'We have enough savings and pensions. We're lucky – we are well set up. I keep telling him he should rebrand the redundancy and call it early retirement instead.'

Steve had taken her advice, but it had hit him hard. He'd spent the first couple of months out of work repainting his entire house, which didn't need doing. Then he'd pruned the garden to within an inch of its life, and applied (unsuccessfully) for an allotment, even though we all knew gardening was not his thing. He'd set himself to read a classic novel a week and had achieved it. He'd offered his services at a charity shop and had reorganised their staff rota and stock storage systems within a fortnight.

No wonder he'd leapt at the chance to find and buy the perfect French château for us! That had 'kept him entertained' as Manda put it, for a good few weeks. But once we'd moved in, what next? He was OK for the first couple of weeks, diverting his energies into organising the unpacking of our three-households' worth of belongings, and exploring the local area. He went out running every day, somewhere different every time, trying new routes that he could recommend to me as walking routes or to Gray for mountain-biking. But when he had to start repeating runs, and when there were no more boxes to unpack or cupboards to organise, he began getting fidgety and irritable.

'He's driving me mad,' Manda confided in me, as we stared up at the top tower window. 'He's always suggesting we go out for the day to some new town or village. I mean, I love sightseeing, but we live here now and there's plenty of time. One day out a week, maybe two, is enough. I want to just enjoy being here in the château for now, not always charging off somewhere. What are we going to do with him?'

'He needs a new project,' I said. But he also needed to learn to relax and slow down a little. Enjoy life, rather than just keep charging on through it.

'Will you talk to him, Lu? Tell him to take things more slowly.' Manda sighed. 'He won't listen to me. But if it comes from you, perhaps it'll sink in.'

I smiled and patted her arm. 'Sure I will.' Why did everyone think I'd be able to make a difference? But maybe if I could think up a project for Steve, it'd help ease him into our new, more relaxed life in France. He hadn't shown any interest in our newly discovered window, but maybe there was something I could come up with to help Steve, and also solve our mystery?

Manda went inside to do some chores. I stayed outside, watching Tom carefully as he climbed down the ladder.

'Well. That's a mystery, isn't it?' he said, as I helped him put the ladder back into the old stables.

Gray was there, pumping up his bike tyres. 'Hey, Tom. Fancy a cycle ride?'

'Sure! Let me run in and change.' Tom charged into the château with youthful energy.

Finding myself at a loose end, I went in search of my husband.

Phil was out in the garden, again. Digging up a patch of ground he'd ear-marked for growing vegetables. It was a great idea – I'd agreed with the others that it would be wonderful to grow some of our own food. But I hadn't expected that it would be Phil doing all the hard work. Why couldn't Steve and Gray do some of the digging? Or Tom, while he was visiting? I took him a glass of iced water with a slice of lemon in to entice him away from the work for a moment.

'Here. You look like you need this,' I said, handing it to him.

He shoved his spade into the earth, mopped his brow with a cloth from his pocket, and took it. 'Thanks. Mmm, cold and wet. Excellent.'

'Love, you are working too hard. And in this heat!' Temperatures had been climbing all week and were now in the high twenties. The vegetable patch was, of course, in full sun.

'Ah, it's not too bad.' Phil followed me over to a couple of garden chairs we'd left under the shade of a large tree. 'Good to have a little rest though.'

'It's too much for you,' I said, firmly. It was time he listened to me. I had visions of him keeling over with another heart attack if he kept this up. 'Get the others to do the digging. I know you're enjoying the gardening but you can do the more gentle jobs.'

Phil laughed. 'Like what? I think all gardening is quite strenuous.'

'I don't know.' We'd never done much gardening in any previous homes. Just a bit of mowing the lawn and pruning shrubs. Certainly no vegetable growing. I pictured my granddad who'd had a veg patch when I was a child, and always seemed to have gentle little jobs to do in it. 'Tying up beans or something.'

'Need to plant them first,' Phil said. 'And before that, I need to prepare the ground. That's what I'm doing.' He drained the rest of his drink and went back to his spade.

'Can't Steve or Gray do this?' I called after him.

He stopped and turned around to face me. 'They both offered, Lu, but I said no. The garden's kind of become my thing. I wanted to do this work. Raising a bit of a sweat, getting some exercise – it's—'

I interrupted. 'It's not good for you. You've had a heart condition. You need gentle exercise only.'

Phil sounded irritated with me. 'Stop fussing, Lu. Honestly, this is all right for me to do.'

'I bet your doctor back in England would have said no.'

'But my doctor here in France says yes.'

I raised my eyebrows. We'd all registered with a local doctor but I hadn't realised Phil had been to see him. 'When was that?'

'Last week. I went for a check-up, to talk about my medical history. And—' Phil fixed me with a stern stare '—to ask if he thought gardening, especially digging, would be all right for me to do. And he said yes, gardening was perfect exercise.'

'Why didn't you tell me about this?'

Phil sighed. 'Because, Lu, you'd have fussed and worried and fretted. Mind you, you're doing it anyway. Please, love, I know you're just concerned for me, but honestly, I'm all right, this is good for me, and I am becoming fitter and healthier day by day since we moved here.'

I had to admit that last bit was true. Phil was slimmer, had a bit of a tan on his face and arms, no longer huffed and puffed when walking up stairs, and was even prepared to walk with me into the village or go on a short, flat bike ride with Gray. He'd never done any of that in England.

I wasn't ready to let the discussion go just yet, though. 'The doctor, did he understand you well enough? How was his English? I mean, did he understand about your heart attack and the stents?'

'He trained in London. His English was near perfect.' Phil stuck his spade back into the soil and stepped towards me, wrapping his rather sweaty arms around me. 'I'm not your mum, Lu. I'm not an invalid you have to take care of – not now. Maybe I was just after the heart attack, but not now. It's all right to let me make my own decisions about what I'm capable of. But thank you for caring. I love you.'

'Love you too. Even when you're hot and sweaty.'

He kissed the end of my nose and let me go. A moment later he was back at it – thrusting the spade deep into the ground, levering up a clod of earth, turning it and breaking it up. I watched for a while, still trying to convince myself he wasn't doing himself any harm. I sighed. It was going to take a bit of getting used to. But perhaps he was right. His heart attack had come so soon after Mum's death, I suppose I'd transferred my worrying and nursing directly onto him. I'd had four years of caring for Mum. It had become a habit.

'He's doing so well, isn't he?' Manda had come out to the garden and was also watching Phil. 'To think what he was like just over a year ago, and now look at him!'

Funnily, as she said it, I looked back at Phil as though with new eyes and saw him as she did. Yes, he *was* doing well. He could have taken the heart attack to mean he needed to stop skiing and spend his life resting and watching daytime television. But he'd treated it as a wake-up call, changed his diet and lifestyle and was now getting himself properly fit. Wasn't that what I had hoped would happen with this move to France?

I nodded. 'He's doing amazingly well. I'm so pleased he's taken up gardening.' As I said it, I realised I meant it. Really meant it. Worrying had become a habit but one I'd need to break.

'I'm pleased too. Looking forward to eating all the produce!' Manda smacked her lips in anticipation and I laughed. I was looking forward to it all too.

Late that afternoon, Steve arrived back from his run with a grin on his face and a wriggling rucksack on his back.

'What've you got in there?' Manda asked, as he went through to the sitting room, calling to everyone.

'Our new housemates,' he replied, opening the rucksack and extracting two kittens. They were about ten weeks old, tabbies, in that beautiful pale-brown colour you often get in Mediterranean countries but which is more rarely seen in Britain.

'So cute!' I said, taking one from him to cuddle. The kitten mewed at me, a tiny, squeaky sound. 'Where did you get them?'

'Gray told me about an advert on the noticeboard in the *mairie*,' Steve said. 'I've named them Flip and Flop. He nodded at the one I was holding, that had a little white bib. 'That one's Flop. Both females.'

'They're gorgeous. You've been wanting cats for ages. Welcome to the château, little ones,' I said. Flop was struggling to get free, so I put her down on the sofa beside me and she crawled over towards her sister, on Steve's knee. I'm not sure why but I felt a pang of jealousy as he moved to allow both kittens to cuddle up on his lap together. He was needed. He had these little creatures to look after. I needed something to look after, too. But I didn't know what.

'There was something else of interest on the *mairie* notice-board,' announced Gray, as we sat around admiring the kittens. 'The annual mayor's fete is coming up. It's on 8th May – a French national holiday.'

'Another national holiday? They had one last week for May Day,' Steve said.

'This one's Liberation Day. We should go along. Tom'll still be here. We're all invited.'

'Oh! Who invited us?' I asked, as I flicked the switch on the kettle to make us all a brew.

'Aimée … I mean, Madame la Maire, of course. Well, everyone in the village and surrounding countryside is invited, but she, um, came out of her office while I was reading the notice board and invited us personally.'

'That's lovely of her.' I narrowed my eyes slightly at Gray – was he showing signs of being interested in the mayor? Surely not – he'd only met her once before, when she'd called round to introduce herself. As far as I knew, anyway. 'Where is the fete held?'

'In the village *salle des fetes,* plus there'll be stalls in the village square. After a little ceremony at the war memorial there'll be a band, some kind of dancing display by the local school, bit of a

117

car boot sale going on – that kind of thing. And the mayor pays for a glass of local wine for everyone.'

'Great opportunity for you all to get more involved locally,' Tom said. 'Better make a good impression on the mayor.'

'I think Gray already has,' I said quietly. He just smiled and looked away.

'Well, that's our weekend sorted then,' Steve said happily.

We walked down to the village all together on the day of the fete, rather than trying to find parking. No doubt all the parking spots would be busy, especially if the main central square was closed off to traffic. The day was warm and bright, and we'd all dragged out our summer clothes. The men were in shorts, Manda was in a loose cotton skirt and T-shirt, and I was wearing three-quarter-length cotton trousers with a loose shirt and a pair of sandals, sunglasses on my head. I felt cool and comfortable, though knew I'd probably feel dowdy and dull compared with the mayor, who no doubt would be in crisp white linen.

'You look gorgeous,' Phil said, kissing me as I took his arm. I smiled at him. It was as though he'd read my mind.

I enjoyed the walk alongside the river. The trees were showing off their bright spring foliage – stunning green against the azure sky. It really was a spectacularly beautiful part of the world.

We arrived in the village just before eleven o'clock, in time to attend the short service beside the war memorial. I had to listen hard to try to understand the gist of the speeches. From what I could gather they were the usual sentiments about remembering the sacrifices of past generations and working together to ensure the horrors of the past wars could never happen again. The words *liberté, egalité* were definitely in there somewhere. The mayor laid a wreath of red, white and blue flowers at the foot of the memorial, flags were lowered for a minute's silence, and then a bugler played the 'Last Post'. I'd attended dozens of remembrance day services when the boys were in the cubs and scouts, and this one seemed much the same – just as moving and thought-provoking, even if I didn't quite understand all that was said.

And then as everyone filed away from the war memorial back to the central village square, a band began playing – a mix of cool jazz and funk. People were talking and laughing. There was bunting up across every street, and the village square was crammed with stalls selling homemade cakes and conserves, bric-a-brac, local crafts. One stall was festooned with the French, EU and Provence flags, and behind it a couple of women were pouring out glasses of wine and handing them to everyone who passed. The non-drinkers were offered Perrier water or orange juice. This was the *mairie's* stall, and Gray made a beeline for it. But I couldn't see Madame la Maire anywhere near.

We split up then – Steve, Manda and Gray headed off in one direction while Phil, Tom and I went the other, browsing the stalls, picking up a few bits and pieces for the château – a gorgeous woven throw in shades of red and orange, a couple of pots containing violets and lavender (all locally grown, the stall holder told me proudly), a pair of old copper pans I thought would look good hung up in the kitchen even if we never used them.

'You realise we will have to carry all this home,' Tom grumbled as I handed him the latest purchases – a whole *saucisson* and a large tub of olives – to hold.

I smiled and nodded. 'It'll be fine, don't worry.' Actually I'd forgotten we hadn't brought a car. I supposed someone could stay in the village with the items while someone else walked back to fetch a car.

'Ah, 'ello, my Eenglish friends! When will you be back in my bistro?' It was Monsieur Christophe. He greeted us like old friends.

'Very soon, Monsieur, very soon.' Phil had shaken his hand and clapped his back, and within a moment or two was discussing the relative merits of different types of tomato with him. I listened for a bit then sat on a nearby bench, feeling the need for a little rest. Tom was waving at Steve and Manda who were also laden with purchases. They came over to join us.

'Hey, how are you getting on?' Manda asked, and I showed her what we'd bought.

'Fabulous! Love that throw. Where's Gray?'

'I don't know.' I looked about for him and spotted him over by the *mairie's* wine stall. 'Ah, over there.'

'Blagging more booze, is he?' Steve laughed.

'No, think he's chatting up the mayor.'

'What?' The others all turned and stared. They obviously hadn't picked up on Gray's interest in the mayor as I had.

'Don't all stare at once! She's facing this way.'

'Bloody hell, Lu, you're right. Look how he's leaning over the table towards her.' Steve shook his head. 'That man has no subtlety. Should we go over and rescue our poor mayor?' He didn't wait for an answer but began striding over. Phil raised an eyebrow and Manda shrugged, as we gathered up our purchases and followed him across the square.

'Hello, everyone!' The mayor greeted us warmly, and this time I was pleased I remembered to kiss her on both cheeks rather than go for a handshake. It'd take a while before it came naturally to me, however. 'Are you enjoying the day?'

'It's lovely. So much going on. We've bought lots of stuff,' I replied, and Manda and Tom held up our shopping.

'And who is this?' the mayor asked, looking at Tom.

'Ah, yes. Our son. Tom, meet Madame la Maire.'

'*Enchanté*,' she said, kissing him, while he blushed and fumbled a little. 'And please call me Aimée. Gray has been telling me you are interested in history, yes?'

'I am. I used to be a history teacher. I'd love to know more about the history of this area.'

'You must visit the library, then. And the museum.'

'There's a museum?' How had I not spotted it?

'Not in Saint Michel-sur-Verais. But down the valley, in the town. There are displays about the Revolution there. I think you may be interested.' She smiled. 'Anything I can do to help, please ask.'

'Thank you, I will.' I noticed Gray hovering at her elbow, clearly waiting until he could have the mayor's attention once more. I smiled in his direction to draw her attention to him, and she turned slightly to include him in the conversation. And, I noted, she touched his arm with a perfectly manicured hand, and almost imperceptibly moved a little closer to him. Was our Gray making an impact on the mayor, the way she had on him?

Chapter 12

Catherine, 1790

The winter had been long and cold. Pierre had never mentioned the climate in Saint-Michel-sur-Verais – Catherine had assumed it would be like Paris, perhaps warmer in the summer. But in the mountains, in winter, it was much colder. 'Because we are higher up,' Pierre told her. The first snow fell at the start of December and stayed on the ground almost continuously from then until March. In some weeks the village was cut off from all neighbouring towns when the roads were blocked by snow. Once food had run short, even at the château, where usually supplies for a winter were stored in the barns, but they'd managed to make what they had last, until the snow melted enough on the roads to allow wagons through.

'We'll stock up over the summer,' Pierre had said. 'In my absence it seems the farms have not been properly managed.' He'd had consultations with his estate manager, and Catherine had heard raised voices from the château's study.

As the winter wore on, Catherine's baby bump grew, and now it was almost due. Pierre had engaged a midwife from the nearby village, and a wet-nurse had already moved into an attic room in the château ready for the birth. A physician had visited a few times and pronounced the pregnancy to be progressing well. But still Catherine was frightened, and more than ever she wished she could have been giving birth at or near Versailles with the Queen's own physician in attendance.

'Madame, all will be well,' Claudette told her. 'Many babies have been born in this valley over the years, including me! The midwife here is good – I remember her. And you will have a physician. Many women are not so lucky.'

Catherine scowled a little at the maid's words. Since the Revolution she had noticed that even Claudette spoke her mind more than before, as though she had taken the idea of equality for all to heart.

At last the day came, a fine, sunny but cold day in late March, when her pains began. Catherine called Claudette and hauled herself up the stairs to her chamber. Claudette helped her into bed, and then ran down to send someone to fetch the midwife. Those few minutes alone, lying on her bed trying to ride the waves of pain that washed over her, were the most terrifying Catherine had ever experienced – even more so than that terrible night when she had fled with the Queen from the Versailles intruders. At least then she had not been alone, and she had had the Queen's example to follow. The Queen had never had to give birth alone. On the contrary, many ladies and gentlemen of the court had been present in her chamber for every birth, as was the custom for royal births. Catherine herself had been present at the birth of the Queen's last child – poor little Sophie Hélène who'd lived less than a year – standing at the back of the room, craning her neck to see what was going on. At the time she'd thought it intrusive having so many people present, but it was better than being alone as she now was. Now, as another contraction hit and she clutched at a bed post, groaning with the pain, she felt small and frightened. Childbirth was dangerous. She'd known of a couple of women who'd died during or shortly after, and they'd had the best doctors money could buy! What chance did she have?

There was a tap at the door and without waiting for an answer, the midwife bustled in, followed by Claudette who was carrying cloths and a basin of water. Catherine sighed with relief. If only the physician could be here too, but he'd told her that she would be in good hands with just the midwife, and he would call to check on her a day or so after the baby was born. And Pierre, although he was somewhere on the estate, had not wanted to be present at the birth.

The labour lasted hours. The midwife had pronounced her barely started, and Catherine had detected a slight sneer as she said this, as though Catherine shouldn't have summoned her yet. 'But as I'm here, I'll stay for the duration,' she'd said, her accent so thick that Catherine could barely understand her. The midwife had sent Claudette to fetch her a glass of wine and some bread and cheese. 'Nothing for you, Madame,' she'd said, as Catherine widened her eyes. 'You're liable to sick it back up, so you must keep your stomach empty until the baby's here.'

Catherine realised that for now, the midwife was in charge and she had better just do as she was told. In any case the contractions were too painful and she was too scared to assert her authority. Another contraction hit her, harder and tighter than any so far, and when it subsided Catherine determined never to have any more children, if she could help it. To have to suffer so much – it was unfair! Claudette mopped her brow, and adjusted a pillow beneath her head, while the midwife checked on progress yet again. 'You're getting closer, Madame. I'd say another hour or two, then you'll be wanting to push.'

Another hour or two of pain! How could she handle it? But somehow she did, with Claudette at her side, comforting her throughout, and in the late afternoon when the sun had moved around so that the room had become cool and dark, the contractions eased for a short while. When they restarted they had a different quality to them – an urgency, a purpose, and the urge to push. And they were more painful than ever. Catherine wanted to die rather than face the next one. She screamed as each one hit, and lashed out at Claudette who was mopping her face, looking worried. The midwife rolled her eyes at her and muttered something about first babies, but got on with the job, and after a particularly painful contraction that made Catherine feel as though she was splitting in two, announced that the head was out and the baby would be born in the next contraction. She was right, and shortly Catherine was handed a squirming, red-faced, swaddled baby boy.

And now it was a different sort of wave that engulfed her – one of love rather than pain. As she gazed into the tiny screwed-up face of her firstborn, Catherine knew that she would do anything in her power to give this little mite the best of everything, the best and safest life. She would lay down her life for him, if she had to. He was the centre of her world.

Pierre, when he met his son a few hours later, seemed equally besotted. 'He is born into a turbulent time, but we shall make sure he is safe and loved at all times,' he said. 'And we will call him Louis, after our beloved King.'

Catherine nodded happily. The perfect name for a perfect child.

In the summer, when little Louis was a few months old, Pierre made a trip to Paris. He had business to attend to, and also wanted to find out what was happening at first hand. The news that reached them in Provence was sketchy at best.

'I'll be safe,' he'd told Catherine. 'I will wear simple clothes and will travel as a bourgeoisie businessman. I will be back within a fortnight.' He'd kissed her goodbye, left instructions with the staff and set off on his horse.

Catherine had spent the fortnight trying to get to grips with running the château. Now that she was not pregnant and had got over the birth, it was time to begin taking charge of her own household. She'd begun by calling the housekeeper Madame Bernard to her, to discuss the changes she wanted to make.

'As Comtesse de Verais, it is my duty to see that the château is run as well as possible. I would like you to help me with this,' Catherine began, trying to sound authoritative. Even after several months she found the housekeeper a little intimidating, even though she was only a servant.

Madame Bernard scowled at her, but nodded and waited for her to continue.

'We will work together to agree all menus each week. I will check the accounts periodically, and expect them to be up to date at all times. You may hire at least two more maids, so that the château is kept immaculate at all times.'

Madame Bernard listened with her lips pinched together in a thin line. Catherine felt herself withering under the older woman's stare. Madame Bernard clearly resented her. Perhaps she had enjoyed looking after an empty château for too many years. Catherine wondered if she should dismiss the housekeeper, though how she would find a decent replacement in this remote corner of France she had no idea. She hoped it wouldn't come to that. Perhaps it would be better to make friends with the woman. She gave what she hoped was a friendly, but still superior, smile.

'Very well, Madame. I shall do what I can,' the housekeeper replied, dipping her knees in an approximation of a curtsy, and leaving the room. Catherine frowned. She had not given permission for the woman to leave. Madame Bernard would not have got very far with that attitude in Versailles, that was for certain. But they were not in Versailles now, and Catherine needed to make the best of things, even if that meant putting up with sullen servants.

Thankfully not all the servants were like the housekeeper. Henri was deferential to them at all times, as though nothing had changed in France. And Claudette was a good nursemaid. Thinking of Louis made Catherine long to hold her son for a while.

She rang the bell and asked for Louis to be brought to her. Claudette fetched the child from the wet-nurse and brought him in, dressed in a white gown and wrapped in a white shawl.

'He's lovely, Madame,' said the maid with a smile, and although it wasn't correct behaviour for a maidservant to speak without being spoken to, Catherine couldn't help but smile back.

'Yes, he really is.' She took her son from the maid and dandled him on her lap, kissing his dear little face, laughing as he tried to push his whole fist into his mouth, melting as he smiled his gummy smile at her. He was an easy baby, and so perfect, so beautiful. She was a good mother too; she remembered that in Versailles some ladies saw their children for only half an hour a day, whereas she would send for little Louis several times a day, and keep him with her for as long as possible – until he began to fret or needed feeding. As she tickled Louis she recalled how Marie Antoinette adored her children too, how she would dress her daughter Marie Thérèse in miniature versions of her own gowns, and would smother her son the Dauphin with kisses whenever he was with her. She smiled at those happier times. Of course she, Catherine, was a marvellous mother. She'd had the opportunity to learn from the Queen herself.

The two weeks without Pierre dragged on, but some things were achieved – Madame Bernard employed the new maids and Catherine met her to discuss menus for when Pierre was due home. She was getting to grips with the running of the château, and Madame Bernard appeared to have accepted her authority. No matter what was happening in distant Paris, it was good to know that servants still obeyed their masters and mistresses as had always been the case. Even if it was done with a bad grace.

At last a commotion in the hallway alerted her to Pierre's

return, and she ran out to meet him. He looked tired and a little dishevelled from the journey, but otherwise well, and she heaved a sigh of relief. He was back, he was safe. He held out his arms and she ran to him, resting her head against his shoulder, breathing in his familiar scent.

'What news from Paris?' she asked, as he released her and followed her through to the drawing room where he sat down heavily on the sofa.

'Ring for some refreshments first. I need wine and food, then I will tell you everything.'

She did as he'd asked, and then settled down beside him. 'Did you see the King and Queen? How are they? Do the people still love them?'

'They are well, by all reports, though I did not see them myself. They are kept within the Tuileries Palace, and do not leave the grounds.'

'Are they locked in?' Catherine gasped.

'They are essentially prisoners of the State,' Pierre said. 'But they are said to be happy enough and are well looked after.'

'And what of the uprising?'

'It's a revolution, my dear. There is no other word. It progresses. The National Assembly are still working on a new constitution. Their latest decrees are not good for us, I'm afraid.'

'What do you mean?'

'They are dismantling the *ancien régime* piece by piece. They have decreed that the hereditary rights of the nobility are to be abolished. That means that titles are no longer handed down from father to son.'

'But that can't be right! How can they abolish our titles?'

Pierre sighed. 'It is all about equality. The Declaration of the Rights of Man states that all men are born free and equal. And, my dear, there are those in the nobility who are inclined to agree with this too. The Marquis de Lafayette, for example. We have no choice. Little Louis will not inherit my titles. He will not be

Comte de Verais. He will still inherit my lands and property, however. He will still be rich.' He turned to gaze at Catherine. 'Talking of Louis, how is he? I should like to see my son.'

Catherine smiled and rang the bell once again. Claudette fetched Louis and handed him proudly to Pierre.

'I believe he has grown!' Pierre chuckled as he cradled the child in his arms.

'He certainly has. And he has discovered how to suck his own thumb,' Catherine said.

'We must give him a brother or a sister soon,' Pierre said. 'I would like him to have playmates as he grows up.'

Catherine was fearful of the idea of giving birth again, but if Pierre wanted more children then so be it – it was her duty and she would do it gladly. She smiled and leaned against him in response. 'Of course, my darling. We will have as many more children as you desire.'

But would their children have a future worth living? They wouldn't have the same privileges Catherine had grown up with, that seemed certain. Things were changing, and she could do nothing about it, other than cling on to the old ways here in her corner of France for as long as possible.

Chapter 13

Lu

The day after the fete, Phil drove off with Tom with a twinkle in his eye.

'What's he up to?' Gray said. I had to agree, there'd been some suspicious mutterings between father and son the previous evening, and Tom had eaten breakfast with a mischievous expression on his face.

'I have no idea,' I replied. 'Neither of them have said a word to me.'

What was also suspicious was that Phil had put a short piece of rope and a large piece of sack-cloth he'd found in one of the outbuildings, in the car. He'd taken our large right-hand-drive Galaxy, rather than the small left-hand-drive Corsa we'd recently bought jointly as it was easier to drive around in our local area. He'd also taken all the back seats out of the Galaxy, effectively converting it into a small van.

The rest of us pottered about all morning, Steve baking again (hurray!), Gray went for a bike ride, and Manda surfing the Internet looking to buy riding jodhpurs and a helmet.

I used the morning to wander down to the village, watch a

few minutes of a *pétanque* match that was going on in the village square, and buy some *saucisson* and local cheese for our lunch. I took the river path to return to the château, put the food away and was about to go out into the garden with a book when I heard a car pulling up. Good. Phil and Tom were back. I wanted to spend some time with my boy. I went out to the hallway and opened the front door ready for them, but they'd driven round the side to the outbuildings. I followed them round the side of the château and was confronted by the extraordinary sight of my husband and son man-handling a goat out of the back of our Galaxy.

'What on earth is that?' I said, unnecessarily because although I'm no expert, I can recognise a goat when I see one.

'This,' Phil proudly announced, as he pulled his sleeve away from the goat who was trying to eat it, 'is Clarabel.'

'But ... but ... why?'

'Clarabel is an excellent recycler. Any food waste, any garden waste – she will eat. Her waste can be fed to the vegetable patch. She will also provide us with milk and cheese. And she will keep me company in the garden.'

'She's a goat,' I said, once again unnecessarily.

'She's beautiful,' Phil said, looking at her with a soppy, besotted expression on his face. She was attractive, as goats go, it had to be said. She was brown and white, with large soulful eyes. One ear stood up while the other flopped coquettishly over one eye. She stood about three feet tall at her shoulder and was currently busily chewing on the sack-cloth that they'd laid across the inside of the back of the car.

Tom just stood there grinning, holding on to a piece of rope that had been tied to Clarabel's harness. 'Isn't she great, Mum?'

'She's ... well, yes, I suppose so ... Where did she come from?'

'Saw her advertised in the window of the *tabac*. Her previous owner is moving away soon, so she needed a new home. He's delighted she's coming to live at the château.' Phil grinned.

Steve, Gray and Manda had heard the commotion and came round to see what was going on. Their mouths dropped open and they all spoke at once. 'Bloody hell, a goat!', 'What on earth …', 'Is that a … goat? Where's it going to live?', 'But … but …'

'Look at those gorgeous eyes!' Manda said. She crouched down and pulled up a dandelion, then approached Clarabel, offering her the weed, which the goat munched appreciatively. Manda scratched her head as she ate. 'I love her. Where will we keep her?'

Phil grinned. 'In one of the outbuildings. Tom said he'll help clear it out. During the day she can be tethered in the garden, disposing of waste, keeping me company.'

'Well, welcome to the château, Clarabel. We hope you'll be very happy here,' I said, plucking up the courage to scratch her head as Manda had. Her coat was softer than I'd expected, and she nuzzled into my hand, hoping for more dandelions I suspected.

'Who's going to milk her?' Steve, practical as ever, wanted to know.

'Me,' Phil said proudly. 'Her old owner's going to come here every day to start with, to show me how. And there are YouTube videos to help. We'll have goat's cheese for lunch within a few days.'

I caught Phil's eye and smiled. So this was the main driver for getting a goat. After his heart attack his doctor had told him to give up eating cheese, but as goat's cheese was lower in fat and contained lots of good minerals and protein, he was allowed to eat it. And Phil was a huge lover of cheese.

Phil had arrived here in France recovering from a heart attack, unfit, wondering how he was going to cope with a new regime that meant no cheese. Now look at him – gardening every day, considering taking up cycling with Gray, acquiring a goat so he could make lower-fat cheese for us all. I was so proud of my husband. But at the same time, I felt vaguely jealous. He had a purpose – gardening – and now a companion in Clarabel. I had … nothing. Nothing of my own, anyway. Just all that I shared with my friends.

With Clarabel tethered to a stake in the garden, I followed Phil in through the patio doors at the back of the château. He wanted to find any edible waste in the kitchen to give to the goat. As I went through the sitting room I tripped on a worn piece of carpet and so very nearly fell – luckily Phil was just in front and I managed to grab on to him to stop myself tumbling.

'You OK? We really need to do something about that carpet,' Phil said, still holding on to me even though I'd regained my balance.

'Whole room needs redecorating,' I said, looking around at the peeling wallpaper and shabby paintwork.

'Not just this room. I suppose we should think about a spot of renovation. Maybe next year.' Phil sounded glum. DIY was really not his thing. We'd generally paid decorators to come in and do the work for us.

'We should eventually do up the whole château,' I said. 'Could do with some new wiring and plumbing, as well as decorating.' There weren't enough sockets in most rooms, and the plumbing tended to make unnerving noises. Well, it was either that or the resident ghost banging on the pipes. Even as I said it, an idea formed in my mind.

Phil turned down the corners of his mouth. 'Going to be a big job. Don't fancy trying to manage that.'

'No, but I know someone who might fancy it,' I said, but Phil had turned away and was already in the kitchen, gathering vegetable peelings and stale bread for Clarabel.

I cornered Steve later that afternoon, when he'd returned from a run, showered and changed, and was in the sitting room, rearranging books by the colour of their spine. Last week he'd arranged them by subject. The kittens were helping by attacking the piles of books on the floor and crawling behind the shelved ones.

'Hey. Can I help?' I said.

'Sure. Pass me anything that's red.'

We had a lot of books between us, and he was going for a kind of rainbow effect. I had to admit it was looking good. 'What are you going to work on next?' I asked him.

He shrugged. 'Not sure.' He sounded a bit despondent, as he always did when one project was coming to an end and there was nothing else lined up, yet. 'Thinking about mapping all my running routes on Mapometer and then producing a little booklet of them all with descriptions. So if anyone visits who likes fell-running or walking, we can hand them the book. I could add Gray's bike routes to it as well.'

'Nice idea!' He'd do it, as well, but I imagined it would only take him a few days to complete. He needed something that would take longer. 'Steve, I was wondering if we ought to start some renovation work on the château. There's quite a lot needs doing – rewiring and plumbing as well as general decorating.'

He shelved the books he was holding and turned to me. 'I had thought about that, Lu. I'd love to take it on as a project, but would everyone want me to? I mean, I know I have a bit of a habit of taking over … Wouldn't want to upset anyone …'

I laughed. 'Steve, I think everyone would be over the moon if you offered to do this. Phil hates DIY. I don't mind – I'll help strip wallpaper and paint, but wouldn't want to manage the project. Gray would help but—'

'He'd be hopeless managing it, bless him,' Steve said with a grin. 'And Manda hates decorating too. So yes, if you think I should do it, I'm more than happy. It'll keep me busy for ages.'

'No rush, Steve! We can work on the château bit by bit over the next couple of years or so. But can we start with the tower room?' I had an idea that when renovating it we might discover how to get to the attic space above.

'Ha ha. No. I think there are other more important priorities than the room we barely use. Right, as soon as these books are back on the shelves I'll go round the château and start a list of what needs doing. With a following wind we could have it done by Christmas.' He bent to grab more red books, working twice as fast now that he had something else lined up.

I put a hand on his arm so that he stopped working and looked at me. 'You know, it's OK to take a rest every now and again. Sit down with one of these books and a cup of tea. Relax. Slow down. Now that you're sixty you need to start taking it easy ...' Manda had wanted me to have a word with him about slowing down.

'Oy! I'm just as fit and active as I was at fifty, or even forty, Madame Marlow!' He dropped to the floor and did a half-dozen press-ups to prove it. I made it harder for him by stacking a few books on his back, but he still managed to complete his set, despite laughing at the same time.

We finished arranging the books, and they looked stunning. I'd pulled a few out that I fancied reading, and was pleased to note that Steve did, too. An hour or two in the garden reading each day would be good for him. And the huge project of château renovations would be beneficial for him too. Another one of us with his own purpose. Plus Manda had the stables and Gray had ... well, his potential relationship with the *maire*.

The next day was Tom's last with us. I felt a little despondent at the idea of him leaving. It had been lovely having him with us – he'd been good company. I had a feeling I was going to be a little bored and lonely once Tom left. Everyone else was so busy all the time. I talked him into spending his last day with me, on another walk to the village. I still wanted to search for the Aubert tomb in the cemetery and this seemed like a good opportunity.

We headed off on the now-familiar path past the old wash house, where I read again the board about Victor Aubert. After coffee and cake at the *patisserie*, and a little mooch around the village, Tom and I headed up the hill on the far side on the narrow street that led to the cemetery. It was packed with graves, some recent but many old, and there were some ornate family plots where many people with the same surname had been buried. Some tombs were adorned with photos of their more recent incumbents. We wandered around, up and down the little gravel paths that separated rows of graves, until Tom called me over to look at a large crypt, with a weathered angel standing guard over it. The word AUBERT was carved across the top, and beneath was a list of names, and dates of death going back to the early 1700s. Victor Aubert was there – he'd died in 1788. Just before the French Revolution, then. Below him were two further names – Louis Aubert and Pierre Aubert, but no other details. I stood in silence for a while, my hand on the stone, wondering if all these people had lived in our château.

I realised Tom was watching me, with a broad grin on his face. 'You should research them. These Aubert people. The history of your château. I mean, you're into history and all that, you've practically got a duty to do it.'

I smiled back. 'Yes, maybe I will, once I'm properly settled in.' I'd always intended to do it, at some point.

'You *are* settled, aren't you?' Tom asked, touching my arm as he spoke.

'Well, yes. I suppose so.' Was I? I was dreading him leaving. What would I do? No one to go for walks with, now that Manda spent all her spare time at the stables.

'You don't sound sure, Mum. Is everything all right?'

To my horror I felt tears welling up. Tom led me to a bench set beside one of the cemetery paths and we sat down. 'What is it, Mum?'

'Oh, I don't know. I'm being stupid. Here I am, living in this fantastic place, and yet I … I don't feel as though I belong. The others have all settled in so well. Your dad's got the garden and the goat. Steve's got kittens and a renovation project. Manda's got her job at the riding stables. Gray seems to spend all his time with Aimée. I feel … well, I don't know what I feel. I'm worried I'm going to be bored and lonely. Especially when you've left.'

'Oh, Mum.' He leaned into me and gave me a hug. 'You know what – you need a dog. Then you'll always have a companion to go for walks with. And, do this local history research. It might help you feel you're more a part of the community as well as giving you a project to get stuck into. That's all you need, I think. Everyone else has got their projects and you need one too.'

I smiled and rubbed the back of my hand across my eyes. 'How'd you get to be so wise? You're probably right.'

'I learned from a master, Mum,' he replied.

History. Yes, it had always been my thing, and Tom was probably right that researching the château's history would be a good project for me. Problem was, I had no idea how to go about the research. Maybe someone at the *mairie* would be able to help me, though the idea of asking the elegant Madame la Maire herself about it filled me with dread.

Before I took early retirement to become Mum's carer, I'd taught history to GCSE level. The Year 9 (that's thirteen-to-fourteen-year-olds) history syllabus was dedicated to 'Revolutions that Changed the World'. We covered the American, French, Industrial, Russian, Chinese cultural and Technological revolutions, spending half a term on each. I did know a little more about the French Revolution than what was covered in the topic of course – you never knew when you'd have a kid in your class who really 'got' the history bug, who'd read around the subject and wanted to know more, asking probing questions.

More usually the kids would yawn and sigh and tell me that what happened in France in 1789 simply wasn't relevant to them today. At which point I'd enjoy telling them about how some parts of the French 1789 Declaration of the Rights of Man and the Citizen (along with the American Declaration of Independence)

137

had been transferred practically word for word into the UN Universal Declaration of Human Rights and the European Convention on Human Rights. 'So you see,' I'd tell them, 'we still live by those documents written hundreds of years ago. The original aims and principles of the French Revolution were honourable – *liberté, egalité, fraternité* – what's not to like? It was a few years later on, when the mobs and the madness of the guillotine took over during the Reign of Terror, that things all went a bit wrong.'

'Mum's going to research the history of the house,' Tom announced, as soon as we were back at the château. We'd found everyone in the garden, where they were unpacking a set of boules that Gray and Steve had bought in the big supermarket down the valley. Phil was online, trying to find out the rules of *pétanque*.

'That's great, Lu!' Steve said. 'I'd love to know everything about it. Just don't want to have to do the work myself.'

'Well, I'll give it a go,' I replied.

'What brought this on?' Manda asked.

'We were looking at the Aubert tomb in the cemetery. I'm assuming they lived here in the château.' I was hoping Tom wouldn't mention my little meltdown – I didn't want to worry the others, especially not Phil. 'Besides, I always like knowing a bit about the history of any place I live in.'

Phil looked up from his computer and nodded. 'She does. She knew everything about the history of Horsell when we lived there. Even the made-up parts regarding its appearance in *War of the Worlds*. Anyway, who's up for a game of *pétanque*? There's six of us including Tom. We can have a knockout competition.'

We'd realised that the flat gravelled area we'd been using as an additional patio to the side of the château was intended as a *pétanque* pitch. It had that fine pink gravel often found in village squares where endless games of *pétanque* take place.

The tournament started that evening. A couple of bottles of

local rosé wine were chilled, and in the evening sunshine we each played each other. You need thirteen points to win a game. When just two are playing, you have three boules each, and roll or throw each to try to be nearest to the little wooden ball. You can score a maximum of three points if all three of your boules are nearer than any of your opponents. We soon discovered techniques such as rolling a boule to try to knock an opponent's out of the way.

'Oi, that's cheating!' said Manda indignantly, when Phil had successfully knocked hers away, leaving his own boule sitting right next to the little wooden ball.

'No, it's not! It's tactics,' he replied, before throwing his last one, which managed to knock his previous one away, leaving Manda's once more winning.

'Yessss!' she cried, fist-pumping the air. Phil looked downcast and the rest of us laughed.

We played until the sun had gone down and it was too dark to see the little wooden ball. Tom won. Then we sat outside a while longer, chatting and finishing the wine.

'Lovely to have Tom visiting,' Manda said, as she watched him help clear away empty glasses at the end of the evening. 'I wish Zoe could come here and see this place. I miss her so much, Lu.'

I hugged her. 'I know. I'm sure she'll visit at some point – when her contract finishes if not before.'

Manda pulled a face. 'That's ages away. And what if she decides to stay in Australia?'

All I could do was hug her more tightly. I knew that was her greatest fear.

Chapter 14

Catherine, 1791

The second winter in the château was easier than the first – a good summer harvest from the farms they owned meant the barns were full and there were no food shortages for them or the local people. When the snow fell Catherine and Pierre hunkered down, well looked after by their army of servants. Madame Bernard seemed to have relaxed a little into the new regime, and was less arrogant towards Catherine. She was accepting her place in life at last, Catherine thought. And as little Louis grew, it seemed Madame Bernard had a soft spot for him. Claudette had been appointed nursemaid, taking the place of the wet-nurse now that Louis was weaned, and Madame Bernard often visited them in the nursery, taking little sugary treats for the child to suck on. Catherine was looking forward to spring and then summer, when Louis would begin to walk. She pictured him toddling around the garden, pulling at flowers, rolling on the lawn, giggling merrily.

An idea occurred to her. She would have a little farm built for him – just like the little hamlet beside the Petit Trianon. Well, perhaps smaller still, child-sized. But yes, a tiny play farmhouse, a couple of paddocks, and she would have chickens and lambs kept there, for little Louis to play with. What a perfect idea! She would enjoy designing it and watching it being built.

As soon as she'd had the idea, she set about sketching plans, and talking Pierre into agreeing to it. She wanted it started as soon as the snow had melted, so that it would be ready for Louis to play in that summer.

'Anything for my little family,' he'd said, and smiled indulgently. 'I remember well how much you loved the little farm at the Petit Trianon. I shall ask the estate manager to set aside some land just beyond the garden. And then it shall be built, in stone, to last not just for Louis but for all our future children too.'

By mid-April the snow had gone and one sunny day Catherine donned her boots and called on Claudette to bring little Louis to her. 'We shall show him the progress on his new farm,' she told the nursemaid. 'You will carry him.'

'But Madame, I fear little Louis is not well today,' the maid protested. 'He has been running a slight fever this morning and seems off his food. I am not sure it is wise to take him out ...'

'Nonsense. He must see his farm. Go and fetch him, at once.'

Claudette curtsied and ran off to do as she was bid. Catherine got herself ready and waited in the entrance hall. Louis wasn't really sick. It was that lazy Claudette – she didn't want to go out. But the fresh air would be good for Louis, and Catherine couldn't wait to check on progress. She pictured the toy farm as it would be in the summer, with snow-white lambs in its paddock, pink or perhaps blue bows tied around their necks, just as on Marie Antoinette's farm. How Louis would gurgle with delight to see them! She must make sure the very prettiest lambs were kept for him.

A few minutes later Claudette came downstairs, carrying a squalling Louis. He was squirming in her arms, and red in the face from crying.

'Can't you quieten him down?' Catherine said.

'I'm sorry. He's hot from his fever, and uncomfortable now

141

that I have put his warm clothes on, Madame. Perhaps he will be all right when we go outside.'

'Well, come on then,' Catherine said. It was annoying. She'd been looking forward to showing Louis the farm, although she knew he was too young to properly appreciate it yet.

They left the château by a door that led directly into the gardens, crossed the lawn, past the kitchen garden and out through a gate onto the hillside. A short way along a track was a flat clearing, and this was where Pierre had suggested the little farm was built. It overlooked the valley and the village. Nearby, a tiny stream ran down the hillside to join the main river at the bottom of the valley, and Catherine had asked for a little stone footbridge to be built across it. As they approached, with Louis now a little quieter though still grizzling, Catherine could see that the bridge was complete. They crossed it, and she exclaimed with delight at the miniature ramparts and pretty arches. After a season or two it would look as though it had been built hundreds of years ago. That was just as she wanted. Beyond it, the foundations were laid for the tiny farmhouse. A couple of men were at work, selecting stones and piecing together the walls. They nodded to her as she approached, and one stood up straight to address her. He was tall and well-built, with muscles outlined through his coarse linen shirt. Catherine felt an unexpected jolt of desire run through her. She saw so few people these days, and this man was so different to her ageing husband. Pierre was kind and good, but didn't excite her physically.

'Good morning, Madame. It'll soon be finished. Might I check, the doorway height is to be this high only, is that right?' He held out his hand at chest height. 'Will be hard to get inside … you'll have to bend.'

'It's for children,' she replied. 'And yes, that will be perfect.' The farm was shaping up just as she wanted it. She could imagine Louis in a few years' time, directing younger siblings in all sorts of games here.

'And the walls around the paddock?'

'Enough to keep lambs and chickens inside.'

'All very small,' he said, glancing sideways at her. She felt herself blushing under the intensity of his gaze and turned away. Out of the corner of her eye she saw the workman smile wolfishly back at her, before making her a flamboyant, mocking bow. She glanced over at where Claudette was standing a little way off, cradling Louis in her arm.

'Put him down, let him toddle around,' she said.

But Claudette shook her head. 'Beg pardon, Madame, but I don't think he will. He seems very sleepy now.'

'Wake him up,' Catherine snapped. 'I want him to see.'

Claudette gently shook the child, kissed his head and whispered to him, but he just wriggled a little and kept his eyes closed. There was a sheen of sweat across his face. Catherine stepped closer and saw that there was a red rash, spreading up around his neck. He really was unwell.

'We need to get him inside,' she said. 'Come on. Quickly now! The poor child is sick. He shouldn't be out here.' She marched off, back towards the château, as Claudette stumbled along behind her. She prayed silently as she hurried back – *please let Louis get well, please, Lord, don't let him die!* Why had Claudette agreed to bring him out?

Back at the château Catherine sent Claudette up to the nursery with Louis, with instructions to put him straight into his crib. She called for Madame Bernard and asked her to send for the physician immediately. Pierre was out on the estate somewhere. A groom was sent to ride out to find him and bid him return home at once. There. She had done all she could. She sat down in the drawing room, but her mind was on Louis, the way his body had seemed floppy as Claudette carried him home, the glazed look in his eyes. Should she go up to the nursery and sit with him? She wasn't sure. She did not want to risk becoming infected herself, with whatever ailed him. Oh, what would the

Queen have done? What did she do when her own child was sick? The Queen had lost children herself, including little Sophie Hélène who'd been around Louis's age. How had she coped? She'd always seemed so dignified through each crisis.

At last, unable to stop herself, Catherine climbed the stairs and entered the nursery, where Claudette had closed the shutters against the bright sunshine and settled Louis into his crib. She was bathing his face gently with a cool cloth and singing sweet lullabies to him. Louis was sleeping, looking peaceful now, but that rash was troubling.

'I have sent for the physician,' Catherine whispered to Claudette. 'Let me care for him now, until my husband gets back.'

'Very well, Madame.' Claudette handed over the cloth and gave up her seat by the crib. Catherine sat down and gazed at her tiny son, silently praying once more that he would get better, as soon as possible. She loved him so much.

Pierre and the physician arrived at almost the same time, and both hurried up to the nursery where Catherine had been anxiously waiting for them.

'How is he?' Pierre asked as soon as he entered.

'N-not well,' replied Catherine, unable to trust herself to say anything more. She cast a pleading look at Claudette, who stepped forward and told the physician how the sickness had begun. He nodded gravely as he examined little Louis, pressing on the rash, placing the back of his hand against the child's forehead.

'It is not good,' he said, at last. 'I have some ointment for the rash, and a potion to put in his milk, but I think … you should call the priest. Has the child been baptised?'

'Of course. But … the priest?'

'In case of the worst.' The physician opened his bag to find the medicines, which he handed to Claudette. Catherine watched in disbelief. It couldn't be that bad, could it? Needing the priest for last rites? She glanced at Pierre, whose face was taut and grim, and then, feeling herself about to crumble, ran from the room.

Pierre followed her, into her private sitting room next to their bedchamber, and sat down beside her. 'Oh, my dear. It is terrible, but we must do as the physician says and call for the priest. Thankfully Père Debroux can get here soon.' He pulled her close and hugged her. 'And the good Père Debroux has not taken the oath of allegiance to France. He is still true to the Church, first and foremost.'

Catherine nodded. That was one small mercy. The Civil Constitution of the Clergy required that all priests take an oath of allegiance to France, but many had objected, saying their primary allegiance was to God and not the country. The Pope had condemned the oath, saying it was against the beliefs of the church. Now the government were denying monies to those priests who were refusing to take the oath. Pierre had promised to support Père Debroux financially if necessary. 'Send for the priest. Let us hope he can arrive in time.'

Little Louis's breathing was shallow and erratic, and he could not be woken from a deep slumber, by the time the priest arrived. Catherine followed him up to the nursery, where the priest conducted the last rites, in the presence of Catherine, Pierre, Claudette and Madame Bernard. Tears streamed down Catherine's face throughout, and she made no attempt to stop them, not caring that it was undignified to be seen crying by your servants. For once she was not thinking of how the Queen would have handled the situation. She was thinking only of little Louis, his pain and suffering. With the last rites over, and Pierre and Madame Bernard leading the priest downstairs for refreshments, Catherine leaned over the crib and stroked her son's face.

'Claudette, if I picked him up, would it hurt him, do you think?'

The servant, who was crying openly too, shook her head. 'No,

Madame. I do not think it would hurt. I think he would like to feel his *maman*'s arms about him, in his ... final hours.' She whispered the last words, as though scared that saying them would make it all true.

Catherine didn't respond. Instead she scooped up her son, tucking a shawl around him, and sat in an armchair cradling him, the child's head against her heart. She marvelled at his beautiful, even features, the delicate curve of his cheek, the exquisite eyelashes against his milky-white skin. He was perfect. Too perfect for this world. His breathing was laboured now, and the gaps between each breath were growing. Claudette knelt at her feet, and stroked Louis's face. She'd loved the child as though he were her own, Catherine realised. Claudette may only be a servant, but she had been a good nursemaid and Catherine had trusted her with that most precious of things – her child's well-being. She forced herself to smile at the other woman.

'It won't be long now. I – I must thank you. For everything you did for him.'

'It was my job, Madame. And I – I love him, truly. So much.' Claudette's voice broke on the last words. Despite herself, despite the gulf between their stations in life, Catherine's heart went out to her and she adjusted Louis's position on her lap so she could reach out and place her hand on the other woman's shoulder. Claudette twisted and leaned slightly, so that her face rested against Catherine's forearm, and there they sat, keeping vigil over the last minutes of little Louis's life.

At last, with a little gurgle, Louis took his last breath and then all was still and silent, save for the sound of birdsong outside. Catherine didn't move. Let her have these last few moments holding her son, while he was still warm. She had not held him enough while he lived, she realised. She had spent no more than an hour a day with him, leaving him to Claudette's care the rest of the time. How she wished she could go back and change all that! If only she'd realised how precious and fragile his life was, she would have spent every waking minute with her child. She could have been the one to feed him, bathe him, dress him, play with him. Claudette had done a fine job, but she, Catherine, had been Louis's mother, and she should have done more for him.

She pulled the body of her baby close, and buried her face in the shawl that he no longer needed for warmth. And at last she gave in to her grief, sobbing uncontrollably, only vaguely aware of Claudette getting to her feet and leaving the room, no doubt to inform Pierre of his son's death.

Catherine sat with the body of her darling Louis for several hours, unable to bear the idea of leaving him, of covering his face with a shawl, of giving him up to the undertaker to put him in a box. How could this have happened, to her son, her only child, for whom she had waited so long? It was Pierre's fault. He was old, less virile, less able to give her a child. And the child he'd finally managed to plant in her had been sickly and was now lying dead in her arms. Pierre had come in briefly, looking grey and older than ever, and had touched his son's forehead and then her shoulder, before leaving her alone again.

She was roused from her mourning only by Claudette rushing in. 'Madame, I am sorry to disturb, but please come …'

'What? What can be so important?'

'It is Monsieur Aubert – he has been taken ill. Oh, Madame, so soon after losing little Louis … The physician has been called for, so has the priest … again …'

Catherine stared at her, barely taking in what she was saying. Claudette rushed forward, taking the body of the child from her, gently, cooing at him as though he were still alive. 'Go, Madame, to his chamber. He needs you.'

As if in a trance she left the room, and then hurried along the corridor to his room. There, Pierre was lying on the bed, half undressed, his face greyer than ever. The physician was standing over him, and the priest was waiting in attendance.

147

'Madame, I had not yet left after attending your son. When Monsieur Aubert was taken ill I thought I had best stay … I have not said the last rites yet. The physician says there is hope. Do you want—'

'No. Not yet. What is happening?'

'It is his heart,' the physician said. 'I believe he will live, if he rests. The shock of losing your son has brought on a minor heart attack, but with care he will make a full recovery. You will need to nurse him. I have left instructions with your servant.' He packed some items in his bag and left.

Père Debroux stayed a while longer, offering prayer and comfort, but Catherine felt too numbed by the events of the day to be able to respond. It was Claudette who took charge. Catherine was vaguely aware of her bustling in and out, speaking in hushed tones to the priest, making arrangements, checking on Pierre, holding a glass of water for him to sip and arranging his pillows, fetching refreshments for Catherine. Thank God for Claudette, Catherine thought. It felt like her first rational thought since Louis had died. She caught hold of Claudette's arm as she passed by.

'Thank you.' Her voice emerged as a whisper, but she knew her eyes showed the intensity of her gratitude.

'It is my duty, Madame.' Claudette bowed her head, and then unexpectedly put a hand on Catherine's shoulder, much as Catherine had done when she was cradling Louis's body. The gesture lent Catherine strength. She rallied herself and took over at Pierre's side.

The days wore on. Pierre improved enough to be able to attend Louis's funeral service. The tiny coffin was placed in the Aubert family tomb in the cemetery. But Pierre was weakened from his heart attack and could do little more than walk around the château, take naps in the drawing room, and haul himself up the stairs at the end of each day. Catherine did everything for him.

148

'It seems so unfair,' she confided in Claudette. 'To lose my child, and then be denied the chance to grieve him properly because I must nurse my husband.'

'Monsieur Aubert is regaining his strength,' Claudette said. 'Soon he will not need much care. You miss Louis so much, don't you?'

Catherine's eyes filled with tears. 'I do. I think you do, too.'

Claudette nodded, biting her lip.

The only tiny good thing to have come out of all this, Catherine thought, was that she now felt she had a friend. Claudette had worked for her for years, but now their relationship had changed. It was no longer one of mistress and servant, but subtly shifting to one in which they were more equal. Perhaps this was the way of things now – the new, post-revolution way.

Chapter 15

Lu

On the morning of Tom's departure, I followed him up to the tower room, peering at the walls around the top of the spiral staircase.

'There must have been some continuation of this staircase, up to the space above,' I said, but I couldn't see any evidence of it. The stairs were built into the thick wall of the tower and stopped at the door to the room. There was no indication at all that they'd ever gone further up, or that they'd been walled up.

'It's weird, isn't it?' Tom said, stuffing his clothes into his rucksack. 'Oh, and Mum, be careful in here. Under the rug the floorboards seem a bit loose – just here, it seems to give a little when you walk on it.'

'Thanks. We're unlikely to use this room much, to be honest.' Although I was planning to come up and have a good look at the ceiling. Perhaps there'd once been a hatch to the floor above. If I brought up a stool to stand on, I'd be able to inspect the ceiling closely for clues.

Tom went over to the window, opened it and leaned out, twisting round to try to see above. 'I've tried this already, Mum.

Can't see the higher window from here as it's too far around the curve of the wall. Hope you'll be able to solve the mystery somehow. I need to know what's up there!'

I laughed. 'Probably nothing other than dead spiders. Just attic space as Steve said. But yes, I'll do my best to find out.'

I drove Tom to Nice airport later and decided to call in at the museum that the mayor had mentioned, on my way back. Might as well get started on the research straight away, rather than sitting around moping now that Tom had left. It was a smallish regional museum, that covered everything about the local area from its geology and stone age inhabitants, the Romans, the Revolution, and the nineteenth and twentieth-century artists who'd made their homes here. I made a whistle-stop tour of all of it, but focused my attention mostly on the eighteenth century and later displays.

The museum's displays were all in French, but with a bit of effort I could translate enough to get the gist of each information board. In one corner was the most interesting part (for me) – a series of paintings of local landscapes, from the 1700s. A couple showed mountain ranges that were familiar – the hills above the Verais valley. One showed the village of Saint-Michel-sur-Verais from an elevated viewpoint somewhere up a mountainside. I enjoyed picking out the buildings I knew that still existed – the church, the *mairie*, a line of cottages on the road up the valley.

But the best was a painting of Château d'Aubert, dated 1770, with a note saying it had been commissioned by Victor Aubert. Maybe it had even hung in the château at one time? It showed the full château – with its now-burned-down eighteenth-century additions as well as the older parts that we lived in all still intact. It had been very grand in those days! I took a photo on my phone of the painting to show the others. There was the tower, the front door looking much the same as it did now, a line of lavender bushes flanking the entrance.

'Imagine living there,' I whispered to myself. 'Oh, actually I do!' I still needed to pinch myself on occasion to realise it was all true, we really had moved to the south of France, we really were living in an ancient château.

And then I noticed something odd. In the painting, the tower had a different number of windows. There were the windows that now corresponded to our kitchen and first- and second-floor bedrooms, and there was the little window of the tower room that Tom had slept in. But that was all. There was no window above the tower room – the mysterious window Tom had pointed out, that we still did not know how to reach. That one was not depicted in the painting.

Had the artist left it out for a reason – perhaps he'd thought the tower looked better balanced without that window? Yet every other detail was, as far as I could tell, completely accurate. So the window must have been added at some point after 1770. It seemed odd – I would have thought it more likely that a window would be bricked up than put in, especially one in an unreachable attic, as I supposed this must be. It was a mystery. I wondered if we'd need to pull down the ceiling in the tower room, perhaps, to discover what was above it. Seemed a bit destructive though, and it wasn't as though we needed the extra space.

My next port of call in my investigations, a day or two later, was to call at the small library in the village and ask to see their archives, as Madame la Maire had suggested. The librarian was delighted to help, and pulled out maps of the area and a few legal documents about the château. I had my phone with the Google Translate app at the ready to help me understand what was written. Most of the documents related to purchase and sale of land, sale of produce from the château's land, etc, and were not very informative. But in among the maps was one from 1795 that I found fascinating.

It showed the château clearly, and marked the burned parts

and the still-standing parts. It seemed the burned-out sections had not been demolished until some later date, but clearly the fire had occurred between 1770 when the painting was completed and 1795 when this map was drawn. Possibly during the French Revolution? I could trace the paths from the château to the village – the lower one beside the river, the mid-level one I'd walked many times and a higher one that contoured around the hillside before dropping down in a series of zig-zags into the village. I knew of the existence of this, but it was so overgrown I had not yet tried to walk it. A job for the future, I decided, was to rope the others into helping me clear the path and bring it back into use.

But this map showed something else. Not far from the château, the path was shown as crossing a small stream that ran down the mountainside into the river at the valley bottom. A small bridge was marked, and then just beyond, a few buildings, labelled *la ferme miniature.* The miniature farm. Intriguing! I recalled a visit to Versailles a few years back, where we had also toured the Petit Trianon palace and its nearby hamlet, that Marie Antoinette had built so she could 'play' at being a shepherdess. Could this miniature farm be something similar? It seemed unlikely. Well, there was something else I needed to explore – as soon as we had the path clear enough to walk, I wanted to search for any remains of these buildings and see if I could work out what they really were. This seemed to be one of those projects – the more I looked into things, the more mysteries there were to resolve.

The day after my visit to the library I decided to start trying to clear the path towards the spot where the miniature farm had been marked on that old map. I'd had no luck persuading anyone else to help, though Phil had said he might help. I went to find him in the garden, to see if he'd come, and found him having a goat-milking lesson from Clarabel's previous owner, Monsieur Giron, watched over by the rest of the crew.

Phil was sitting at the goat's side, while Monsieur Giron held her harness tightly. As I watched, Clarabel twisted out of Phil's grip and turned to glare at him.

'Sorry, old girl,' he said, and offered her a handful of potato peelings from a bucket at his side.

'Leetle more *doucement*,' said Monsieur Giron.

'Yes, *oui, bien sûr*,' Phil replied, looking a little sheepish, if you can look sheepish when dealing with a goat. He had another go, and this time Clarabel stood still, munching her peelings, as a jet of milk splashed into the bucket beneath her.

'Vairy good, you 'ave it now. Keep going, I not need come again.' Monsieur Giron stood up and scratched the goat's head. '*Au revoir, ma chèrie.* Be 'appy.'

'Thanks so much,' Phil said, shaking the man's hand. He looked nervous at the prospect of being in sole charge of Clarabel now, but also pleased to have had the praise. He walked Monsieur Giron to the door and then returned, to find Clarabel with her nose in the bucket of peelings. 'Hey, those were supposed to be your dinner!'

'Aw, leave her, she must be hungry,' Gray said.

'She's always hungry.' Phil stroked her, lovingly.

I refused to be jealous of a goat, but it was obvious Phil was not going to be able to help me clear the path today so I set off alone, armed with gardening gloves and a pair of secateurs in my back pocket, hoping I'd be able to fight my way through far enough.

In places it wasn't too bad. The path had clearly been in use in the not too distant past. Maybe when the château was an *auberge* the owners might have kept the path clear to provide their guests with a selection of easy local walks. I'd always tended to head the other way, further up the valley away from the village. There were other ruins in that direction – what looked like small farm-worker's cottages.

I was able to cut back brambles and break off a few small

branches of saplings growing near the path, and with a bit of effort I managed to trace the path a few hundred metres. Not quite as far as I wanted to – I had not reached the stream or bridge which were before the little farm. But it was a good start.

I returned from my exertions to find Madame la Maire in our sitting room, sipping tea. Gray was sitting opposite her, and the others were also in the room.

'Hey! How did you get on?' Phil said, as I entered and leaned over him to kiss him.

'Pretty good, thanks. It's not as bad as I thought it might be. Hi,' I said to the *maire*, as she rose to air-kiss me on both sides as usual. I felt I'd never get used to this, but at least I managed to remember to go to the left first to avoid a nose-bump.

'Hello, Madame Marlow. You like to walk, yes?'

'Please, call me Lu.' She sat down again, and I sat beside her. 'I do love walking, yes. And it is such a beautiful area. I've been clearing the old path that leads along the hillside to the village today.'

She smiled. 'Ah, yes, no one has gone that way for years, since the *auberge* closed.'

'We're hoping to bring it back into use. Usually I go the other way, up the valley and then up to the top of the mountain. Fantastic view from there. Have you been up it?'

Madame la Maire grimaced slightly. 'I climbed it once. Only once. So high! I do not like to walk up hills.'

'Neither do I,' said Gray, 'but you can't keep our Lu away from them. I prefer cycling.'

'Ah yes, on a bicycle. I like that, as long as the roads are flat.' The *maire* smiled, and Gray grinned at her.

'Nothing nicer than a pootle along flat country lanes, with a picnic in your bicycle basket, is there?' he said. And unless I was seeing things, I do believe he winked at her. Gray, winking at the *maire*? Was it acceptable to wink at a mayor in France? Manda had clocked it too, and raised her eyebrows at me. I had an insane urge to giggle.

'Lu wants to get a dog,' Steve said. 'To accompany her on her walks. You can't take a dog on a bike ride.'

'Ah you can, though,' Gray said. 'Either take a small one in a basket, or a large one on a lead running alongside.' He turned to the *maire*. 'Is that allowed, in France?'

'I think so.' Her expression was thoughtful. 'Madame Marlow, ah, excuse me, Lu – you want a dog, yes?'

'I'd love one. Company on my walks!'

'There is a dog … he is four years old and he is a very good dog, but his owner is in hospital. He has broken his, what is it in English?' She tapped her upper leg on the side.

'Thigh? Hip?' I offered.

'Hip, yes. He is an old man, he has fallen and now has to have the operation. I have the dog at my house for now, but I don't like to walk, not like you. The dog needs to exercise. Perhaps you take the dog as a test? When Monsieur Baudin is out from the hospital the dog can go back to him. It is a good plan, is it not?'

I looked around the room at my housemates. Personally I thought it was an excellent plan. We'd talked, back in England, about all the animals we'd like to have, and had already acquired Clarabel the goat and the kittens Flip and Flop. Borrowing a dog, to help out an old man, sounded perfect. Manda was smiling at me. Steve nodded and Phil raised his eyebrows. Gray, I noticed, had his eyes fixed firmly on Madame la Maire.

'Actually,' I said, 'it sounds like an excellent plan. What sort of dog is it?'

'He is a *chien bâtard* – I do not know the English word. About so big, with a friendly face.' She held her hand about two feet from the floor.

'A mongrel,' Steve translated. 'I like the sound of his friendly face. What's his name?'

'He is called Felix. He is very friendly. I will bring him to you?'

'He sounds lovely. We'd love to have him. But no need for you to bring him. I can drive over and collect him.'

'Or I could,' said Gray. 'Any time. Want me to come and get him later today? Whatever suits you.'

'Why don't you come tomorrow to meet him, and then if everything is good, take him then? I will need to talk to Monsieur Baudin of course, to be sure he is happy for Felix to live with you for now.'

'Of course. Good idea.' I felt ashamed I hadn't thought she'd need to check with the owner. 'Would you like me to visit Monsieur Baudin and talk to him about it?'

She nodded. 'I think that would be nice. I will write down the name of the hospital, and my address. I will telephone him at the hospital so he will expect you.'

Before she left, we arranged that I would visit Monsieur Baudin that afternoon, and if he was happy, Gray and I would call at the mayor's house in the morning to collect Felix and his belongings. Manda added dog food to the shopping list. Interesting but not surprising, I thought, that Gray was so keen to go to collect the dog.

I was already planning a first walk with my new companion. I hoped Tom was right – that starting the research project plus going on more walks would help me settle better, the way the others had. It'd be good too to meet Felix's owner and get to know another local person.

As suggested by the mayor, I went that afternoon to the hospital to visit Monsieur Baudin about his dog. Phil came too. The hospital was not in the village – it was way down the valley, not too far from the large supermarket where we did our 'big' shops. We planned to call in there after visiting the hospital and stock up.

Monsieur Baudin was in a geriatric ward, or whatever they call them these days. It was a bright, modern hospital with gleaming cream floor tiles and fresh paintwork. His bed was one of four in a bay, by a window that looked out onto well-maintained gardens where shrubs flowered around a pretty fountain. All in all, I thought, not a bad place to be.

Madame la Maire had given us a note to take to Monsieur Baudin, to introduce ourselves, but she'd also promised to telephone him if she was able to. It seemed she had, as the nurses were expecting us and took us straight over to see him. He was sitting up in bed, a drip attached to one hand, wearing blue striped pyjamas that were neatly buttoned up. He had a mop of grey hair that looked like someone had tried to tame it but failed. He smiled broadly as we approached, and I felt my nervousness vanish in an instant.

A young nurse was with us. 'Monsieur does not speak the English good, so I will … what is the English word?'

'Translate?'

'*Oui*. Yes. Translate.'

She turned to Monsieur Baudin and introduced us. I understood her well enough to realise she'd called us 'the English people from the château, who will love your dog'.

He smiled and nodded and put out a hand to shake ours – the English greeting! I was glad, it would have felt odd to bend over him in the bed to kiss his cheeks French-style.

'*Enchanté pour faire votre acquaintance*,' I said, using French that sounded oddly formal, but his smile broadened yet more as he seemed to appreciate my attempts to use his language. I warmed to him at once.

'*Voulez-vous prendre mon chien? Voulez-vous le soigner?*' He spoke slowly and clearly, and I was pleased to find I understood. Would we take the dog? Would we look after him?

'Please tell him, we will look after his dog for as long as needed, until he is home from hospital.'

The nurse translated, but to my horror Monsieur Baudin shook his head. He said something in French, speaking too fast for me to follow.

'What's wrong?' I asked the nurse.

'He says, if Felix … is the dog name?'

I nodded.

'… if Felix like you, then he want you to keep Felix.'

Monsieur Baudin said something more, his rheumy eyes fixed on me as he spoke. The nurse translated once more: 'He says when he come out of hospital he will not be in his house. He will be in a … small apartment, for the old people …'

'Sheltered accommodation,' I said, and she nodded.

'He cannot have a dog there. So you must keep Felix.'

I smiled and nodded at the old man. '*Nous serons heureux de garder Felix.*' I hoped that meant we'd be happy to keep Felix. It must have been close enough, for he visibly relaxed and smiled and reached out a hand to mine.

'*Il a trouvé un bon foyer.*'

Yes, I hoped he'd found a good home with us. I realised I'd not yet met the dog. All depended on Felix and I getting on well together.

We spent a few more minutes with Monsieur Baudin, talking about the dog's needs and habits, until the nurse began checking her watch. Then it was time to say goodbye, and now I had no hesitation in leaning over to kiss his cheek, and he squeezed my hand with a surprisingly strong grip. I told him I'd make arrangements with the mayor to fetch Felix the next day, and Phil and I left the hospital feeling excited.

'You know, I've always wanted a dog,' I said, as we drove to the supermarket. Top of our shopping list was dog food – Monsieur Baudin had told us Felix's favourite brands.

'Really? Why didn't you say?'

I shrugged. 'We were always so busy. Work, the kids, then looking after Mum … I suppose it felt as though there wasn't really enough room in my life to take one on. But here' – I gestured to the mountains behind us – 'there seems to be more space. Around us, but also in our lives, to do more. Be more.' As

I said it, I realised I meant it. Was I beginning to settle down at last?

Phil put an arm around my shoulders and squeezed. 'I know what you mean. Who'd have thought I'd take up gardening and get myself a goat?'

Chapter 16

Catherine, 1791

'What news from Paris?' Catherine asked Pierre as he read his correspondence over breakfast one morning. She did not usually ask for news. She was aware that Pierre tried to keep the worst from her. It was all too depressing, and she feared too much talk of the Revolution could bring on another heart attack. Pierre's health had steadily improved as the year wore on, and now, in summer, he was almost back to himself again. Not so the health of the country. The King and Queen had been confined to the Tuileries Palace for nearly two years now, and the possibility of returning to the old ways, the *ancien régime*, seemed more remote than ever, although Catherine had not given up hope. While Paris was still gripped in revolutionary fever, the rest of the country went on as it always had, more or less. Certainly very little had changed here in St Michel-sur-Verais.

Pierre sighed as he put down the letter he was reading and looked at her. 'Not good. It seems our dear monarchs engineered an escape attempt. They had amassed loyal forces on the Austrian border and planned a counter-revolution to restore themselves to power.'

Catherine gasped. 'An escape! And have they got away? I do hope so, for they have done nothing wrong.'

But her husband shook his head sadly. 'No, my dear. It seems it has failed. They were in disguise, as bourgeoisie, but travelled in a conspicuously large carriage pulled by six horses. They spoke to people en route and were recognised. Word was sent ahead, and they were arrested at Varennes, not far from where they were due to meet the commander of their forces.'

Catherine's heart sank, and she covered her mouth with her hand. 'Oh no. The poor dear Queen. So near and yet ... what will happen to them now?'

'They have been returned to the Tuileries, with less freedom than before.' Pierre stood up and paced about the room. 'Had they been successful, they might have been able to garner support and overthrow the reactionaries in Paris. There would have been civil war, but it may have resulted in a restoration of the King's authority, as he wanted, with perhaps a few concessions to ensure the people didn't rise up again. But now ...' He slammed the coffee cup he'd been drinking from down onto the table. 'Now all is lost. I fear the worst, now.'

'The worst?'

'The end of the monarchy. Oh, foolish, foolish Louis! Why travel in such a huge coach? Why not employ more secrecy? My correspondent says the Queen believed they were still loved by the common people outside of Paris. She was travelling in the guise of a governess to her own children, and yet she handed out silver plate as a thank-you to some helpful person. Silver plate! Has she no sense? Of course they were recognised. Stupid, stupid people!'

Catherine was astonished to hear him speak so strongly, so vehemently against their beloved King and Queen, and in front of her, too. But it did sound as though their escape attempt had been ill-judged and poorly executed. And what now? Would this mean the end of the monarchy as Pierre seemed to think? 'Perhaps they will try again, and do better,' she began, but Pierre cut her off.

'No, they will not get another chance. Their guard has been increased, and the people of Paris are now turning even more against Louis. There is open talk of abolishing the monarchy and setting up a republic. Louis's only hope now is foreign intervention.'

'In what way?'

'War with Austria. Humiliating French defeats would perhaps turn the people against the Revolution and back to wanting restoration of the old ways.'

'But how can Louis engineer war, while he is under guard? And how can he even want war where French soldiers are to be defeated?' It seemed like a far-fetched scheme, wanting your own armies to lose, in an attempt to destabilise the government.

Pierre shrugged. 'I don't know. I suppose he is able to correspond with loyal generals, and maybe the Queen is writing to her brother, the Austrian emperor. I would expect their mail is censored but perhaps they have some way of getting letters out safely. There are still some in Paris who are loyal, and some of those presumably work at the Tuileries as guards. But it is not good news. And not good for us, my dear. We may need to think about going into exile. Many of the nobility have already done so.'

'Leave France?' Catherine was aghast. How could she leave the country of her birth, the only country she had ever known? 'But, we cannot!'

'Ssh, my sweet. It may not come to that. I hope it won't. But we must be prepared.'

That word – prepared. Like their flight to Provence after the attack on Versailles. He'd prepared that beforehand, and it had paid off. But surely leaving France would never be necessary?

If it was, it may be as well that they had no babies to bring with them. Tragic though little Louis's death had been, if they did have to move quickly it would be easier to do so if there was only herself and Pierre to think about. The Queen's escape attempt was presumably made so much more difficult by the presence of her children.

Père Debroux visited them weekly in the château now, to allow them to celebrate Mass. He was no longer allowed to perform Mass at the church in the village, as he had not taken the oath of allegiance. There was no new priest, and the church had been boarded up. Catherine had heard that it had been looted – silver candlesticks and artwork taken. She occasionally walked to the church to visit the cemetery behind it, and pay her respects at little Louis's grave, and had noticed some of the stained-glass windows were broken. What was becoming of her country?

Père Debroux had agreed to visit the more wealthy of his old parishioners in their homes, for communion and to collect a small stipend from each. He lived now in a small cottage on Pierre's estate, high in the hills. It would do for the summer, Catherine thought, but how the priest would manage in the winter she did not know. She resolved to speak to Pierre, and perhaps offer him room here at the château when the weather turned. She hoped that doing so would not put them in any danger.

One Sunday when the priest arrived, he seemed distracted, more worried even than usual. He administered communion rather more hurriedly than usual, but afterwards still accepted their usual offer of hospitality – to eat dinner with them and share a bottle of wine from Pierre's well-stocked cellar.

'Thank you,' he said, as they sat down to eat. 'It means a lot. I am increasingly struggling to make ends meet. All my rights have been taken away, as I won't swear that damned oath.' He shook his head sadly. 'It is a sorry state of affairs when a man must choose between God and his country. But for me there is no choice. I will always put my allegiance to God above everything else.'

'The Pope agrees with you,' Pierre said.

'Yes, and that makes me more certain that I am right. But it is hard for me to continue my work as a priest. I can no longer preach in public, or celebrate Mass apart from privately, as today. I am told that once a replacement for me has been secured, a priest who has sworn the oath despite the dictates of the Pope, then I will no longer be allowed to perform any priestly duties, even privately.'

'How will they know?' Catherine asked. 'If you were to, say, visit us as friends, to dine with us, who would know if we quietly took communion with you while you were here?'

'Your servants would know. We do not know who we can trust.'

Catherine considered this. She'd assumed that Madame Bernard, Claudette, Henri and all the rest were loyal and faithful to her and Pierre, and therefore could be trusted. The thought that perhaps she was wrong, and they would tell the authorities if Père Debroux broke the new laws, was upsetting. 'What would happen, if you were discovered?'

'I do not know. But it is not a path I would like to tread. I will continue celebrating Mass with you for as long as it is safe to do so. After that, well, I have a cousin in Piedmont and I think I will cross the border to him. This country is not the one I knew and loved. The reforms ... well, I had thought they were just and fair, but I fear now they are going too far. Where will it all end?'

'Only God knows that,' Catherine said quietly, and the priest nodded silently.

It had been two months since little Louis's death and Catherine was bored. On a fine summer's day, she decided on a sudden whim to walk up to the little farm. Had the workmen finished building it, she wondered? She'd given no instructions. She assumed they would have completed it according to plan, as no one had told them not to. She and Pierre were hoping for another child, and so eventually the farm would be in use.

She summoned Claudette to accompany her once more. A lady should not walk alone outside of the gardens of her home. Claudette could carry her parasol, holding it over her to keep the sun off, just as Marie Antoinette had always had a servant to perform this duty. They may be far from Versailles but when possible, Catherine liked to try to keep to the old ways.

'Come, Claudette. The sunshine may not last for long, and I want to take a look at my little farm. I shall call it *La Ferme de Louis*, in memory of my poor dear son, who never had the chance to enjoy it.' Catherine crammed on a bonnet and strode out of the door, with Claudette hurrying along behind.

They walked along the track that led to the farm. It was a little overgrown in places. Catherine made a note to ask the workmen to cut the vegetation back, so that her skirts were not in danger of being snagged. The little bridge was still in place, though the stream it crossed had dried out.

'Why is there no water running beneath here?' Catherine said. It had looked so pretty in the spring, with the water burbling and splashing over the rocks.

'Madame, it has been dry. I imagine it only flows after rain, or in the spring with meltwater from the snow.'

'But I want it to flow all year round! It is the water supply for my little farm. I shall speak to the workmen.'

Around the corner of the track the farm came into view. Catherine gasped to see that it was incomplete; in fact, the building work was no further on than it had been on that terrible day when Louis had become sick. The cottage was half-built, with no roof, and bushes growing up inside. The land that had been cleared to make space for the little paddocks had grown over with vegetation. The work would have to be done again, before any lambs or chickens could be kept there. Catherine was furious.

'Why is this not complete? Do you know what has happened here, Claudette?'

'No, Madame. I do not. I have not been up here since the last time I came with you, with little Louis, God rest his soul.'

'Well then, do you know where we can find the workman who was here then? What is his name?'

'Madame, his name is Jacques Valet. I believe he lives in the village, but I do not know where. Now, he is probably at work. I do not know where.'

Catherine frowned. 'I shall have to ask Pierre. Well, let us return to the château. I am not at all pleased.' It was that man, Jacques Valet, who had looked at her in that obscene way, as though he was undressing her with his eyes, the last time she'd been here.

That evening, Catherine told Pierre of the lack of progress on the farm.

'Why has it not been completed? Dearest, did you perhaps set the man to work on something else? I know that with little Louis gone, there was no urgent need for it to be finished but I think if it was done, it would cheer me up. I would go daily to play with the little lambs and feed the chickens.'

'I didn't give orders for the work to be stopped, no. But I suppose Valet assumed that after Louis's death the farm would not be needed. I shall send word to him to return and complete the work. Do not worry yourself, my sweet. It will be finished, and it will be ready for use long before we have another child.'

Catherine smiled. 'Then I shall call the dressmaker and have her make me a shepherdess gown. Remember the beautiful one I had at Versailles? Perhaps I shall have another, just like it. What do you think, dearest?'

'Whatever you want,' replied Pierre, smiling. 'I want only for you to be happy.'

The following day, Pierre informed her that work had resumed on the farm. Catherine decided to go and see for herself – alone this time, for Claudette was busy with other chores. She put on a lightweight shawl and set off walking the high path up to the site of the farm.

As she approached she saw that Pierre was right – work had resumed. And Jacques Valet was there, shirtless, swinging a scythe at the overgrown vegetation. She stopped short of the site and watched for a while, finding herself guiltily enjoying the spectacle of a well-toned, young, muscular male body. So unlike Pierre, who with lack of exercise after his heart problems was running to fat.

After a moment he stopped, put down his scythe and mopped his brow. As he did so he caught her eye, and she blushed at having been caught watching him. He shifted position to stand square on to her, as though wanting to show her his body in all its glory.

'I-I came to check on progress,' she called, as she took a few steps forward. 'When I came before, work had stopped, and it made me angry.'

He smirked. 'You, angry? That would be a fine sight. With your child dead I assumed this place was not needed. There was other work more important. Shepherds' huts up in the mountain need repairing. Walls around the low pastures. My own cottage roof. All more important than your plaything.'

'We are paying you well to build this.'

'You could pay me better. Not just in money.' He held her gaze, defiantly but with a challenge in his eyes. She understood immediately what he was suggesting. For a fleeting moment she wondered what it would be like, with such a man? What would it feel like, to run her hands over that fine, muscular body, his hands pulling at her clothes, his mouth upon her neck. And then she remembered her place – she was a married woman, the Comtesse, and his employer. While at Versailles the ladies of the Court had frequently taken lovers, it was not with men as lowly and coarse as this one. She raised her chin and stared back at him, keeping her expression as haughty and aloof as possible, until at last the man looked away and returned to his work.

She'd won this little battle. But there was something about him that unnerved her.

Chapter 17

Lu

As agreed, Gray and I went the next day to the *mairie*, where Madame la Maire was waiting for us. I gave up the front seat of the car so she could sit beside Gray who was driving, on the journey to the mayor's home to collect Felix. I felt like a kid in the back seat, especially as I was watching for signs of what I was sure was a growing attraction between Gray and Madame la Maire. He kept glancing over at her as he drove, so much so that I feared we'd end up in the ditch on the twisting lanes. As for her, she laughed at his jokes, made teasing remarks of her own, and altogether simply flirted with him the whole way. I sat back and watched, amused but also very happy for my friend. He deserved a chance of happiness in his love life.

Madame la Maire lived in a glorious large house, down the valley from the village. It was set back from the road, with a curving driveway, immaculate lawns and a swimming pool. A verandah ran round two sides, and it was there that Felix lay, on an old blanket in the shade, tethered on a long leash with a bowl of water within his reach. He raised his head as we approached, and thumped his tail against the decking in greeting. He had the look of a collie, but a little larger, coloured brown, black and white, with intelligent-looking brown eyes and a happy expression as he let his tongue loll out, panting.

'Hello, Felix,' I said, putting out a hand for him to sniff, which he did and immediately followed it with a lick. I scratched his head and then crouched down to his level and fussed him a little, eliciting more vigorous thumping of his tail on the deck.

'He likes you,' said the mayor.

'I like him, a lot,' I said. 'Well then, old boy, fancy coming to live with me for a while then?'

He stood and pressed himself sideways against my leg as though in response. Madame la Maire had gone inside the house to fetch his belongings, and Gray had followed her in. I untied Felix's leash and took him on an experimental lap of the garden. He sniffed at everything, cocked his leg on a lupin, but behaved impeccably. 'Oh yes, I think you and I are going to get along very well indeed,' I told him.

Aimée came out of the house with a bag of dog biscuits, and Felix's ears pricked up and he gave a quiet woof, as though to say, 'please may I have one?'. She laughed and passed me the bag, so I could be the one to treat him. Without being told, he sat in front of me waiting for his treat. I was pleased he was clearly so well trained, but realised I'd probably need to use the French words for commands such as 'sit' and 'stay'. Or maybe he'd learn some English and become a bi-lingual dog.

He took a bit of persuasion to get into our car, but with Aimée encouraging him and me enticing him with dog biscuits he finally clambered into the back seat, and I got in beside him. Then he lay down in the footwell, with a dejected expression on his face.

'Aw, poor boy, won't be a long journey, honest,' I said, as I fondled his ears.

'Probably thinks he's going to the vet's.' Gray climbed into the driver's seat after putting the dog gear in the boot.

'It has all been very strange for him.' Aimée had locked her house and climbed in; we gave her a lift back to the *mairie* before going straight home to the château with Felix to introduce him to everyone.

As we entered the sitting room, I caught hold of Felix's collar. The kittens were on the sofa with Steve, who was working on a spreadsheet of renovation costs.

'Whoa, careful, mind the cats,' Steve said.

I let Felix inch forward, until he was nose to nose with Flip, or was it Flop, on Steve's lap, but kept a tight hold of him. He sniffed and then to our delight the kitten stuck out a paw and cuffed him on the nose. Felix flinched, then gave the kitten a gentle lick, before lying down and rolling over submissively.

'I think that means he's accepted who's in charge,' I said, with a laugh. I released his collar, and Steve and Gray let the kittens down on the floor. We watched closely as they made friends. Felix was delightfully gentle with them the whole time.

'Aimée said he'd be fine,' Gray said. 'Monsieur Baudin always kept cats. They've been rehomed with his neighbour.'

Manda was grinning. 'So, Phil's got his goat, Lu's got a dog, Steve's got cats – so now can I have a pony?' She took on the whine of a spoiled child as she said the last words, and we all laughed.

'A pet for everyone. Just me without one now,' Gray said, sticking out his bottom lip in a mock pout. 'What shall I have?'

'A lady mayor?' I said quietly, eliciting a roar of laughter that even Felix joined in with. The kittens seemed not to mind his barking.

Felix was an instant hit with everyone, and excitedly went from person to person sniffing, licking their hands, thumping his tail against their legs. Phil laughed. 'He's going to be a great addition to our family, isn't he?'

'I certainly hope so,' I said, smiling.

'Do you think the pets will help keep us young?' Gray said, as he began a game of tug with Felix, using an old tea-towel.

'Definitely! How could they not?'

Maybe it was because Gray was a single bloke, but of all of us, he was the one who seemed to hate the ageing process the most. You might think it'd be Phil – after all he was the one who'd had the worst health scare. Or me – when caring for Mum I was closest to seeing just what age could do to a person.

But it was Gray who was upset at his greying hair and the way he couldn't cycle as far or as fast as he once could. It was Gray who'd peer in the mirror, wondering whether his wrinkles were deeper than the day before. Gray who spent more than any of the rest of us (including Manda and me!) on facial creams and hair serums to prevent hair loss. Actually he was lucky in that regard – although it was beginning to thin, he still had a full head of hair – unlike Steve who was completely bald but didn't care in the slightest.

When Gray began experiencing knee pain the doctor sent him for an X-ray. The verdict was a bit of age-related wear and tear; in other words, osteo-arthritis. We all have a touch of that. But for Gray, you'd have thought it was a death sentence. He was depressed for weeks. It was Steve who made him snap out of it, urging him to keep his weight down to lessen the load on his knees, eat oily fish, use knee supports for more strenuous activities and apply ibuprofen gel whenever his knees were particularly sore. 'It's about managing it, mate,' Steve had told Gray. 'What we need to do is deal with the bodies we have *now*, not the ones we used to have. We're all ageing. And that's a good thing.'

'Good? How can ageing be good?' Gray asked, frowning.

'Good when you look at the alternative,' Steve said with a chuckle. 'You either get old or you die.'

I wasn't sure that comment had actually helped Gray much.

We were there for him. But, frankly, he had to deal with this himself.

On Felix's first day with us, we kept him in the château and allowed him a few turns about the garden on a leash. He met Clarabel, tried to encourage her to play with him, but she just ignored him and carried on munching her way through the pile of vegetable peelings Phil had put in her bucket.

'Ah well. Maybe she'll pay him more attention when she's finished eating,' Phil said, giving Clarabel a scratch on the head.

The next day I decided to try taking Felix for a walk. Monsieur Baudin had told us he liked long walks, and so did I. We could be a match made in heaven. I put him on the lead, not yet trusting him to come back to me when I called. I needed to find out whether he was the sort of dog who'd chase after rabbits. Or marmots, common in the higher mountains around here. I'd decided to follow the high path towards the village – the old path that was marked on the maps I'd seen in the library. That marking showing '*la petite ferme*' was still intriguing me. I'd cleared a bit more of the path and it was passable for quite a way now.

Felix seemed to think that was a great idea too, and was eager to get going, pulling slightly on the lead as we headed out of the garden, up the winding path I'd already cleared, and onto the higher track that contoured around the hill down the valley, towards the village. 'Oy. Heel!' I called, but he ignored me. Pulling out my phone and doing a quick Google of French dog commands, I came up with '*Au pied*,' and was delighted to find that worked. He stopped pulling and trotted neatly by my side, earning himself a dog biscuit from a bagful I had in my pocket. 'Good boy,' I told him, scratching his head. He could learn the English for that, I decided.

It was about fifteen minutes from the village, into the parts of the track that were still overgrown, that we came across a little bridge over a stream. It was made of stone, wide enough for two people to walk side by side on, and over-engineered for such an infrequently used path. Maybe in early spring the snow melt-waters made such a bridge necessary, but normally on a path such as this one there'd be just a few stepping stones in the stream, or perhaps a couple of wooden planks balanced across. It was as I crossed it that I remembered the old map marked a bridge, and I pulled out my phone again. I'd taken a few snaps of the map, and opened those up, zooming in on the area. Yes, a bridge over a stream was shown, near to the *petite ferme.*

'We're not far away, Felix!' He gave a little woof as though picking up on my excitement.

And then, just another hundred metres or so along the path, Felix, no longer walking to heel, pulled me to one side as he sniffed around the hip-high undergrowth. The vegetation here was a mix of broom, bracken, small shrubs and ash and oak saplings. I looked to see what had caught his attention and real-ised there was some stonework there – in among the shrubs, almost completely hidden.

'Felix, good boy! I believe you've found it!' I said, and began pushing the vegetation out of the way. There was definitely a wall there, about waist-high. Thankfully none of the vegetation around it was prickly, and I was able to push through, and put my hands on the stonework. Peering over, I could see this wall was one of four, that made a small square. Inside, if you could call it inside, there being no roof at all, the vegetation was just as dense as outside. But I could make out a couple of small openings, perhaps intended as a door and a window. They were tiny. If this was indeed the little farm, it looked as though it had been built for midgets. 'Or children!' I said, out loud, earning myself a quizzical look from Felix, who was enjoying himself sniffing around this odd structure.

'Think we'll need to come back with the secateurs,' I said. It would be the only way to work out what this place was, and how much of it remained. But I was certain this was it – the *petite ferme* marked on that eighteenth-century map. Who had built it, and why?

Felix and I headed back to the château after finding the farm, but then went up a different path – one I knew was clear and easy to walk, and which led to the top of the hill behind the château, and where I could give the dog a decent walk. He deserved it. From the summit was my favourite view – of the entire valley, the château, the village down below, the hills across the valley, and to my right, just visible, the glint of light on the horizon that I knew was a glimpse of the Mediterranean. As always, I relished the fact that we were among mountains yet so near the sea. Overhead an eagle soared, and I stood to watch it for a while, until it was out of sight. Felix was sniffing at a marmot burrow, but if its occupant had any sense it'd stay deep inside.

The dog came to sit at my side, panting still from the climb, and apparently enjoying the view as much as I was. Or just too tired to go sniffing and exploring. 'You're going to like living with us, aren't you, boy?' I said, and he licked my hand in response.

But lunchtime was approaching, my stomach was rumbling and it was hot. I'd come out without so much as a bottle of water. Time to head back down. Felix would be thirsty too. I must remember, I realised, to always bring water, for both of us, on any long hikes over the summer.

I went upstairs to shower and change after my walk, and while in the shower found myself thinking once more about that mysterious window. It was time I investigated further. As soon as I was dressed again I found a stool of a suitable height and carried it up the spiral stairs. Time to inspect the ceiling. Felix followed me up the stairs but refused to come into the little room. Instead he lay down at the top of the spiral stairs, just outside, whining a little. I looked up at the ceiling of the little room. There were numerous cracks in the plaster – was there a hatch that had been plastered over? If I could get up close to it, I reckoned I'd be able to tell.

I placed the stool near the door first, climbed up and ran my fingers along each crack, prodding at it, trying to see if it covered a wooden hatch that might give a little when I pushed at it. Plaster dust rained down on me, getting in my eyes and coating my hair.

'Should have done this before showering, silly woman,' I told myself, but the damage was done and I might as well continue.

I moved the stool along a little, methodically covering the whole ceiling. The blow-up bed and rug we'd put down for Tom's visit were still in place. I bundled the bedding out of the way so that it wouldn't also get covered in plaster dust, moved the stool onto the rug, and climbed back onto it.

Just then, one leg of the stool gave way, tilting over and sending me flying. I landed half on, half off the blow-up mattress, sprawled across the floor with the stool on top of me. Felix gave a little bark, but still didn't come into the room.

'Ouch,' I said, inspecting my left wrist which had taken the brunt of the impact. That and my left hip. Both were sore.

The stool was intact – it wasn't its leg that had broken as I initially thought. Too late I remembered Tom's warning about the sagging floor. There was a deep dip in the floor under the rug. I pushed the stool away with my right hand, keeping my injured left wrist close to my body, then pulled back the rug. The floorboards beneath had given way, broken and crumbling. As I shifted position, I felt more give way under me. The whole floor was unsound. I crawled, commando-style, back to the door, reaching it just as Steve and Phil appeared, having heard the crash and my scream as I fell.

'Lu, what happened?' Phil made to rush into the room, but I stopped him.

'Don't come in – floor's not safe.' Felix obviously had more sense than I had, in keeping out.

Phil reached down and helped me to my feet at the top of the stone-built stairs. It felt good to be back on a solid surface. I rubbed my sore hip.

'Are you hurt?' he asked.

'A little. Bruised hip and my wrist hurts a little.' I held it up to show him.

'Jesus, Lu, what were you doing?' Phil began leading me down the spiral stairs, going ahead of me backwards, one hand reached out to steady me in case I stumbled. Not so very long ago it was me helping him navigate stairs. Now I was the invalid. I suppressed a wry smile.

Steve was kneeling by the door, looking closely at the floor. 'Riddled with woodworm. The whole floor's unsafe. God knows how it lasted when Tom was sleeping in here.' Behind us he closed the door firmly then followed us down.

'I was looking for evidence of a hatch in the ceiling,' I said, once we'd reached the bottom of the stairs. 'There must have been some way of getting into the room above.'

'Well, the room's out of bounds until we can get it treated for woodworm and the floor replaced. Possibly the joists, too,' Steve said. 'I'll add that to the list of work we need to do.'

'You hear that, Lu? Your window mystery will have to wait.' Phil rubbed his forehead in a way I knew meant he was worried and stressed. 'God, you might have gone right through the floor.'

'I'd have ended up in bed,' I said, with a feeble attempt at a laugh. Our room was the one directly below the tower room, that incorporated the curve of the lower part of the tower.

'You'd have ended up with a broken neck, then where would we be? Anyway, let's get that wrist seen to. Can you move it?'

I could, although it hurt. We went downstairs, where Manda fussed over me, decided it probably wasn't broken, and bound a bag of ice-cubes around it to help reduce the swelling. 'I've got a wrist support somewhere, from when I fell off a pony and sprained my wrist,' she said. 'You can use that. And take some ibuprofen.'

'Yes, nurse,' I said. Phil was still glaring at me for hurting myself, then he shook himself, made us each a cup of tea, and put his arms around me.

'Promise me, no more searching for ways into the top of the tower?'

'Not until the floor's fixed anyway,' I said, squeezing his hand. Steve had come back down. 'Steve, how long will it be?'

'Don't know. What's the French for woodworm? I'll need to research relevant tradespeople.' There was a gleam in his eye. Another project for him.

The next day, Felix's second day with us, I took him for a walk along by the river, into the village. My bruised hip was stiff but I knew it would loosen up with a walk, and as long as I didn't hold Felix's lead in my left hand, the sprained wrist would not be a problem. I wanted to call in at the *mairie* and show Aimée how well Felix was doing. Setting off out of the front door of the château, I glanced back over my shoulder as I so often did, and up at that infamous window in the tower.

This time, as I looked up, I had a shock. There, outlined in the glass of that top window, was a distinctive face. A white oval, pressed to the glass. A dark shape of a mouth, open as though crying for help. I'd thought I'd seen something on the day Tom first noticed the window, but had put it down to a trick of the light – the sun reflecting off the glass. That had to be the explanation. I stared up at it and had the distinct impression the face was staring down at me. Felix, at my feet, looked up and growled quietly, a deep rumble.

'Ssh, boy, it's all right,' I told him, bending to stroke his head. I'd never heard him growl before. Maybe it comforted him for he stopped, whined a little and then began pulling on the leash as though to say, come on, let's get going. I looked back up at the window. The face, if that's what it was, had disappeared. The sun had also gone behind a small cloud.

'Trick of the light, Lu,' I told myself. 'Nothing more.' But why had Felix reacted to it? He was such a good-natured dog.

We walked the riverside path into the village, and up to the *mairie*. Aimée was as delighted to see Felix as he was to see her. She even let him jump up, putting his paws on her silken blouse just above waist height. Thankfully he didn't leave any muddy marks. Actually she'd encouraged him to jump up anyway, even though I'd been saying, 'Down, Felix!' Or rather, when I remembered, '*Couche!*'

'So, all is going well?' Aimée asked, and I nodded, giving her a quick resumé of all that Felix had been up to since I collected him, including meeting the kittens. 'Ah, yes, Gray asked me how Felix would cope with *les chats*,' she said, with a smile. 'Oh, what have you done to your poor hand?'

'A silly fall. It's nothing.' I didn't want to tell her the exact circumstances, but I did tell her about the mysterious upper window in the tower.

'A window?'

'Yes, but one we can't reach from inside. And it doesn't show up in a painting I found in the museum.'

'The tower was perhaps extended upwards after the painting was made?'

I shook my head. The tower had not been made taller, but maybe an attic had had a window added. But still, how did you get into that attic?

'And something more.' I blushed, but I wanted to talk about that face. 'I thought I saw a face at the window. Felix too – he growled.'

'I think I told you the old owners said the château was, what is the word? *Hanté*. Maybe it was *le fantôme* that you saw?' She laughed. 'But it is all just fairy tales, of course.' She shook her head. 'No. A *tour de la lumière*, it must have been. Not real.' She smiled, and at that moment her phone rang, and with an apologetic shrug she turned away to answer it.

Now, I wondered. Was there really a ghost in our château? One that messed with the electrics on occasion (still, even after having them all checked and some rewiring done since we moved in), one that banged on pipes and made odd noises at night (we were getting used to those) and that showed her face at the tower window on occasion? Her? Why had I thought 'her face'? I couldn't say. Just, somehow, I felt the face was female. If it was a face at all.

Chapter 18

Claudette, 1791

It was early October, and the leaves on the trees were beginning to turn as the days cooled and the summer ended. There had been a good harvest and the barns were full. Claudette was pleased – the local people would not go hungry this winter, as long as Monsieur Aubert was generous with his stocks. He was a good man. She believed he genuinely had the welfare of the people at his heart. Even Madame was changing. She'd been selfish and naive when Claudette first worked for her, back in Versailles. But now she seemed to be growing up a little, learning to care about people other than herself, about issues of more consequence than what colour ribbons she should wear.

The little farm, Madame's plaything, had been completed. Over the summer Madame had walked up to it frequently, to check on progress. When it was finished she'd furnished the tiny house as a chicken coop and acquired some hens, and then went every day to collect the eggs. The farm was a frivolity, but at least it was now providing them with fresh eggs. Claudette had expected Madame to quickly bore of collecting the eggs, but she was showing no sign of doing so yet. But one day the priest had arrived just after Madame had left for her walk up to the farm, and Madame Bernard had dispatched Claudette after her. She'd hurried along the path, getting glimpses of Madame Aubert as she rounded each corner just ahead, but out of calling distance. Eventually she'd reached the farm, and realised Madame was not alone. There was a man with her – Claudette recognised him as Jacques Valet. Claudette stopped and hid in some bushes, watching as Madame approached the man and said something to him. Jacques bent over her – from Claudette's vantage point it looked as though he was kissing her – and then they went inside the tiny farmhouse, with Jacques having to bend double to get through the little doorway.

Claudette gasped, and hurried back to the château, telling Madame Bernard that she had not seen Madame Aubert. 'She must have walked another way,' she said. 'I went all the way to her little farm but she was not there.'

How long had this been going on, she wondered. Should she tell poor, kind Monsieur Aubert? She decided against it. He worshipped his young, pretty wife, and there was no reason to spoil that for him. Besides, for all she knew, Madame Aubert might have been just pointing out a defect in the structure to the workman. Maybe it was all innocent, after all.

News had come from Paris that King Louis had accepted the new Constitution of France. It provided the principal topic of discussion for weeks – among the château's staff, the villagers and between Monsieur and Madame Aubert. Claudette overheard them talk about it on several occasions. Predictably, Madame Aubert saw it as meaning they might yet return to the old ways.

'We can all live happily again now, can't we, Pierre? Now that he has accepted the changes that the Assembly wanted, they will surely set him free, and perhaps allow him to return to Versailles? And if he returns, then so can we, and all the other noblemen and women? It'll be just as it was.' Monsieur and Madame Aubert were in their drawing room, sitting by the fireside.

Claudette was busy tidying away some tea things they had used, and stoking up the fire. She hid a wry smile at Madame's words. There was no going back – the King accepting the changes had been inevitable and was a step forward in this revolution. It seemed Monsieur Aubert agreed for he shook his head at his wife and smiled indulgently. 'Ah, my sweet, how little you understand. It is good that he has ratified the Constitution, though to be honest he had little choice but to do so. But he won't be allowed to return to Versailles. That place is too much a symbol of the *ancien régime*, and there would be a fear that if he lived there, he and the Queen would return to their old, profligate ways. Louis is bankrupt, my dear. He has been so for years, and now he can no longer borrow from the State to finance his whims. He may be a king but he lived beyond his means, and that is a large part of the reason why we got into this mess.'

'So we have to stay here in the south?' Madame Aubert sounded like a petulant child, annoyed at not getting her own way. Claudette bit her lip to stop herself responding.

'Yes, my dear, for now we must stay. Things are perhaps better than they were, but we are by no means out of danger. Think for a moment about poor Père Debroux. He is practically in hiding. He dare not hold a public Mass. And yet it is his vocation – his reason for being!' Monsieur Aubert shook his head sadly. 'We can but hope that Louis's acceptance of the Constitution is the beginning of the end of this terrible period.'

Madame Aubert smiled at her husband. 'I hope you are right. You must be. All will be well in the end, I suppose.'

Claudette, having finished her chores in the room, dipped a small curtsy as she left to take the tea tray back to the kitchen. It was interesting, listening to the Auberts' conversation. She did not entirely share their hope that this was the beginning of the end. For so many people, life had not yet changed for the better.

The promised equality and liberty had not fully materialised. She suspected there was some way to go before the end of this period of upheaval, and where would they all be by then?

A few weeks later Claudette was helping Madame get dressed one morning when Catherine winced at the tightness of her bodice.

'I am sorry, Madame, I shall let it out,' Claudette said, although she had laced it to the same tightness as usual. She realised Madame's breasts were fuller than usual. Could she be pregnant again? And if so, was the baby her husband's? Or if Claudette's suspicions about Madame and the man Jacques Valet were correct, then might he be the father?

It appeared that Madame Aubert at least believed the child to be her husband's for soon she had told him her news, and Monsieur Aubert was walking around the château with a broad smile on his face, clearly delighted with the prospect of becoming a father again. Claudette entered the breakfast room one morning, thinking they had finished, interrupting him congratulating his wife.

'… something to focus your attention on. I am so pleased for you, for us both …' He broke off, realising Claudette had entered.

'I am sorry, Madame, I thought you had finished.' Claudette began to back out of the room but Madame Aubert gestured to her to come in.

'It's all right. I have just been able to tell my husband some wonderful news. And you will need to know in time, so I shall tell you now. I am expecting another baby. Isn't that marvellous? You shall be nursemaid again!'

'Oh, Madame!' Claudette smiled. She'd already known, of course, but it was good to be told officially. 'That is wonderful news! I am very pleased for you both.'

Pierre stood up. 'Well, I will leave you ladies to discuss babies, then.' He kissed Catherine and strode out of the room.

Catherine poured herself another cup of coffee. 'It is exciting, isn't it? How I miss little Louis. I hope this one will be another boy, but perhaps it'll be a girl.'

'Madame, I will be very happy to work as nursemaid again. I love children. I loved little Louis so very much. I am so very glad you are to have another child. I always thought …' Claudette broke off, blushing. She'd been about to speak her mind, but perhaps it was not the right time.

'You always thought what, Claudette? Pray tell me. I want to know.' Catherine smiled.

Claudette took a chance. 'I thought, excuse me Madame, but I thought that perhaps you would want another chance at being a mother. Perhaps you regretted not spending as much time with Louis as you might have, and with another child you could do things differently …'

'But I spent a lot of time with Louis! Far more, girl, than the ladies of the court of Versailles ever spent with their offspring! Ladies of the court who were mothers, would only see their children for a few minutes each day. I spent much more time than that with Louis.'

'But still less than an hour each day, Madame. A common mother from the village would be with her baby almost all the time.' Claudette began stacking plates and clearing the table. She'd said her piece and was not going to say anything more. Let Madame think about what she'd said.

Catherine picked up her coffee cup and flounced out of the room. Good. Claudette's words had hit home. Maybe this next child would get to know his or her mother a bit better than the last had. Motherhood was not about building miniature farms for babies, but about spending time with them, giving them love and attention. While Claudette looked forward to acting as nurse-maid again, she believed that children should be with their own mothers as much as possible.

Chapter 19

Lu

It was my turn to shop at the village market, which was once a week on a Thursday morning. We were producing a fair bit of veg and salad and fruit from the garden now, not to mention the first cheeses from Clarabel, of which Phil was rightly proud. But I still had a list as long as my arm – from selections of olives that we seemed to eat by the bucketful, to *saucisson* which we were all rather too fond of although Phil had to take it easy. I decided to drive – it was a hot day and there'd be too much to comfortably carry back on my own with only one fully functional arm. So to Felix's utter disgust I picked up the car keys rather than his lead, and headed off with a couple of baskets to carry the purchases.

It was at the olive stall that I met Monsieur Christophe. Usually we only saw him in the bistro on our weekly visit there, and he'd be too busy to stop and chat. But today he greeted me like an old friend and gestured to me to sit down on a nearby bench which was thankfully under the shade of a spreading plane tree.

'You like the market?' he asked.

'I love it. Markets in England are not nearly as good.'

He smiled. 'Ah we French know 'ow to grow the best produce, and 'ow to sell it the best way.'

'You certainly do.'

'You 'ave settled in OK?' He asked this every time he saw any of us, and we always answered the same.

'Yes, we are very happy here.'

'A shame the *auberge* closed down. They 'ad problems.'

I frowned a little. 'What problems?' Was there some difficulty with the plumbing that we'd only discover in the depths of winter or something?

He waved a hand vaguely in the air. 'Noises. The lights going off.'

'Oh, those.' I smiled. 'We've had those too.' Should I tell him about the face at the window as well? I decided against it.

''Ave you 'eard,' he said, conspiratorially, 'about the family Aubert, who lived in the château during the Revolution? They say'– and here he leaned closer – 'that Pierre Aubert 'aunts the château still.'

'Haunts?' I remembered Aimée's use of the French word. 'You mean *il hante le château*?'

'*Oui.*' He looked pleased with himself. 'It was 'is 'ome. He died in the time of *le terroir*. Those noises are made by 'im, trying to get back inside. Maybe looking for 'is wife.'

'What happened to his wife?'

Monsieur Christophe gave a huge expressive Gallic shrug. 'No one knows. She vanish. Pouf! Like that.'

I recalled what Steve reported the estate agent had said about a woman who'd disappeared. That must have been Pierre Aubert's wife. 'What was her name?'

'I do not know. This is all I know. Pierre Aubert 'aunts the château, and 'is wife *disparu*.'

'During the Terror?'

Again that shrug. 'She disappear then. Or she escape. Many escape to Italy to avoid Monsieur Guillotine.'

I shuddered. I knew about the Terror of course – the period in 1793–94 after the Revolution, when the original idealistic aims became smothered by a desire to root out all those who'd supported the King and Queen, all ex-nobility, and anyone who had hidden or aided them in any way. Anyone considered to be anti-revolutionary. It had begun in Paris but spread to other towns and the country. Mobs had rampaged through, rounding up anyone they had any suspicions about, subjecting them to summary trials and then executing them by guillotine. It had happened everywhere. But for some reason I hadn't imagined it had happened *here*, in our quiet little village high in the Alpine foothills. Perhaps it had – the village central square was named Place de la Révolution, after all. Had a guillotine once been erected there?

'Monsieur Christophe, do you know if anyone was ever, you know, guillotined here in Saint Michel-sur-Verais? Is that why the square is called Place de la Révolution?'

He laughed and shook his head. 'No, I do not think there was a guillotine 'ere. Every single town in France 'as a Place de la Révolution. And a Place de la Résistance. As if those are the only two things that ever 'appened in France.'

I laughed too.

Monsieur Christophe stood, to continue his shopping. I glanced at my watch – we'd sat there long enough and some stalls were already beginning to pack up. I'd barely started. I bade the bistro owner goodbye and rushed round the stalls, thankfully managing to buy everything even though half my attention was once again on Pierre Aubert and the events in the château around the time of the Revolution and the Terror. Always more to research. Well, I'd taken a history degree then taught the subject for over thirty years. It should be right up my street. If this was England, I'd go to the nearest large library, and take out as many local history books as I could find. But here – the books would be in French and reading them would be a struggle.

But perhaps still worth doing. And it'd be good for my French skills, too.

Across the valley was another path, signposted with a brown footpath sign, with various intriguing sounding places listed including a couple of villages in the next valley, and what I assumed was a mountain summit. I'd had my eye on this route for a while, and now that Felix had settled in with us, now was the time. After returning from the market I donned my boots – to Felix's excitement; he'd already learned what this meant – and packed a rucksack with a few snacks for us both, a flask of coffee and a couple of bottles of water. And a rain mac, for although the forecast was for wall-to-wall sunshine, I am far too used to hiking in Britain to be brave enough to set out into the mountains without preparing for all weather conditions.

'Right, we're off out for a long walk,' I told Phil, who was sitting in the garden with Clarabel tethered nearby.

'Oh, all right. You want company?' He looked at me quizzically. I knew that look. It meant, *please don't say yes, I'm comfortable here.*

'No, it's all right. I've got Felix. See you later, then.' Phil probably still wasn't fit enough for what I was planning anyway.

'You've got your phone?'

'Yep.' I tapped my pocket. And off we went. Down the château's long driveway, across the road and along it for a few hundred metres, then when we reached the signpost we turned off up a track. Felix pulled on his lead a bit, and I had the impression he knew this walk well. Perhaps Monsieur Baudin had brought him up here when he was fit. There were a couple of farms and cottages with their entrances off this track, but gradually we left them behind and below us, and the track grew rougher until it was only suitable for walkers or perhaps mountain-bikers. I let Felix off his lead here. He pranced around in delight for a moment, before setting off upwards, sniffing at everything, marking his route, and looking back every few yards to make sure I was following. I smiled. I was no longer fearful he'd run off.

The walk was an absolute delight, as we left the farmed land behind and came out onto the open hillside. At this time of year the Alpine flowers were magnificent, bordering the path on both sides; yellow gentian, saxifrage and rosebay willowherb all jostling for attention, with the occasional small oak tree dotted around. There was a delicious scent – it took a while before I realised that the low growing, purple-flowered plant that covered the ground was thyme, and every step I took released its fragrance into the atmosphere.

One of the traditional *herbes du Provence*, I told myself. I wondered if we had any in the garden yet. Perhaps Phil could grow some and we could become self-sufficient in herbs, as long as we wanted everything thyme-flavoured.

As we climbed higher the land became rockier and the plants smaller. The view was constantly changing – the village rooftops were visible one moment then disappeared behind a rocky outcrop the next. Once they were out of sight it felt as though I had the entire Alps to myself. The hills I knew well – those behind the château – were joined by a more distant, higher range of hills and then, peeking out over those I could see the snow-capped peaks of the high Alps. The path zig-zagged its way up a steep section and finally reached the summit plateau, the high point marked by a stone cairn. Felix immediately slumped down in the small amount of shade it offered, and I poured some water into a plastic bowl for him to refresh himself. When I straightened up and looked around, I was delighted to realise there was a 360-degree view. To the south, the Mediterranean, shining a deep blue. The coast line – I could pick out Antibes, the airport at Nice, the mouth of the river Var, the outskirts of Nice itself. Further west more hills, some on a promontory under which I knew the town of St Tropez nestled. Looking east, the hills beyond Nice would be part of Monaco and further on, Italy. Nice itself had been part of Piedmont at one time, I vaguely recalled, and pulled out my phone to check facts. Yes, until 1860 Nice had not been French. After the Revolution. But Saint-Michel-sur-Verais had always been part of France – the old border ran to the east of here.

As I sat down on a flat rock and poured myself a coffee, I wondered why Pierre Aubert and his family had not escaped into Italy during the Revolution. So many French aristocrats had gone into exile then, most of them returning to France later on, in Napoleon's reign. Given how near to the border they were, it would have been relatively easy to get across, I would have thought. As Monsieur Christophe had suggested, perhaps Pierre's wife had managed to escape, perhaps on foot through the mountains. I hoped so. Maybe she was the mother of the baby Louis whose name and dates were on the family tomb. I found myself feeling sorry for Pierre Aubert, hunted down by the revolutionary mob and somehow dying as a result. His only crime, quite likely, was the accident of his birth into the nobility.

'Lovely up here, isn't it?' I said to Felix, who'd come sniffing around me as though wondering if I was carrying any dog biscuits for him. Or human biscuits. Or any kind of tasty treat – we had discovered he was really not at all fussy. 'Hungry? Well here you are then.' I pulled out a packet of digestive biscuits I'd stuffed into my rucksack and gave him one, which disappeared in a single gulp. I made my own last a little longer, despite having to eat it while Felix sat panting hopefully in front of me, his head cocked slightly to one side in the cutest possible way. It worked. I gave him another biscuit from the pack before putting them away. 'I'm too soft on you, aren't I?' I scratched his head and felt a surge of love for this animal who I'd only known for a couple of weeks, but who felt like part of the family already. When Monsieur Baudin was discharged from hospital and in his retirement home I vowed I'd take Felix to visit him. It'd be good for both of them.

'Shall we descend?' I asked my canine companion, and received a soft woof in reply, as he jumped to his feet. But first I walked across the summit plateau a little until I could see down into the next valley. There was a pretty looking village perched on a rocky outcrop part way down – all jumbled medieval buildings, terracotta roof tiles and tiny twisty streets. Another day I'd go on, explore that village, and then walk back over. Maybe one to do with one of the others – Steve, perhaps, though he'd probably want to run the route rather than walk it. Gray would rather use a mountain bike, Manda would want to be on horseback. And Phil would rather stay in the garden, unless it was all snow covered with a chairlift going up so he could ski down it. I chuckled. 'Good job I've got you, isn't it, Felix?' Having the dog was certainly helping me settle in.

We were sitting at the breakfast table the next morning, drinking coffee while I told the others what Monsieur Christophe had said about Pierre Aubert's wife, when Manda's phone buzzed with an incoming message, at the same time as Steve's. They looked at each other and both reached for their phones.

'It's Zoe, on our family group chat,' Steve said, to answer the questioning look we had all given him.

'She wants us to ring her. Now, before she goes to bed.' It was evening in Australia. Manda looked worried, as she stood up and gestured for Steve to follow her to another room where they could talk to their daughter in private.

Steve returned on his own about ten minutes later. His expression was mixed – there was joy in there but also worry. 'What is it, Steve? Is Zoe OK?' I asked.

'She's fine. Absolutely. She had some news for us though, which Manda isn't quite sure how to react to.' Steve poured himself another coffee and sat down.

I frowned. 'Oh? What is it, can you tell us?'

'Zoe has met a chap in Australia. She'd spoken about him a

few times but it seems it was more serious than we realised. They've got engaged.'

'But that's lovely news!' I'd blurted the words out before I remembered what Manda had told me about her greatest fear being that Zoe would meet someone and decide to settle in Australia for good.

'It is, yes. He sounds like a good, solid chap. Ryan, his name is.'

'Fantastic news, mate!' Phil clapped Steve on the back.

Gray gave a little cheer. 'First of our offspring to get engaged!'

'Is Manda pleased?' I asked.

'Yes … and no. She's happy for Zoe, of course. Zoe sounds over the moon about the whole thing. But Manda's really scared Zoe will never come back.'

'Should I go and talk to her? Or does she want to be left alone?' I stacked up plates as I spoke, ready to take them through to the kitchen and load them in the dishwasher.

'Yes, you go. A bit of magical Lu-wisdom might help her come to terms with it. I mean, I miss Zoe too, and would prefer her not to stay in Australia, but if it's what she wants then it's what I want for her, too,' Steve said. But I could tell he was saying what he thought he ought to be saying, rather than how he really felt. I suspected he was just as keen as Manda that Zoe should come home at the end of her contract. I tried to imagine how I'd feel if Tom or Alfie emigrated to the other side of the world. But I would be happy to jump on a plane and go to see them every year. So would Steve, but he'd be alone. Manda had never been able to contemplate long-haul air flights.

I found Manda lying stretched out on a sofa, a balled-up tissue in her hand. 'You OK? Steve told us the news.'

She sat up, to make space beside her and I sat down and put an arm around her. 'Oh, Manda. I know it was what you feared would happen. But it's good that Zoe's happy, isn't it? As parents that's the thing we want most – our kids to be happy.'

She sniffed loudly. 'Of course. I'm happy for her. Really. But, Lu – this is it. I'll never see her again.'

'Yes, you will. She'll come to visit.'

'Every two or three years at most. She won't be able to afford to.'

'You can send her the money.'

'She wouldn't take it. Oh, why couldn't she have met a British bloke?'

'Ryan is Australian then, is he?'

'Yes, I assume so. He works for the same company as her in Sydney. They've got lots of interests in common – surfing and hiking. They're having a whale of a time out there, spending every weekend at the beach or in the Blue Mountains.'

'It's good she's making the most of her time. Another nine months or so on her contract, isn't it?'

Manda stared at me. 'Yes ... but then she'll probably extend it.'

'Has she said so?'

'No. But she will, now she has Ryan. She's bound to. Then they'll marry. I won't be able to be at my own daughter's wedding!' Manda broke down and wailed at this, so loudly that Steve came through to see what was going on. I shrugged at him. So much for Lu's wise pep-talks – Manda seemed more upset now than when I'd come in.

'Ah now, ssh,' I said, putting my arms around her and rocking her like a child in need of comfort. 'Don't be trying to second-guess the future. She might want to marry in England – it's where all her friends are, after all.'

'Except the friends she's made in Australia, and all his friends and family, and all their work colleagues and mutual friends.' Manda sniffed again. 'No, they'll have more people in Australia and will decide to get hitched there, I know it.'

'Then we'll find a way to get you there. Maybe by ship. Maybe lots of short hops with a day or so between each flight. There are ways, Manda. But listen, don't be worrying about it. Zoe's happy and healthy and living her best life.'

'I know. I sounded pleased for her when she told us, honestly. Only started crying when she was off the phone. I'd hate for her to think I wasn't happy for her.' Manda managed a weak smile.

'That's good. So let's see what happens, eh? Send her a congratulations card, and we can cross each bridge as it comes.' I squeezed her shoulders, and she wiped away the last of her tears and nodded. Behind her, Steve gave me a smile and a thumbs-up and left the room.

'Yeah. Thanks Lu. I feel better for talking about it.'

'Any time, pet. Any time.'

Chapter 20

Pierre, 1792

Pierre was worried. France was at war with Prussia and Austria, and he was becoming increasingly concerned for their safety. He wished he had insisted they go into exile at the time when so many other nobles had. At least it might have been one upheaval rather than two. But Catherine hated the idea of leaving France, and he had not the heart to force her. He was not sure his health would stand another long journey. Besides, she was heavily pregnant now. He'd made her flee once, while carrying a child, and he could not do it to her again. She still seemed not to accept that the old ways were gone, and the new regime was increasingly against all those who owned land or property or were titled, by accident of birth. Indeed, all noble titles had now been abolished. He had tried to change things here in St Michel-sur-Verais. He paid fair wages to all those who worked for him. He no longer expected them to do everything he said without question – indeed he encouraged them to discuss their problems with him and he would do what he could for them. Most seemed to appreciate this. Hadn't he given the Barniers a cottage on his estate, after their roof had collapsed? He'd loaned the Duchamps money to pay for the physician after their child had fallen gravely ill, and then he'd paid for the child's burial. And he'd shared the harvest last year, with every person getting a more-or-less equal share. So what if he'd kept some in reserve at the château? It was exactly that – a reserve, in case it was needed.

But some, like that Jacques Valet, were still hostile to him and his family. Pierre had heard that Valet agreed with the view that the nobility should be stamped out completely. How this was to be achieved, no one could say. Pierre supposed they wanted people like himself to give up all their lands, all their rights, to open up their properties to whoever wanted to live there, and to live themselves like the peasants did, in one room along with their animals. Wearing rough clothes infested with lice at the seams. Unwashed. Uneducated. Well, that was a step too far. Pierre believed that no matter what, there would always need to be someone to manage the lower classes. Someone to keep them employed, to organise their work, and keep them in check. And it was the nobility who had the knowledge and skills and education to do this. So while he agreed with the aims of the Revolution to an extent, he felt strongly that it should not be allowed to go too far.

And yet it *was* going too far. Pierre had news from Paris, that a new punishment was being used. A Monsieur Guillotine had invented a machine that chopped off a man's head, cleanly and neatly. This machine was being used in Paris, to execute those who were deemed guilty of crimes against the State. And from what Pierre could gather, crimes against the State were many and varied, and new ones were invented almost every day. It did not bode well for them.

In addition, so many of the local men had gone to fight in the wars that Pierre worried there were not enough people left to work in his fields. Food stores were low – the Army had passed through, requisitioning most of the supplies that were to last the community for the rest of the year. Wherever he looked, to Pierre it seemed there was nothing but worry.

But there was better news, too. Catherine's pregnancy had progressed well, and on a fine afternoon in early summer, he arrived home from an exhilarating ride in the mountains to a château in uproar, with maids running hither and thither and a feeling of excitement in the air.

'What is happening?' he asked Claudette as she ran upstairs with a pail of water.

'Sir, it is the Madame, she is giving birth!' The maid dipped a curtsy, managing to slop water from her bucket as she did so, and Pierre waved her away, grinning. Soon he would be a father again. He was very much looking forward to this and having a baby to care for would be good for Catherine.

Birthing rooms were no place for men, although back at Versailles when the Queen gave birth there would be any number of people, men and women, in the Queen's bedchamber to witness the birth of an heir to the throne. He shuddered. He'd never had to be present at such an occasion, and nor did he want to. He retreated to his library where he sat with a book, a pipe, and a glass of brandy, to await the hopefully happy outcome of proceedings upstairs.

Hours later the mood in the château was more that of worry than excitement. Pierre paced the hallway, accosting any servant who hurried through, but the news was always the same. Catherine still laboured, the baby had not yet been born, Madame seemed tired but otherwise all right. The physician was called for, but he spent only a few minutes in Catherine's bedchamber before joining Pierre in the library for a brandy.

'Baby is breech,' he said. 'That's why it's taking so long. Nothing I can do, and the midwife doesn't want me there anyway.'

'Will they be all right?' Pierre said. He hadn't for a moment thought that Catherine's life might be in danger. She had done well with her first birth, and he'd assumed this one would go well too.

The doctor shrugged. 'Only God knows that. If the baby is born in the next couple of hours, then I would say both will be well. But the longer it goes on, the more danger there is. For both.'

Pierre felt a band of ice around his heart at these words. 'Is there nothing you can do to help?'

'Your wife needs to push, the midwife needs to guide her, and with some effort, the baby will be born. Breech births happen all the time, Monsieur Aubert. Most are successful, but some fail. Let us hope your wife is strong.'

Strength was not a quality Pierre normally associated with Catherine. He found himself doing what she did so often – wishing they were back at Versailles, with all the advantages of being among the court, with the country's best physicians on hand. How the lower classes managed at all, he had no idea. Those who could not afford the services of any physician, or even a midwife. Those who had no comfortable château, with a plentiful supply of food and fuel. How any peasant child survived birth and the rigours of childhood was nothing short of a miracle. But that aside, this was his child being born, his wife in danger, and he had money and influence, and by God he was going to use it to make sure they had the best treatment available!

'Sir, I require you to attend the birth until it is all over, whatever might happen. I can pay you, of course. I will pay you double for your time. But I want you upstairs, in the chamber now.' He fixed the doctor with a stern glare.

'Alas, the midwife does not want my presence.' The doctor raised his hands in a gesture of submission.

'It's not her decision to make. It is mine. Now go, and do what you can for my wife. Or you will not be paid for today at all.'

The corners of the physician's mouth turned down, but he put down his brandy glass and left the room. Pierre heard his tread on the stairs and sighed. He'd done all he could now, to help

Catherine. It was up to her, the midwife and the doctor. And God, he realised. He rang the bell for a servant and sent a boy to run for Père Debroux at once. The priest lived in a rough cottage on Pierre's estate now, rent free, as he no longer had an income from the State. While he waited for the priest's arrival, Pierre paced back and forth, muttering prayers.

It seemed hours until the priest arrived, hours in which there was no more news from upstairs, and only occasional cries of pain and anguish, turning to screams, from Catherine. Each cry broke Pierre's heart. He could not lose her! She was such a sweet, gentle soul. He had promised to protect her always, and he had done so, but he could not protect her from the terrors of childbirth. Only God could do that. Oh where was that damned priest?

At last the priest arrived and was shown into the library. Pierre explained the situation, and the two men knelt to pray.

'I will stay until the outcome is known,' Père Debroux said. 'In case there is some further service I can perform.'

He meant delivering the last rites, Pierre realised. For either Catherine or their child or both. Pierre's heart sank at the thought. No, it could not be! 'Let me offer you some refreshment while we wait,' he said, and rang the bell to order as fine a meal as the kitchen could prepare, under the circumstances.

They were halfway through eating, served by Madame Bernard herself, when Claudette came rushing into the room, without knocking. Her face was red and sweating, her eyes wide but there was an expression of joy on her face.

'Oh, sir, come at once! It is over!'

Pierre jumped to his feet, knocking his chair over. 'And? What is the outcome, girl?'

'A son! Fine and healthy.'

'And my wife?'

Claudette's face fell a little. 'She is alive. But exhausted, and she has lost much blood. The next couple of days are critical, says the doctor.'

Pierre took the stairs two at a time, closely followed by Père Debroux. He barged into his wife's bedchamber, and fell to his knees at the bedside, kissing her ashen face, holding her limp hand. 'Oh, my sweet! Well done! A son, I am delighted!'

Catherine gave him a wan smile and lifted her hand to stroke his face. 'I am so tired, Pierre.'

'Of course. You must rest. Sleep, and when you wake you shall hold your son.' Catherine turned her face away and he realised she was already asleep. Only then did he look around the room for his child, who was swaddled and cradled in the midwife's arms.

'It was a difficult birth,' the midwife told him. 'But I've never lost a breech baby yet, so I wasn't going to start today.' She pulled back the shawl to show him the baby's face, red and mewling like a kitten, and Pierre's heart was filled with love for this tiny being, who had so nearly taken his mother's life. Still might, he realised. He looked at the physician, who was standing in a corner, away from the bed.

'And what can you do for my wife?' he said.

'She needs rest, and I can offer this potion to help her sleep,' the doctor said, taking a small bottle out of his case.

The midwife scoffed. 'She needs nothing to help her sleep. She needs someone to sit with her, though.'

'I will do that,' said Claudette, stepping forward and then blushing.

Pierre nodded at her. She was a good, loyal servant. He appreciated her help. 'Thank you. I will have some food sent up for you. Is there anything else you need?'

Claudette shook her head. 'No sir. I will do what I can for Madame. And you can leave the baby here too, so that he is here when she wakes up.'

The midwife nodded her agreement. She was collecting up her things, preparing to leave. Nothing remained to be done but to pay her and the physician, send for the wet-nurse and then leave Catherine in Claudette's care and God's hands.

Chapter 21

Lu

As the summer wore on, Gray's relationship with Aimée progressed nicely. He even stayed away from the château on a few occasions, coming back the following morning whistling cheerfully. Aimée had never yet stayed over at the château though. She'd come for dinner on several occasions but always Gray would stay off the alcohol and drive her home.

'It's as though,' Phil said to me late one night after Aimée had been for dinner, 'he's treating us like his daughters. Not wanting a girlfriend to stay when we're in the house. It's a shame.'

'He needs to get over that. Aimée is perfect for him. There's no problem with her staying here now and again,' I said. Phil was right. For years Gray had kept his relationships separate from his daughters, even though it led to his break-up with Leanne all those years ago. And now, apart from the odd dinner, he was keeping Aimée at arm's length when the four of us were around. 'His girls are coming to visit next week, aren't they?'

Phil nodded. 'Think so, yes.'

And they did come. An excited Gray drove to Nice airport on Saturday afternoon and arrived back with Hope and Clemmie in the back seat, both looking glossy and gorgeous, giggling with excitement as Gray showed them around the château. They were delighted by everything, and had brought thoughtful gifts for us all – things for the château, and a couple of bottles of champagne which went down very well on their first night with us. They'd even bought a squeaky toy for Felix, stuffed mice toys for the kittens and a huge rosette for Clarabel. They shared a guest room. We had enough space for them to have a room each, but they insisted on sharing. 'Like old times, eh, Clemmie?' Hope said. 'We can have pillow fights and midnight feasts and everything.'

'Aw, can I come to the midnight feast?' asked Gray.

'Course not! You're an adult!' Clemmie said. 'You're supposed to tell us off for having it!'

'Um, you're both adults too,' Gray pointed out. 'Twenty-six and twenty-four, if I remember correctly.'

'Not as adult as you though, Dad. Not *alpha* adults.' Clemmie stuck her tongue out at him, and Gray chased her around the garden, followed by Felix who thought it was all a wonderful game, while Clarabel skipped nimbly out of the way and watched them with disdain. It was good to see Gray still had such a great relationship with his daughters. I wondered whether he'd introduce them to Aimée or not. So far, he hadn't mentioned the *maire* in their presence, and following his lead, neither had the rest of us.

But he had to – a couple of days later when we were with the girls in the village, shopping at the market, we bumped into Aimée who was buying olives. Gray, Hope and Clemmie and I were there, the others had wandered off to buy cheese and vegetables at other stalls.

'Aimée, good to see you,' I said, kissing her on both cheeks. Over her shoulder I could see Gray blushing horribly. 'Aimée, this is Hope and this is Clemmie. Girls, this is Madame la Maire.'

'A woman mayor, that's awesome,' Hope said, taking Aimée's hand. 'Dad, you never said you were friends with the mayor. Mixing with important people!'

'Ah, I am not so very important,' Aimée said with a smile, then she turned to greet Gray. 'Hello. I hope you were not too hungover after our night out last week?'

'Er, um, no, not at all,' he stuttered, blushing yet more furiously. I noticed a look pass between Clemmie and Hope – they had clocked his confusion and that he'd had a night out with Aimée, as well as her squeeze of his shoulder as she kissed his cheeks. They'd put two and two together and their maths was good.

'I'm thinking the mayor is actually quite an important person at least to Dad, am I right?' Clemmie said, so that only I could hear. I smiled and gave a tiny nod.

It was a day or two after we'd met the *maire* in the market that Clemmie asked Gray whether we'd be inviting her for dinner at all while she and Hope were visiting. We were washing up after breakfast – me washing and Clemmie drying. Gray was clearing up and putting things away.

'Because we only got to meet her very briefly in the village,' Clemmie said. 'And I think we'd both like to get to know her better.'

'Why? She's just … the mayor,' Gray stuttered.

'I think she's more than that to you, isn't she?'

I glanced at her and she winked at me.

'Why, who's been talking to you? Lu, what have you been saying?' Gray's tone was a mixture of fake outrage and confusion.

'Me? I've said nothing, have I, Clem?'

'Dad, no one's said anything. But your face when we met the mayor said it all. Honestly, Dad, if there's something going on between you then we both think that's brilliant, don't we, Hope?' Hope had walked into the room bringing a few coffee cups from the patio.

'Yeah, fabulous! Invite her for dinner. That'd be OK, wouldn't it, Lu?'

'Of course. We love having Aimée here.' Oops. I'd let on now that it wouldn't be her first visit.

'And maybe she could stay the night,' Clemmie went on.

Gray shook his head. 'Ah no. That wouldn't be … no. That's just not right.'

Clemmie put down her tea-towel and went over to her father, wrapping her arms around him. 'Dad. We are grown-ups. We don't mind. We want you to have a relationship, a sex life. It's good for you. And Aimée seems lovely.'

'She is lovely. But she can't stay here, not when …'

'Not when Hope and I are here? Maybe after, then?'

Gray shrugged and turned away to put some coffee cups back into the cupboard. He'd clearly decided the conversation was at an end. But at least he now knew that the girls knew about Aimée and were happy for him.

'How about Friday?' I blurted out, without really thinking. 'Aimée could come then. It's the girls' last night with us, and we were planning a big dinner anyway. There'll be enough for one more.'

'Sure. I'll text her,' Gray said, without looking at me or Clem. He closed the cupboard door and left the room.

'Grumpy sod,' Clemmie said. 'But thanks, Lu. It's time he grew up where we're concerned. He could have had fifteen years of marriage to Leanne if he hadn't been so squeamish about Hope and me knowing what was going on. We call her "the one that got away".'

I laughed. 'So do we.'

'So is Aimée as nice as she seemed? Do you think she's right for him?'

'She is, yes. She's lovely. Very sophisticated compared with us lot, but genuinely nice. Whether she's right for him – well, that's up to them, isn't it? They just need to let their relationship progress naturally and see where it leads.'

Clemmie nodded. 'Tell him that, will you? He thinks you're wise. He'll listen to you.'

'Me, wise?' I laughed. 'But yes, I'll try to find the right moment for a heart to heart.'

Clemmie hugged me. 'Thanks, Lu. He's lucky to have you, and the others, as friends.'

'We're lucky to have him, too. And he's lucky to have you two lovely daughters. You're coming back over for Christmas, right?' I hugged her back.

'Definitely.'

We sat outside that evening, enjoying the last of the sunshine as it dipped down behind the mountain, and sipping our glasses of wine. It was one of those evenings when I'd look around me – at the château, the garden which was beginning to look beautiful, the surrounding mountains and of course, my best friends – and think how very lucky I was to be here, living like this. It had been hard to settle at first, but I was getting there.

Our conversation had somehow drifted around to all that we had achieved since we moved to France. We'd looked back on where we'd been on that fateful night when the idea had been conceived, and where we were now. Clemmie and Hope had wanted to hear the full story of that night.

'Take Phil, for example,' Gray said. 'He was a fat bastard with a heart condition. And now he's fit and healthy and fast becoming the greatest gardener in the Alpes-Maritimes.'

'Ha! And look at you – from sad loner to having snagged the Alpes-Maritimes' most eligible lady mayor,' retorted Phil.

'Yes, it's all working out for us, isn't it?' Manda looked at me. 'What about you, Lu? Back then you'd just come out of years of being a carer – first for your mum, then for Phil. Always helping other people. Only ever as happy as the least happy person around you. Now you can spend your time on yourself at last.' She leaned over and gave me a quick squeeze.

I was surprised. Is that how they saw me? Always doing things for other people and not myself? Since moving to France, I felt I'd had loads of me-time – all those walks with Felix, plenty of time sitting with a book or researching the history of the area. Possibly too much me-time. I still felt at times that there were too many hours to fill each day. The project I really wanted to get on with was solving the mystery of the tower room but that would have to wait. We'd had the woodworm treatment done but were still waiting to replace the floorboards and repair damaged joists.

'You still miss teaching though, don't you?' Steve said. He missed project managing, and tended to assume we all missed our old day jobs.

I thought about it for a moment. 'Yes, I suppose I do, some-times. I did enjoy teaching. The thrill when students really got what you were telling them. Knowing that at the end of term they were in a better position for their future lives than at the start, partly because of what you'd taught them. Enriching lives. Not much beats it.'

'Shame there's no way you can use your teaching skills now, really,' Phil said. 'It'd be good for you.'

'My French is not up to teaching here, and I wouldn't have the right qualifications, anyway.'

'Teffle,' said Clemmie.

'You what, love?' said Gray.

'Perhaps Lu could do TEFL. Teach English as a foreign language. That'd make use of her teaching skills.' Clemmie smiled at me.

'How does that work, then?' Gray asked. 'Wouldn't she need better French to be able to teach?'

Clemmie shook his head. 'I have a friend who did it in Spain for a summer. It's basically conversation classes for people who already know English but want to improve. The whole class is run in English.'

'Sounds good,' Steve said. 'What do you think, Lu?'

I shrugged and smiled. 'Don't know. Maybe. I'll find out more about it.'

'You'd be great,' Manda said. 'You're a born teacher.'

I tuned out of the conversation then, and sat quietly sipping my wine and wondering. Was teaching English something I could do? Something I should do? It was worth investigating. I did miss teaching. Of everyone, I'd been the first to give up my day job, to care for Mum. I'd effectively retired far sooner than I would have, otherwise. Was I ready to come out of retirement and teach again? It would certainly help keep me busy, and would allow me to get to know more people locally.

In bed that night I asked Phil his opinion on the idea, as we turned out the lights and snuggled under a lightweight duvet. 'Do you think I should give it a go?'

'Sure, why not? If you need something more to do. Either that or you could help me in the garden …'

'Hmm, no thanks,' I replied. 'You'd only give me all the heavy, boring work to do.'

'Yep, of course. No point having an assistant if you can't give them the lousy jobs!'

I gave him a bash with my pillow for that. 'So I thought I'd go and enquire at the *mairie* tomorrow, to see how to go about getting involved in that. I guess that's the best way to start.'

'Uh huh,' he replied, and I realised he was already close to sleep. Always takes me ages, but oddly I find the sound of Phil's gentle snores relaxing. I lay back and planned a first lesson.

The following day I took Felix on the walk beside the river into the village, past the old wash house and round to the *mairie*. It was a hot day, but the village square was shaded by large plane trees and the ubiquitous game of *pétanque* was in progress beneath them.

At the *mairie*, I tied Felix up outside in a shady spot. Aimée's assistant told me she was out at the moment. Gray had gone out early today too – neatly dressed and wearing an abundance of aftershave. Maybe it was just a coincidence, but who knew?

I asked the assistant – a young man in his twenties, named Pascal – about the possibility of teaching English locally. His eyes lit up.

'Yes, Madame! We have much need here. We often get the enquiry about who can lead a conversation class. Give me your details – I make a poster. You will have a full class in no time.'

'Marvellous! Would people expect me to be fluent in French too? Because I'm not ...'

He shook his head. '*Mais, non*. People who come will want to speak only the English, to practise. I will come. I am wanting to work in London one day.'

Pascal seemed open and helpful, so I sat down to discuss how these classes should run. Pick a conversation topic each week, he said, and lead the conversation. Make sure everyone is encouraged to join in. Ask questions. Try to use future and past tenses. Set homework – optional – of preparing a short talk on a subject for the next lesson.

I could do all that, I thought. I'd been a teacher for thirty years. Lesson plans, leading discussions, ensuring everyone had a chance to be heard – these things were bread and butter to me. The only difference was not all the conversations would be about history. Though some would. It occurred to me we could use one week to talk about local history. I might learn something too ...

I'd already decided I'd run classes on Tuesday evenings and Friday mornings. The latter probably for retired people, the former gave those with jobs a chance to attend. Pascal nodded, jotting down the details, and we agreed a start date of two weeks' time.

'Where will the classes be?' he asked. I realised I had not arranged a venue. The château was too far out of the village. I needed somewhere central. 'You could use the *salle des fetes*,' he suggested, consulting a diary. 'Yes, it is free at that time. How much will you charge?'

'Oh! I don't want to be paid,' I said. 'Or only enough to cover the cost of the hall.'

'The hall will be free for you if you are not charging your students,' he said, smiling. 'This way the whole village benefits.'

'*Parfait*,' I said. Already I was looking forward to holding my first class.

'I will see you at your first lesson, then!' Pascal smiled and shook my hand.

I collected Felix, bought a few items in the *patisserie* (it was always hard to pass it by without going in) and headed back to the château with my news.

Chapter 22

Catherine, 1792–93

As summer progressed into autumn, and autumn into winter, Catherine gradually regained her strength, though she felt as though she would never be completely whole again. But little Michel brought her much joy. He looked just like his father – Pierre. Catherine remembered with a shudder the time when she had briefly contemplated starting an affair with Jacques Valet. Thank God she hadn't. She had not seen the man for many months, and nor did she want to. It had been a difficult time – little Louis's death then Pierre's illness had put her under a lot of stress. Jacques' attentions had provided an escape from her worries. That was the only explanation she could give herself.

As Claudette had suggested long before he was born, Catherine had taken on more of this baby's care herself. She spent hours each day cradling him, letting him sleep on her lap as she dozed in an armchair. She had still hired a wet-nurse – it wasn't healthy for a baby to be fed by its own mother, she felt – but she occasionally even bathed and dressed the child, enjoying his giggles as she tickled him, laughing at his gurgles and marvelling at the perfection of his tiny fingers and toes and that perfect little curl of hair on the top of his head. Why hadn't she spent more time with little Louis, she wondered, with regret. She'd been so convinced that she'd been doing everything right then, but now she realised that there were other ways to raise a child, ways which were so much more rewarding. Perhaps the lower classes had it right all along.

Michel thrived, and Claudette proved herself to be once more a fine nursemaid, although this time the child's care was shared between them much more than before. Claudette seemed to approve of this, though why Catherine cared what she thought, she couldn't say. But the household was a happy one on the surface at least, although news from Paris, reported to Pierre by letters from friends, continued to be worrying.

'I should go to Paris,' he said, one evening as they sat beside the fire, Catherine dandling little Michel in her lap. 'I should see for myself what is happening.'

'No!' Catherine was aghast. 'You keep telling me it is not safe, that we are not safe even here. Why would you want to go to Paris? Think of your health!'

'I need first-hand information, to decide what is best for us to do.'

Catherine was terrified the long journey to Paris might be too stressful for him, and bring on another heart attack. Without Pierre she would be so vulnerable. At Versailles, a young widow had always been able to find another husband or lover as a protector, but here there was nobody. 'Please, Pierre my love, do not go. Do not leave me. I would be terrified to be here on my own. Besides ...' She looked sideways at him. Perhaps this was the right time to tell him her news. She'd kept it quiet for a few months. 'I am once again with child. I am scared, after Michel's birth. I want you to stay here with me.'

He fell to his knees at her feet and wrapped his arms around her waist. 'Oh, my darling. Of course I will stay, then. If you need me, I am here.'

At Christmas, when the first snow had fallen and there was no chance of Pierre going anywhere, there came two pieces of unwelcome and unsettling news. One a local event, and one national.

Pierre had ridden down the valley through the snow to collect his mail. He returned ashen-faced, having opened and read it in a café on the way home. Catherine was in the drawing room, embroidering clothes for her new baby which she was sure would be a girl, when he flung open the door and strode in, slamming the door closed behind him.

'What is it?' she said, putting her work down, and patting the seat beside her for him to sit.

'The King is on trial.'

Five words. That was all he could say, before he stood again, pacing the room, and finally with shaking hands picked up a bottle of brandy and a glass and poured himself a large measure.

'On trial? But, for what?' Catherine knew that the King had been arrested in the summer, but Pierre had told her that was all for show, and they would not actually put him on trial.

'For many things, which he has denied. But chiefly for conspiring with foreign armies to start a counter-revolution. His exiled brothers were raising troops, ready to march on Paris and reinstate the monarchy.'

'Is this true?' Catherine felt a flutter of hope. Of course, if one of Louis's brothers was able to fight, and restore things to how they were, there was hope yet … Though as time went on she was beginning to understand that things could never go back to how they were. This revolution was like a boulder rolling down a hillside. It could not be stopped or reversed.

Pierre nodded. 'I believe it is, yes. Louis – Citizen Capet as they are calling him now – denies it, but there is no denying that when he made that ridiculous escape attempt, he had amassed troops at that time ready to march to Paris. It does not look good for him, Catherine. My informer wrote this letter before the defence had been heard, but …'

'What? Tell me!'

'There are suggestions that if found guilty he will be ... executed. By guillotine.'

Catherine clapped a hand to her mouth. She felt sick. How could the State kill the King? In the old days, he was beholden only to God. How could a court of mere men find him guilty? It was all wrong. 'But surely he will not be found guilty? If he denies the charges, then they must believe him! He is the King! He is our ruler!'

'*Was* our ruler, my dear. Not any longer. He is just an ordinary citizen now, they say. As is the Queen, and her children.'

At the mention of Marie Antoinette, Catherine could hold back tears no longer. The dear Queen – how was she coping with having her husband on trial? What would she do if he was found guilty ... if he was executed? It did not bear thinking about. For a moment Catherine wished she had never left Versailles. Perhaps she could have supported the Queen through these difficult times. But at what cost? Their own safety, probably.

'There's more bad news, I am afraid,' Pierre said. His voice was softer now, and he sat down beside Catherine and took her hand. She steeled herself to hear it.

'The Queen?' she whispered.

Pierre shook his head. 'She is safe inside the Tuileries for the moment. They will not harm her. There are no charges that can be brought against her. No, my dear. The other bad news is closer to home.'

She looked at him questioningly.

'It is about Père Debroux. He has been arrested. We have no priest now, not one that has not sworn the oath, at least.'

'What will happen to him?'

'He will remain locked up, I believe, until or unless he agrees to take the oath of allegiance. There are many priests imprisoned now, across France.'

Catherine closed her eyes for a moment, in silent prayer for the priest. That he would not suffer while incarcerated. That he would find strength in his faith. 'And what of us? How should we worship?'

'We either no longer take Mass, or we attend church in the village along with everyone else.'

'With the new priest who has sworn the oath? Who supports the Revolution?' It went against everything they believed in.

'We have no other choice. And I fear that we will be looked upon badly if we do not go to church. Those who support the non-juror priests are deemed to have committed crimes themselves.'

'But that's us! We have supported Père Debroux!' Catherine stared at him in horror. Was he saying that they themselves were now criminals, for feeding and housing a priest?

Pierre rubbed a hand across his forehead and nodded. 'So we should go to church, with this new constitutional priest, and make it look as though we now accept the Constitution, and all the changes, ourselves. If we do not, I fear that we may find ourselves in danger. We need the local people to love us, to accept us as their own.'

'But they do, don't they?'

'I'm not sure they all do. We must take steps to address this. On Sunday we will walk to the village and attend Mass there.'

There was no arguing with him. He had made up his mind, and she must do as he bid. It would be the right thing to do. Pierre was always right about these things.

Even so, when Sunday morning came around it was with trepidation that Catherine donned her boots and her warmest cloak, and set off for the walk through the snow to the village, across its little central square, and into the church. She had not set foot in it since Père Debroux had been forbidden to lead public worship. She had not even set foot in the village since those days, either, other than a few visits to little Louis's grave. As they entered and walked to the front of the church to take their places in the front pews, as was their right as the local nobility, all heads turned in their direction. She spotted Jacques Valet leaning against a wall, and felt herself colouring as he stared insolently at her. Catherine steeled herself to keep her gaze forward and her head high. They had done nothing wrong. They were guilty of nothing, save the accident of their noble birth. But still, she thought she heard mutterings from the people, mumbles of 'shame' and 'get rid of them' and 'traitors to France'. As she slid into a pew beside Pierre she whispered to him.

'They cannot really think we are traitors to France, can they?'

'Ssh. We will talk about this later. It is not safe to do so here.'

It was the longest church service she had ever sat through. The priest's sermon seemed more of a political speech, including many references to the new order, loyalty to the State and the Christian duty of showing brotherhood to one's neighbours. He was a tall thin man, with a piercing gaze, that he turned frequently in their direction as he spoke about the desire for liberty and equality for all men. Catherine thought hard about his words. Liberty for all she agreed with. No man or woman should be a slave. Only criminals should be denied their freedom. Brotherhood – well yes. Hard to argue against helping out one's fellow humans who were in need. She and Pierre always did that, did they not? They had certainly stuck their necks out to help Père Debroux.

But *equality*? These peasants, these uneducated, illiterate farmers and shepherds, they were not the equal of herself and Pierre, surely? To be truly equal, everyone would have to have the same level of schooling, to own the same things, have standard, equal housing. Equality meant the end of the nobility, as well as the end of the monarchy. If all men had the same things, there would be no incentive for anyone to work harder to better themselves. No, Catherine thought, as the new priest droned on, equality would not work in practice. There would always be a need for a hierarchy. One where she and Pierre were at the top, as was their right. Their God-given right; at least it had been, under the *ancien régime*.

Christmas was a subdued affair. Catherine dared not attend church again, using her delicate condition as an excuse to stay at home, but Pierre went every Sunday and made a point of speaking to the local people at every opportunity, treating them, he reported back to Catherine, as though they were indeed equals. 'As though,' he said, 'I am a bourgeois merchant, rather than as though they are nobility, of course. They do not know the etiquette we used to adhere to at Court. They have not the knowledge of how to behave in polite society, so to be equal I must reduce myself to their level, rather than expect them to raise themselves up. And I believe it is working. They smile at me. They are friendly. We chat of this and that, and I believe they like me and also still have respect for me. Even the fellow Jacques Valet nodded respectfully at me.' Catherine suppressed a shudder at the mention of that man. How could she ever have found him attractive?

January was long and cold, and Catherine felt isolated, confined to the château by the snow, her pregnancy, and her fear of the local people. At the end of January came news from Paris, reaching Pierre by letter just a day before it reached the villagers. He told Catherine in his study, in private, making sure no servants could overhear them.

'The King has been found guilty and condemned to execution.' He did not look her in the eye as he told her. Catherine was stunned at the news. Despite Louis's trial she had not believed he would be found guilty, and even if he was, she'd been so sure that it would just mean he was kept locked in the Tuileries for a few more years or perhaps sent into exile, until the country came to its senses at last.

'They won't actually do it, will they?' she whispered.

Pierre's mouth was set in a tight line. 'They will.' And then he strode out of the room, leaving her alone to try to take in the news.

Less than a week later another letter arrived, confirming that the King's execution had taken place in the Place de la Révolution in Paris, by guillotine. Catherine took to her bed and wept for a week, for the quiet, gentle man she remembered from her days in Versailles. He had not deserved this. He was guilty of nothing, beyond trying to govern the country as best he could, following in the footsteps of his grandfather Louis XV and all his forebears. It was not fair. Damn this revolution! Her heart went out to Marie Antoinette, imprisoned in the Tuileries with her children, now widowed. If only that escape attempt had worked! If only they had been able to get themselves into exile, raise an army and quash the Revolution. But now she increasingly wondered if it could ever have worked. They might have fought back for a while but in the end the revolutionaries had the support of the masses and were bound to win. She realised that the King's only chance had been to work with the Revolution, not against it.

'Sometimes things just don't work out the way we want,' Pierre had said, sadly, when she had voiced her frustration to him. He looked older, she thought. His hair was grey and thinning, and there were lines on his face – a deep furrow between his eyes – that had not been there back in their days in Versailles.

As the snow melted and the spring flowers blossomed on the hillsides, Catherine's pregnancy came to term. She was attended by the same midwife as before, but no doctor. She gave birth to a daughter, and this time her labour was uneventful and thankfully quick, taking just three hours from her first pains.

'We shall name her Marie,' she said to Pierre, but he shook his head.

'No. We must not mark ourselves out as royalists. I have been pretending we have no sympathy for the plight of the Queen, when speaking to the local people. We cannot name our daughter after her.'

He was right, she knew it. In the end he suggested they call the infant Jeanne. A fine, Christian name, recalling a heroic woman who fought for her faith. Perfect for this new France they found themselves living in. Catherine remembered another Jeanne – Jeanne de la Motte – the woman whose actions in the affair of the diamond necklace had helped turn the people against Marie Antoinette. But she smiled and nodded and agreed on the name for their infant.

Claudette was delighted with the new addition to the family. 'I love little girls,' she said. 'And Michel is so happy to have a sister.' Even Madame Bernard smiled as she gazed on the baby for the first time and nodded her approval.

The year wore on, the news about the Revolution became more and more worrying, but Catherine felt safe in her château, with the small number of servants who had stayed – Madame Bernard, Henri, Claudette, the cook, a couple of other maids, and two lads who worked in the stables and the kitchen garden.

France seemed to be at war with everyone – against the British and the Dutch now, while the war against Austria rumbled on.

In the summer, as Jeanne learned to smile and suck her toes and Michel was running everywhere, babbling and beginning to learn a few words, Pierre's correspondents and the few newspapers from Paris they were able to obtain, began mentioning a man called Robespierre. France, one letter said, had been on the verge of falling apart, the Revolution failing. But Robespierre, a member of the Committee of Public Safety, had mounted a campaign against all enemies of the Revolution, and in late summer, declared that a Reign of Terror had begun, and all those guilty of conspiring against the Revolution would be hunted down and executed. Even many who had been members of the original National Assembly and part of the Revolution of 1789 were now deemed enemies, and had to flee for their lives.

'Paris is emptying,' Pierre told Catherine. 'I am glad we are here, so far from it all.'

'And are we safe here?' she asked, for the thousandth time since their flight from Versailles.

Pierre nodded, but with less conviction than usual, she thought. He'd been a member of the aristocracy, a member of Louis XVI's government, and these were now crimes, it seemed. Along with harbouring a non-conformist priest. But he was far from it all, and in this remote, difficult-to-reach spot, surely he would not be found? Catherine bit her lip. She could only pray she was right.

October brought two significant pieces of news. The first, read in a newspaper, seemed to exasperate Pierre. 'They have changed the calendar. We no longer have *Janvier, Février, Mars* and so on, but *thermidor, fructidor, prairial* and who knows what else. It is ridiculous. They are changing everything. Next they will say the Earth no longer goes around the sun, but must go around the moon instead.'

Catherine laughed with him, but it was a hollow laugh. How far would this revolution go? Her thoughts turned as so often to the poor dear Queen, still imprisoned with her children in the Tuileries. What would become of her?

The answer came a couple of weeks later. On trumped-up charges, chiefly of indecency against her own son, Marie Antoinette had been found guilty and sentenced to death by guillotine.

'She was dignified to the end,' Pierre told a weeping Catherine. 'Her last words were to apologise to the executioner, for stepping on his toes as she ascended the scaffold. But the crowd cheered, and now she is gone.'

'I cannot bear it. She would not have hurt her son. That is all lies! She committed no crime.'

'She was a symbol of the *ancien régime*, my dear. Her spending was part of the cause of Louis's bankruptcy, one of the original causes of the Revolution. Being Austrian meant the people never really loved her.'

'I loved her,' Catherine said quietly.

'Madame, shall I light a fire in here?' Catherine turned in shock and clapped a hand over her mouth. Madame Bernard had entered the room. Neither Catherine nor Pierre had noticed – they would never have spoken so openly about the royal family in front of anyone. As far as they were aware, no one locally other than Claudette knew they'd been part of the Court.

'Ah, no, thank you, Madame Bernard. We are warm enough.' Pierre, thankfully had kept his cool and acted as though the housekeeper hadn't heard anything. He even smiled and bowed to her.

But Catherine noticed how the woman's eyes were glittering with hate as she turned her gaze towards her.

'You have heard the news?' she asked Catherine. 'That the Austrian bitch is finally dead? It is good news, no? We are all celebrating in the kitchen. I imagine you will want a bottle of your best wine with dinner tonight.'

'We have heard, yes. So now France can move on to a glorious republican future. France will be the greatest country on earth. That is indeed something to celebrate,' Pierre said.

Madame Bernard looked confused, as though working out whether or not he'd agreed about celebrating the death of the Queen. She looked as though she was about to say something more, but in the end simply left the room.

Catherine breathed a sigh of relief. 'Did she hear? What I said about loving the Queen?'

Pierre crossed the room and took her in his arms. 'If she did, what can she possibly do about it? Winter is coming. Soon we will be snowed in as usual. There will be no revolutionary action here over the winter. And in the spring, my darling, we will take our money and our jewels, and leave. It is time to seek safety elsewhere. Perhaps in Piedmont. No, Switzerland, I think. I have a cousin there, who will offer us shelter.'

Catherine felt too exhausted by it all, too upset about the news of Marie Antoinette, to argue with him. They'd lose the château, they'd lose their land if they left – that had happened to other *emigrés*. The State would seize it all. But they had the children to think about. Michel and Jeanne deserved the best chances possible, and it did seem that leaving France would be the safest course of action now. Just one more winter to get through, and they could leave when the snow melted.

Chapter 23

Lu

When the next Tuesday rolled around it was with some trepidation that I drove into the village, parked outside the *salle des fetes*, and went inside armed with a lesson plan of sorts for my first English conversation class. I'd planned this first session to be an introductory one – getting to know each other, finding out what people expected from the class – to help me shape future lessons. If everything dried up I had an idea to talk about animals – people's pets. Everyone liked talking about their pets. I'd brought photos of Felix, Clarabel and the kittens just in case.

I was early; I collected the key from the caretaker and opened up the hall twenty minutes before the class was due to start. There was no one waiting in the tiny car park, but that was to be expected. They'd all be local, and turn up just at the last minute, perhaps walking here. *If* anyone turned up. I felt like a kid anxiously awaiting my own birthday party, terrified that no one would attend. But Pascal from the *mairie* had said he'd come, and he'd seemed sure there were plenty of people who'd be interested. In my mind, a class of six to eight would be perfect.

Enough to show there was a demand for this, but not so many that I couldn't remember everyone's names.

The *salle des fetes* was like small function halls anywhere – stacks of chairs and fold-up tables along one side of the room, a tiny stage, a little kitchen area in which coffee could be prepared and mugs washed up afterwards. Being France, there was a decent capsule coffee machine and a large pot of capsules, with an honesty box – 50c for a coffee. I'd brought biscuits, and there was a cupboard housing an assortment of small coffee cups.

I set out some chairs around a table, picked one for myself, and laid out paper and pens. I was pleased to see a clock on the wall that would allow me to keep an eye on the time. Then all I could do was sit and wait for people to turn up.

Pascal was the first to arrive, and he brought with him three friends, all around his age. I was delighted to see him. If no one else came, at least there were four, enough for a lively class. But I needn't have worried. A middle-aged couple came next, and a couple of teenagers were pushed giggling through the door by their parents.

Once everyone was settled, I made a short speech in French that I had prepared. Basically, I said that this was the only French I intended speaking, as I wasn't very good at it, and that we would use English for the whole session. And then I introduced myself in English.

'My name is Lu Marlow, and I live in the château up the valley with my husband and friends. I moved to France three months ago. I have a dog called Felix and I love to walk in the mountains. I hope we can use this class to help you learn English and to make friends. Now, please could each of you tell us a little about yourselves?'

We went around the table and each person did as I'd asked. Pascal and one of his friends had the best English – I felt there wasn't much they would learn but the practice would be good for them. The teenagers were the worst. They were here, they said, because their parents said it would help them pass their school exams. The middle-aged couple were planning to take a motorhome on an extended trip to Britain and Ireland the following year.

It all went well, the mix of people helped, and the first hour flew by. We broke for coffee, and stood around in the little kitchen chatting while we waited for the coffees to brew. I had to give stern glances to the different groups as they lapsed into French chatter.

'If you are stuck for an English word, use the French but then try to continue your conversation in English,' I told them. 'Or try to find another way to say it.'

We talked about pets for the second half, as planned. One of the teenagers spoke for a long time about a cat she knew from school that'd had kittens, and it was after some time that I realised Steve's kittens, Flip and Flop, had come from this litter. She was delighted to hear how well they were doing and how they had asserted their authority over poor Felix within moments of meeting him.

When it was time to pack up they all helped with the washing up and putting away of the tables and chairs. I was delighted how well it had gone, and had lots of suggestions (from them all) for topics for future sessions. All were planning to come back the following week, although I had the impression I'd only see the teens until their exam came around, then they'd be off.

'It went well, yes?' Pascal said, as we stacked the last chairs.

'I thought so. What did you think?'

'I think it was excellent,' he said, and I smiled. 'And I think I will like a session to talk of local history.'

'I *would* like a session,' I corrected him. 'I'd like that too. I'm very interested in the local history, especially anything relating to the château or the people who lived there around the time of the Revolution – the Aubert family.'

'I studied history at university,' he said. 'I have some books on the history of this place.'

My eyes lit up. 'I'd love to borrow them, if I may?'

'Of course. But they are in French. I could help you understand them, perhaps? In return for these English lessons.'

'*Parfait!*' I said, grinning. A perfect swap.

'If you come to the *mairie* tomorrow I bring the books for you.'

'I *will* bring the books.' I was still in teacher mode and couldn't help but correct him again.

'I will bring the books,' he said with a smile. '*Au revoir*, Madame Marlow, and thank you.'

I called at the *mairie* as Pascal had suggested the next day. He handed me a box full of history books, in which he'd helpfully inserted Post-it notes in the pages where Saint Michel-sur-Verais was mentioned, or Château d'Aubert.

'You can take them home, and perhaps after the next English lesson I can explain them to you,' he said.

'Great idea. Thank you so much!' Now I had homework too.

'Also I think there are records in the church that might be helpful.'

I stared at him. Of course – just like in England the church would have records of baptisms, marriages and burials. At least from before the Revolution. After that, when the revolutionaries had tried to remove all power from the church, there would be civil records.

'Thank you! I will go and enquire.'

'And from after 1792 there are records here in the archive,' he said. I detected a glint in his eye. Pascal looked as keen as I was to find out more about the Auberts. And he didn't know yet about the mysterious window in the tower, or the face in that window ... I decided to wait and talk about those later, in case he thought I was just some mad old Englishwoman.

'An archive! Brilliant! May I look at it now?'

He glanced at the clock, and then nodded. 'Yes. I have time now to help you. Come this way.'

He led me upstairs, into a room that was lined with shelving filled with box files. I thought he was going to start pulling down boxes but instead he sat at a computer in one corner, and pulled up a chair for me. 'Our records are online. I show you.'

I grinned. It was always so much easier when records had been digitised. And indeed, starting from the date of the French revolution, within a few minutes he'd found records of baptisms for two Aubert children – Michel and Jeanne, in 1792 and 1793. Their father was listed as Pierre Aubert and their mother as Catherine Aubert. 'You've found them already!' I said, and Pascal smiled.

'I am sorry but I must return to work. I show you how to make the search, and then you can continue, yes?' He showed me how the website worked and left me to it. I had a notepad and pen in my pocket and began making notes. Civil records had begun in 1792, and before that there were the local church records, all digitised. It was thrilling to discover these two children. And then I found Pierre Aubert's burial record from 1794, and the burial of a child named Louis Aubert in 1791 – the other name on the Aubert tomb. Louis must have been Michel and Jeanne's older brother. The poor mite had died as a baby. Nothing more for Catherine. I searched for marriages and deaths but there was nothing. She'd vanished, or maybe moved to a different *département* or even a different country.

Giving up on Catherine, I searched for her children, Michel and Jeanne. Had Michel grown up and inherited the château? Unlikely. It would have been seized by the State in 1793 or 1794, around the time of Pierre's death. Maybe searching for the children was pointless, as their father had died and I couldn't find their mother. They were so young at the time of their father's death. If Catherine had survived, the children would have gone with her, wherever she went.

Yet … after a bit of searching, I found a marriage for Jeanne, some twenty years later. And another for Michel. Both had stayed in the local area and married local people – Jeanne's husband was a baker, and Michel's wife's father was the local miller. So the children at least had integrated into the local society – renouncing their nobility as was necessary after the Revolution. What had become of their mother, though? Perhaps I'd never know.

I jotted down all the details and all the many questions which occurred to me. It would be interesting to try to trace Michel and Jeanne forward. Had they had children? If Michel had a son, that would mean a continuation of the Aubert name. There were no more Aubert names on the tomb in the cemetery after Pierre's, but perhaps there'd been no one able or willing to pay to use that grave plot after the Revolution.

It was Catherine who was getting under my skin, though. She'd lost her husband, but what had happened to her? She had been the last of the aristocratic Auberts. Her children had survived to adulthood, but she seemed to be nowhere in the records. Another mystery.

Time was getting on, and I had errands to run and dogs to walk, so I closed down the website and went back downstairs. Pascal was busy with someone else, so I sat to wait until he could spare a moment.

'Did you find what you want?' he asked.

'I found some interesting things, but of course there are always more questions than answers.' I told him about the Aubert children and the lack of information on Catherine Aubert.

'Maybe she was a … *emigré* … sorry I do not know the English word.'

'We often borrow the French word! Yes, I think perhaps she left the country. But why did she not take her children with her?'

'Maybe she think they are safer here in the village.' He gave a Gallic shrug.

'You may be right. Well, perhaps I can continue to search for them, now I know the websites to use. I'll read your books too, and see you next Tuesday.'

'*Bon chance,* Madame Marlow, *et au revoir.*'

As I left, I reflected on how Clemmie's suggestion that I try teaching English had led me to Pascal, who'd led me to the archives. Making an effort to fit into the community and keep myself busy had helped me progress my research project. Funny how things worked out.

The sun doesn't always shine in the south of France. We discovered that over the next week, when the wind picked up and storms raged over the whole Alpes-Maritimes area. Apart from dashes to the village in the car to buy bread we pretty much stayed in the château, even lighting a fire in the wood-burning stove one day when it felt decidedly cooler. Even the ghost, if ghost it was, seemed miserable, howling at us down the chimney, playing havoc with the electricity despite Steve's efforts to get it fixed. The lights flickered endlessly in the evenings.

Phil sat beside the patio door, looking disconsolately at his garden where much of his late summer produce was being flattened by the rain. 'I should have harvested the last of my lettuces,' he said. 'They'll be mush.' He'd brought Clarabel into the stables and provided her with straw bedding. She still had plenty of kitchen scraps to eat daily, and Phil paid her regular visits to scratch her ears and top up her food bucket. She didn't seem to care about the weather. As long as she had plenty to eat, she was happy.

The same could not be said of Felix. Or me. We longed to be able to get out into the mountains. I tried a short walk, but the paths were muddy and slippery as torrents of water gushed down the mountain sides. It seemed unsafe, and all it achieved was to give me another job to do – bathing Felix. I decided to stay home and concentrate on researching Pierre and Catherine's descendants instead.

It took a lot of work. Even though the *département's* records were all online, it's always more difficult to trace a person forwards in time rather than backwards. If you are going backwards, you know that a person who died or got married must have been born, so there must be a birth record for them. And that person certainly had parents, who probably married and definitely were born, so they too can be traced. But going forward, looking for what happened to a person after they were born is far harder. Did they marry and change name, move away, or die? They could have died at any time, as a baby or as a ninety-year-old. Did they have any children? But with diligence I gradually began to find some details for both Michel and Jeanne Aubert. I'd already found that they'd stayed in the village and married – this had meant a change of name for Jeanne of course. They had children – four for Jeanne and three for Michel, so then there were a host more names to follow. Sadly some of the children died in infancy. But I kept at it and gradually a chain emerged, with some lines dying out if a person had no children and others disappearing – presumably people who'd moved away.

'Have you bought shares in Sellotape?' Gray asked, when he came into the dining room where I was working, and saw my sheets of A4 taped together, with the Aubert family tree scrawled all over it.

'Not yet. But I might. Look, this is the Auberts' family tree.'

'The who?'

'The people who lived in this château around the time of the French Revolution. Pierre Aubert had been Comte de Verais until the revolutionary government abolished the nobility.'

'Oh! Cool. Is this what Aimée was helping you with?'

I smiled as I noted the goofy look he took on at the mention of Aimée's name. 'She gave me some pointers, then her assistant Pascal has helped too.'

'What are you hoping to find?' Gray sat down beside me, studying the papers.

I shrugged. 'Not entirely sure. What I really want to know is what happened to Catherine Aubert. Her children stayed in the village but I can't find any death record for her. It's as though she vanished.'

'Moved away? Married again and changed her name?'

I shook my head. 'I've checked for a marriage. Can't find her on any French genealogy website. She may have moved to another country, but why leave her children?'

'Maybe they were grown-up?'

I frowned. 'When their father died, in 1794, they were just babies. I'm kind of assuming Catherine disappeared or moved away around that time, too. Almost certainly she'd have stopped living here – the château would have been seized by the State. But I suppose you could be right. Maybe she just lived quietly somewhere locally until her children were grown and then moved to another country.'

Gray stood up. 'The simplest explanations are usually the right ones, even if they're boring. Cup of tea?'

'I'd love one.' Yes, boring, but probably right. There was me wanting an explanation for our ghost. Maybe it was Pierre after all. Though that face at the window had seemed female to me, somehow.

Thankfully the weather the next day was back to business as usual, with the sun shining, the sky blue, but just a slight nip in the air reminding us autumn was just around the corner.

'Come on, boy,' I said to Felix who was lying on the kitchen floor, head on paws, moping because he hadn't had a decent walk for a couple of days. 'Let's go back to *le petite ferme* and check it out some more.' I had a feeling that the farm was somehow connected with Catherine. The clues I had fitted – the date of the map I'd seen it on.

Felix was of course delighted by the suggestion, so very soon we were out, tramping along the path, a pair of secateurs in my pocket so I could trim back some of the undergrowth and get a better look at the structure. The dog bounded ahead of me along the path. I trusted him now to come when he was called, so there was no need to put him on the lead when we were out in the countryside. Unless there were sheep around, and even then he seemed to ignore them.

We reached the little bridge, crossed it, and then we were at the farm. Felix ran on up the path so I had to call him back. 'We're going to hang around here for a short while, all right?' I gave him a dog treat, then he began happily sniffing around the broken-down walls of the little building. I followed him, tracing the remains of the walls, running my fingers over the stonework, trying to imagine what it looked like when complete, with a little thatched roof, doors and windows. Had it been furnished at all, I wondered? I went inside the little structure and crouched down among the undergrowth, feeling on the ground to see if there were any remains of a floor. Felix came in too, sniffing, and then began scrabbling at one corner, pushing his nose into the foliage, scratching at the ground. He'd obviously spotted something he wanted to dig up. I left him to it, and went round the outside, cutting back some of the shrubs that were close to the walls. My thoughts ran to Marie Antoinette's hamlet at Versailles, where she'd 'played' at being a shepherdess.

'Imagine if this was something similar,' I whispered. 'If Catherine was trying to emulate the Queen.'

Felix gave a little woof, then emerged from the tiny building with something in his mouth.

'What've you got there, eh?' I asked him, holding my hand out.

He dropped it at my feet. Whether he wanted me to inspect

it or use it for a game of Fetch I didn't know, but it made me squeal. He'd dug up a bone. A sizable one. I crouched down to look at it more closely, not wanting to pick it up. I'm a bit squeamish about bones. What was it from?

Thoughts of the missing Catherine Aubert flooded through my mind. What if she'd also been running from the mob, as Pierre had, and had hidden in the little farm? Could she have stayed in there, undetected, dying from some injury, being covered in time by vegetation? I shuddered. What a horrible way to die. I went back into the little building and kicked around cautiously in the corner where Felix had been digging. There were definitely more bones there.

Chapter 24

Pierre, 1794

Spring arrived, the snow began to thaw, and Pierre stepped up his plans to take his family out of France and into Switzerland for their own safety. He had written to his cousin to tell him to expect them. He had sewn most of Catherine's jewels into pouches hidden inside their clothes – the clothes of ordinary bourgeois merchants. He had a small carriage stocked with provisions stored in a barn further down the valley, all ready to go. He was waiting only for Catherine to recover from a slight fever she'd had for a week or so, for his own health to improve and give him a respite from the chest pains that had plagued him on and off for years, and for the roads to become more easily passable. He had breathed not a word of his plans to anyone, not even the most loyal of their servants. Not even Claudette or Henri. You could not know who to trust in these turbulent times.

And then, one day as he was making lists of provisions to take with them, Henri knocked on his study door and entered without waiting for permission.

'Sir, they are coming. You must hide, or I fear ...' The old man looked flustered and was out of breath.

'Who's coming?'

'A mob. Many people from the village. Someone has informed on you – said you are an anti-revolutionary. They're saying too that you were part of the old King's Court. They accuse you of aiding an enemy of the State – the old priest. They want blood, sir. Yours. Come quickly!'

Pierre cursed. 'From which direction are they coming?' He was thinking hard. Could they get to the carriage he'd hidden unseen, and before the mob reached the château?

'Directly up the road from the village. They will be here in minutes. You can escape them perhaps by the high path, from the top of the garden …' Henri was wringing his hands. Pierre realised that he too might be in danger, for his loyalty to the family. Claudette too. And what of Madame Bernard? Or had she been the person who'd betrayed them?

Pierre leapt to his feet. 'Henri, you must go. Leave by the high path, as you suggest. Get to a friend's house.' He took the old man's hands in his and kissed his cheeks. 'And thank you, dear friend, for your loyal service over all these years. I pray to God we will meet again.'

Henri nodded, overcome with emotion. 'Get those babies away to a place of safety. Send them with Claudette, to her mother's, perhaps.' Then he turned and hurried out of the room.

Pierre followed, in search of Catherine who was in her bedchamber, still recovering from her fever. He burst into the room. Thankfully she was alone. He knew there was no way she would be able to rouse herself, get dressed, and then walk that high path out of the château grounds. No, he had another plan to guarantee her safety. One he'd planned for years, should this sort of occasion arise.

'Catherine, we must hide! Henri tells me a mob are coming for us. We must put our plans in action, but we cannot get to the carriage today. We need to hide for a day or two first, until we can slip away.'

'Pierre, I am so unwell, I cannot …' His wife's eyes were wide with fear, and she clutched her bed shawl tightly around her shoulders.

'You are improving, and in a few days you will be well enough to travel. Until then we must hide.'

'Where? Oh – in the little farm, perhaps?'

He shook his head. 'No. That would not work. We will hide within the château – there is a place.'

'But they will find us …'

Pierre shook his head. 'No they won't. There is a secret place. I had it built soon after we arrived here, in secret. The entrance is well concealed. Come. Come quickly.' He tugged on her hand to get her to leave her bed.

'The children. What of the children?'

'I will send them with Claudette. To her mother's. Claudette is loyal. The mob will not harm babies, I am sure of it. I will ask Claudette to bring them to us, at the barn where the carriage is stored, when it is safe for us to leave. Do not fear, my love. All the preparations are in place. But hurry now – we have only minutes before the mob come.' He opened her jewellery casket, and grabbed the jewels that had been left in there, stuffing them into his pocket.

'Don't send the babies with Claudette alone! She cannot carry two of them, and Michel cannot walk that far!' Catherine was slipping her feet into shoes and gathering shawls as she spoke. Pierre realised she was right – Claudette could not carry two children.

'I will go with Claudette. By the high path – the one that leads past your little farm. We can carry a child each, and then I shall come back for you.'

'I'll be alone in the château when the mob come? Pierre, no, I can't!'

'They'll soon leave when they think no one is here. Come now.' He led her by the hand out of her room, along corridors to the tower, up the narrow spiral stairs to the circular tower room. There he moved a cabinet and pushed aside a tapestry. Behind was a door concealed in the wooden panelling. He led her through it, up another set of stairs and through a door into a tiny circular room at the top. It was furnished with a thin mattress on the floor, a pile of blankets, a large pitcher of water and a basket of food – all of which Pierre had religiously replaced each week since he'd had the room built, ready for just this occasion.

'Who betrayed us, Pierre?' she said, as he settled her onto the mattress. 'Was it Madame Bernard? She has always hated me. And she overheard me saying I still loved the Queen.'

'I don't know. Possibly.'

'How could she?'

'Ssh. Now, stay quiet, and don't come out of this room until I return, whatever happens. Lock the door. Open it only to me. Promise me, my love? I will take the children to safety and rejoin you here as soon as it's safe for me to re-enter the château. I will tell Madame Bernard we are hiding in Père Debroux's cottage. If it is she who has betrayed us, she will direct the mob there.' He held her tight, kissed her, and smoothed her hair away from her forehead. She looked so vulnerable here in her nightie, her hair undressed, her face not made up. Still, so beautiful. He felt he had never loved her as much. And yet he must leave her now.

There was no time to lose. As he left the room, Catherine called out to him. 'Tell Michel and Jeanne I love them very much, won't you?'

'I will,' he replied, his voice choked with emotion. 'But you will be with them again very soon, my love.'

He closed the door at the top of the hidden stairs, descended, closed the concealed door, behind the tapestry and pushed back the chest that helped hide its location. And then he ran to the nursery, where Claudette was caring for Michel and Jeanne.

'Claudette! Come quickly! We must take the babies and go. It is not safe here for any of us.'

Claudette's eyes were wide, but she scooped up Jeanne without a word, and also grabbed a basket which she hooked over one arm. Pierre picked up a squealing Michel and bade her follow him. 'We will go out through the gardens, and along the high path. Will your mother help?'

'She will. She would not see children harmed,' Claudette said.

They were almost out, unseen, when suddenly Madame Bernard appeared, coming out of the kitchen corridor. She gasped when she saw them. 'What is happening? Henri says there's a mob coming …'

Pierre thought quickly. Her terrified reaction seemed genuine but he had no idea whether he could trust this woman. He'd tell her a partial truth. 'Claudette is taking the babies to her mother's. Madame Aubert and I will hide.'

'Where will you hide?' Claudette asked.

'The priest's cottage,' Pierre replied. The cottage was in the opposite direction to where he had stored the carriage, and a good twenty minutes' walk away. By the time the mob had been there and found no one, he and Catherine might be able to make their escape.

Madame Bernard nodded. 'I am leaving too. It is not safe for me here. Good luck, Monsieur Aubert.' To his surprise she curtsied, and her eyes were shining with tears.

'Sir, we must go,' Claudette said, and indeed Pierre realised he could already hear chants and shouting coming from the lane that led to the village. At least Catherine was safe in the tower.

With a child each in their arms, Pierre and Claudette hurried out of the back of the château, across the gardens and out through the gate that led onto the hillside. The path was wet underfoot from the snow's meltwater, and badly maintained, since Catherine had given up her interest in the little farm. Claudette was struggling a little, trying to carry the basket she had snatched up along with Jeanne. He was struggling too – his chest was painful and he was struggling to catch his breath. Even so, he reached out a hand to help Claudette.

'Here, let me take the basket,' he said. 'What is in it?'

'Some things for the children,' she replied, as she handed it to him. 'Clothes, their toys, a little food.'

'How did you come to have it all ready to go?' Pierre said, frowning.

Claudette stuttered a little as she answered. 'I-I have been fearing something like this for a while … I had it ready … and my mother is expecting us. Monsieur, you will then go to the priest's cottage?'

'Yes, to meet my wife there,' he replied carefully. How had the girl had the foresight to pack a basket? Had she known something in advance about the attack? Had Madame Bernard told her? Or …

'Claudette, you are loyal to us, are you not?'

'O-of course, Monsieur, of course.' Claudette stumbled a little as she spoke, over an exposed tree root that ran across the path. Pierre put out a hand to steady her, but she flinched at his touch.

'I am wondering who it was that betrayed us. Madame Bernard, perhaps? She has made no secret of her dislike of Madame Aubert, at least.'

'Oh, no Monsieur, it was not her,' said Claudette forcefully.

'Who, then?' Pierre shifted the weight of Michel on his hip and hoisted the basket up his arm.

'I do not know. Monsieur, we must hurry,' she said, and strode forward, hoisting Jeanne up against her shoulder. 'The people will not harm your children. It is only you and Madame they want. I heard talk in the village. They will put you on trial. But your children will be safe with my *maman* and me. Trust me.'

He had to trust her. And he had to hope that the mob would

give up when they found both the château and the priest's cottage apparently empty.

It was almost an hour before they reached Claudette's mother's house, on the far side of the village, part way up the hillside. It had been slow going, burdened as they were with the children, who had both cried throughout much of the journey. They'd had to hide from villagers a couple of times, once darting into a stable, hands over the children's mouths, once into bushes as a group of labourers passed by, and once in Catherine's little farm. At last they reached a rough cottage, its door covered with peeling blue paint, its shutters firmly closed. Claudette led him round to the back of the cottage and in through a second door.

'*Maman*? We are here,' she called out, and a stooped woman with white hair stepped forward. Pierre guessed that despite her appearance the woman was probably only about fifty. Younger than himself. Peasants aged quicker than aristocrats, it seemed.

'And these are the babies? Come to *Grand-mère, mes petits*,' cooed the old woman. 'And who is this?' She waved a finger at Pierre.

'The babies' father,' Claudette said, and Pierre noticed a look pass between the women.

'Thank you for taking the children,' he said, forcing his voice to remain calm. 'I will pay you, of course.' He pulled out a bag of coins, it wasn't much, but all he had with him. 'There will be more, when I am able to access it. I will return for the children as soon as I am able.'

Claudette took the money from him and tucked it into the basket. 'Your children will be safe with us. Now, go to your wife. Good luck, Monsieur.'

Her voice wobbled on the last words. Making a sudden decision, Pierre pulled out a handful of Catherine's jewellery and passed it to her. 'In case I-I can't return, for some reason.' She stared at him and nodded silently.

240

He planted a kiss on each child's head, realising that Catherine had not had a chance to do the same. 'Michel, Jeanne, your parents love you, and we will return for you as soon as possible. Be good for Claudette, now.'

'Papa, don't go! Please!' squealed Michel, clinging to Pierre's coat.

'Papa must go. It won't be long before I return for you.' With a breaking heart, Pierre prised his son's fingers away and left the cottage without looking back, praying silently that he would be able to keep his promise and return soon. When the mob failed to find them at the château or priest's cottage, and found out where the children had been taken, surely they'd watch Claudette's mother's cottage? He and Catherine might have to go into exile alone. Pierre realised it might be a very long time before he'd see his children again.

Chapter 25

Lu

Felix helpfully carried the bone he'd found in the little farm back to the château for me, as my aversion to bones meant I couldn't bring myself to handle it.

'What's the dog got there?' Phil said, as we came through the gate in the back of the garden. 'A bone? Give it here, boy.' He held out his hand and Felix obediently dropped the bone at Phil's feet. He picked it up. 'Hmm. A sheep's femur, I'd say.'

'Sheep?'

'Most likely, if you found it up the mountain.'

I stared at the bone. Had I honestly been hoping – or fearing? – that it might be human, and possibly belong to Catherine? I was daft. How could her remains have stayed undiscovered in that little farm building for over two hundred years? Of course it was the bone of some animal who'd taken shelter in there and then died. Probably in the last year or two.

'Well, Felix was very proud of having found it,' I said, but the dog had lost interest in it now, and was prancing around Clarabel, trying to provoke her into butting him.

'I'll break it up and chuck it on the compost,' Phil said, tossing it onto a pile of garden waste.

I went inside, my mind still on Catherine Aubert. Maybe I'd just Google her, and see what turned up.

I made myself a cup of tea, fired up the laptop and began running Google searches on the names 'Pierre Aubert' and 'Catherine Aubert'. They threw up a number of matches; some I was able to discount quickly. A Pierre who lived in Canada and worked for an electric company; a Catherine who'd put numerous photos of herself with a small dog on Facebook. But in among the misses were some hits – mentions of the Auberts in a number of blogs about the area, and in Wikipedia articles about the French court. I read them all. The ones about the French court intrigued me – had my Auberts been a part of Louis XVI's court, then? I'd assumed they had spent all their time in the Alpes-Maritimes, and it was too far from Paris to be able to make easy, regular trips to Paris or Versailles.

'Maybe they came here to the ancestral home to escape the Revolution,' I muttered to my laptop.

'Hmm? What's that?' Gray said. He was sprawling on a sofa, feet up, reading a cycling magazine he subscribed to.

'The Auberts. Seems they were part of the royal court.' I guessed she and Pierre travelled to Saint-Michel-sur-Verais during 1789 or 1790. After the 'women's march' on Versailles in the autumn of 1789, the royal family had been taken into Paris and held under house arrest in the Tuileries Palace, and around that time many other nobles had gone to their country residences or into exile. Maybe this was what the Auberts had done.

I clicked on another link, and gasped. 'Oh, wow!' It had led me to a photograph of a painting held in the Louvre. 'Come and look at this, Gray!'

He grunted as he heaved himself upright and came to look over my shoulder. 'Who's she?'

'Catherine Aubert!' The caption was *Catherine Aubert, Comtesse de Verais, in Versailles, painted 1786.* The picture showed a woman in typical costume for an aristocrat in the late eighteenth century – her gown was a confection of frills and lace and ribbons, her hair elaborately piled on her head and decorated with more bows and flowers. Her face was oval, with a beauty spot on one cheek, possibly painted on. The portrait had that agelessness of so many from that era – Catherine could have been any age from fifteen to fifty-five when it was painted. But still I thought I could detect a haughtiness in her eye, pride at her place in the world, disdain for the lowly artist who was capturing her image. Or was it simply the fashion of the time, to give portraits an expression of aloofness? Gazing at her picture, I wanted more than ever before to discover what had happened to her and her children.

'Excellent!' Gray said. 'Now you have a face for the name.'

'Yes. I just need to find out what happened to her.' It'd be lovely to resolve one of my mysteries. That made me wonder about the tower room – work had begun on replacing the floor. I decided to pop upstairs and check on progress.

A carpenter was at work on the second-floor landing – cutting new joists to strengthen the floor. We'd had it all treated for woodworm, and the carpenter had pulled up and disposed of the old floorboards. I couldn't enter, but standing at the top of the stone stairs I could look around the room.

'Hey, Lu,' Steve said, as he came to join me, having handed the carpenter a cup of coffee to keep him going.

'Pleased with progress?' I asked.

'Yes, he's doing well. It'll be done in a week.' He clocked me grinning, and smiled back. 'I know you're desperate to get in there again, Lu.'

I nodded. 'I am, yeah. Did the carpenter find anything? Under the old floorboards, perhaps?' I don't know why but I'd had this vague idea there could be some clue there.

'No. Just dust and dead spiders. Sorry to disappoint.'

I wasn't sure what I had been hoping for. A lace handkerchief with Catherine Aubert's initials. A diary, tucked under a loose floorboard, detailing Pierre's fears of what might happen to his family as the Revolution progressed. A child's rattle, that might have belonged to one of Catherine's children. Perhaps I'd been reading too many novels. Real life was never quite so exciting, even when you lived in a château which had a mysterious window in its tower.

Later that evening, Gray and I were sitting outside, enjoying the last of the sunset. The evenings were getting cooler and the rest of the gang had gone inside to put a DVD on. Gray and I had decided to finish the bottle of wine and watch the stars come out. We'd grabbed fleece blankets from the sofa to curl up in.

'You really like Aimée, don't you?' I said.

He nodded. 'I do, yes.'

I smiled. 'She's perfect for you, I would say.'

He nodded again and bit his lip.

'Gray? Is there a problem?'

He shrugged. 'It's easier, sometimes, to not find a perfect woman. I mean, we had this all sorted – the five of us, moving here, living a fabulous life all together. And then ... Aimée comes along, and ... Lu, I'm all confused.'

'You can have us *and* Aimée,' I said. 'We're not mutually exclusive.' I was wondering if perhaps one day he'd want to move in with Aimée, in which case we'd need to buy out his share of the château, or if he'd want her to move in with us. Which would not be a problem as we had loads of space and she was a lovely person to be around. Maybe I'd get some fashion tips from her.

'I know, I just don't know quite how ... or if ...' He shrugged again.

'How to commit?'

'Er, yeah. I guess that's it. Never been very good at it, since Melissa …'

'Not sure you ever fully committed to her, either.' He'd never married the mother of his daughters and had managed to keep up a pretty independent lifestyle even when he was living with her.

'No, probably not. But Aimée – she's different.'

'She's amazing.'

'Yes.'

'Your girls loved her, too.'

'Yes.'

'Does Aimée like you as much as you like her?' I thought I probably already knew the answer to this, but it would be good to hear it in Gray's words. He took a sip of wine before answering.

'Yes. Think she does. Actually, Lu, I think we are both in love.' I glanced at him. Either he was blushing or the last of the sunset was reflecting in his face.

'That's wonderful. Here's to love.' I raised my glass and clinked it against his.

'So … what next?'

'That's the problem. I don't know. I don't know how to do this next bit.'

'Hmm. You've had too many years of keeping girlfriends at arm's length,' I said, gently.

'Yeah.' There was a sadness, a regret in his voice as he answered me.

'I do understand why,' I said, shuffling my chair a little so I was facing him. 'You wanted what was best for the girls. So they didn't have to suffer a stream of potential stepmothers, like you did.'

'There'd probably only have been one.' He pressed his lips together for a moment. 'I messed up with Leanne.'

'That's in the past, Gray. Don't go fretting about that, now.

Think about the future instead. You've a real chance, here with Aimée.'

'I'm scared I'll fuck it up, Lu.'

He sounded like a frightened adolescent. I put my hand on his knee, and he grabbed it with both of his. 'You won't. Just … follow your heart. Wherever it leads.'

'But the girls … need stability …'

'They're grown up. They don't live with you any more – they'll make their own stability. All they want is your happiness.'

'And you lot …'

I grinned. 'We are also grown-up. You might have noticed. We can cope if you bring Aimée here for a night. We can cope if you stay away at hers for a night. We can cope if the two of you go away on a holiday together.'

'A holiday …' he said, as if the idea had never occurred to him before.

'Yes – holidays with your partner are a good way of finding out how compatible you are when you are together twenty-four seven.' It felt like I was coaching a teenager in his first relationship.

'We can also cope, Gray, if you and Aimée decided you wanted to live together.'

'What, here?' He seemed horrified.

'Or at hers. Either. There are ways we could make it work. Not that I think you should rush anything, but …' I squeezed his hand and made him look at me as I continued. 'You must understand that whatever you choose to do is OK by the four of us. I know I speak for us all. You mustn't let our living arrangements get in the way of your long-term happiness with Aimée. Just keep that in mind, as your relationship progresses, all right? Don't use us and our shared château as an excuse not to get close to her.'

'I think I used to use the girls as an excuse,' he said.

'Yes, you're right, you did. But no need to any more.'

'You're so wise, Lu. Should have listened to you years ago.' I had tried, when he was with Leanne, but we were in our thirties back then and we all thought we knew everything, and Gray was not good at taking advice.

'There you go again, trying to change the past. Gray, you gorgeous boy, you can only shape the future.'

'I can, that,' he said, and now there was laughter in his voice. We clinked glasses once again. I shivered – it was dark now and a chill breeze had got up. 'Shall we go inside? They're watching *Mamma Mia.*'

I rolled my eyes. 'Again. Third time this month, isn't it?' It was Steve's favourite film, and if the rest of us said 'don't mind', it was inevitably the DVD that got put on.

'He'd watch it three times a day if we let him,' Gray said, as he followed me back inside. I smiled to myself. I hoped our little heart to heart had done some good.

The next day I spent more time reading the books Pascal had lent me. They were really helpful, though it took me a long time to read and fully understand the short sections they contained that mentioned the village or the château. The château had originally been built in the seventeenth century, with a large addition built by a Gustav Aubert in the early eighteenth century. I noted his name down – was he Pierre's grandfather perhaps? I'd be able to check on the church records – but then I remembered I had a photo of the Aubert tomb. I opened that up on my laptop and zoomed in on the image. Yes, a Gustav Aubert was listed, above Victor Aubert and Pierre. So almost certainly Pierre's grandfather, judging by the dates.

But what interested me more than when the château was built, was the news that the fire that had totally destroyed the large newer wing happened in 1794. Right around the time Pierre died, during the time of the Terror. Had he perished in the fire, perhaps? And Catherine alongside him? If so, surely her remains would have been found?

The books held no clues. One stated only that the only remaining part of the château was the older, original wing with its tower. The other went into a little more detail, saying that it had been owned by the Auberts but became State property in 1794 after the fire. Pierre was mentioned briefly in this one, as having been the last Comte de Verais and as having died during the Terror. I already knew all this.

So at least now I knew the year the château had burned. None of the books gave any hints as to what had caused the fire.

I decided to take a closer look at the grounds, and the remains of the burned-down wing. Since moving in we'd always taken it a little for granted – there were a few low walls, some flattened gravel areas (including our *pétanque* pitch) but I'd never actually tried to work out the layout at all. I had a photo of the painting of the château in its heyday – the one where the top window of the tower was missing. One of Pascal's books contained a grainy reproduction of that painting too. I studied it closely, noting where the additional wing joined onto the still-existing building, then headed outside to look more closely.

It seemed odd – we'd lived here for months and only now was I investigating in detail the outside of the building. Other than the tower, and that odd extra window, and general glances upwards now and again, I'd never paid a lot of attention to the fabric of the château. But, as I turned right out of the front door and followed the wall around, now that I was looking for clues I could clearly see where a wall had been dove-tailed into the existing one, where remains of mortar that would have sealed the gap between new and old were still attached, and areas of blackened stone on the side of the château where the other wing had been. Also a patch of lighter stone at ground floor level – where I guessed a doorway had been knocked through to link the old and new sections, and then filled in after the fire and the demolition of the burned sections. It seemed amazing that just one wing had burned. Perhaps the fire had spread into the older parts, but just not damaged it so much, leaving it salvageable.

I followed the wall of the château around and looked more closely at our *pétanque* pitch. It was the size of a large drawing room, and the low stonework that surrounded it were clearly the remains of the room's walls. I realised that a recess along one long side, that now housed a bench, had originally been a fireplace. And the gap in the walls we used as an entrance was a doorway. Beyond, I could trace a few more walls but then the stables and garages had clearly been built over the old remains. Actually, now that I looked closely, I realised the back wall of the stables, that was made of stone, had probably been part of the château wing. It too had black marks as testimony to the fire.

I fetched an A4 pad of paper and a pencil and had a go at sketching the floor plan of the remaining bits of wall. My mind kept running on the fate of Catherine and Pierre. Had they been in one of these rooms when the château burned? I shivered as I walked across the *pétanque* pitch. Where we played our games and drank and laughed, one or both of them might have died a hideous death. It was a sobering thought.

My other ongoing project was tracing Catherine's descendants. The family tree had become pretty unwieldy, and I had resorted to transcribing the lot onto some online software. That had taken ages. And the weather had been good, so Felix of course wanted lots of walks. Steve was working his way through the château on his renovation project, and we'd all needed to chip in to help strip old wallpaper, sand the walls, and paint them. Not to mention the English classes which took up quite a bit of my time – preparing plans and taking the lessons. So for a while I'd made no further progress with the research.

Until a day came when the others were all out, choosing paint for Steve and Manda's bedroom which was the current one being worked on. Gray was out with Aimée, and Phil had gone along with Steve and Manda for the ride. Felix had had a walk and was lying contentedly on his dog bed, so I decided to push on with the research. There were a few lines of descent I had yet to follow to the end – either to living descendants or until I got stuck, whichever came first. The one I chose to work on first petered out quickly. Just one more generation on from where I'd left it, brought me to a family with just one son who'd died in 1944, fighting for France's liberation. Next, I chose a line that had originated from Jeanne Aubert. She'd had a number of grand-children born in the 1850s and 60s, and although I'd come to dead ends with most of these, there was one strand still going – a family who'd stayed in the area. One of their daughters, I then discovered, married a man named François Baudin. I gasped as I read the name. It was a surname I knew. But perhaps it was a common one? There could be hundreds of Baudins around. It would surely be too much of a coincidence if this Baudin had any connection to the one I knew.

As though he'd read my mind, Felix came over to nuzzle at me, placing his head on my thigh. 'What do you think, boy?' I asked him. 'Could your previous owner be descended from the Auberts? And wouldn't it be amazing if he was?'

Next step – look for children of François Baudin. The marriage was around 1925, so I was looking for children born after that date, in the area. I was working quickly, fired up now, impatient to find out if there was really a connection. Moving forward from 1925 looking at birth records I found a string of children born to François, including a few who had sadly died as young children. It took a while to work through them all, and I kept telling myself none of them would be 'my' Baudin. But then, as I was about to give up for the day, I found a boy born in 1937 and named Jean-Paul. I felt the hairs on the back of my neck stand up. This was him!

'There he is, Felix! I'm thinking we will have to pay him a visit, won't we?' Monsieur Baudin had been a long time in hospital, with bouts of sickness complicating his recovery from the hip fracture, but Aimée had said he was very soon going to move into a nursing home where I would be allowed to bring Felix to visit him at last. I'd been to the hospital a couple of times to report on Felix's progress, but despite pleading with the nurses there I had not been allowed to take Felix in. Monsieur Baudin had had to be content with the many photos of the dog I had on my phone.

But now there were two reasons to see him as soon as he was discharged – to take Felix and to talk about his ancestry. I couldn't believe it. A descendant of the Auberts, still living locally, and someone I already knew!

Chapter 26

Pierre, 1794

Pierre knew he needed to run, and not be seen, as he hurried back to the château. With luck the mob would have discovered it apparently empty, and would have gone in search of them elsewhere – at the priest's cottage if they'd questioned Madame Bernard. If the château was deserted, he'd be able to slip inside and up to the tower room to rejoin Catherine. When they would be able to leave for good, he didn't know. Neither did he know when they'd be reunited with their children. How he would break this news to Catherine was another unknown, but the most important thing was that the children were safe.

He kept telling himself this as he hurried through the village, keeping out of sight, and on to the high path back to the château that he'd taken with Claudette and the children only minutes before.

But there were people coming down that route now. A handful of men, armed with pitchforks. Men he knew, who'd worked on his farms. They were carrying the flag of the Revolution, the tricolour, and singing a rousing marching song. He ducked into a small barn attached to the side of a cottage on the edge of the village. It was home to a cow, tethered to her stall, and he squeezed in beside her, praying the men hadn't seen him. If they were coming to the village by the high path, it meant they had not been taken in by the pretence that he and Catherine would hide in the priest's house. Perhaps Madame Bernard had told them where he was taking the children, and the mob was hoping to catch him on the way back from Claudette's mother's.

He held his breath as the men passed. He could hear voices, among them some he recognised. Jacques Valet. The doctor. All laughing and jeering as they spoke about what they would do when they found him, how his trial would be swift and his execution by guillotine inevitable.

'All he deserves,' shouted Jacques Valet, as they passed. 'Done me out of my full wages. So much for equality, eh? And his wife – nothing but a cock tease. I should know!' There was raucous laughter at his words.

Pierre wondered what he meant. It was true he'd not paid Valet for a while – when work on the little farm had ceased. But what did he mean by calling Catherine a cock tease? Surely she hadn't … no. He refused to believe she'd had anything to do with such a coarse man. He knew, being so much older than her, and with precarious health, that she would almost certainly outlive him. But he intended making sure that she and the children would be well provided for after his death. He loved her so much.

The men were still shouting. 'Valet – she'll never have you now, after you've denounced her and her feeble husband!'

'I wouldn't have her now if she begged me for it!'

'You won't want her anyway, without her head on her shoulders!'

So it had been Valet who'd betrayed them. Though how Valet had known anything about them, Pierre had no idea … unless Catherine had told the man? Pierre recalled her frequent visits to the little farm after work on it had resumed. But no. She wouldn't have … He shook his head. Even if there had been

254

something going on, during that terrible period after the death of little Louis, that was all in the past. Catherine loved him, and he loved her, and that was all that mattered.

Pierre stayed in the barn until all was quiet, and debated staying longer, but someone would come to milk the cow soon, and besides, she had begun pressing up against him, pinning him between her flank and the side of the stall. Struggling to breathe, he heaved against her and at last she shifted position, releasing him. He squeezed out, checked up and down the lane, and ran once more. Not safe to go by the high path, or via the main road back to the château. There was only one other option – the path along the riverbank, which was seldom used beyond the wash house, and quite overgrown. Plenty of vegetation to hide in, if he needed to. As long as he could fight his way through the undergrowth.

He managed to get to the river path unseen, and started along it, but there were voices behind. He'd been spotted, and the same gang, the one containing Jacques Valet, were running towards him, gaining on him. He began to sprint. The path followed the river around a bend and he'd be out of sight there – perhaps he could find somewhere to hide while they raced past?

The wash house. It was up ahead, and Pierre would reach it before the men came around the corner. He could hide in there – it was a sturdy, stone-built structure that his father had provided for the women of the village to do their laundry in the river. He prayed there'd be no one using it now and darted inside. It was empty, but he quickly decided it was no good as a hiding place. There was no door, and anyone hurrying past only needed to glance inside to spot him.

Looking around in a panic, he realised there was only one option. The wash house had a wooden floor that could be raised and lowered, depending on the height of the river. If he got into the water, underneath the floor, and kept very quiet, making no splashes, then anyone entering the wash house would not see him. There was no time to lose. It was his only chance. If the mob caught him, it would be the end.

He slipped into the river, gasping as the icy water soaked his clothes. The wash house floor was a hand's length above the surface of the river, enough space to breathe. He eased his way under the floor, slowly, trying to disturb the surface of the water as little as possible. Thankfully here it flowed fast enough to cover any ripples he might make. Under the floor he had to turn his head sideways so that his mouth and nose were both above the water, and his head was pressed against the wooden floor. It was desperately uncomfortable, and cold, so very cold! The pain in his chest intensified, feeling like an icy band tightening around his heart. He knew he could not stay like this for long, but hoped he wouldn't need to. Once the mob passed by, he could come out again, and either get back to the château or find some better hiding place to hole up for the night.

'Please God, let Catherine be safe,' he whispered, as he heard the thumps of men's boots, running along the path, getting closer and closer. 'And the children. Please God, look after them.'

And then there was the clatter of boots on the floor above his head, the shouts of the men as they checked the dark corners of the wash house and looked up and down the river.

'He'll not be in the river, this time of year,' said a man. Pierre thought it was the doctor. 'Cold would kill him in minutes. His heart's weak, anyway.'

As if responding to the doctor's words, at that moment Pierre's teeth began chattering with the cold, and he clamped his jaw shut. Too late – a mouthful of river water had got in, and he choked a little, trying not to make a sound that could be heard over the noise of the men and the gurgling river.

'What was that?' a voice called. The voice of a man standing directly above. 'Thought I heard someone coughing …'

'Ah, only old Giraud,' someone else said, and whoever that was obligingly coughed, and the men laughed.

Pierre bit his tongue, trying to stop his teeth chattering and his throat constricting in a cough, and it was cold, so very cold. His hands were numb, the right side of his face, that was in the water due to the way he'd twisted his head on one side, was freezing. The doctor was right – he could not stay like this for long. But the men were still there, he could hear their voices; if he came out of the river now, he would be caught and it would all be over.

'We need to find the bugger,' a voice said.

'Ah, we have old Henri. He'll be on trial for his part supporting them. Only thing that can help him is if he gives us information now that helps us find him, but the old fellow is keeping quiet. That won't go well for him. Wouldn't want to be in his shoes now.'

They had Henri. It made no difference to Pierre – Henri did not know where Catherine was hiding, or anything about their plans to go to Switzerland. But Henri had been a faithful servant for so long – serving Pierre's father before him, and then Pierre himself. He'd been a good friend when Pierre was a child. Pierre sent up a silent prayer that the mob would be kind to the old man. He didn't deserve this.

'Good job we caught the old priest too, before he went over the border. He's to be executed tomorrow. I'm going to see it. Anyone else?'

'Yeah, me too.'

'Nah, unless we've caught Aubert by then. That's more important.'

Pierre shivered. He had hoped that Père Debroux would be found not guilty and released, or at the very worst kept in prison. What kind of new state was this, that it would execute a priest, whose only 'crime' was to stick to his beliefs, putting God above country?

He had no idea of the passage of time. Had he been in the river for minutes or hours? He had forced himself to stay quiet, and stay awake, listening to the sounds above him. After an eternity, with his hands and feet and the side of his face so numb he could barely move them, there were new voices above – women's voices, bantering and joking with the men. And then the men were leaving, calling their farewells, blowing kisses, and the women were giggling.

Could he leave if there were only women there? It sounded like just two women, and even if they were hostile, he'd be able to overpower them. He'd be stronger than them, despite the increasing pain in his chest. When he could no longer hear the men's voices or boots, and judged that only the women were there, Pierre began to ease himself out from under the platform. But his coat was caught in something. In the chains at the edge of the floor, that raised and lowered it. He tugged at it, but it would not come free, and his hands were so cold he could not grip the fabric properly. He needed to slip the coat off, but it was difficult to do this, in the water, while trying to keep his head up in the tiny breathing space.

Worse, and with horror, he realised the floor was being lowered. The women must have brought some washing, and were lowering the platform closer to the water. The pressure on his head grew, forcing his face into the water. He tried to turn onto his back to keep his nose and mouth above the surface, but still the platform lowered and still his coat would not come free, and he couldn't get out of his coat. The water closed over his face, the wooden platform now meeting the surface of the water. He had a lungful of air. He had to get free while that lasted. The icy water numbed the whole of his face, and in a panic he thrashed around, anything to free himself, anything at all, not caring if the women heard him – if they heard him they'd raise the platform, he'd be freed – but his movements were underwater, not breaking the surface, and under the platform wouldn't be noticed. He raised his arms

258

and tried to bang on the underside of the floor, but forcing his numb arms through the water he could not make enough of an impact to be heard, and the water was entering his mouth, the urge to breathe was burning his lungs, great bubbles of precious air left him in a final gasp in which he took in a lungful of water. One last heave at his jacket but to no avail, and then the blackness came and the cold was no more and he slipped into oblivion, his last thoughts being of Catherine and his children.

Chapter 27

Lu

Aimée phoned one evening a couple of weeks later, with the news that Monsieur Baudin had at last been discharged from hospital and settled into a nursing home. He was back on his feet, though he had to use a walking frame now. 'He's ready for visitors, when you have time, and I know he would love to see his friend Felix,' she said.

'Of course,' I told her. 'I'll go tomorrow. I have something else I would like to chat to him about as well, if he is well enough.'

'He is very well in his mind. Just an old body.'

I told her the time I'd be able to go, and she promised to let the nursing home know. It was situated some distance from the village – down in the wide valley where the large supermarket was. Not too far from the hospital he'd been in. I wondered if he'd miss the feeling of being up in the mountains, the views, the clear fresh air. But I guessed he'd find the milder winters at those lower altitudes easier to handle.

The following afternoon I ushered Felix into the car and set off on the drive. I stopped in the village to buy some chocolates and flowers – who knew what Monsieur Baudin would like but

I guessed if they weren't to his taste, the nursing home would be able to give them to someone else. 'You're what he really wants,' I told Felix as I drove down the valley.

The nursing home was an attractive modern building, set in landscaped gardens with small ponds, winding flat pathways and benches placed under shady trees. There was the obligatory *pétanque* pitch and parking for half a dozen visitors. I pulled into a space, clipped Felix's lead on, and led him to the door where a receptionist buzzed me in. She made a fuss of Felix. 'All the residents will be pleased to meet your dog,' she told me, in French.

'He used to belong to Monsieur Baudin, who I have come to see,' I explained, and she grinned.

'He will be the most pleased, then.'

She led me through to a day room where a couple of ladies sat knitting, while an old gent snoozed in front of a TV turned down low. Monsieur Baudin was in a chair beside a patio door that looked out on the garden, and with a view beyond to the mountains, I noted. Felix recognised him immediately and began pulling on the lead, giving a quiet little woof of excitement that alerted Monsieur Baudin to our approach.

'Felix! *Mon Dieu! Mon vieil ami!*' The old man reached out his hands and I let Felix run into them, to be fussed and patted and stroked and nuzzled. Monsieur Baudin leaned down over the dog and rubbed his face against Felix's head. I stood quietly by, watching the reunion. It had been months, but clearly neither had forgotten the other. Felix was turning in small circles, trying to get as close as possible to his old owner, pushing against his legs, head on the old man's lap, licking any part of Monsieur Baudin's skin that came in reach. I couldn't help but smile at the sight, and if there was a tear in my eye, what of it?

'*Merci, Madame! Il a l'air si bien!*'

I nodded. Yes, he did look well. In halting French, I told Monsieur Baudin all about Felix's regular routines, the walks I took him on, the way my four housemates all doted on him too, the way he submitted to the kittens' will at all times. Monsieur Baudin laughed at this, and said, yes, Felix had always been a little wary of anything smaller and furrier than himself.

We chatted happily for a while, until the tea trolley came round. I took a cup of mint tea while Monsieur Baudin had coffee. And then I broached the subject of my research, and my discoveries about his ancestry. He listened intently as I stuttered my way through my explanation, in what I suspected was very poor French. I just hoped he was understanding me.

'So you see,' I finished, 'I think you are descended from the people who owned the château, at the time of the Revolution.'

He nodded. '*Oui.*'

I blinked at him – the way he'd responded was as though he wasn't particularly surprised by my news. 'Did you … already know something of this?'

'Yes,' he replied in French. 'There is a family legend that says our many-greats grandparents were once the Comte and Comtesse. Your château perhaps is mine, then?' He laughed, throwing his head back as he did so, and causing Felix to bark a little in excitement. 'Sssh, Felix! You cannot bark in here, my boy!'

'You are welcome to come and visit your heritage, any time,' I said. I couldn't believe he already knew about this. 'I could collect you and bring you for a visit?'

'Ah, thank you, but I don't travel so well at the moment,' he said. 'And I would not want to take your château. There must be hundreds of descendants since the Revolution?'

'You are the only one I have managed to find. And you, I already knew!' If he'd said something when I'd visited before, perhaps it would have shortened my research. But I'd enjoyed tracing all Catherine's descendants down through the ages, and ending up finding someone who was already a friend was an added bonus.

We chatted a little longer about it all, while Felix settled down for a nap across Monsieur Baudin's feet. Maybe it was my imagination, but between the joy of seeing his dog again and the pride he showed in his ancestry, I felt the old man looked younger, happier, fitter when I left that he had when I arrived. I promised to come again with Felix in a week. Felix whined a little when it was time to go, unhappy at leaving his old master, but Monsieur Baudin whispered something in his ear and then Felix trotted obediently to heel, with a backwards glance as we left the day room.

Felix and I became regular visitors to Monsieur Baudin's nursing home, going to see him most weeks. The dog was always overjoyed to see his old master and would lick his face then sit leaning against his legs while we chatted. It was lovely to see. My French was improving but I still needed to resort to Google Translate every now and again. After a month the old man was able to move out of the nursing home and into his retirement flat where he could live more independently, although he still had carers visiting twice a day. We continued visiting him there – it was a beautiful complex with communal gardens and lounges alongside self-contained flats with a full-time warden on hand.

Monsieur Baudin often had a small job he'd ask me to do for him. Change a light bulb, replace a clock battery, put away some laundry, buy a newspaper. I always did it happily.

'You like being a carer, don't you?' Manda said when I returned from one visit. 'And it's nice that this time it is not taking over your whole life. You're a star, you really are, for what you did for your mum, and then Phil so soon after.'

I laughed. 'Phil doesn't let me care for him any more. I'm not allowed to so much as bring him a cup of tea when he's gardening.'

'He's done so well, recovering. He's really turned himself around.'

'A health revolution. We've all had a revolution of sorts, since moving here, haven't we?'

Manda grinned. 'We have indeed.'

I realised she was right – Phil was as fit as any of us now, and no longer needed any special treatment. And my natural inclination to fuss around people had indeed been transferred onto Monsieur Baudin, someone who both needed and appreciated it. Add to that the satisfaction I had from my teaching job and all in all I felt happy and fulfilled. I just wished I could resolve the mystery of what had happened to Catherine Aubert. She'd really got under my skin.

By mid-autumn, with all the main living rooms and the bedrooms that were in regular use newly painted, Steve turned his attention to the smaller, lesser used rooms. I wondered what he would do once the entire château was renovated, but Phil told me not to worry.

'In a building of this age there will always be some project that needs doing. It'll keep Steve busy for as long as he wants to be. But you never know, he might learn to relax and rest, once he's got all the rooms done.'

I raised my eyebrows. The thought of Steve sitting down and resting seemed entirely foreign. He was always doing something. A great flatmate to have!

'Hey all,' he announced over dinner one evening, 'I thought I'd tackle the little tower room next. What do you think?'

'At last!' I said. I'd been longing for him to get round to that room.

'It's got that damaged, painted panelling in it,' he went on. 'With a bit of paint stripper and some repair work, I think it could be restored. And if we install some wiring up there so we can have lights, I think it'd make a great little snug – a kind of reading den or something.'

Gray frowned. 'Nice idea but how will we get a sofa or any furniture up those narrow spiral stairs?'

'We can get flat-pack bookcases up, and I thought floor cushions or beanbags would work well.'

I smiled. 'I love that idea. It'll be a lovely place to escape to, if someone wants peace and quiet.'

Steve nodded. 'Exactly. So, I bought some paint stripper, and thought I'd get going on that tomorrow. Anyone fancy helping me?'

I put my hand up. 'I've got nothing on. I'll give you a hand.' I had a few spare days and definitely wanted to be there if we uncovered anything. I felt a frisson of excitement. That room held secrets, I was sure of it.

'Fantastic. Right then, we convene at 9am in the tower room, wearing rubber gloves and a face mask.'

'Do I need my own or do you supply them?'

He laughed. 'I bought two sets today. Just turn up and I'll kit you out.'

And so, the following morning after a good night's sleep and a breakfast of croissants and local cheese, I put on my oldest jeans and T-shirt. Phil was going out for the morning – Clarabel was producing more cheese than we could eat now, so Phil delivered the surplus to Monsieur Christophe in the bistro in return for a discount whenever we ate there.

I made my way up to the tower room. 'Ready and reporting for duty, sir,' I said to Steve, with a mock salute.

'Great. Right then, Corporal, first job is to chip off that plaster. See over there, where part of the panelling has been plastered over and it's all cracked? Put these on.' He handed me a set of clear goggles to protect my eyes from flying chips, and a pair of gloves. 'And use this blunt chisel and hammer to gently chip away at it. Should come off fairly easily, you can even pull some bits off with your fingers, see.' He demonstrated, and a large piece of plaster fell away, throwing up a cloud of dust as it landed on the floor.

I coughed, and Steve handed me a face mask to wear as well. 'A dirty job, but worth doing. From what I can see, this panelling could be lovely when we've restored it.'

Once I got started, and discovered the best techniques to use, progress was surprisingly quick. While I chipped off plaster on one half of the room, Steve got going with the paint stripper on the other half, where the panelling had only been painted over. I was glad of the face mask – that stuff stank, and mixed with the plaster dust I was creating the atmosphere in there was pretty awful. We opened the small window as wide as it would go, and thankfully there was a bit of a breeze blowing in to improve the air.

The most difficult part of my job was when I reached the mouldings around the edge of each panel. I had to go carefully so as not to damage it at all, and frequently resorted to picking at it with my fingernails. The plaster was crumbling with age so came away fairly easily, but in chunks of about a square inch each time it was going to be a long job.

We broke for lunch when Manda called up to say there was fresh soup ready (made with butternut squash from Phil's veg patch). We were shouted at for entering the kitchen covered in plaster dust, and Manda pushed us out to the terrace to brush ourselves off. 'We should make you two eat out there,' she grumbled. 'You're filthy.'

'Job's going well though, isn't it, Lu?' Steve said, and I nodded.

Back to work, and after another half-hour I spotted something odd. 'Steve, take a look at this.'

'What?' He put down his paint stripper and came over to my side of the room.

'Looks like a huge crack in the wood panelling. Is that repairable, do you think?'

He ran his fingers along the line I'd discovered, that followed the edge of some moulding. 'I guess so. We'll need to put in some wood filler. Hopefully we can find some that matches the wood. Shame, as that's quite a wide crack.'

He went back to his task and I carried on chipping off the plaster. The crack went all the way down beside the moulding, right to the floor. As I moved up, I realised it went higher too, to near head height. And then I discovered a second crack running horizontally, again just beside a length of moulding.

By the time I had stripped all the plaster from that area I'd found a second vertical crack, parallel to the first, one panel width away. 'Steve, come and have another look. These cracks look deliberate to me.'

He came over again and looked closely. 'Hmm. Yes, it looks almost as though …' He felt his way around the edges of the panel.

'As though what?'

'As though … it's a kind of opening, or something.'

'A hidden doorway?'

'Cupboard, more like. Some kind of priest hole, perhaps? Did they hide priests in France?'

'After the Revolution, some non-conformist priests went into hiding.' I had a sudden thought. 'Steve, you know that mysterious window in the tower, above here?'

'Ye-es?'

'Just wondering if …' Oh God. I couldn't voice it, but my excitement was growing. Was this a secret doorway, that would lead to a way up to whatever was above us?

Steve was tapping at the panelling. 'Certainly sounds like there's a void behind here. See, it sounds different to when I tap the previous panel.' He began pressing around the edges, then picked up a screwdriver and gouged out more plaster from the crack, all the way around. It became obvious it was some sort of door, but one with no handle, no way of opening it. 'Must be some way into this,' Steve muttered, as he kept pressing and pushing, all the way round.

Suddenly, with no warning, the wood creaked and gave way, opening inwards, releasing a cloud of dust that sent us reeling backwards into the tower room. Behind the door, revealed as the dust settled, was a narrow spiral staircase, leading upwards.

Chapter 28

Catherine, 1794

When Pierre closed the door of the little room in the tower, leaving her alone, Catherine felt rising panic. She turned the key in the lock as he'd told her, and leaned her forehead against the wood of the door. She was alone, a mob were coming, looking for her and Pierre, no doubt intent on capturing or even killing them both. Pierre had tried to hide the worst of the news from Paris, but she knew what went on. She'd heard of heads being hacked off and carried on pikes. Of people dragged through the streets tied to horses, until all their skin had been flayed off on the cobbles. Was that to be their fate? All she could do was trust that Pierre was right, that the mob would never find this room, would think the château was deserted and would look for them elsewhere. And she had to have faith that Pierre would return to her, after he'd got the children to safety.

The children. Sweet little Jeanne, not yet one year old and dear, funny Michel. She had not had chance to say goodbye to them, or tell them she loved them. If all went well, she'd be reunited with them within a day or so, but she would have liked to be able to kiss them, cuddle them, reassure them that she'd see them again soon.

'Pierre, my sweet, I hope you do that for me. Tell my babies their *maman* loves them, please,' she whispered. Would it have been better to keep them with her, to bring them up here to hide, rather than split the family? The four of them could have stayed in this little room … Why hadn't Pierre suggested that? But who knew how long they would have to hide. There was very little food and water here, and if the mob came into the château, they'd need to be quiet. No, Pierre had been right to take the children away to Claudette's mother. They would be safer there.

Dear Pierre. He'd only ever had her best interests at heart. She felt deeply ashamed of the resentment she'd felt when she'd had to nurse him after little Louis's death. He'd been a good husband. He was *still* a good husband – why had she thought of him in the past tense? He would return to her, they would survive this, surely? They had to. For the sake of the children.

She sat down on the thin straw mattress that lay on the floor. There was a pile of blankets at one end. She pulled the top one off and wrapped it around her, feeling the chill through her thin nightdress. She shivered. Perhaps she was still feverish. There was a pitcher of water and a cup – she poured herself some and drank thirstily, then stopped herself. How long would that water need to last? When Pierre returned it needed to do for two of them. She poured the rest of the water back into the jug, and set down the cup. Under a cloth was some stale bread, a plate of dried meat and some apples – last year's, their skin wrinkly and unappetising. She was thankful she did not feel hungry.

There was one small window lighting the room. She stood, crossed to it, and peered out. Gasping, she saw the mob approaching the château. They were just a hundred metres down the lane now. There were about a dozen men. They were carrying weapons – pitchforks, and one or two had blazing torches.

What of Madame Bernard? Would she go out to greet them,

to tell them that Pierre's plan was for them to hide in the priest's cottage? If so, would they simply turn around and make their way up the hill to the cottage? She watched from the window, taking care to keep herself as hidden as possible, though she wasn't sure that anyone would see her from down there, even if they did happen to look up.

The mob approached, she could hear chants and yelling, and the leader hammered on the door of the château. From her window Catherine could not see who opened it, but someone must have, or perhaps it had been left unlocked, for the men went inside and she could see and hear them no more.

She tried to imagine what was happening – they'd be splitting up, running from room to room, searching for Pierre and herself. Was Madame Bernard even in the château any more? Catherine risked another glance out of the window, and saw a figure appear from around the back of the château, running back down the lane. It was Madame Bernard. She had hoisted up her skirts and was running as though her life depended on it, looking back over her shoulder. Not the actions of a guilty woman, of an informer in league with the mob. Catherine frowned. Was Madame Bernard not the person who betrayed them after all? Who, then?

Catherine sat down again on the mattress, head in hands, and then on a whim twisted round onto her knees, clasping her hands together in prayer.

'Please let Pierre have got my children to safety,' she whispered. 'And bring him back to me.' How long would it be until the mob gave up here, and went elsewhere to look? If Madame Bernard was not the informer then who would tell them to go to the priest's cottage? With horror she realised Pierre's plan had depended on Madame Bernard betraying them, and telling the mob where to go. Without that, they would search the château more thoroughly, or perhaps go to the village and search there … where Pierre and Claudette had taken the children, and from where he'd be making his way back …

'Don't let them find him, oh Lord,' she added to her prayer. She prayed too for Claudette, her loyal servant, who perhaps she had not always treated as well as she might have. Claudette had been with her for so many years. She was more than just a servant. She was a confidante, an adviser, a friend. And most of all she prayed for her children.

There was nothing more she could do. Pray, wait, hope. She had never felt so helpless. She tried to comfort herself with thoughts of beloved Marie Antoinette, who no doubt had suffered much worse before her execution, and yet by all reports had borne it with dignity. Catherine lifted her chin. Whatever happened, she too would bear it all with her head held high and with as much dignity as she could muster. She pulled in dismay at her nightdress. If only she'd had the chance to dress and arrange her hair. If the mob did find her, she'd have preferred to look her best. It would lend her strength.

But no. They wouldn't find this room. The entrance was well concealed. You had to know it was there. Anyone just walking into the room below would find it empty and see no other way out other than the door they'd entered by. She would be safe.

Even as she told herself this, she heard sounds from below – muffled voices, thumps of boots on the wooden floor, crashes as furniture was knocked over. She kept completely still and held her breath. It all depended on them not searching further, not moving the tapestry, not noticing the section of panelling that was actually a door.

'Don't find the door, please don't find the door.' She mouthed the words, not daring to even whisper them aloud. Sweat was pouring down her – whether from the fever or fear she did not know. Her thoughts a moment ago of wishing she was properly dressed seemed ludicrous now. She was in danger of her life – who cared what she looked like?

And then the sounds below her faded, and all was quiet again, other than a shout or two from outside. They had not discovered the secret door. They had left the tower. She was safe – for now, anyway. She let out the breath she'd been holding and collapsed down onto the thin mattress, exhausted.

She must have slept, for she woke feeling groggy and confused, to sounds of shouting from outside. She hauled herself to her feet, stumbling a little, and crossed over to peer out of the window. There was a crowd outside, cheering and singing. It was late – it was growing dark – but there was a strange glow she could just make out, coming from the newer wing of the château. She craned her neck, trying to see what was happening there, and realised with horror that the château was burning. The mob must have set fire to it – at least to the other wing. She collapsed back onto the mattress in horror. If the château burned, how would Pierre get back to her? Would this older wing, and the tower, burn too? Perhaps not – perhaps the fire would not spread this far. But all their good rooms, the library, the drawing room and dining room, their bedrooms, the nursery – all were housed in the newer, west wing. If the fire really took hold – and it seemed from the glow she could just make out from the tower window that it had – all those rooms would be lost.

Her clothes – for the second time in her life she was to lose all her clothes, all her possessions. Pierre had hidden her jewels somewhere, so that they could sell them when they reached Switzerland. But where had he put them? If they were anywhere in the château, they too might be lost. All she had with her was her garnet wedding ring.

Where was he, anyway? She imagined him hiding some way off, watching helplessly as his home burned and the villagers, once his friends, cheered. She risked another glance out of the window. The mob were all watching the flames, not looking up at the tower. She scanned the crowd for faces she knew, but she was too high up and the light was failing to make out their features. Even so she thought she saw the tall, strong figure of Jacques Valet.

She watched as he brandished a lit torch, shouting something, and realised that he was a leader of this mob. Bile rose to her mouth as she recalled how she had once found this man, who was now calling for her blood, attractive. Thank goodness she had never given herself to him.

Why was it only now, trapped alone in her home, in danger for her life, that she realised how much she truly loved Pierre? How much she had always loved him?

What could she do now? Only wait, hope that the fire burned itself out before it reached the old wing and the tower, pray for her children's safety and then wait for Pierre to return to her. He would do so, as soon as it was possible. She had faith in him. He had never yet let her down. She would not contemplate for a moment the idea that the mob might have caught him.

Another glance out of the window showed the fire was spreading – she could see licks of flames now. It was spreading towards the older parts.

'Not here,' she whispered, 'don't burn here!'

It wouldn't, surely? The old parts were built of stone, surely there was little that could burn. The tower was stone too, only the floors were wooden. And the panelling, and furniture, carpets and tapestries.

With rising horror she realised that wisps of smoke were curling under the door of her room. Pierre had said to stay there, to not leave the tower room until he returned, but he hadn't expected this, had he? She ran to the door of the room, thinking to run downstairs and out of the back of the château. The mob were at the front – she'd be able to get out across the gardens, the same way Pierre had. She could run along the high path and would probably meet him coming back. Yes, that was the answer. That was the right thing to do. No matter that she was in a nightdress and had nothing on her feet. She unlocked the door, grabbed hold of the handle and opened it, then staggered backwards, coughing, as a wall of acrid smoke billowed up the stairs.

Choking, she slammed the door closed, locked it again as though a lock could keep out the flames, and fell back onto the mattress. There'd been no sight of flames on the stairs, but that smoke was too thick to fight her way through. The water – could she use the pitcher of water? Could she wet a cloth to hold over her mouth? She fumbled for it – it was getting dark and the increasing amount of smoke in the room made it hard to see, and then she felt it, but in her confusion knocked it over. She rolled over on the now sodden mattress and covered her face with her hands. The water would not save her. The smoke was still curling under the door, rising and filling the room. She could not stop coughing, as it stung her eyes and the back of her throat. She could only lie here, and wait for the fire to go out and the smoke to clear. This room was to have been her salvation, but it had become her prison cell.

As she pulled a blanket over her, she thought that very likely the room would become her coffin, too. Thank the Lord that it was only her here, and Pierre and the children had got away to safety. As long as they survived, she could accept her own demise. The children were all that mattered. The children … the children … She had not had a chance to say goodbye to them, to hold them one last time, breathe in their baby scent, feel their little arms around her neck. Her children, her reason for existing …

She finally drifted off into a deep, black sleep, thoughts of little Michel and Jeanne with her until the last.

Chapter 29

Lu

Steve and I just stared at each other, and then back at the spiral staircase.

'Why on earth was it hidden? That panelling …' I shook my head in confusion.

'I'm wondering if the entrance was always hidden – maybe it was meant to be secret. Even before the plaster was put on, if you didn't know this part of the panelling opened, you wouldn't know there was a door here. And if a piece of furniture or a wall-hanging was in front of it …'

'Well, are we going up or just going to discuss it?' I said. I couldn't wait to go up and see what was in the room above.

'Sure, but … I need to fetch a torch first. It's pretty dark and that staircase might be unsafe. Stay here – don't go up alone.'

I peered through the doorway at the stairs. They were made of stone, like the ones from the lower floor up to the room we were in. They looked firm enough. A little blackened, as though from soot – had the fire reached here, then? Or the smoke at least? But Steve was right – it was too dark to attempt to climb them with no torch.

He was back in minutes, with Manda, Phil and Gray right behind him.

'Wow, a secret staircase! I feel like suddenly we're in the middle of a *Famous Five* mystery! Where's Timmy the dog?' Gray said, with a laugh.

'More *Scooby Doo*, I'd say,' Phil added. 'Lu can be Velma, Steve is Shaggy.'

'Calm down, chaps. Chances are there's nothing up here. Just a dusty attic room. Don't get too excited,' Steve said.

But I was already extremely excited – something told me this was going to be a significant discovery. The hairs on the back of my neck were all standing on end. 'Who's going up first?'

'You or Steve,' Manda said. 'You found it.'

'All right.' I held out my hand to Steve for the torch. I didn't mind going first.

'I think just one at a time, in case the stairs are fragile,' Manda said.

'They're stone – I think they're OK.' I switched on the torch and shone it up the spiral. It didn't reach far, but I could see the steps looked sound enough. I ducked through the doorway – it was lower than normal – and began ascending, holding the torch in my left hand and feeling my way up the spiral with my right. The stairs turned once, twice, and then stopped. In front of me was a door – wooden, solid but like the stairs, blackened.

I called down to the others. 'The stairs are safe, but up here there's a door.'

'Can you open it?' Phil's voice.

I couldn't see a handle. I shone the torch around the edges, then spotted it. A ring, recessed a little into the wood. I grasped it and pushed – nothing. Pulled (carefully so I didn't topple backwards) – no movement. I tried twisting it, one way and then the other, but no joy. And then I spotted a keyhole, just beneath the ring. 'I think it's locked.'

'Ah, darn it! So near, yet so far.' Gray's voice.

But then I realised there was a strip of light shining from beneath the door. Just a sliver, as though the light from the window was finding its way out. The gap at the bottom of the door was sizable – unlike the door in the panelling, it was not a close fit. I angled my torch through the keyhole and gasped. It looked as though the key was in the lock – the other side. Locked from the inside. Locked by whom?

The gang's talk of *Famous Five* and *Scooby Doo* gave me an idea. Steve had come up behind me – feeling his way and using his phone as a torch.

'Can you get me a sheet of newspaper and some stiff wire – like a coat-hanger or something?' I asked him.

'What for?'

'I think the key's in the lock, the other side.'

He raised his eyebrows but went back down – backwards as there was no easy way to turn around on the narrow spiral. A minute later he returned. I unfolded a sheet of the newspaper he'd brought and pushed it through the crack under the door. It slid through easily enough – nothing stopped it. Shuffling it about I made sure it was right underneath the lock. And then I took the piece of wire – Steve had quickly cut off a length of wire from a coat-hanger – and pushed it into the keyhole, jiggling it about.

'Picking locks a speciality of yours, is it?' Steve asked.

'Not picking it, just trying to push the key out,' I replied.

'Where did you learn this trick?'

'An Enid Blyton book, I think,' I replied, and he laughed. 'I've no idea if it'll actually work.'

But it seemed to be working – I could feel the key beginning to shift, and then suddenly with a clatter it fell out of the keyhole. Had it landed on the newspaper? That was the burning question now. I handed the wire and torch to Steve, and took hold of the newspaper with both hands, tugging it carefully back through the crack under the door. Slowly, slowly. It felt heavier – that meant the key had landed on it and not bounced off. Gradually it came through, and with it, the key. It was a large old iron key, almost three inches in length. 'Bingo,' I said.

'What's going on up there?' called Phil.

'Hold on,' I replied, as I fitted the key into the lock and attempted to turn it.

'Is it working?' Steve asked.

I shook my head. 'Won't budge an inch.'

'WD40?'

'Worth a try.'

So poor old Steve once more went backwards down the stairs, down to our tool store and returned a minute later with a can of WD40. I squirted some oil into the lock, jiggled the key, and had another go. And this time, it worked. The key turned, the lock clicked. I put my hand on the ring and twisted it, pushing at the door, and it opened, stiffly, with a creak and a sigh, as though it was happy to be giving up its secrets at long last.

'It's open,' I said, sounding breathless even to myself.

'Go on, then,' Steve said, giving me a gentle nudge. 'I can't get past you, so you'll have to go in first, but be careful, in case the floor isn't sound. Use your torch.'

'It's well lit.' The sun was streaming in through the little window. The air however smelled stale and musty as I pushed the door open wider. Behind me I could hear the others coming up the spiral staircase, and Steve was right behind me as I took a cautious step into the room. My first impressions were that it was a similar size and shape to the one below. My second was that there was a pile of rags against the far side of the room. I moved away from the door, allowing space for Steve to enter, and looked more closely at the rags.

And then I gave a little scream.

'What is it? Lu, are you all right?' Phil called from the stairs.

'Yes, I'm fine, it's just …'

'What?' Steve was beside me. 'Oh! Oh my God!'

There, on a thin mattress and covered with a rotting blanket, lay the remains of a woman. Her long auburn hair partly covered her face – or what would have been her face. Now it was just a skull, the eye sockets staring blindly at us. Some sort of white fabric covered her upper body, then the grey blanket covered the rest of her. A bony hand lay across her chest. It was as though she'd lain down there to sleep, and never woken up.

'Christ!' Phil, Manda and Gray had all entered the room. Clearly we were happy the floor was sound, then.

'Ugh!' Manda said, her hand over her mouth as she retreated to the doorway. 'Not sure I want to look any closer. I'm going back down.'

'How long has she been here?'

'Who knows.' But I thought I did know. Could this be the missing Catherine? Had she been here since revolutionary times? It's funny – I had a bit of a fear of bones usually but I felt quite calm crouched beside this complete skeleton. I felt as though she was glad she had been found at last. As though she felt she'd soon be at peace.

Phil had come to stand at my side, gazing down at her. 'Did she get trapped in here do you think?' He shuddered. 'What a horrible way to die.'

'I don't think she was trapped. The door was locked from the inside.'

'How did you open it, then?'

'Ah ha. My little secret.' A thought occurred to me. Maybe she had been trapped, but not by being locked in. The fire – it hadn't burned this part of the château but perhaps she'd been up here when it was burning, and unable to get out. I looked closely at the walls. There was some blackening – could it be soot? If Catherine had come up here to escape the fire, then succumbed to the smoke … But why come up to a tower room, better to get out of the château if it was burning. And why lock herself in?

I guessed we'd never know. And of course, we didn't know for certain that it was Catherine. I crouched beside the skeleton and looked more closely, gently easing the rotting blanket away to see more. Among the bones of one hand lay a ring. A large red stone, garnet perhaps, with a ring of small diamonds surrounding it, set in gold. I reached out and picked it up, then held it to the light. Inside there was an inscription. I went to the window and peered at it, but no use. I'd need my reading specs which were several floors beneath me.

'Here, let me look,' Steve said. He's short-sighted. He pushed his glasses up onto his head and held the ring inches from his nose. 'There are some initials. C.A. and P.A. And a date – *Juillet 1784.*'

I felt a rush of excitement. 'C.A. could be Catherine Aubert. And P.A. could be Pierre Aubert. If they married in July 1784 ...'

'... That would mean this is your Catherine, and that's her wedding ring,' Steve finished for me.

'Yes! Well, I hopefully will be able to find when they married,' I said. It was pre-revolutionary so I'd need to rely on church records, but there were plenty of searchable websites that might have the information.

'What are we going to do with the poor woman?' Phil was standing quietly beside her, his hands clasped together in front of him, almost as if he was at prayer.

'I suppose we need to inform the *gendarmerie*,' Steve said.

'Or start with the *mairie*. Aimée will know what to do,' Gray added. 'I'll call her.'

'I think she deserves a proper burial. Perhaps with Pierre Aubert, in the Aubert tomb in the cemetery.' Assuming I could confirm this was Catherine, that felt like the right thing to do. 'Poor woman. She's been waiting to be found for so long.'

'Our resident ghost, do you think?' Gray said.

I nodded. 'I'd assume so. Trying to let us know where she is. We've found you now, Madame Aubert. We'll reunite you with your husband. And that ring of yours – perhaps your many-greats grandson would like it.'

Perhaps it was my imagination, or perhaps it was just a draught finding its way in through the little window somehow, but I thought I heard a gentle murmur of thanks, a sigh of relief, as I spoke.

Chapter 30

Claudette, 1794

'So, young lady, what are you planning to do with these children?' Claudette's mother was standing with her hands on her hips, watching Michel as he curled in a corner of the cottage's kitchen with his thumb in his mouth, whimpering quietly.

Claudette sat at the battered table that took up most of the space. She was cradling Jeanne, trying to rock her to sleep.

'I'll look after them, *Maman*. They will be safe. I promised as much.'

Her mother shook her head. 'You know the Auberts will never come back for them, don't you? They won't be able to. Despite Monsieur Aubert's brave words, he'll be caught along with his fancy wife, and they'll be tried.'

'Ssh, *Maman*. Michel is old enough to understand what you are saying.' Jeanne was asleep now, so Claudette took her through to the tiny room she'd used as a bedroom as a girl and laid her on the bed. She returned to the kitchen, scooped up Michel and held him tightly.

'Where is Papa?' Where is *Maman*?' the little boy was saying.

Claudette sat down with the boy on her knee. 'They have had

to go away for a while. You and Jeanne will live with me and my mother. It is an adventure, no?'

'I want my *Maman*,' he whimpered, but he clung to Claudette in a way that told her he would soon get used to it and accept his new place in life. She held him tight. Thank God both children were used to her caring for them. If the worst happened and their parents were not able to return for them, it made it all a little easier. They would not feel completely abandoned, the poor little mites.

It was a difficult situation. She believed in the Revolution. It had been well past time to get rid of the monarchy and nobility, to make things fairer and more equal, and to share the lands of the nobles and the church among the common people. And yet it was hard to see how it was affecting these innocent children, and their parents who had committed no real crimes.

'They'll be executed, you know,' her mother was saying. 'They'll be found guilty and put to the guillotine.'

'No! Not the guillotine. They'll just be imprisoned.'

Claudette's mother shook her head and folded her arms. 'Not what I've heard. The Comte de Custine was executed just last week. His trial only lasted half an hour, they say, and they chopped his head off the very next day. Wham, bam, all done.' She made a chopping motion with her hand as she said these last words, and Claudette winced.

'But Monsieur and Madame Aubert have not committed a crime. Only the crime of their birth.'

'You said they were members of the old Court! You said Madame Aubert still loved the Austrian bitch. And they helped a non-conformist priest. You told me that, in this very room!'

Claudette felt her eyes fill with tears. It was all true. What she was not so sure of now, was whether those facts were genuine crimes or not. Whether it was right that the parents of these children, who she loved as though they were her own, should die just because of the accident of their birth.

'Well, whatever, it's happening now,' her mother continued. 'One way or another those Auberts will be caught and tried, and these children will end up as orphans. You'd better find yourself a husband who's willing to adopt these two mites. I can't see another way. Good job you have some money to get yourself started, and those jewels he gave you.'

Claudette sniffed, and nodded. Her mother was right. That was the way ahead. She bent over Michel's soft head and kissed it. No matter what, the children would stay with her and she would do all she could for them. They were no doubt safer with her, than if they'd stayed in the château with their parents. Sooner or later the mob would come for the Auberts, no matter what. She had done the right thing, for this way the children would be saved.

As she sat there cuddling Michel, she made a silent promise to him and his sister. She'd tell them, when they were older, and when things had settled down in France, who their parents really were. She'd make sure they knew they were Auberts, and that had things been different, they would have been aristocrats, living in a grand château. But she would also make sure they were brought up to be good, kind and fair. New citizens for this new France.

It was a couple of days after Claudette and the children had left the château that the grisly discovery of Pierre Aubert's body beneath the wash house floor was made. Temperatures had risen, sending more meltwater down the mountainsides into the river, and there'd also been a night of rain. With the river level high, washerwomen had tried to raise the floor but had struggled, as there seemed to be something caught in the mechanism. Upon investigation, Pierre's bloated body was found. No one knew how he'd got into the river. His remains were retrieved and buried in his family tomb. Claudette used a little of the money he'd given her to have his name inscribed beneath that of little Louis.

'What happened to his wife?' Claudette's mother asked her. 'Will we find her in the river too? Perhaps washed further downstream. Or did she burn in the château?'

'The remains of the château have been searched for her body, but she's not there,' Claudette replied. She'd assumed Catherine perished in the fire too, but it seemed not. She was nowhere to be found – not in the priest's cottage or anywhere else in the château's grounds. What had been discovered, however, was a carriage supplied with clothes and food and items for the children, and with jewels and money hidden within, stored in a barn a little way down the valley. It was clear the Auberts had planned to make their escape at some point, and perhaps go into exile. The men were saying it was just as well they acted when they did, or the Auberts might have got away and never faced justice. It was just a shame Madame Aubert couldn't be found.

Claudette found herself quietly hoping that Madame might have got away. Who knew where, or how, but perhaps she had, and was living quietly, hidden, biding her time until she could come back for her children. Meanwhile, Claudette would make sure they wanted for nothing.

The château was only partially burned – the newer parts, built by Pierre Aubert's grandfather, were destroyed but the original structure including the tower had survived and were habitable. It was declared public property, and a couple of families moved in, relishing living in the grand château, but soon they moved out again, declaring it uncomfortable and draughty. They reported strange unexplained noises at night, and rumours began that it was haunted, presumably by the ghost of Pierre Aubert.

Claudette could not bring herself to walk past the château. If she needed to go that way, she would take a detour rather than look upon her one-time home. A year later she married a man from a neighbouring village and moved there. He knew where the children had come from, but her new neighbours were all told they were hers, by her first husband who had sadly died. No one questioned her, in these troubled times. The children grew up strong and healthy, bringing her joy. They called her *Maman*, and although she would often tell them the story of their real parents, they treated it just as a fairy tale, and would beg her to tell them another tale of the Auberts and their magical children.

Chapter 31

Lu

Aimée was amazing. She came round to the château within an hour of Gray calling her, accompanied by the local chief of police. He had a look at the body, but Aimée declared she did not want to go up there. To be fair, she was wearing white linen trousers – completely unsuitable clothing for climbing up that soot-blackened narrow staircase. She remained in our sitting room with Gray and Manda, while the rest of us took the chief of police up. He came down pretty quickly – he only needed to confirm it was indeed an ancient body and not someone one of us might have killed. We gave statements, he filled in forms, and left, saying he'd soon be in touch again with Madame la Maire, who would then advise us on how to proceed regarding disposing of the remains.

'I'd like to think we can bury her,' I said. 'With her husband.'

Aimée stared at me. 'Does this mean you know who she was?'

I explained about Pierre and Catherine, and what I'd found out about Catherine going missing, and then I showed her the ring. 'So you see, I am pretty sure she must be Catherine. I wonder if she got trapped up there when the château burned, perhaps.'

'What a sad way to go.' Aimée shook her head and reached for Gray's hand. 'But yes, it would be nice to put her with her husband. There is a family Aubert tomb in the graveyard, I think?'

'Yes, there is.'

'I will speak to the priest for you.'

'Thank you. One thing I can't quite work out is how her children survived.' It had been bugging me since we found Catherine. Why was she locked in the tower room alone, without her children?

'Did they survive? How do you know this?'

I explained about the research I'd done, helped by Pascal. 'They stayed in the area, married and had children of their own. I have not been able to trace all their descendants, but I found one. You're not going to believe this. It's Monsieur Baudin.'

Aimée actually clapped her hands with excitement at this. 'That is wonderful! So this poor lady can have a relative at her burial service. Perhaps we can bring Monsieur Baudin here for the service. And he will enjoy seeing Felix again, no doubt.'

Two days later, everything was arranged. The police had formally handed over the remains to us, Aimée had arranged a burial service with the local priest, and I had telephoned Monsieur Baudin to tell him what we had found, and to invite him to the burial and to a party afterwards in the château.

It had been strange, being in the château and knowing there was a dead body above us in the tower. 'Not a body, a skeleton,' Phil reminded me. 'And she's been there all along.'

Nevertheless, I was glad when the undertakers arrived to remove her. They brought her down from the tower wrapped only in a sheet, which Manda had donated, as there was no possibility of carrying a coffin up those narrow stairs. But they treated her with the utmost respect at all times, and when she was eventually laid reverently in her coffin in our hallway I shed a few tears. Before they closed the coffin, I gently arranged her hair so that it fell in waves over her shoulders. The sheet was tucked up under her chin.

'You can rest now, Catherine. And tomorrow you will be with Pierre and your firstborn again, for all time,' I whispered, before stepping away from the coffin to allow the undertakers to close and fasten the lid. Phil took hold of my hand and squeezed it. I had the impression he was as choked up as I was.

The burial service was brief but moving. Monsieur Baudin came, in a wheelchair and attended by a carer. Before Catherine was placed into the Aubert tomb he asked to be pushed close to it, and he put a hand reverently on the simple wooden coffin, closing his eyes as though saying a private prayer for his ancestor. He existed because of this woman, who'd been lost for so long but now was found. I was pleased we had been able to help resolve her mystery.

Felix had attended the service too – sitting as good as gold at Monsieur Baudin's side, leaning against him, as the priest said a few words that I was pleased to find I could understand. My French had improved so much since coming to live here. Sadly Monsieur Baudin could not come to the château afterwards, as his carer could not spare the time. But I managed to invite him for a pre-Christmas party a month later, promising we would arrange his transport.

'Thank you, I would be pleased to come,' he said in French, squeezing my hand. His carer was looking at her watch and beginning to look fidgety.

That was when I remembered about the ring and pulled it out of my handbag. 'Oh yes. I must give you this. As Catherine Aubert's direct descendant it belongs to you. It was found with her remains.' I showed him the inscription on the inside.

He looked up at me with misty eyes. 'This is beautiful. I have a daughter – she is far away in California but she will visit me soon. She would like to have this. Thank you.' He took the ring and raised it to his lips, kissing it. I loved that he now had a tangible link to his ancestry, and that the ring would be cherished by future generations. Catherine's story would live on.

It had taken quite a bit of work and a lot of keeping quiet – something I am not entirely renowned for being good at. But finally all the arrangements were in place. Phil, the only other person who knew, had sworn secrecy but he had a habit of winking at me every now and again which made me blush. The others would make lewd jokes if they spotted the wink and blush. 'Hey up, you two, get a room!' Gray quipped on more than one occasion.

But as Christmas approached the time was getting near. We were all busy making the spare rooms ready for all our guests – Tom was coming, as well as Clemmie and Hope, and Alfie was making his first visit to us too. Everyone had lots of plans for the period – Clemmie and Hope wanted a shopping trip in Nice; Tom, Alfie and Phil had tickets for a rugby match in Toulon against Munster; Gray was intending taking Aimée for a weekend in St Tropez. Manda was doing a grand job of putting on a brave face – she was looking forward to having the four youngsters with us but of course sad that her Zoe couldn't be there too.

Little did she know!

Zoe and I had Skyped many times making the arrangements. It was her idea to keep the whole thing secret from her parents. 'I want to surprise them,' she'd said. 'Mum's face – it'll be awesome. And if I tell Dad, he won't be able to stop himself telling Mum. So will you help, Lu?'

I had grinned from ear to ear as we chatted that day, and on the various other occasions afterwards. I'd had to commandeer a corner of the tabac in the village to use when talking to her, to reduce the risk of Manda, Steve or Gray walking in on us.

I'd quietly made the lower tower room ready for a guest. Interestingly, Felix had been happy to enter that room while I worked on it, and curl up for a nap. He'd always seemed to hate it before our discovery of Catherine's remains. It'd probably be Tom using the tower room – I couldn't imagine Zoe would want to take it after our grisly discovery up above, but Tom wouldn't mind. I'd already asked if he'd mind taking that room again and he'd leapt at the chance. It had a power supply now, so he'd have lights and sockets and an electric heater. The electrics in the château seemed to have settled down at last. So while Manda thought Tom would be sleeping in one of the newly decorated second-floor guest rooms that she'd made up, those would be taken by Clemmie, Hope, Alfie and Zoe. And by the biggest surprise of all.

At last, on the Saturday before Christmas, the day for Zoe's arrival came round. I'd planned to be the one to collect her from Nice airport but Clemmie and Hope, who'd arrived the day before, had roped me into helping them make a chocolate cake as part of their present for Gray, and then Alfie had pestered me to play board games with him and Tom, and there seemed no easy way to get away without making people suspicious. Phil, meanwhile, had loudly announced that he needed to drive to a garden centre for sacks of compost, and had winked at me as he passed through the kitchen where I was pulling bags of sugar and flour out of the larder ready for the cake-baking.

I frowned, excused myself for a moment and went out to the hallway to see what he wanted. 'I'll fetch Zoe,' he whispered. 'I don't need any compost. You make sure Manda and Steve are here when I get back in a couple of hours. And maybe put some bubbly in the fridge.'

I hugged him. 'Thanks, darling. That's a real help.'

He'd left, and I'd helped with the cake making and played a couple of board games. I'd put Prosecco in the fridge as requested and then by mid-afternoon when Phil was due back, we were all in the sitting room drinking tea and coffee, chatting and laughing. Aimée had arrived, and unbelievably she'd brought a small suitcase which Gray had quietly taken up to his room. It was beginning to snow outside, just lightly, and I was hoping Phil would be back before it became heavier. I'd spotted Manda and even Steve looking wistfully at the four kids, who were hoping the snow would become heavier so they could make a snowman and go sledging, and had had to bite my tongue to stop myself saying, 'Just you wait!'

And then there was a clattering at the front door, Phil's voice calling out, 'Hey honeys, I'm home!' and some muttered whisperings which I think only I caught, being the one nearest the door and also being the only one expecting Phil not to be alone. The door to the sitting room opened and in they walked. Zoe, closely followed by a grinning Ryan who looked impossibly handsome and tanned, and then Phil.

'Hi, Mum and Dad,' Zoe said, dropping her handbag onto a sofa and holding her arms out to Manda.

'Zoe? Oh my GOD!' Manda squealed, knocking over a cup of tea as she hurried to her feet and threw her arms around her daughter. 'Oh my God, oh my God, oh my God you are HERE!' She was jumping up and down, crying and grinning and squeezing Zoe so hard I feared the poor girl would barely be able to breathe.

'Zoe, wow, what a surprise!' Steve wrapped his arms around them both and if I'm not very much mistaken there was a tear in his eye too. 'How did you ... I mean when ... well, how long are you staying?'

'Mum, Dad, let me introduce my fiancé Ryan,' Zoe said, disentangling herself from her parents.

'Hi, it's fantastic to meet you both,' Ryan replied, in what was unmistakably an English Midlands accent.

'Good to meet you too,' said Steve, nudging Manda who was standing with her mouth open.

'Er, yes, hello Ryan. And congratulations to you both.' Manda kissed Ryan's cheeks in a French-style greeting.

'So, Mum, if it's OK with you all we'll stay here for a week then go to the UK for a week to see some friends over New Year. Then back to Australia.'

'A week!' Manda looked both delighted and disappointed. A week she hadn't expected with her daughter, but only a week.

'Then, Mum, it's only another three months till my contract is up. And we've decided' – Zoe looked at Ryan, smiled and took his hand – 'that we'll then move back to Europe. Not sure where – either England, or Ryan quite fancies working in France if we can find something ...'

'ZOE!!!' Manda squealed so loudly Gray, Aimée and I all put our hands over our ears. 'That is amazing!'

'Fantastic!' Everyone was up on their feet, all talking at once, congratulating the engaged couple, asking after life in Australia and wedding plans. I quietly slipped out to the kitchen, followed by Phil, and came back with a tray of champagne glasses and the two bottles I'd put in the fridge to chill. Clemmie and Hope whispered to each other and then fetched the chocolate fudge cake they'd made earlier, some plates and forks and a knife. 'Let's have this to celebrate,' Clemmie said to me. 'We'll make another for Dad. I seem to remember Zoe likes chocolate fudge.'

'Oh, I do indeed,' she said, picking up on the end of Clemmie's comment.

It was a very happy, noisy party for the rest of the day. At one point Manda came to sit beside me. 'This was your doing, was it, Lu?'

'Zoe's idea. But I facilitated it, yes.'

'Best. Christmas. Ever,' she said, feasting her eyes on her daughter who was now chatting to Hope.

I had to agree. For all of us, this first one in the château looked like being one to remember. As the snow fell outside I looked around at my husband, sons, best friends and their children, Felix and the kittens and felt supremely contented. We'd all been successful making a new life for ourselves here in France as we entered the 'third age' of our lives. It had taken me a little longer than the others to settle in, but I'd done it. I'd learned the language, got myself a job, solved a mystery and acquired a dog. It had all helped me begin to feel that Château d'Aubert and this corner of France were home.

We were lucky, we knew, to have been able to do all this. To have the money, the opportunity to retire early, and the freedom of movement to come to live here. We'd built, in a way, on the efforts of those who'd come before – people who'd fought for freedom and equality, who'd fought so that future generations could have equal chances in life, not constrained by their class or circumstances of their birth.

We were living our best life, and the years ahead promised to be the best yet.

Author's Note

I well remember enjoying learning about the French Revolution at school, aged about 14, as part of a history curriculum covering 'Revolutions that Changed the World' – just as Lu used to teach. The events at Versailles and Paris in this novel are all true to history; however, the Auberts are fictional, as is their château, the village and its environs.

Chapter One was inspired by a rather drunken evening with my own set of old pals from my university days, during which we did indeed find ourselves Googling for French châteaux that we might all live in communally. Unlike Lu and her friends, we did not go ahead with the idea. (At least, we haven't yet!)

Acknowledgements

Firstly, huge thanks to my editor Abigail Fenton who helped pull a messy first draft into a much better shape. She managed to see the story I was trying to tell and her feedback was invaluable in turning this one into a readable book.

Thanks also to my husband Ignatius and son Fionn, who as always were the first readers of this novel – that messy first draft. Ignatius wants us to buy Château d'Aubert together with our friends. I have had to break the news to him gently that it's a fictional place.

Thank you to Rachel Gilbey for her help arranging blog tours for this and previous novels. You really are the best! Thanks also to the community of book bloggers. You are all very much appreciated.

I must also thank all the team at HQ Digital for another stunning cover and for all the other work that goes into producing a novel. Sometimes I think writing the story is the easiest part of the process.

And finally, thanks to all my readers for your continued support. I'm so glad you enjoy my books, I love hearing from you, and hope you like this one too!

Dear Reader,

We hope you enjoyed reading this book. If you did, we'd be so appreciative if you left a review. It really helps us and the author to bring more books like this to you.

Here at HQ Digital we are dedicated to publishing fiction that will keep you turning the pages into the early hours. Don't want to miss a thing? To find out more about our books, promotions, discover exclusive content and enter competitions you can keep in touch in the following ways:

JOIN OUR COMMUNITY:
Sign up to our new email newsletter: hyperurl.co/hqnewsletter
Read our new blog www.hqstories.co.uk
🐦 : https://twitter.com/HQDigitalUK
🅕 : www.facebook.com/HQStories

BUDDING WRITER?
We're also looking for authors to join the HQ Digital family!
Find out more here:
https://www.hqstories.co.uk/want-to-write-for-us/
Thanks for reading, from the HQ Digital team

Keep reading for an excerpt from
The Stationmaster's Daughter ...

Prologue

For a moment he was frozen, unable to move, unable to react to what had just happened. Time stood still, and he stood with it, not seeing, not hearing, doing nothing.

And then as his senses returned he registered screams of horror, followed by the sight of that broken and twisted body lying at the foot of the stairs. How had it happened? Annie was screaming, lung-bursting screams of pain and terror. His instinct was to rush to her, gather her up and hold her, but would that make things worse? There was no going back now. No returning to how things used to be, before … before today, before all the horrible, life-changing events of the day. It was all over now.

The screams continued, and he knew that the next minutes would alter his life forever. He knew too that even without the broken body, the screams, the fall, his life had already changed irrevocably. The door to a future he had only dared dream of had been slammed shut in his face.

He allowed himself a moment's grief for what had been and for what might have yet been, and then he shook himself into action, hurrying down the stairs to deal with it all. Not to put it right – that wasn't possible – but to do his best. For Annie.

Chapter 1

Tilly – present day

It was her dad's voice that Tilly Thomson could hear, outside the room she'd been sleeping in. Her dad. What was he doing here? She rolled over and buried her face in her Disney Princess pillow. She didn't want to see him. No, that wasn't true, she *did* want to see him – she wanted nothing more than to be scooped up in his strong arms, and for him to take all the pain away. But she didn't want him to see her like this. Broken, sick, deep in a pit of despair. No parent should see their child in this sort of state. Even if that child was 39.

There was a tap at the door, and then Jo entered. Jo was Tilly's best friend, the person who'd saved her life and given her a place to stay. She'd moved her two little daughters into one room to make space for Tilly, after she was discharged from hospital.

'Tils? Your dad's here.' Jo stepped into the room, her face taut with worry. 'I know you said you didn't want to worry him, but listen, mate, he's your dad. So I phoned him. Don't be cross at me. Let him help.'

Before Tilly could summon the energy to answer, Jo stepped aside and Tilly's dad, Ken, entered the room. He looked stressed, much older than when she'd last seen him. That would be her fault, she supposed.

'Hey, Dad,' she managed to croak.

'Oh, pet. What's up? Jo said you were in a bad way?' He looked about for a place to sit down, and pulled out a small stool upholstered in pink to perch on.

'I'll, um, leave you two to talk,' Jo said. 'Did you want a cup of tea, Ken?'

'Thanks, Jo. I'd love one.'

Jo closed the door quietly behind her. Tilly took a deep, shuddering breath, and closed her eyes. The pain on her father's face was too much to bear.

'What's up?' he said again, his voice hoarse. He was fighting back tears, she realised.

'Just … all got a bit much for me, I suppose,' she whispered. She couldn't tell him the whole truth. Not now. Not yet.

'You should have talked to me! I'd do anything for you, you know that, pet? Jo said you were … having a breakdown of some sort. God, when I heard …'

Tilly didn't want to think about how he'd have felt. A pang of guilt coursed through her, adding to the pain, pushing her deeper into that dark pit of misery. 'Sorry, Dad. I … didn't want you to be worried.'

'Of course I worry. Just want my girl to be happy again.'

She forced a weak smile to her face and reached for his hand. Her lovely dad, just trying to do what was best for her. But he wouldn't be able to fix everything. 'I know you do. Thanks.'

'Look, pet, we have a bit of a plan. I think you should come home with me. Down to Dorset. I'll sort out the spare room for you, and then you can rest and relax as much as you need. Jo's been so good, but you can't stay here forever. She's got her own family to look after.'

Tilly tried to imagine life with her dad in his bungalow by the sea. He'd lived on his own since her mum died nearly three years ago. He spent all his spare time helping with the restoration of an old railway. He'd probably try to get her involved in it too, but right now, she couldn't imagine doing anything other than lying in bed, under a thick duvet to insulate her from the rest of the world.

'It'll be good for you, pet. Sea air. The views from the cliff top. Getting away from London and all … everything that's happened.'

'He's right, Tils.' Jo had come back in with a couple of mugs of tea. She handed one to Ken, put the other on a bedside cabinet then perched on the end of the bed and took Tilly's hand. 'Listen, mate, you know you can stay here as long as you want. I'm not chucking you out. But have a think about it. New surroundings, living by the coast in Coombe Regis, a slower pace of life a long way from Ian and the rest of it. Might help get your head straight.'

'I'm not sure it'll ever feel straight again,' Tilly said, but regretted it when she saw Ken wince. He didn't know all of it. Unless Jo had told him.

'It will, in time. Believe me.' Ken put his tea down on a plastic toy crate and slid to his knees beside the bed. 'Come here, pet. Let your old dad give you a cuddle. Can't promise to make it all better in one go, but the Lord knows I'll give it my best shot.'

And then he scooped her up into a sitting position, wrapped his arms around her and held her tight. Tilly held on to him, letting his strength seep into her, resting her head against his shoulder and finally giving in to the urge to cry – huge, ugly sobs that shook her body and wracked her soul, but which somehow he seemed to absorb, so that when she finally calmed herself and pushed him gently away, she felt just a tiny bit better, just a touch more able to face the world. Perhaps he and Jo were right. Perhaps a stay on the Dorset coast with Ken would help. It certainly couldn't make her feel any worse.

*

Ken slept on Jo's sofa for the next two nights, until Tilly felt ready to face the journey. She felt scared to leave the cocoon of Jo's house, that comforting little pink bedroom in which she felt like a child being cosseted as she recovered from a bout of chicken pox. But 5-year-old Amber deserved to have her bedroom back.

At last it was time to leave. After dropping her kids off at school and nursery, Jo had made a trip to the house Tilly had once shared with Ian, and filled a suitcase with clothes. 'I picked up mostly jeans, T-shirts, fleeces,' she said. 'I guessed you wouldn't want your smart work clothes. If you need anything more I'll go and fetch it, and bring it when I come to visit.' She hugged Tilly. 'Which won't be too many weeks away, I promise.'

Tilly's eyes filled with tears. Jo had been such a good friend to her through all this. There was no way Tilly could have faced returning to her old marital home to pack, even when Ian wasn't there. And although Ken had offered, Jo had insisted he stay with Tilly rather than risk a confrontation with his son-in-law, which would almost certainly end badly. 'Thanks, Jo. I can always buy anything else if I feel I need it.' Though right now all she felt she'd need was a few pairs of warm pyjamas and maybe a dressing gown.

With effort, she dragged herself into the shower, washed her hair, and dressed in some of the clothes Jo had fetched. When she came downstairs, she found her father and Jo sitting in the kitchen, talking seriously. About her, no doubt. They cared, she reminded herself, even if she no longer cared about herself.

'There you are. You look better for having that shower,' Jo said, with a smile. 'Cup of tea before you go?'

Tilly shrugged. Recently she'd found it impossible to make even the simplest decision. Ken put out a hand to her and squeezed her arm. 'Thanks, Jo, but I think we'll get going. It's a longish drive, and I want to get home before the evening rush hour. Ready, pet?'

She nodded, numbly, and allowed him to shepherd her out to the car. Jo gave her a hug. 'Look after yourself, Tils. Listen to your dad. Do whatever he suggests, promise me. I'll be down to see you in a couple of weeks, I promise. Love you, mate.'

'Thanks, Jo,' Tilly managed to say. The words seemed inadequate, but the effort required to find more was too much. She climbed into the car, put on her seat belt and leaned back against the headrest. Outside, Ken was hugging and thanking Jo, and loading his bag and Tilly's suitcase into the boot. And then he was in the driver's seat beside her, starting the engine, and they were on their way, leaving Jo standing on her driveway, dabbing at her eyes with a tissue. Even Ken's eyes looked suspiciously moist. Far too much crying was going on, Tilly thought, and all of it her fault. But right now, she didn't feel she could do anything about it.

*

The journey passed uneventfully. Ken found a classical music station on the radio, and Tilly let the music wash over her as she stared out of the window at the passing countryside. It was February, the fields were brown and bare and the sky was a dismal grey. The scenery and weather were a perfect match for her frame of mind. Soon it would be spring, there'd be new growth in the fields and hedgerows, birds would sing and lambs would be born, and everyone would look forward to the warmth of summer. Would she? Was there anything to look forward to? She'd lost her job, her husband, her chances of having a family. But now she was here, with her dad, and somehow she had to find a way forward.

She knew she shouldn't dwell on these thoughts. All it did was make her more miserable. She fumbled in her jeans pocket for a crumpled tissue, but it wasn't enough to soak up her never-ending tears. Ken glanced over, then rummaged in his pockets and pulled out a cotton handkerchief. 'Here, pet. It's clean, and it'll be easier on your skin than those tissues.'

She took it gratefully. The cotton was soft from having been washed hundreds of times. It had been folded in four and ironed, just the way her mum always used to iron handkerchiefs. An image of her dad standing over the ironing board, carefully ironing and folding hankies flitted through her mind, and despite her misery she found herself smiling faintly.

'That's better, pet. Breaking my heart to see you so upset. When we get home I'll make up the spare bed for you. Then I'll make us shepherd's pie for tea. You always loved your mum's shepherd's pie. I've learned to cook since she ... went.' He bit his lip. 'I've had to.'

Tilly reached out to pat his shoulder. Dad had never cooked so much as beans on toast the whole time she was growing up. Mum had done everything. When she died, Tilly had wondered how he'd cope on his own, but she'd been so caught up in her own problems at that time that she'd never asked. To her shame, she realised this was her first visit to Dorset since the funeral. And this wasn't so much a visit – more like a rescue.

'Thanks, Dad. Looking forward to it.' Looking forward. Well, it was a start.

The roads became narrower and more twisty as they drove deep into Dorset. Not far from Coombe Regis Ken slowed down as they passed through a village. 'That's Lynford station house,' he said. 'The first station the restoration society bought. We've laid some track here and we're open at weekends and school holidays, running trains up and down.' Tilly glanced across at the building he was indicating, and saw a sign: *Lynford station: Home of the Michelhampton and Coombe Regis Railway.*

'Is that where you spend your time?' she asked.

He nodded. 'Well, there and Lower Berecombe, which is the next station on the line. Actually, I'm usually at Lower Berecombe.

We've not owned it as long, and there's more to do there. Anyway, I'll give you a tour of both as soon as you feel up to it.'

She forced herself to smile at him, then stared out of the window in silence for the remainder of the journey. Thankfully they were soon in the outskirts of Coombe Regis. She'd been here before – her parents had bought their cliff-top bungalow after they retired, and she and Ian had visited a few times.

Ken drove down a steep street that she remembered, that led straight down to the tiny harbour in the heart of the little town. There, they turned right, past some shops and a small beach, and then through a residential area, heading uphill once more to the cliffs on the west side of town. This part was familiar from her previous visits, and soon they turned into her dad's driveway and she saw the stunning view across the cliff top to the sea. Even with the low grey cloud and sporadic rain, it was beautiful.

'Here at last, then, Tillikins!' Ken jumped out and began unloading the luggage from the boot.

'Great,' she replied, turning away. His use of her old childhood nickname had made her eyes prickle with tears.

She got out of the car and followed Ken inside. It was exactly as she remembered it – exactly as it had been when her mother was alive. A small table stood by the front door, with an overgrown spider plant on it, its offspring dangling down to floor level. Her mother's deep-red winter coat still hung from a hook in the hallway, and as she passed, Tilly reached out to caress it.

'I should send that down to the charity shop, I suppose,' said Ken, noticing her action.

'Not if you're not ready to,' she replied, and the way her dad turned quickly away told her he wasn't.

'Go on into the sitting room,' he said. 'Give me ten minutes to sort out a bedroom for you.'

She did as he said and sat on a sofa that was angled to make the most of the view of the cliff top and sea. There was something calming about resting your eyes on a distant horizon, she thought. It would help, being here.

A few minutes later Ken came back. 'So, you're in this room,' he said, leading her along the corridor and into the guest bedroom, the same one she'd stayed in before with Ian, but her father had decorated it since she'd last been here. It had a double bed with crisp white bed linen, pale-blue painted walls that on a good day would match the sky outside, a dark oak chest of drawers and a chair upholstered in vibrant blues and greens. The floor was a pale laminate, with a fluffy cream rug beside the bed. The whole effect was restful and calming. Ken had put her suitcase on a low table and laid a blue-and-white striped towel on the end of the bed.

Tilly felt tears come to her eyes again. 'Thanks, Dad. This is really nice.'

'I tried to think of what your mother would have done, and did the same,' he said.

'She'd be proud of you.'

'Thanks, pet.' A gruffness in Ken's voice betrayed his usual discomfort with emotional scenes, so Tilly said no more, but set to work pulling clothes she had out of the suitcase, putting her wash bag on the chest of drawers and tucking her pyjamas under the pillow.

'Right then, a cup of tea, and then dinner in about an hour?'

'Got anything stronger? I feel the need … well, it's been a long day.'

Ken nodded. 'There's some wine, but are you sure, after—'

'I'm fine. I won't overdo it.'

A few minutes later, with a glass of buttery Chardonnay in her hand, Tilly was standing by the picture window in the bungalow's sitting room, gazing at the view. The rain was beginning to clear, and dusk was falling. To the west, over the sea, there was a strip of clear sky, turning ever deeper red and purple as the last of the light faded. There was a path along the cliff behind her father's garden.

'Did Jo pack your walking boots or a pair of trainers? It'd be good for you, to get out there and walk along the cliffs. Helps put things in perspective. Well, it helped me, after … you know.' Ken had come to stand beside her, watching the sunset.

'Yes, maybe I will. Some day.' Tilly topped up her wine. Right now, the only thing she wanted was to drink enough to blot out the world and then crawl under a duvet.

DIGITAL

If you enjoyed *The Secret of the Château*, then why not try
another gripping historical novel from HQ Digital?